"With poignant moments, touches of m͓
Darkest Shores by Carolyn Miller reur
and an injured war hero. I thoroughly en͓͓ͦ ͓͓ ͓͓͓͓͓ ͓͓͓͓͓͓͓ ͓
and their humorous, teasing banter as the two gradually progress from
acquaintanceship to friendship to true love."

JULIE KLASSEN, author of *A Castaway in Cornwall*

"*Dusk's Darkest Shores* brings Regency England to life with a charming
and inspiring romance that is sure to warm readers' hearts. They will
fall in love with the strong but wounded hero, Adam Edgerton, and
the kind and caring heroine, Mary Bloomfield. This wonderful story
will keep you turning pages until you reach the very romantic and sat-
isfying ending. Well-written and highly recommended!"

CARRIE TURANSKY, best-selling author of *No Ocean Too Wide*
and *No Journey Too Far*

"From the first page, I was caught up in the journey of a wounded war
hero facing a new battle as his once-certain future crumbles around
him, and a woman both gentle and capable who has built a purposeful
life and relegated love to a girlish dream. Carolyn Miller's authentic
portrayal of real-life struggles, raw pain, and faith in the midst of difficult circumstances will resonate with readers. A heartfelt and satis-
fying novel sure to captivate fans of inspirational Regency romance."

AMANDA BARRATT, author of *The White Rose Resists*

"*Dusk's Darkest Shores* is all about coming into the light, a joyful journey of restoration amid the lush beauty of England's Lake District.
Mary and Adam will seem like not only book characters but beloved
friends. The Regency Wallflowers series has a beautiful beginning!"

LAURA FRANTZ, Christy Award–winning author of *Tidewater Bride*

"Carolyn Miller has penned another absolutely beautiful novel. With
profound messages of hope and faith, along with charming wit and a
sweet romance, *Dusk's Darkest Shores* will captivate Regency readers.
An excellent start to what will surely be a series to remember."

JOANNA BARKER, author of *Otherwise Engaged*

"Carolyn Miller's main character, Mary, is delightfully unique and fascinating for the era. I was pulled in immediately by her personality, and then by the well-crafted setting and beautiful language. The intrigue and conflict led me quickly along, and although I loved the beginning, I was blown away by the end."

JEN GEIGLE JOHNSON, author of *A Torn Allegiance*

Darkest Shores

Dusk's
Darkest Shores

CAROLYN MILLER

KREGEL
PUBLICATIONS

Library of Congress Cataloging-in-Publication Data
Names: Miller, Carolyn, 1974- author.
Title: Dusk's darkest shores / Carolyn Miller.
Description: Grand Rapids, MI : Kregel Publications, [2021] | Series:
   Regency wallflowers ; 1
Identifiers: LCCN 2020049995 (print) | LCCN 2020049996 (ebook) | ISBN
   9780825446535 (paperback) | ISBN 9780825476839 (epub) | ISBN
   9780825468490 (kindle edition)
Subjects: GSAFD: Love stories.
Classification: LCC PR9619.4.M565 D87 2021 (print) | LCC PR9619.4.M565
   (ebook) | DDC 823/.92--dc23
LC record available at https://lccn.loc.gov/2020049995
LC ebook record available at https://lccn.loc.gov/2020049996

ISBN 978-0-8254-4653-5, print
ISBN 978-0-8254-7683-9, epub

Printed in the United States of America
22 23 24 25 26 27 28 29 30 / 5 4 3 2

To all those who dare to believe God

. . . on the shores of darkness there is light,
And precipices show untrodden green,
There is a budding morrow in midnight,
There is a triple sight in blindness keen.

John Keats, "To Homer"

Chapter 1

Music and laughter swirled through the assembly room, a shiny, animated scene within a life-sized bauble. Smile stiffening, Mary Bloomfield surveyed the event, which bulged with all the notables of the district. Couples twirled under the candles of enormous iron chandeliers, candlelight flickering across the features of the polished and assured. Excitement suffused the faces of the young, the old, the newly married, the long married, the hoping-to-soon-be-married, all those complacent in their bubble of ease. Mary relaxed as Emily Hardy drew near, her pretty face aglow.

"Oh, Mary," she gasped, clutching Mary's arm as she laughed, the soft sheen of cream satin gloves a marked contrast to Mary's brown kerseymere sleeve. "Isn't this all so delightful? I am sure I have not sat down for a single dance!"

"You have been much sought after."

Emily's blue eyes softened, as if in pity.

Before Emily could speak her sympathy, Mary hurried on. "These musicians are rather good, aren't they? I do not think I have ever heard Mr. Pendle play the flute so well."

"I am certain I have never heard anything quite so pretty. We must have this trio play at our wedding soon. Do you think Adam will agree?"

"I'm sure Adam will agree to anything you suggest, and his parents will likely also. They are quite as besotted as their son, it appears." Mary glanced at Mr. and Mrs. Edgerton. Their plump features shone with delight, as much with pride in their prospective daughter-in-law as with the pride naturally expected of parents of a war hero.

The Edgertons' beaming faces turned. Their smiles widened yet further in elated approval as they regarded Emily. But really, what was there not to approve? Emily was the very picture of perfection. From the top of her carefully coiffed golden curls to the tips of her beribboned slippers, she was everything charming and pleasing to the eye.

Mary curtsied as they drew near. "Good evening."

"Oh, good evening, Miss Bloomfield." Mr. Edgerton nodded. "Such a lovely dance, is it not?" Before she could answer, he continued. "But I have not yet seen you dancing."

A corner of her mouth tipped up. Nor was he likely to. There were few unattached gentlemen here in Amberley, the legacy of the town's enthusiastic response of sending its sons to the war against France. Such a patriotic demonstration, disproportionate to Amberley's population, meant the higher number of women would forever advantage gentlemen seeking partners with whom to dance. Or with whom to partner in life. A fact, at the ripe old age of nine-and-twenty, she had long grown reconciled to.

"Perhaps you might offer Miss Bloomfield your arm," his wife suggested kindly.

Mary demurred. "I'm sure he would much prefer to dance with his daughter-to-be."

His eyes brightened, and he turned to Emily, whose countenance quickly approximated his. He asked the question, and, after an apologetic glance at Mary, she accepted prettily, and they both moved to join the dancing.

"And how is your son?" Mary asked Mrs. Edgerton.

"Oh, did Emily not tell you? Adam will soon be returning home! We received a letter just the other day."

"How wonderful for you all."

"Yes. It will be marvelous to see him, especially as he and Emily have spent so little time in each other's company these past years. We can now start planning for their wedding."

"Forgive me, but I did not realize that the situation in the peninsula allowed visits home just yet. Robert has certainly never mentioned any such thing."

A crease appeared between Mrs. Edgerton's brows. "I don't believe they were serving in the same regiment."

"That must be it," Mary agreed easily.

Mrs. Edgerton shifted to answer a neighbor's query on the other side, leaving Mary to watch the dancing once more. The music picked up pace and volume, as if celebrating the inclusion of Emily and Adam's father, as if recognizing them with extra favor due to their connection of loving and being loved by one of the district's favorite sons.

Adam Edgerton. Where was he now? Basking in the triumph of the latest victory in Spain? Lapping up the adulation of London? Sometimes it was difficult to reconcile her brother's playmate with the formidable soldier he had become, the man whose rise from the ranks to commissioned officer had accompanied several bouts of heroic exploits, including a daring rescue under enemy fire of another of Amberley's own sons. Her brother had never achieved such heights, but Robert's need for spectacles had meant his inclusion in the armed forces had been more a surprise than a certainty, even if he were only allowed to work in the medical corps. Of course, Father, a practitioner of medicine himself, had been cautiously gratified to see his son included in such ranks, to know the legacy of his occupation continued.

Beyond the dancing figures, Mary's stepmother sat with others of her acquaintance, no doubt good-naturedly gossiping about the prospects of her daughter. Mary's own mother she could scarce remember, her death occurring when Mary had been but two. Her father's second marriage a few years later had resulted in a kindly mother Mary regarded quite as her own and, eventually, a sister ten years Mary's junior. Joanna resembled neither of her elder siblings, possessing the physical qualities of height, ruddy locks, shining eyes, and clear skin that had eluded her brother and sister. Mother hoped a match might be made this year should Mr. Peters finally come up to scratch. Father, it seemed, was not quite so determined to see his daughter married off to a legal clerk, even if he were the second son of Amberley's third biggest landowner. But his mild protests fell on deaf ears.

As if summoned by Mary's thoughts, Joanna appeared in the whirling couples, laughing as the candlelight glinted off her tresses. A clearly smitten Mr. Peters led her to the end of the rows with a gratified expression. Little wonder when the youngest Bloomfield possessed a tendency to flirtatiousness that made some suspect her motives. Perhaps that was what had kept Mr. Peters from proposing, a hesitation until he could be certain that Joanna's heart was truly his.

A disturbance at the door drew most eyes to the figure of an agitated-looking Mr. Croker, who stood hat in hand, clearly not dressed for the assembly. The music changed, and her father hurried towards her. "Mary?"

"It is time?"

He nodded, and together they made their farewells and moved to Mr. Croker, whose air of relief threaded concern within.

"How is Sally?" she asked him, her short legs struggling to keep up with the farmer's long strides as he exited the building.

"She be asking for you, miss." He glanced at her. "And you, too, sir," he added, in an almost apologetic tone.

Father chuckled softly and shook his head. "I know it is my daughter that Sally wants." He retrieved his medical bag from their hired carriage and issued instructions that the servant wait for his wife and daughter. "We shall travel with Croker, here."

"Yessir."

Mary grasped Mr. Croker's outstretched hand, and he hauled her up into his gig. She clutched her shawl around her shoulders. Thankfully, the March evening was unusually mild. "How long between her pains?"

"She said it was time."

After five children, Sally would know. Mary glanced at her father, whose presence tonight served more as precaution than anything else. Mrs. Liddell's role as midwife and Mary's role as nurse during births were generally preferred by all, save the occupants in the house on the hill. Lord and Lady Carstairs preferred the London mode of medical practitioners, or so Father had said, as Mary never had visited the great metropolis herself. But after a difficult birth last time and a pregnancy that had necessitated bedrest for many weeks, Father had insisted he be nearby when Sally Croker's birthing time arrived.

Mary spent the remainder of the short journey praying for Sally, for the babe, for Mr. Croker and his other children. Within minutes they arrived, and she was helped down. Her brown skirts swished as she moved to the open door, reminding her of the need to exchange her best gown for something more practical. Though judging from the whimpers of pain coming from the bedchamber, there was no time for anything save the white apron which the eldest Croker lass held out to her.

"Mama said you might need this," Betsy whispered, blue eyes large.

"Thank you," Mary murmured, efficiently wrapping the large pinafore-like apron around her, only pausing long enough to stroke the seven-year-old's cheek affectionately. "You will have a new brother or sister soon. Won't that be wonderful?"

"I hope it's a girl. I want a sister," she confided. With four pranksome, noisy brothers, it was hardly a surprise.

"I'm sure God will give your family just what you need." Mary leaned down. "But I'd like for you to have a sister, too."

Betsy's smile held a note of conspiracy as Mary tied the apron's long ribbons around her waist. The apron's size suited Mrs. Croker's girth far better than Mary's thin frame. Still, it would protect her clothes effectively.

With an encouraging smile for the children peeping from their sleeping pallets, she pushed open the bedchamber door.

Mrs. Liddell peered underneath the blankets obscuring Sally's lower body, the village midwife muttering to herself. Father stood holding Mrs. Croker's wrist, an expression Mary recognized as worry wrinkling his brow.

"Hello, Mrs. Croker, Mrs. Liddell." She hurried to the bed and grasped Sally's other hand.

Sally's reddened face eased. "I'm that glad you're here."

"There's nowhere else I'd be."

"Oh, go on with you. Such a lovely, soothing voice you have—oh!"

Another pain gripped Mrs. Croker, and she squeezed Mary's hand tightly. As the pang passed, the grip eased, and Mary offered a sip of water, which Mrs. Croker swallowed eagerly.

Mary glanced at her father, whose worried expression had smoothed. "Her pulse is not as rapid now."

Thank You, God. Bring Your peace here. Help this child be born soon.

"I be thinking it's near time." Mrs. Liddell's dark eyes flicked from Sally to Mary. There were some who said Hannah Liddell reminded them of a witch, with her crooked back and twisted features and her knowledge of birthing and healing and herbs. Of course, there were some who said similar things about Mary, because of the times she had prayed and seen God intervene. Mysterious ways tended to lead the ignorant to superstition.

Mary nodded, then bent to Sally's face, gaze fixed on hers. "You know what to do. Your body will be ready to push soon, so rest as much as you can between contractions."

Sally closed her eyes, as if to summon strength.

Mary placed her hand on Sally's shoulder, praying aloud for God's power to cover the situation.

Sally's body stiffened, sweat beading her brow as another contraction swelled. She clutched Mary's hand, squeezing so tightly Mary had to suppress a gasp.

"I can see the baby's foot." Hannah's voice held a note of concern.

Father hurried to the end of the bed as Mary worked to ease the panic filling Sally's eyes. "You will be well, the babe will be well," she comforted, with a calmness her heart did not feel. But underlying the concern was the certainty that God was here, was intervening, was helping. "You need not fear. God is present with us."

Sally released a shuddery breath, even as the movements at the end of the bed hastened.

Father gestured to Mary, and they moved to the side of the room, out of earshot. "The baby is in the breech position. We shall have to manage things carefully and maneuver it to achieve an effective position. I'm afraid this will be very painful for poor Sally."

"What's happening?" Sally called, fear lacing her voice.

Mary hastened to her side, offering a smile even as she repossessed Sally's hand and held it firmly. "I'm afraid your baby is being a mite stubborn and must be manipulated into position."

"Will it hurt?"

"Of course," Hannah muttered in her ever-caustic way.

"Yes, I'm afraid it will," Mary said quietly. "But remember, you can do this. God is with us. He cares for us."

Father returned to the room, followed by Mr. Croker, whose fearful expression mirrored his wife's. "What's happening? Is Sally going to be all right?"

"Come, sit." Mary pushed him gently into the wooden chair beside the bed. "Sally will appreciate your support. And your prayers."

He flushed. "But I don't know what to pray."

"Pray for peace. Pray for Sally's strength. Pray for your new child."

He nodded, eyes fixed on his wife's face as she gave another gasp, one that turned into a groan.

"Mama?" Betsy peeked in the partially opened door.

Mary rushed to her. "Betsy, my dear. Come, we must let the adults be. Your mama is a little busy helping your new sibling into the world."

"Sister?"

"We don't know yet." Mary pulled the door shut behind her and wrapped an arm around Betsy's thin shoulders as she smiled at the other children dressed in faded, much-patched nightgowns, wearing identical expressions of fear. "Your mama and father need you to be very good, as Mrs. Liddell and my father help your mother's new baby arrive safely."

"Your da's the doctor," Tommy said wisely.

"Yes."

"And Mrs. Liddell is a witch." He nodded.

"Indeed, she is not," Mary said. "She is a very kind lady, helping others as she does."

"She looks like a witch."

"She cannot help her looks any more than I can help having brown hair, or you can help having blue eyes." Mary tapped him tenderly under the chin. "We should be kind to others and speak kindly of them."

"That's what Mama says," Betsy said, solemnity in her wide eyes.

"Your mother is very wise. Now, if we want to be kind to others, per-haps you can help your father by everyone hopping into your beds and closing your eyes. Then when he returns, he might be so pleased that there might be currant buns for you tomorrow."

"Really?"

"Really." Well, only if she remembered to include currant buns in her delivery of baked goods to the Croker house tomorrow. *Lord, help me not to forget.* "But only if you snuggle into bed now."

"Will you tuck us in?" Tommy asked. "Mama always does."

"Of course."

Mary tucked and prayed and kissed the tiny brows, the pleasure of such a task tugging at an unexpected knot deep in her heart that she might never do so for children she called her own. Still, she would be a good aunt, a good friend to those who needed her. "Good night, dear ones," she murmured, twisting the oil lamp's wick to low. "I'm sure we shall be out shortly."

"And we'll pretend to be asleep," Betsy reassured.

"Your father will be pleased to know he has such obedient children." She waited a moment longer, then reentered the bedchamber.

Sally panted, grunting with exertion, the veins on her neck bulging with the effort.

"Good, come here." Father signaled Mary near. "She is losing blood, and her pulse is getting weaker. Hannah and I are at a loss."

Mary glanced at Sally writhing on the bed. *Lord, what do we do?* She stilled, listening for the small voice within.

Over.

Over? She frowned. Very well. "Perhaps . . . turning her over, on all fours, would help the baby release."

"Yes." Her father looked surprised. "Hannah? What do you think?"

"Aye." She jerked a nod at the bed. "We should get Sally upright, but Fred can barely think."

Mary turned her attention to where Mr. Croker sat, slack-jawed, watching the proceedings with glassy eyes.

"Croker," Father snapped.

The farmer jerked and seemed to come to himself.

"Mr. Croker, please help me assist Sally. She needs to shift onto her hands and knees, so she can push this baby out." Mary wrapped an arm around Sally's thick shoulders and lifted but was barely able to move her. "Mr. Croker." Her voice sharpened. "Now."

He blinked, rose, and wrapped a meaty hand around his wife's shoulders, then obeyed Mary's instructions to help Sally to the bed's side and turn her so she could be supported by the bedframe.

Hannah Liddell scurried near, examined Sally again, and barked instructions.

"Sally." Mary crouched, waiting until the exhausted woman's eyes met hers. "We need you to focus. It's time. Let's meet your precious baby. Ready?"

The poor woman looked drained, her features sagging, her gaze dull. She nodded limply.

"Now push."

Sally's eyes closed as she concentrated. She released a thin screech of exertion.

"Help hold her, Croker," Father commanded.

One push.

Please, God.

A second push.

"I can see its legs."

Sally was weeping, puffing, her face red and tight. "I can't do this. I can't—"

"You can." Mary gripped Sally's hand. "And you will. Now take a breath and try again."

Sally obeyed, then squeezed shut her eyes and concentrated, straining away.

"Good, good," Father said. "We have the legs out. Congratulations, Sally, it's a little girl."

"Hear that, love?" Mr. Croker said. "A little girl."

"Betsy will be pleased," Sally gasped.

"So help her meet her sister. One big final push. Ready?"

Sally nodded, new determination filling her eyes. She gritted her teeth, crying out in a groan of pain as Mrs. Liddell helped tug the babe free, and Father scooped the infant into his arms and commenced his ministrations.

"Oh, congratulations, Sally." Mary rubbed her shoulder soothingly. "You've done very well. Your babe will be as bonny a lass as Betsy."

"Can I see my baby?"

The swift look from her father shot a spike of fear inside Mary. The baby needed to cry, needed to breathe. *Lord, please touch her now.* "In just a moment," Mary said, her encouragement meant to distract the new mother for a moment. "Let's first get you comfortable in bed."

"Wait." Mrs. Liddell held a damp cloth.

As Hannah performed the needed ablutions, Mary hurried to where her father rubbed the infant's limbs with a dry towel.

"She must start breathing." He slapped the tiny girl on the bottom, eliciting a weak cry.

"Thank You, God," Mary murmured.

"Amen." Her father's glance held a wealth of understanding.

"My baby?"

"She's being wrapped now," Mary called, as her father efficiently swaddled the infant in the muslin wrap that had seen use by the Crokers' other children.

Delight suffused the parents' exhausted features as their new child was placed in Sally's arms. Mary smiled. "She's beautiful."

"Of course she is." Fred gazed at his wife, adoration shining in his eyes. "Just like her ma."

Tears pricked, and Mary turned away. "I will go make some tea." She escaped the room, nearly bumping into Betsy's nightgowned form near the door.

"Is Mama all better?"

"Yes." Mary smoothed her tousled curls. "And I think you will be very happy."

"I have a sister?"

"You might need to go and see." She opened the door. Surely Sally would be thrilled for Betsy to see her longed-for sister.

Betsy slipped into the bedchamber as the other children remained fast asleep, Tommy's thumb stuck in his mouth.

Mary's heart twisted again and, after kindling the fire to resume boiling water, she slumped into the wooden chair beside the table, allowing the rush and tension to slowly ebb away. It was foolish to hope, to dream that motherhood would one day be hers. Best to stifle such feelings. God was enough for her. He had blessed her in so many ways. To want more was selfish, was greedy, was wrong.

She should be content.

"I *am* content," she whispered fiercely in the gloomy shadows.

So why did something within persist in wanting more?

Chapter 2

On a mild spring day such as today, one could hardly indulge in the discontent induced by private darkness. Indeed—Mary eyed the shining lake, nestled as a pearl between green velvet hills—there could be few finer vistas in all of England.

With reluctance she withdrew her gaze and carefully snipped rosemary flowers from the garden that lined the road, placing them in her basket. The benefit of this garden was twofold. It provided a lovely view for those of Father's patients whose needs necessitated a longer stay in the rooms of their home used for such purposes, as they overlooked the garden and the peaceful hills and vales beyond. The garden also contained a wealth of flowers and herbs, nearly all of which were used to provide traditional compositions in accompaniment with the oft-expensive medicines and powders that had to be transported from London, or sometimes down from Glasgow.

For many of the poorer laborers, opportunity to rest and be fed healthy meals and elixirs at Father's cottage infirmary was healing enough. For those of greater income, Father's reputation as an Edinburgh-trained apothecary-surgeon meant his advice was not only sought out but embraced, even if some with greater social aspirations than sense considered him rather less than gentlemanly, due to his practical administrations of medical treatments rather than the prescribing nature of London physicians.

She moved to collect some stalks of lavender. When the flowers were boiled with cider and water, a most versatile and soothing solution was produced and used for everything from sleep troubles to toothache to hair tonics. She lifted a cut sprig and inhaled its spicy-sweet scent.

Beyond the low hedge a gig rumbled by.

She straightened in time to catch Emily wave a hand, a beaming smile filling her features.

Of course. She must be heading up to the Edgerton farm. No doubt the family wanted her there for the special homecoming, or at least to discuss further details of such things. For the return of the war hero was all any of the village wanted to talk about.

Following her morning visit to the Crokers to check on Sally and the new baby, and to give the children the promised currant buns, she had fulfilled her mother's request and visited the milliner's in the village and been informed by no fewer than three persons about the arrival of Adam Edgerton on the morrow.

"Oh, Miss Bloomfield, is this not exciting? Can you believe we are so fortunate in our little village to have one of England's heroes return to us?"

"I'm sure none would be so filled with anticipation as Mr. and Mrs. Edgerton."

"Oh, and brave Albert Jamieson. He owes Lieutenant Edgerton his life, after all. I'm sure that will be quite an occasion."

"As will be the reunion with Miss Emily Hardy. She and Adam Edgerton will make such a handsome couple, don't you agree?"

"Indeed, they will."

All sorts of festivities were rumored to be planned, from a turtle dinner for the notables of the district to a special picnic for the village's younger members.

Mary's age and station meant an invitation to either event was unlikely. Not that it mattered. She might have once trailed her brother and his friend as they walked the various hills overlooking Windermere, but that was long ago, and her interest in Adam had long been only as her brother's friend. Emily, eight years Mary's junior, was closer to Joanna's age, but seemed to possess a maturity yet to be seen in her sister.

Poor Joanna. When they had finally returned from the Crokers' last night, it was to discover Joanna had faced some challenges of her own.

"Finally, you are back!" Joanna's petulant expression never boded well.

A glance at their weary mother held no further clues, as she quickly excused herself.

"I cannot believe that man!"

Had Mr. Peters overstepped? Mary removed her gloves and stretched her neck.

"You missed it, having left shortly before it happened. Joseph Beecham asked me to dance and, well, I had no choice but to refuse him. Dance with a butcher's son? I'd sooner die!"

Mary's eyes widened. "Oh, but Joanna—"

"Don't look at me like that, Mary. I know you think I should have accepted him, but ugh, I simply cannot stand the sight of him, let alone the smell. Can you think where those hands have been?"

"Joseph Beecham does an honest job—"

"Don't try to defend him, Mary. You don't know what he did next."

Mary willed her expression to appear penitent, and awaited her sister's next cause for outrage.

"When I refused, along came Mr. Jamieson, and I was never more grateful to accept his hand. Well, you should have seen the look Joseph Beecham gave me. I declare if Mr. Benjamin Jamieson had not been supporting me, I might well have fainted!"

"But surely you know it is impolite to refuse one gentleman's offer to dance, then accept the next."

"Hmph. Such rules are ridiculous in the extreme. So many men seem to think young ladies have no mind of their own. *I* certainly don't think a young lady should be obliged to dance with a man just because he has a nerve to ask her. And Joseph Beecham seemed to have some nerve!"

"You must be aware such an attitude appears very rude. And what about Mr. Peters? I thought he was your choice."

"Oh, he is pleasant enough, I suppose. But I must say he does not seem to have a lot to say for himself at times. I found Mr. Jamieson a far more interesting conversationalist. After all, with a brother who has gone to war and had such exciting experiences, one can hardly expect otherwise."

Mary blinked. "But you have encouraged poor Mr. Peters to think you'll accept his suit. Do you want to be labelled as a flirt?"

"I don't mind saying, Mary, that it seems rather petty of you to make such observations. But then I suppose it is inevitable, especially when I was fortunate enough to receive invitations for every dance, when others, well . . ." She eyed Mary with a sly look from under her eyelids.

That expression always caused a slight hardening of Mary's heart towards her foolish, headstrong sister. Yes, Joanna was young and impetuous; yes, Mary was supposed to love her sister, but sometimes Joanna seemed to possess a very selfish core. Had she been overindulged, much fussed over as the child born ten years after Mary? Or was it simply her looks and pretty ways that had blinded others to her less attractive qualities?

"I did not dance last night, that is true," Mary finally replied, thankful for the calmness in her voice that had a tendency to dampen her sister's taunts.

"I suppose next you will say you had no desire to." Her sister sniffed and turned her head.

"If I had been asked, I would have accepted, regardless of who asked me."

"I suppose that is your way of saying you are better than I!"

Mary stifled a sigh, regret kneading her heart at her o'er hasty words. "I'm sorry you think that of me. I am certainly well aware of my faults."

"Like the fact you never care about your clothes." Her sister eyed the brown gown critically. "Don't tell me you wore that to the birth."

"Very well, I won't."

Joanna gave an unexpected snort of laughter, her humor restored by Mary's dry response. "If only you would follow my advice and wear something that flatters your complexion, surely you would have suitors galore."

"Once again I must thank you for your interest, but I assure you I am resigned to being the most delightful of aunts for your children."

"Really?" Joanna's voice possessed an element of doubt.

"Really," Mary said firmly. "That is, if you ever decide which suitor you wish to marry. Tell me more about Mr. Peters. Has he proposed? Do you think him likely to soon?"

Her sister's brightened expression led to yet further conversation, amid Mary's smothered yawns. Mary had been extremely glad to finally achieve her own bedchamber and, after a quick wash and exchange of garments, had tumbled into bed and slumber.

Sleep had proved elusive, as the events of the night chased the emotions her sister's words provoked. Would meek Mr. Peters be strong enough to curb her sister's headstrong tendencies? Somehow, she doubted so. They would certainly be a mismatched pair.

Mary drew in a deep breath, willing the fresh morning air to refocus her thoughts to return to the present and the tasks of the day. The sun sparkled on the lake a half mile away, shining jewellike, holding a promise of boating adventures in a few months' time. In the distance Emily's gig slowly trundled past the Oakley smallholding, then began to ascend the great hill to the Edgerton farm, the windswept location that overlooked the valley and commanded one of the district's best views of Windermere.

By all reports Emily and Adam were well suited, their respective backgrounds and their fathers' status as friends meaning this alliance had not been wholly unexpected. But whether Emily's tender years and country innocence would knit well with Adam's seasoned experience with war remained to be seen. Mary could only hope—and pray—that their union would be a happy one.

And that the return of the conquering war hero would be everything that it ought.

The carriage clattered and swayed, the miles near interminable. His head throbbed, his eyes ached, his body was so wearied of travel. But soon he would be there. Soon he would—*please, God*—gaze out over the fields and valleys he remembered. Had it really been four years? It seemed a lifetime ago.

"Adam?"

His head shifted in the direction of the speaker. "Yes, Ted?" His ears, sharpened by the demands of these past days, heard the note of impatience in his own voice, and he sighed. He'd need to sort out this agitation before his return. Thank God for his Yorkshire friend, whose forbearance—and willingness to escort Adam all this way from London—made this journey more tolerable than it could have been. The fact his friend had even been in London and traveling north had proved something of a godsend. But Edward "Teddy" Bracken's agreeable nature was sometimes easy to take advantage of, and Adam would not have his mother, or, worse, his betrothed, upset because he'd forgotten how a gentleman ought to behave. "What is it?"

"I simply asked how you are feeling, but your response made it quite clear."

"Forgive me."

"No forgiveness necessary," Bracken replied easily, his patience befitting his status as Adam's friend of longest years.

Though perhaps not longest years. Robert Bloomfield still served that role, even though he hadn't seen the man in several years, save for a glimpse at a medical tent near Lisbon.

His mind tracked back to the days when the two of them would scale the great hills, or fish, or boat on Windermere's glassy waves. Such innocent pleasures. Neither of them had ever dreamed war would steal away such simple dreams.

The carriage dipped with sudden force and stopped, slamming his head against the thinly padded headrest.

He winced, as the thudding in his head resumed its loud tattoo. "What is happening?"

"It seems a large pothole has swallowed a wheel," Bracken said. "I'm afraid we might need to get out and help push. Well, *I* might." An apologetic note rang in his tone.

Adam nodded, then wished he hadn't, the action searing fresh pain up his spine to rim his brow. He gritted his teeth, clenched his hands, and waited for the episode to pass, refusing to let the smallest sound escape.

The carriage swayed as Bracken exited, the sensation drawing both a new bout of nausea and Adam's now-familiar regret at his inability to help. *God, heal me*, he begged. Then life could resume as he'd previously known it, life could resume as it ought.

There came the sounds of grunts and heaves, sounds that drew awareness that freeing the wheel would be much easier if he weren't still seated inside. Why hadn't anyone said?

Adam slid his hand along the carriage door, reached for the handle, twisted it, and gingerly inched his way outside. One booted foot dangled in thin air—

"Edgerton, what on earth—?" Bracken said. "Get back inside now."

"But I can help."

"You won't be helping anyone if you fall."

Adam's arm was clasped, and he was gently pushed back into his seat. "But I'm too heavy for you to move the carriage."

"You cannot afford to be further . . ." Bracken's voice trailed off, but Adam knew what he'd been about to say.

Truth be told, Adam was tired of fighting him. He waved a hand, aiming for an insouciance he did not feel. "Have it your way, then."

"Finally," his friend muttered.

Adam slumped against the squabs, willing patience to appear, counting the seconds until the carriage jerked upwards and forwards, the door creaked open, and Bracken's voice came again.

"We're getting faster at digging ourselves out, I think."

"I doubt we could get any slower."

Bracken chuckled. "I did not realize the roads would be quite so bad. At least they're not covered in snow."

"Have you seen any snow?"

"Occasional traces on the peaks, that is all."

"Perhaps the winter wasn't as hard here as it was on the Continent."

"Perhaps." An element of doubt tinged Bracken's voice.

Well, perhaps not. It wasn't as if they had not had this discussion before.

"How much longer do you suppose until we arrive?"

"It's hard to say. The coachman thinks we might need to travel a little slower, just as a precaution."

Adam's lips compressed. No good complaining. "It will be what it will be."

"Ever the fatalist," Bracken chided gently. "Don't you hope for more?"

"Hope?" Adam's thin veneer of ease slipped. "What do you think this trip is about, if not hope?"

Bracken was silent, perhaps thinking on what they talked about previously. Of course this trip was built on hope. But it was also built on reality, and the reality was that certain people would struggle to see past the man he was now.

A man who most certainly was not the same kind of man who had proposed to and been accepted by the prettiest girl in Amberley. A man who held grave doubts about his future with the farm. He might hope, but he'd overheard enough doctors' coded whispers to know his hopes should not be raised terribly high. The sickness that had first struck in Walcheren had gradually worsened in the past year, leading to several weeks in a hospital as his fever raged and the doctors worked in vain. He'd heard later that he'd been muttering all sorts of mad things, his memories of Cumbria mingling with scenes from the peninsula, the confusion of his mind the merest echo of that which he had lived.

His regiment had endured abysmal conditions in the Netherlands as part of the Walcheren Campaign, where thousands of men had died due to fever, before withdrawal, when those deemed fit enough were sent to the peninsula. His status of "healthy" had proved optimistic at best, but he'd still been able to man a rifle and engage in the kind of bravado people awarded medals for. If it hadn't been for men nursing him—men like Captain Balfour, Captain Stamford—he most certainly would have died.

One day he hoped to meet his fellow soldiers again to thank them, but he'd been told that both men were still involved in the fighting. His lips twisted. Only the most desperate cases were shipped home to England, those deemed useless to employ in fighting . . . the maimed, the mad, the diseased.

And those men who could no longer see.

Chapter 3

Mary glanced across the congregants to where Mr. and Mrs. Edgerton sat, eyes fixed to the front as the minister ascended the pulpit. The Sunday service at Amberley possessed a special energy today, the excitement swirling around the promised return of Adam Edgerton akin to the promise of a visitation by angels. Mary shook her head, as if shaking off the uncharitable thought.

It wasn't Adam Edgerton's fault the anticipation surrounding his arrival had only heightened due to an unfortunate delay. Everyone in the village had fully expected to see him in services today, to offer their congratulations, their best wishes, but when Mr. and Mrs. Edgerton had arrived *sans* heroic son this morning, the palpable disappointment humming through the gathered congregants had drawn Mr. Edgerton's apology.

"Unforeseen circumstances necessitated the delay of a day or two."

Or so he said. But there was something else in his eyes, something about the way his half smile did not light his eyes, that made Mary wonder while Mr. Ponsonby lectured from the pulpit.

As Mr. Ponsonby pontificated on—it would be unjust to call his message a sermon, as it seemed to consist more of instructions for personal betterment than any real inspiration from the Scriptures—her heart continued to ponder.

What was the matter? Surely a father should be thrilled to see his son return from war. Father never stopped praying for Robert's safe return, and made sure to include prayers for him in their morning and evening devotions. Why was Mr. Edgerton not sounding overjoyed?

"Let us pray."

She bowed her head dutifully, but as the minister began his usual spiel of focusing on their utter wretchedness and sinful state, she focused her attention on the Edgerton family, pleading for God's mercy to be shown to them, and that whatever worry creased Mr. Edgerton's brow might be trusted to the care of their loving heavenly Father.

The final hymn was sung, and they joined the other congregants in the aisle, waiting their turn to be greeted by the minister at the door.

Mr. Ponsonby's round halo of white hair seemed at odds with his piercing dark eyes, and he seemed to hold her hand rather more tightly than usual. "Ah, Miss Bloomfield. I was most gratified to see your fervent interest in the sermon today."

She tugged back her hand and offered a polite smile that encouraged nothing more. She would not lie and flatter him about his message. "I believe the best part was concerning the saving power of Jesus Christ. In fact, I would dearly love to hear more sermons spent exploring such things. Imagine if people believed that what is spoken of in Acts amongst the believers could actually happen today. Just think how remarkable it would be if God would choose to use us to heal the sick and see the lame walk. Don't you think that would be wonderful?"

He coughed, his face turning an interesting shade of puce.

Before he started questioning her theology, she quickly moved on. Rumor had it the recent widower wished to see someone take up the position of Mrs. Ponsonby soon. Likely the woman would act more as an unpaid housekeeper than any real helpmeet, and she had no desire to take on either role.

She smiled to herself. Such pronouncements as today's would likely disqualify her from further interest.

Outside, the congregation milled in the cold air, and again a clutch of interested villagers surrounded the Edgertons. Again, that knot centered Mr. Edgerton's brow. She moved past the crowd to speak with Mr. Croker, who was busily accepting congratulations from his own little crowd of well-wishers.

After speaking of Sally's health, he extolled the good behavior of his children. He fielded a question with a nod and an "Aye, Hannah attended her. And the doctor. And Miss Bloomfield, of course."

Several villagers echoed, "Of course," prompting Mary to hurry away before more could be made of her endeavors. She had no use for such praise, not when she merely followed God's prompting.

She moved to stand quietly beside her father, placing a hand on his arm as they waited for Mother and Joanna to finish their conversations.

He patted her hand. "Old Ponsonby didn't seem to know what to say to your comments before."

"No."

Father chuckled. "I rather think he wouldn't ever dare believe God might want to move in today's world, let alone do anything so unscripted as to perform a miracle."

"Not everyone believes as we do."

"That is for certain." He turned to her, eyes narrowing. "You are well? You seem a bit tired. I hope the activities the other night were not too strenuous for you."

"I had strength enough for the Crokers. Perhaps because I did not dance earlier," she added dryly.

"Yes, I heard your sister mention it." His brow creased. "She is a little tactless sometimes."

"Joanna is young."

"Hmm, yet older every day. Well, I cannot but be thankful that you accompanied me. Mrs. Croker has not ceased to sing your praises. Even if it has wearied you more than you admit."

Her smile of assurance grew wry. "I have not the happy talent to make my features appear other than what they are."

"No." He eyed her thoughtfully, as Joanna and Mama approached. "Ah, we are here. Shall we depart?"

"Oh, please, Father." Joanna clasped her hands. "Emily requested I share luncheon with her today. Please say I may go. I would dearly love the opportunity to chat with Emily before she soon makes the county's most advantageous match."

Well, not quite the county's *most* advantageous match, as just then

Mr. Josias Payne and his pompous son Charles strode by, the magistrate's aquiline features strongly marked in his heir's raised nose, as if he considered those around beneath his dignity. Charles might have an exaggerated opinion of his personal importance but, with the promise of a moneyed estate, he was generally held by all and sundry to be the catch of the county. At least he had, until Adam Edgerton's war exploits had reached Amberley's ears and the young ladies accounted a handsome war hero—who had a medal from King George himself!—as worthy of more attention.

Mary caught the twinkle in her father's eyes and swallowed her amusement. "But whatever will your suitor say?"

"My suitor?"

"Mr. Peters. Was he not invited to dine with us today?"

"Oh." Her face looked so crestfallen Mary had to bite back another smile. "I forgot about him."

"My dear Joanna," Mama said. "How can you say such things? Have you not encouraged his attentions these past weeks? No, it is simply out of the question. Mr. Peters has been invited, and it is to see you, my dear, so there is to be no more talk of abandoning our luncheon plans simply because of a foolish whim. Do you want him to cry off?"

Joanna sighed. "No."

"Then let me hear no more. Ah, Mr. Peters." Mama smiled warmly as that gentleman drew near. "Here you are now."

As he exchanged greetings with Mary's parents, Joanna murmured to Mary, "I don't suppose you can entertain him sufficiently for me, should I endeavor to leave soon after luncheon?"

"I don't know if he would deem my entertainment as sufficient, but I could try my best," Mary said meekly.

Joanna tilted her head. "When you use that tone, I sometimes think you are roasting me, but right now I am too glad to care. Thank you. I will make it up to you."

"How exactly? By drawing attention away from one of my unwanted suitors?"

"Obviously not that." Joanna chuckled.

No, obviously.

"Joanna, my dear," Mama protested in a hushed aside, as Father talked with Mr. Peters. "I do think you should be more circumspect with your words. Truly, you can seem unkind at times."

"Mary knows I do not mean it."

Mary raised her brows.

"Well, I don't! Anyway, I see Emily and the others are waiting for me. I shall tell her it must be later this afternoon."

Mary exchanged looks with her mother as Joanna huffed off. She pressed her lips together as Mr. Peter's countenance fell at Joanna's departure, then brightened as she drew near again.

"Mr. Peters," Joanna murmured, slipping her arm through his, "how glad I am that you are coming today."

"I'm so pleased for the invitation." His cheeks flushed to the color of Mary's shawl.

"You must forgive me. I needed to tell poor Emily that I must forgo her very kind invitation, as I had plans already. Plans with you," she added brightly.

"Oh, but I do not want to intrude on your pleasure—"

"Truly? Oh, I knew you'd understand! See Mama, Mr. Peters does not mind if I spend time with Emily today. Oh, you are *such* a kind person." She squeezed his arm in an appearance of affection, which caused the young man to appear flustered.

Mama protested. "My dear—"

"I'll just hurry now and tell her I can come after all." And without waiting a moment longer—no doubt to escape the censure in Mama's tight jaw and eyes—she hurried back to where the Hardy family awaited.

"Enjoy yourself, Miss Joanna," Mr. Peters called.

Joanna turned with a mischievous smile and a flutter of her hand. "I always do."

"That girl," Mama said in a low voice, her expression mingling frustration and resignation.

Yet there would be no scenes forthcoming, Mama's reluctance to harness her youngest's headstrong tendencies stemming from a lifetime of averseness to confrontation, Papa's ongoing busyness meaning he had even less time or energy to care.

A slight frown appeared on Mr. Peters's face, as though he'd suddenly grown aware of the consequences of his burst of charitable generosity.

Mary stepped forward. "Mr. Peters, I wonder if you would mind telling us about your recent visit to York."

He nodded, and shared about his time at the symposium for those in the legal profession as Mary and her parents walked with him the short distance to their home on the village outskirts, the dark slate roof gleaming wetly in the sun after the night's rain.

After a cold collation at lunch, and entertaining Mr. Peters to the best of her ability—which surely had fallen sadly short of both Mr. Peters's and Joanna's standards and expectations—Mary retired to her room, thinking over the morning.

Silly, foolish Joanna. While Mary could understand her younger sister's disinclination for Mr. Peters's dry conversation, he did still hold Joanna in high regard. How, when her sister was so cavalier with his attentions, Mary could not comprehend. Perhaps such was the nature of love, that one could be blind to the folly of the chosen object of affection.

Would that someone she admired held her own self in such esteem. But no. She would not feel sorry for herself. It was best to not ponder those things that would never be. Instead, she'd turn her thoughts to what could be.

Did she truly believe what she had said to the reverend this morning? What if God did want people to trust Him to act in miraculous ways today? Was it presumptuous to believe in healing miracles? Or was it faith?

She closed her eyes, opened her hands. "Heavenly Father," she whispered, "I know I am not much, but I do believe You are real, and that You love people, and that You want to make a tangible difference to people's lives today. Use me for Your purposes, I pray."

In the quiet that followed, something subtle shifted in her soul, as if a breath had been released. The next minutes she spent in silence, listening for that small voice that so often guided her steps, a voice that guided her days. Some had called the inner promptings she heard superstitious and questioned why she turned up just as their child had fallen from a tree, or when an extra pair of hands was needed to assist. She believed, as did her father, that this voice was the Holy Spirit, and the number of times she had seen situations transformed for good when she had obeyed only reaffirmed crediting these promptings to God.

Mary continued to pray. For her parents. For Joanna. For Robert. For Mr. Peters. For the Crokers. For the Edgertons. Even for scarce-believing Mr. Ponsonby.

That her village and its loved ones might know God, might know His mercy, and might know His power to save and to heal.

A faint scream woke Mary from light slumber.

Mary sat up, pushing her hair from her eyes, blinking against the darkness. Had that sound been real or just imagined? A person or a crow? Deep shadows hid the room, though a slight fluttering came from the curtains shrouding the partially opened window. Was it evening or morning? She had eaten supper, had she not? She thought back to the rest of the evening. Joanna's return had seen tossed-off apologies for abandoning them earlier, and exclamations about Emily's beautiful wedding trousseau, and a plaintive desire for an eligible gentleman to make her a bride. Mary had wryly suggested Mr. Peters stood as an obvious candidate, only to be met with derision and a flounced-off departure from Joanna to bed. How many hours ago had that been?

After what seemed an age, the thumping in her heart eased, only to be replaced a few minutes later by a thumping up the stairs. She tensed. The scream had been real? There came the sound of voices, one higher pitched, one lower. She had heard such sounds before.

A tap came at her door. "Mary?"

"Yes, Father?"

The door was flung open. "Oh, good, you are awake. You must dress quickly. We are needed."

"Of course."

Within two minutes she joined her father in the gig, stepping around a lantern at their feet. He snapped the reins as she fastened her cloak. "It is the Oakley girl. She has been attacked, so the servant said."

"Oh no, poor Susan! And without a mother to lend her support."

"Hence why I asked you."

Because Mama's softhearted sensibility did not always lend itself to the hard tasks such visits would imply.

Dear God, be with Susan. The lass could not be older than sixteen. *Help her, help Mr. Oakley. Give us wisdom.*

Her prayers sliced through the emerging dawn as they drove the quarter mile to where the Oakley farm subsisted. There were lamps aglow, running figures, the barking of a dozen dogs, a scene of chaos and confusion. Her stomach tensed.

"In here," a man yelled and ran to hold the horses.

Her father jumped down, offering her a quick hand to assist her descent before they hurried inside the cramped stone farmhouse. "Where is she?" he called to the bustling room.

A wide-eyed servant girl pointed to a closed door, which they pushed open. There lay the curled and weeping figure of young Susan Oakley on the bed, being patted awkwardly on the shoulder by her father.

"Thank God you're here," Mr. Oakley said, his features drawn and pale.

"Susan?" Father moved to her. "It's Doctor Bloomfield."

"Get away! Get away!" Susan cried, shuddering.

"Susan, it's only the doctor, come to help you," Mr. Oakley said. "Oh, and Miss Bloomfield, too."

"I can't, I can't—" She curled more tightly upon herself.

At Father's gesture, Mary moved closer to the bed and knelt. "Susan? It's Mary. You are safe now. No one can hurt you."

Whimpering, Susan shook her head, face still turned towards the wall. "I'll never be safe. Never!"

Mary laid a hand on Susan's shoulder, felt her stiffen, then relax. "You are safe now," she assured, silently praying for Susan to experience God's peace and comfort.

After several minutes the girl's weeping quieted, her shudders ceased, and she drew in several raspy breaths.

"Would you tell me what has happened?" Mary asked gently.

A nod. "But not when they're here. I'm so . . . so ashamed. Oh, Papa." Her voice broke, and she started crying again.

Mary glanced over her shoulder at the clearly distraught Mr. Oakley and her father.

Father met her gaze, nodded, and quietly escorted the farmer from the room, leaving Mary alone with the still sobbing girl.

"I'm sure you have nothing to be ashamed of." Mary softly rubbed her shoulder. "It is only us now."

Susan shook her head. "I . . . I do not . . . I cannot—" She rolled over, her scared brown eyes meeting Mary's in one quick moment. "Oh, Mary!"

Mary bent, and the next moment Susan was sobbing into her shoulder, offering broken whispers about waking to find a man in her room, about how he covered her mouth with his hand, threatened to kill her if she screamed, before doing the most heinous of things and forcing himself on her.

Heart clenching, Mary hugged her harder, as if she could protect her from the memories. "You poor, dear child."

Susan's tears had wetted her gown, her sniffling making Mary long for a handkerchief. "I didn't know! I didn't see—"

"You did not see who did this to you?"

"No. It was dark, he was heavy—oh." She retched, and Mary snatched up the porcelain chamber pot just in time for Susan to release her stomach's contents.

Compassion wrung her heart. When Susan had finished, Mary offered her a cloth to wipe her mouth, and encouraged her to sit on the bed, wrapped in Mary's own shawl.

"Susan." Mary held the girl's hands and squeezed them gently, looking her in the eyes. "I'm afraid my father will need to examine you."

"No. I don't want him to."

"Of course you don't. But the magistrate will need to ask both you and your father questions. I'm so sorry. I'm sure it will be unpleasant, but it must be done."

"But I don't want people to know."

"I understand. And I'm sure people will do all that they can to protect your name from being linked to anything sordid. But in order to catch the man who did this, the authorities will need to find out what they can."

"No, no." Susan shook her head. "I can't—I don't want anyone to know—"

"Susan," Mary said, her voice firming. "You have done nothing wrong."

"But I should have woken earlier, I should have screamed—"

"You have done nothing wrong." Mary eyed her firmly. "Nothing wrong."

Some of the panic seemed to leave Susan's eyes, and she gulped. Blinked. A new tear traced the contour of her cheek. "Will—will you stay here with me?"

"Yes. I will not leave you."

"Promise?"

"Of course." Susan gave a tiny nod, and Mary squeezed her hand and opened the door. "Father?"

He looked up from the table where he was speaking with Mr. Oakley. "The magistrate has been sent for."

She nodded, glancing at Mr. Oakley. "She does not want it spread abroad that she was attacked."

"But I cannae let the man who damaged my daughter's virtue go free!"

"Perhaps it need not be spread about that her virtue was affected, but merely that there was an intruder. The magistrate must be told the truth, of course, but perhaps we can persuade Mr. Payne to the benefits of not spreading things further."

Her father looked at her askance.

She shrugged. One could only hope for the best as far as that man was concerned. And hope—indeed, pray—that the Oakley's few servants would have sense enough not to noise abroad the terrible circumstances affecting their master's daughter.

She joined her father in the room, doing all she could to distract Susan as she was carefully examined and the various scratches, bruises, and other signs of injury were noted.

"You do not remember anything about the man?"

"No," Susan said dully. "He was heavy, that is all."

"You did not recognize his voice?"

"No." Susan glanced at Mary. "Will this be finished soon?"

"Very soon," Mary promised. Daylight seeped past the curtains. "I hear a carriage, which suggests the magistrate has arrived. He will likely ask you questions, and then it will be time for a nice long sleep."

"But not here. I can never sleep in this room again."

Mary glanced at her father, who gave a sharp nod. "If it is all right with your father, then perhaps you might like to stay with us. You'll be safe and protected, and a change of scene might do you good."

Susan nodded, and lowered her skirts, just as a knock came. The door opened and Mr. Oakley looked in. "The magistrate is here to see you— oh, Mr. Payne."

"Thank you, I do not need to be announced." Mr. Josias Payne walked into the room, eying Susan and Mary with a narrowed gaze.

He was not known for his compassion, and Mary could only pray he might see fit to use some today.

"Bloomfield."

"Mr. Payne." Father acknowledged him with professional courtesy. Theirs was a strange relationship, where the rich landowner barely tolerated the man who had studied medicine in Edinburgh, but whose successful treatment of his wife and sons had resulted in a measure of grudging respect. Such respect was all the more necessary when Mr. Payne needed him in cases like this.

"How's the girl?"

"Quite shaken," Father said.

Mary stayed silent through the interrogation, holding Susan's hand as promised, not letting go even when Mr. Payne asked what she was doing here.

"Miss Bloomfield is my friend," Susan attested. "I will not speak unless she remains."

"Hmph." He eyed Mary askance but said nothing more until the end of the accounting.

"Seems a hopeless case, if you have nothing with which to describe him," Mr. Payne said dismissively.

Susan blanched, and Mary squeezed her hand.

"Susan is welcome to shelter at our house, as she does not feel safe here anymore," Father said.

"Yes." She glanced around the room and visibly shuddered. "Take me away from here."

"Oakley? Do you understand?" At the farmer's nod, Father continued. "Payne, I trust if you have further questions you will address them there. I wish for Susan to be removed before too many villagers are awake and curious."

"Very well." Mr. Payne proceeded to examine the room, studying the stained bedclothes, rattling the locked window. "Locked, was it?"

"Aye," said Mr. Oakley.

"Hmph." Another glance about the room and he exited, followed by Father and Mr. Oakley.

Mary turned to Susan. "Are you sure that you wish to stay at our house?"

Susan nodded. "I'd rather be anywhere than here."

"Perhaps you could gather some of your clothes to bring." Mary's own gowns were unlikely to fit Susan's more statuesque form.

Mary exited to find the men seated at the table, Mr. Payne discussing the difficulties of finding the villain.

"Excuse me, sir," Mary said, "but would it not be possible to learn if there were any eyewitnesses or to question people about their whereabouts in the early hours of the morning?"

He snorted an unpleasant-sounding laugh. "And just who do you expect to be out at such a time? This isn't London, Miss Bloomfield. We've no night watchmen here. Besides, what would you expect anyone out at such an hour to say? They will all say they were in bed, as all good Christians were when this young person claims to have been attacked."

Mary's hackles rose. Surely he didn't suspect Susan of being immoral, of being less than a good Christian? "Please, sir, we request that you do not advertise the entire nature of the attack. If you would be so good as to say there was an intruder, rather than it was Susan who was attacked, that might help preserve her reputation."

"I believe that would be wise." Father nodded. "There is no need to further ruin the poor girl, is there?"

This last was said with an even look at the magistrate. What *had* previously transpired between them?

"I suppose not," Mr. Payne said, in an almost regretful tone.

"We shall go, then." Father rose and put out a hand to Mr. Oakley, who clasped it. "Rest assured Susan will be well cared for."

"Aye." The farmer offered his daughter another helpless gesture, patting her shoulder.

Within the half hour Mary had tucked Susan up in the bedchamber adjoining hers, the sleeping draught administered by her father having worked effectively. Mary tiptoed from the room and found her father in the kitchen, his stockinged feet stretched towards the welcome warmth of the fireplace.

"What a start to the day." Father rubbed the back of his neck. "Poor girl. We can only hope—"

"She is not with child," Mary finished for him. *Dear God, please no.*

He shook his head. "Sometimes I wish you were not so wise to the world. But if you weren't, then I suppose you would not be so valuable in moments like these."

A yawn escaped him—little wonder, he'd been out visiting patients for much of yesterday—so she kneaded his tight shoulders.

"Ah, you're a good girl. Just a little to the left—ah, thank you."

The crackle and hiss of the flames and the early morning birdcalls were the only sounds for a lengthy moment.

"Such a tragedy." He shook his head. "Who would have ever thought our little village would see such a thing? And against little Susan Oakley of all people. That family has had a hard enough time as it is these past years."

The loss of Susan's mother to typhoid three years ago had tipped Mr. Oakley's focus from his only child to his farm and dogs, a self-protective measure, Father surmised, as if Mr. Oakley couldn't bear to have his heart rent again.

"At least Mrs. Oakley was spared the knowledge of this happening to her daughter," Mary murmured.

"Indeed, indeed." Father sighed heavily. "What is the world coming to, I wonder?"

Mary ceased her massage and leaned down to rest her chin against the top of his head. "We shall pray God will heal her body and soul."

"Yes." He patted her hand resting against his shoulder. "I fear poor Susan will not be the only one in need of such mercies."

But further questions could not be asked as the cockerel crowed and Ellen bustled in to begin the breakfast preparations.

Chapter 4

After a few hours' sleep followed by instructions to Mama, Ellen, and a wide-eyed Joanna that gave them some—but not *all*—knowledge of the situation, Mary felt rather more the thing. She needed to visit Mrs. Croker, to deliver an elixir to Mr. Crowdey, to see how Letty Jamieson was getting on, and it wouldn't hurt to see if the haberdasher had the new muslin Mother had ordered.

A knock came at the door. Mary peered through the kitchen window and answered it. "Oh, hello Emily."

"Mary, is it true?" Emily pushed in, forcing Mary to take a backwards step. "It's all over the village about what happened to Susan Oakley."

Oh dear. Mary gestured for Emily to go into the small dining room. "What happened?"

"You cannot deny it—you were there, or so Mr. Payne said. He called in to see my father this morning and told him in the *strictest* confidence that poor Susan had been ravished!" Her eyes were huge. "I cannot believe it!"

Mary clamped her lips as heat ballooned within her chest. How *dare* Mr. Payne speak so?

"Oh, don't look at me like that." Emily's features took on the semblance of contrition. "It was simply because Mr. Payne is such a good friend of my father's that he felt he should warn us, seeing as we are somewhat isolated, although not as much as the Oakley farm, of course. He just wanted to make sure we—that is, I—should be kept safe."

"He communicated such news as an act of neighborly concern, did he?"

"I suppose you could say so," Emily said, apparently unaware of the irony.

"Well, I hope no one else will feel it necessary to spread such tales."

"But is it not true? Do you mean to tell me that Susan made up such a story?"

"I mean to suggest nothing of the sort." Oh dear. How had her efforts to protect poor Susan's reputation descended to this? "Now, was there a message you wished me to communicate to her? Perhaps you had some flowers you wished to leave, or a kind word you wished to offer?"

Emily's blue eyes grew shiny with tears. "Are you suggesting I indulge in gossip? I thought you were my friend."

Mary compressed her lips. Had her words proved so very unfortunate?

"People might say you are kindhearted, but I know exactly why you are still unmarried. It's because of your nasty tongue!"

Mary flinched. "Emily—"

Emily shook her head and flounced out.

Mary made no further effort to stop her. Her lips pushed to one side. Perhaps Mary wasn't the only one thought to own a nasty tongue.

At a sound in the hall behind her, she turned to encounter Joanna's disappointed face.

"I was upstairs and thought I saw Emily leaving."

"I'm afraid so."

"I thought she wanted to speak with me. I'm surprised she left without saying anything."

Oh, Emily had said enough. "I suspect she might be a little distracted with Lieutenant Edgerton's return."

"Ah, that would explain it. But why did she call in?"

"I believe she wanted to convey her best wishes for Susan's recovery."

"That was kind of her." Joanna reached for an apple from the bowl on the dining room sideboard. "How long do you think we shall have Susan here? Not that I mind terribly much. It's not as if I shall be expected to nurse her or anything, but I wondered if others might be a little put off by knowing she was here." She bit into the apple with a loud crunch.

"*Others* meaning your suitors?"

Joanna flushed and looked away.

Mary's brows rose. "How wonderful to see your concern for Susan's well-being does not derive from self-interest."

"I *am* concerned." Joanna swallowed. "Really, Mary, if you haven't anything nice to say to me, then perhaps you should heed Mama's advice and not say anything at all." With a smirk that could only be described as triumphant, Joanna turned on her heel.

Both her sister and Emily claiming a certain acidity was responsible for Mary's continued single state? Were they correct?

Not that such a thing mattered at all.

❦

Following visits to the Crokers and old Mr. Crowdey—visits that proved to Mary she most certainly *did* know how to speak with kindness—she made her way to visit Letty Jamieson, the sister of both Joanna's "rescuer" from the dance the other day, and Albert, the corporal whose rescue in Spain had done so much to bring Lieutenant Edgerton acclaim.

"How are you getting on?" Mary asked Letitia, as they sat in the Jamiesons' sunny kitchen.

"Oh, Alby is that pleased Lieutenant Edgerton is returning, and cannot wait to see him. I'm sure they will have much to discuss."

"I'm sure. And Albert has recovered?"

"Ah, poor Alby will always have a limp, that is so, but then, considering he got a ball to the hip, it's a wonder he can walk at all."

"Thank God he can."

"Oh, he does, and we do. And we thank God that Alby was where Lieutenant Edgerton could drag him to safety. What a brave man."

"Yes." Mary took a sip of tea and opened her mouth to enquire after the state of Letty's own health.

Letty's other brother walked through the back door. "Good day, Miss Bloomfield."

"Good day, Benjamin."

His eyes lit. "Is Miss Joanna with you? We had such a good chat the other day at the assembly, and I would like to see her."

"She mentioned enjoying her conversation with you, but I'm afraid she's visiting elsewhere today." Visiting the Peters family with Mama, but he would likely not appreciate learning that.

"Ah. Well, if you could please pass on my regards, I'd be grateful."

"Of course."

He smiled, a sight that elicited a slight tug within. She could see why Joanna enjoyed time with him.

"Have you spoken to my scapegrace brother?"

She chuckled. "I would hardly consider your poor brother a scapegrace."

"Hear that, brother?"

A clumping sound signified the crutches and swung boots of the third Jamieson sibling. He came into view, his grin reminiscent of his brother's. "Good day, Miss Bloomfield."

"Hello, Alby. How are you feeling?"

"Much better since that tincture your father prepared for me."

The one she had prepared, actually. "I'm so glad. It has eased some of the aches?"

"Some."

She discerned a tiny pinch pleating his brow. "But not all."

"I'm sure it will get better with time."

"We will pray for you."

"Thank you." He dipped his chin. "I will admit I'm looking forward to seeing Lieutenant Edgerton's return."

"Of course."

"Did anyone ever tell you exactly what he did?"

"I've heard that he—"

"Oh, Miss Bloomfield, you never saw such a thing!" He rushed on as if she hadn't spoken. "We were surrounded by the French, and out of nowhere it seemed we had these cannonballs raining down on us, dust and smoke everywhere. Men were getting hit left, right, and center, which is how I got this lead in my leg." He rubbed his hip, eyes feverishly bright. "I was lying there, in a field surrounded by my fallen comrades, when suddenly Edgerton and Captain Balfour led a charge and swooped in and carried us away, all under enemy fire. It was the bravest thing I ever saw."

"He must be a very brave man indeed."

"That he certainly is. I can't wait to see him, and offer my thanks, and wish him all the very best."

"He shall return to a true hero's welcome."

Albert suddenly frowned. "But that is the thing. I can't help but think it strange he returns now and not with the rest of the troops. Do you not think that odd?"

"I cannot profess to be an expert in these things, but it does seem unusual." And may well account for the concern she'd spotted in Mr. Edgerton, senior. "We shall simply have to pray that all is well, and he returns to us safely."

"Aye, I'm sure you are right. He'll be safely back in no time."

His brother nodded. "No need to worry at all."

⚮

"Are we nearly there?"

The headache throbbing since Kendal on Sunday had worsened to this near parlous state, where his body and mind felt suspended between reality and nightmare. Not that he wished to alarm Bracken. His friend was alarmed enough already, having witnessed too many of Adam's pain-filled exclamations he'd been unable to stifle. Their trip had been delayed yet further days after Bracken insisted that Adam rest at various inns along the way. But the noisy inns with uncomfortable beds were hardly conducive for repose, much less sleep, and this rocky road ensured that whatever respite Adam managed to snatch was fast eroded by the constant jolting and bumping of the carriage. No doubt the lack of sleep had contributed to this feeling of nausea and unease.

Of course, such things were made worse by the bandages wound around his head. He recalled other journeys made easier by at least being able to see where he was going. Now, he had to rely on his other senses, on his hearing, on his sense of smell, on his body's roll and sway. Since the bandages had been placed over his eyes, he'd noticed such perceptions working extra hard as if to compensate for his lack of vision, and it seemed as if his thoughts never stopped their racing. It wouldn't be forever, God willing, for his mind and his body were utterly exhausted.

Another sudden jerk of the carriage slammed his nose into the carriage door.

"Edgerton?"

Hands on his arm, his shoulder.

"That was a nasty knock."

He couldn't speak. His nose was clogged, forcing him to tilt his head and breathe through his mouth.

"Oh, it seems you have a bloodied nose. Allow me."

At the ineffectual dabbing near his nose, he seized what he presumed to be a handkerchief from Bracken and held it to stem the blood. Wonderful. Another flaw to add to those qualities his betrothed would exclaim over. How he hoped she might prove a sensible lass and not one prone to hysterics. His brow wrinkled. She would be sensible, wouldn't she?

Another wave of nausea rippled, followed by a fresh rimming of pain around his crown. He swallowed. Felt the prickle of heat line his brow, slide down his neck.

"Adam?"

He ignored Teddy. Just needed to not move, not speak. Just needed to keep still else Bracken's shoes might be soon wearing Adam's last meal.

"Adam? Can you hear me?" Bracken's voice now seemed to be coming from very far away.

Adam exhaled slowly, willing the nausea to subside. How much longer?

"I say, you really do not look at all the thing. You look quite done in, and your face—what isn't black and blue or red—looks rather green. Do we need to stop?"

No. Adam gritted his teeth, managed to mutter, "Continue."

The sooner they got there, the sooner he need never ride in a coach again. Especially such an ill-sprung coach as this one.

"Well, if you want to stop, you simply need to say so. I'd rather that than see you cast up your accounts."

He forced himself to steady, to focus. Soon he would be home. Home among the lakes, the hills, the wind, the fields. Soon it would be summer, and he would enjoy the crisp freshness of the Cumbrian land-scapes, revel in the world he'd enjoyed since a boy.

And soon he would be married, if dearest, sweetest Emily still wished to have him. His brow furrowed. Was it right to even expect she would want him to fulfill his promise? What would she say when she saw him, when she realized he was not the man she'd made promises to? Was it more noble to ask her to forget him?

But what if the doctors had been wrong, and a cure could be found, and his sight restored miraculously as in Bible days? What if he called things off only to have his sight return? Wouldn't that be even worse for Emily? Oh, what was the gentlemanly thing to do?

He pressed his hands to his temples. Why did he doubt? Surely dear, sweet Emily's promise would not waver just because he was not quite the man he'd been when he had left. Wryness tweaked his lips. "Not quite as he left" was something of an understatement. He wouldn't blame her for second thoughts. He would seek her best—but what *would* best be? A life bound to him, playing nursemaid, or should he set her free?

A shiver wracked his body, the questions swimming in his brain relentless, a constant push and pull of pain that matched the ebb and flow low in his gut. Sweat trickled down his back.

God, give me wisdom.

Did God even hear him? His prayers these days seemed devoid of any faith.

Another bump, another savage pain. He groaned. Then swallowed a spurt of sick.

"Edgerton? You do not look at all well. I think it will be straight to bed when you return home. I cannot think your good mother will allow you to stay upright a second longer than necessary. I remember when I visited once during term break—do you recall? She was always so good to us, although inclined—not unnaturally, I might add—to fuss."

"I remember," Adam rasped.

Days of chasing sheep and clouds, and long treks to the fells and tors. Days of fishing on Windermere, then returning to Mother's relieved concern. Days of flirting with local lasses, pretending he was more experienced to show off to schoolfriends. Carefree days that were now gone forever.

Dear God. His head lolled to one side, his neck seeming to have lost all strength.

"Adam?" There was a note of panic in Bracken's voice. "Adam? Can you hear me?"

Hot. He was so hot. So thirsty. Why didn't they stop at a public house? Even plain water would do. He tried to lift his arm to tug at his too-tight neckcloth. Couldn't. No strength. No energy. Too warm. He was prickling hot all over.

"Adam." A hand rested on his forehead. "Oh, you have a raging fever. Poor chap. Can you hear me?"

Now he was too cool, too cold. He shuddered. "C-cold."

Sounds of shifting, a dip in the seat beside him. "Let's have you lie down here, that's right. And you can have my greatcoat to cover you, if you promise not to soil it."

He feebly grasped the coat, tried to drag it but it was too heavy. What a weakling he'd become, scarcely better than a wee bairn. The coat slipped, and a blast of cooling air taunted his neck, his back. He shivered again.

A hand pressed against his brow. Too heavy, hurting.

"You're burning up."

The pressure released, and the slam of a window opening ricocheted through his head. Oh, how wretched was he.

"Can you hurry? He's taken unwell again."

The carriage lurched forward once more, jerking fresh pain through his head, teasing his stomach to release its contents.

"Now, now, my friend, we'll soon be there. Just hold on an hour more."

An hour? He might die. He wished he could die. Or that he *had* died. This pain was not something to wish on his worst enemy. If only the doctors could diagnose him accurately and provide a remedy. If only God would heal him. If only . . .

God, help me. The carriage jolted, and he tumbled into oblivion.

Chapter 5

The sun had barely begun its noontide descent when Mary heard movement from the guest bedchamber. She hurried to the room beside hers. "Susan?" she called through the closed door.

"Mary? Is that you?"

"Yes. Please unlatch the door."

There came the slight scrape and rasp of the door latch hitching up, then the door inched open.

Poor girl. Susan had spent much of yesterday closeted within, her red-rimmed eyes testament to her sorrow and lack of sleep, hence her rest now. How long would it take before Susan felt safe? "How are you feeling now?" Mary moved into the bedchamber, held out a hand that Susan quickly grasped as they sat on the bed.

"A little better. But I had such awful dreams." Susan's eyes were shaded with fear. "Will they ever stop?" she whispered.

"I cannot say." Mary squeezed her hand. "But you know that here you are safe, you are protected. No one can harm you."

The dark head bent, then eventually nodded.

Compassion twisted her heart. *Lord, help Susan know Your healing, Your comfort, and Your peace. Help her—*

"Oh, what is that?" Susan glanced at Mary's hand. "Your hand feels so hot!"

"I . . . I don't know."

"It happened earlier, too. When you were praying. I felt most peculiar."

The way Susan looked at her—brow knit as if worried—twisted uncertainty inside. Did Susan suspect Mary possessed qualities more like Hannah Liddell than like Jesus? "In what way most peculiar?"

"Oh, I don't know." She shrugged, glanced away. "One moment I felt a kind of terrible churning inside, then it seemed to stop. Or at least not churn quite so badly."

"Susan, I believe that is—"

A pounding at the front door interrupted her and drew Susan to her feet. "Oh, miss! Do you think that's him? You said he'd never find me, that he'd never be able to hurt me again. Please, don't let him hurt me!"

"Ellen will answer the door, so you need not worry. In fact I—"

"Miss!" Ellen's voice trailed up the stairs. "Miss Mary!"

A trickle of fear raced up her spine. The last time Ellen's voice held that pitch the minister's wife had suddenly sickened and Mr. Ponsonby had summoned urgent help, but they had been too late, and had arrived to find the still form of Mrs. Ponsonby lying on the bedroom floor, hands clutched claw-like at her chest.

The servant hurried up the stairs and gasped, clinging to the door-frame. "Oh, Miss Mary! Your father wants you immediately. Up at the Edgerton farm."

The Edgerton farm? "Of course." Had the joy of the son's return proved too much for Mrs. Edgerton? She did have something of a frail heart, so Papa had said.

"Oh, and he said bring both the syrup, and a specimen of featherfew and powder of dropwort and toadflax."

"Of course. You will stay to ensure Miss Oakley is safe and well?"

"Aye."

"I'm sorry, Susan. Ellen will look after you, and my mother and sister will soon return from their luncheon engagement. If there is anything you require, you need only ring this bell."

Susan glanced at it dubiously. "But what if—"

"Sorry, miss," interjected Ellen, "but the doctor said it was urgent-like."

"Then I best not keep him waiting. Excuse me, Susan." She raced down to the distilling room, where Father kept the herbal preparations, and hurriedly searched through the stores until she found what had been requested. Clutching the basket containing the herbs and two small glass bottles, she hurried outside to the dour afternoon skies. Oh no. She would need to walk the steep mile up the hill to the Edgerton farm. It would take much longer than the urgency demanded. *Lord, please help.*

A cool breeze teased at her hair as she hurried along the muddied road, doing her best not to stumble on the slippery stones. A clattering sound came behind her, and she turned to see Mr. Croker's welcome face as he slowed his cart and horse. "Oh, Mr. Croker! Would you please help me? I must get these medicines up to the Edgerton farm immediately."

"Jump up."

She grasped his hand and he pulled her up to the wooden seat beside him.

"I gather this means young Adam has returned."

"I do not know for certain, but I suspect so."

They passed the Oakley farm, from which came the ever-present sound of dogs, but over which bleakness seemed to have settled like a gloomy cloud. Her prayers for Mr. Oakley were interspersed with spurts of impatience as she silently begged Mr. Croker's too-placid animal to hurry. Father had rarely summoned her in this way.

They slowly ascended the steep hill, passing the green fields bordered by stone walls that denoted the Edgerton farm. Then they were moving past the twin stone pillars that marked the yard of the white farmhouse with its blue-painted square windows and red door. A gig waited nearby, the horse's reins tied loosely to a wooden post.

"Thank you, Mr. Croker," Mary said, as he helped her down. "I'm so thankful you were passing by at that precise time. Please send my regards to Sally."

"Aye, miss, I'll be sure to do so. Oh, now don't forget your potions."

"Oh, thank you." She grasped the basket containing the special herb bottles Father had requested and hurried to the front entrance, only to be met by a weeping Emily, supported by her mother. "Emily? What is it?"

"Oh, it is terrible! Oh, I can't believe it." She sobbed, dragging in great noisy breaths, careless of who observed.

"Now, now, Emily, that is no way to behave," Mrs. Hardy admonished, with a sideways look at Mary. "I suppose you are here to give those"—she glanced at the bottles askance—"to your father." She shook her head. "Much good they'll do him."

What had happened? "If you'll both excuse me—"

"Nothing will help. It's all over for him now."

All over for whom?

"We should never have countenanced such a thing." Blackness tinged Mrs. Hardy's features. "It's all your father's fault."

Mary stiffened. "I beg your pardon?"

"But I *love* him," Emily sobbed brokenly.

Mary's eyes widened. "You speak of Adam?"

"Who else?" Mrs. Hardy sniffed loudly. "He's not long for this world, much the pity."

What? She stamped down the surge of emotion. "Excuse me. My father needs me." Mary pushed open the front door and moved into a long dim hallway. After a moment her eyes adjusted, and she saw young Meggie Smith, the Edgertons' part-time maid, holding a tray at the hallway's far end, hesitating at the closed door as if wondering whether to enter the room or not. "Meggie?"

She jumped, setting the tray things to rattle. "Oh, Miss Bloomfield! I did not know you had arrived."

"Is my father within?"

"Aye. He and the master and mistress and the young master. Terrible sick he be, too." Her eyes rounded. "They say he might die!"

Mary's breath caught. No wonder Emily was distraught. Mary slowly exhaled, eyed the tray. Glasses. What looked like light wine or whiskey. "Are these supposed to be taken inside?"

"The master asked for them, but I didn't want to bother them none."

The whiskey was likely more for the father than the son, perhaps as a special medicine to numb the pain of loss. Still, if Mr. Edgerton had requested it . . . "Shall I manage the door for you?"

"Oh, thank you, miss."

Mary opened the door, holding it so Meggie could pass inside, then followed behind her.

The room, a man's bedchamber, held a bed and six persons: her father, Mr. and Mrs. Edgerton, another man unknown to her, a male servant, and the prone figure of Adam Edgerton. A sickly, musty scent filled the air, one exacerbated by the fire in the corner. The room was too hot.

Meggie placed the tray on a small table near Mr. Edgerton, but he ignored her, his eyes fixed on the motionless figure in the bed. Mrs. Edgerton sat in a low chair on the other side, her fingers intertwined with her son's. They seemed to be listening to the unknown man speak.

". . . At a place called Walcheren. Didn't seem to get better, or so they said at St. Thomas's." He held out a paper to Mr. Edgerton. "The doctor sent notes."

Mr. Edgerton stared at the paper, his blank expression such that Father asked to see it.

Receiving no response, Father gently tugged it from the man's fingers and perused it intently. "Ophthalmia," he muttered. "I have heard of this sickness, a painful inflammation of the eye accompanied by a fever that comes and goes. Some say it originated in Egypt." Father nodded, stroked his chin, before snapping into authority. "Well, as I said before, the first thing we must do is get this fever down." He glanced behind, noticed Mary. "Ah, Mary, good. You brought the toadflax?"

She nodded.

"I have already administered laudanum, as the poor lad has been in such pain. But before he drops off completely, I shall need you to add a measure of the flaxseed to this dram of wallwort and cinnamon here." He motioned to the table beside the bed, where a small glass of pale yellow liquid sat, then leaned over the prone body again.

With shaking hands she carefully added the toadflax powder to the glass and stirred carefully, then handed it to her father.

The unknown man glanced at her curiously.

"My daughter." Papa raised Adam's head slightly, easing the glass to his lips and tipping it so he was forced to drink.

"Something of a healer," Mrs. Edgerton murmured, her face drawn with fatigue.

Mary stole closer to the bed. Breath suspended. The upper part of Mr. Adam Edgerton's head was surrounded by bloodied bandages, with only his mouth and chin visible. "Oh my goodness!" she whispered. "What happened?"

"He was injured in battle, then grew sick with fever. It's affected his eyesight, but that's the least of our concern now," Papa said. "If we don't get the fever down, he won't be needing his eyesight."

Oh, dear God, no. "Of course." Mary suppressed her emotions and moved into place beside her father, helping him as he stripped away the bloodied bandages.

"This blood looks fresh."

"I, er, am afraid that happened on the journey here," the man said. "It was one bump too many for his nose."

Mary winced, then glanced at Mrs. Edgerton, whose face wrinkled as if she might cry.

"Mr. Bracken accompanied Adam in the coach." Mr. Edgerton cleared his throat. "Indebted to him."

"Least I could do. Adam has long stood as my friend," Mr. Bracken said, the frown pleating his brow suggesting this was so. He glanced up, met her gaze, and dipped his chin.

She acknowledged him with a nod.

Her father muttered about the room's heat. "It wouldn't have helped, not with all this bandaging. Kept him too warm."

She laid two fingers on Adam's hand, sure such an action would not meet Mr. Bracken's approval. "He is very warm."

"We shall have to strip his shirt. I'll need some help," Father said to the manservant. His strained features melded into a small smile as he spied her. "Mary, go make a poultice with the bruised featherfew now, that's a good lass."

"Yes, Papa." She glanced at Mrs. Edgerton. "Would you like a cup of tea, ma'am?"

The words seemed to penetrate the bubble of shock in which the older woman seemed to be suspended, as she blinked, and nodded. "Yes. Yes, please."

Mary nodded, and followed Meggie to the kitchen, where Mrs. Parr,

Meggie's aunt who worked as the Edgertons' cook, had water boiling in a large black pot over the fire. After requesting sweet tea for Mrs. Edgerton, Mary withdrew the pungent featherfew from her basket and separated the parts with a knife. The root and stalk she gently bruised with a mortar, then carefully poured some of the water over the fibrous parts before wrapping the whole in a small piece of muslin.

She returned to the sickroom to see Adam freshly clothed, now tucked between white sheets. He seemed more awake, moaning, though his bandaged eyes gave no clue as to how alert he really was.

"You have the poultice?" Father asked.

"Here." She handed it to him, and he drew back the sheet and placed it on Adam's midsection.

Adam flinched.

Oh no. The compress worked best when warm, but had she made it too hot? She averted her eyes, more for Mr. Bracken's sake than her own, and pretended to busy herself with rearranging the bottles on the side table. Propriety was scarcely her concern—in her years working by Father's side, she had seen many things people would deem unsuitable— though she had no desire to deliberately offend a person's sensibilities by her presence here.

"Mary, make up more of the laudanum, please."

She silently obeyed, focusing on her movements but unable to ignore the whimperings of the man in the bed.

"Em'ly."

Her heart twisted at the desperation in his rasping voice.

"Don't . . . stay." He groaned. Gasped. "No."

"Please, Bloomfield, do all you can do," implored Mr. Edgerton. "I cannot stand to lose my only child."

"Rest assured I will."

The door opened, admitting Meggie holding a tray with tea things.

Mary hurried to assist her, making sure Mrs. Edgerton's tea was sweetened as Father always recommended for shock. The men might prefer the stronger liquids on offer to take the edge off their upset.

God help us, God help them, God help him.

And Mary and her father pressed on.

The scream billowed inside. He had to escape, to be free. If he didn't escape the prison of these binds, he would go mad. Perhaps he was mad already. Was he mad? Would anyone ever tell him so, or would they treat him as he'd seen others treated in the hospitals in Spain and London, spoken to softly, patted on the head like an old, sick dog nobody had any use for?

Where was this place, anyway? Was Bracken still here? The interminable swaying and tipping of the wretched carriage ride seemed to have stopped, although the dizziness striking unawares might be compensating for such things. Maybe they were at an inn. He could smell alcohol. Whiskey? How strange that something he'd never really acquired a taste for he could now recognize.

At least he could breathe better now. The blood clogging his nose had been cleared away. Bracken's doing, or someone else? He should probably thank his friend for providing services no friend should ever have to perform.

Where *was* he? Who else was here? He coughed. Fire ripped through his chest, his lungs, his head. He groaned.

At once a cool, small hand rested briefly on his brow. Then came an easing, a soothing of the agitation he'd known for too long now.

"Mr. Edgerton," a low, gravelly voice murmured near his ear. "Adam. Can you hear me?"

He swallowed. Tried to speak. Couldn't.

"Adam," another voice now, one he vaguely recognized. "The doctor is here, Dr. Bloomfield. Remember him?"

Not really. Bloomfield? He'd once known someone by that name. Who? It hurt to try to remember, so he stopped.

"I say, Adam, you really should try to answer your father." Now he recognized *that* voice. Bracken's.

He cleared his throat. "Te . . . Teddy?"

"One and the same." There was a chuckle. "Well, you certainly had us going. We thought you might be dead to the world. Oh, sorry. Pardon my careless tongue."

Had he really been that sick? The muffled exclamations in the background suggested further confusion.

"Adam? You are back in your home in Amberley." The gruff voice. "Your father and mother are very pleased to have you return."

Hadn't someone else been here? He remembered crying, tears, dramatic exclamations. It had hurt his ears.

"I'm right glad you are returned to us," the other voice said.

Adam's skin prickled. He recognized it now, his father's voice. He licked dry lips. "Mother?"

"I am here, too," a softer voice said. "We are so wonderfully glad to have you returned to us." There came a sound, like a broken sob. "I didn't realize you were in such a bad way."

"I only told her you'd received a slight scratch," Father said.

"Apologies, sir," came Bracken's voice. "He wasn't this bad when we left London."

"The sickness comes and goes, does it not?" The gruff voice came again.

"Yes," Adam rasped.

Bracken and the doctor continued discussing his condition in low tones, and he was left with the familiar frustration of being the object of people's scrutiny, the subject of their conversation, yet ever unable to respond. If only he could see!

"Mr. Edgerton." A new voice, low, soft, cool. Female. "Adam."

Who was this who spoke so familiarly? His intended? He did not recall Emily possessing such a sweet voice. He caught a trace of lavender.

"You must be very tired."

That was true. He was starting to feel very heated again, too. He pulled feebly at the bedclothes, felt the cool hand from before cover his own.

"You need to rest."

A gentle heat passed from her hand to his, a strange, urgent heat that somehow both clutched his heart and soothed. "What—?"

"Here." The gruff voice again. "Before you rest you need to drink this. It will help bring down the fever."

A hand grasped at his shoulders, another arm rested behind, hefting him upright. His head screamed in protest at the movement, his body felt weighty, clumsy, strange. Who was the other woman here? A maid? A nurse? Why did she call him Adam?

"Open wide."

He grimaced at the instruction, at the way he was treated like a child. Still, he opened his mouth obediently, half-hoping the woman wasn't there to see him in such a vulnerable position.

Something vile was shoved into his mouth. He choked, swore.

A cleared throat, a wisp of lavender suggested the woman remained near, was likely witness to his shameful outburst.

"Excuse my son, Miss Bloomfield. He's not himself."

"He need not be excused," the soft voice said. "It is a taste most foul, yet it helps bring relief."

He certainly hoped so. He had no desire to repeat the experience, although he suspected it would prove to be among the least of the trials he might be forced to undertake.

Miss Bloomfield? Did this mean she was the doctor's daughter? His brow wrinkled, eliciting a fresh wave of pain, but he forced his thoughts to track on. He remembered a Bloomfield from long ago. Who? "Robert," he rasped.

"Robert Bloomfield is my brother," came the soft voice.

Robert Bloomfield. Ah, the lad he'd tramped and swum and rowed with. The one who had also gone to war.

Had he a sister? Why did he not remember? "Who are—?"

"My name is Mary, sir. The little girl who used to trail behind you both when you would walk the fells."

Ah. A knot within his chest released. Little Mary Bloomfield. He had hazy memories of a plain face, brown hair, nutmeg eyes, and short stature. A lass who showed quiet kindness to all.

A lass he'd never really noticed.

A lass opposite to Emily in every way.

A lass his mother had always described as the wallflower.

Chapter 6

Today held the promise of spring. The oaks boasted a fuzzing of green, the meadow's scent drifted to her, and the light breeze offered a hint of warmth. Mary paused at the vantage spot on her way to the village. From these heights Windermere shimmered below, the color and serenity a promise for those wishing to venture on water today. Mary's thoughts drifted to her brother, whose love for sailing was only equaled by his love of learning. Many the days had been when Mary had been hard-pressed to find Robert, only to learn he was on the water with one of his friends, fishing or boating. Certainly his days were not filled with such carefree leisure now. What would he be doing at this moment? His letters were few and seemed determined to cheer their recipients. She could not imagine his task was very pleasant, though his efforts were so necessary.

"Mary?"

She turned at the voice. Emily. Her heart sorrowed. "Good morning."

"Is it?" Emily's face had lost its vivacity, the luster was gone from her eyes. "I find it hard to think anything is good today."

"I am so sorry that Mr. Edgerton is unwell." Mary gently touched Emily's arm.

"Do you know anything?"

"No more than you."

At Mary's denial she pressed eagerly, "But surely your father—"

"I'm sorry, Emily, but I cannot satisfy your curiosity." She hoped her smile conveyed regret. "Father does not like to discuss his patients with us." Well, not with Mother and Joanna, anyway.

"But you were there."

Was that a hint of accusation in her voice? The sharpened gaze seemed to suggest so. "I was with my father, and he asked me to stay and assist him—"

"So, you have seen Adam and I still have not."

"Forgive me, but I thought you had seen him. Yesterday, it seemed your mother and you . . ."

Emily vehemently shook her head. "They wouldn't let me go in. Said it was too distressing. Oh, how wretched I am."

Mary laid a hand on her arm. "Not wretched, and certainly not unwanted. You surely know Mr. Edgerton simply wants to spare you from the pain of seeing him in such a condition."

Something flashed in Emily's blue eyes. "Adam told you this, did he?"

"His father thought it best."

"Oh." Her voice, her posture drooped.

"I'm sorry I have no better news to give you."

Emily shrugged, the twist to her mouth giving her a petulant look, making her appear much younger. "I know it is silly for me to be envious of you."

"Envious? Of me? Why, you absurd creature. You are quite right to call yourself silly for such a thing."

Emily's lips lifted in a reluctant smile. "It is not as if he would ever have any thought of someone like you, anyway. Oh!" Her hands covered her mouth. "I didn't mean that to sound quite like that."

"I know what you meant." Mary chose kindness even as her heart stung.

"It's . . . it's simply that I'm so terribly worried about him. I would hate to think he might be permanently affected by this."

"Of course. It's quite understandable." She patted Emily's arm. "Now, it's probably best you go and do something useful with your time. Is there someone else you can visit? No good will come of thinking only on Adam."

"But he *is* all I think about. How can you ask me to be so unfeeling? I cannot help but wonder will he live? What will happen?" Her voice, her hands, rose in fluttering agitation. "What am I going to do?"

"You are going to pray for him," Mary said firmly, "that God would heal his body. And his mind. I imagine it too has suffered a degree of damage."

"He has not left my prayers," Emily assured her.

"Good."

Adam Edgerton needed all the prayers he could get.

Emily's attention was stolen by another passerby, and when she soon launched into another exposition of her worry and ill-usage and rejection, Mary quickly made her farewells and hurried away to complete the tasks set before her.

Funny how grief manifested in varied ways. Some, like Emily, seemed to need to talk and talk and talk. Others, like poor Susan, seemed to prefer silence as they withdrew into themselves. Still others, like Mr. Ponsonby, seemed almost in denial in their rapid resumption of duty and tasks. Father had discussed this with her before, acknowledging the way different temperaments and personalities adjusted to pain and change, before patting her hand and saying, "Not everyone is so fortunate as to possess your calm good sense, my dear."

Her lips curved at the memory, but she wondered at it sometimes. Was she missing something not to experience the grand emotional highs that seemed the wont of girls like Emily and Joanna? Granted, such flights of ecstasy generally seemed to be followed by equally grand lows, where their emotions were laid bare to all, and seemed to have a way of infecting those around them with misery and woe. Had she ever been like that? Somehow she didn't think so. But did the lofty heights make such misery worth it, after all?

Too much introspection. She really needed to hurry home and assist Mother with the herbal preparations that Father had requested.

Later that night at dinner the family conversation—for Susan refused to join them at meals—turned once more to events facing the villagers. After some talk about the upcoming market and this year's sadly low prices for sheep, Joanna, restless as ever, who had spent much of the day with friends, put her fork down with a clatter.

"Father, what I and many others really want to know is when Adam will be better."

"That I cannot say."

"Because you do not know, or is it that you simply do not wish to discuss your cases with us?"

"I'm afraid it's too soon to say, my dear. He's been home but a day."

"Oh, Father, please. You cannot know how trying it is to be forced to deny to all my friends and neighbors that I do not know."

"But you aren't denying anything, dearest, because you do not know anything," Mary said quietly.

Joanna's gazed lifted to the ceiling. "You know what I mean." She returned her attention to Father. "Please, can you not give a crumb of hope I can offer to poor Emily? She was so distressed when I spoke with her today."

Mary lowered her utensil. "When did you see her?"

"Oh, it must have been early afternoon. I was just leaving Sophia Drayton's—did you hear that she has a cousin, who now lives with an old schoolfriend, who lives in a castle in Northumberland? I have never heard of anything so wonderful! She is sure to be married—probably to someone most fantastical due to all those wonderful aristocrats she'll be forever meeting. There, tell me have you not ever heard anything more amazing?"

"Sounds like a fairy story to me," Father said.

Mary smiled.

Joanna shot her a sudden glare. "I don't know why you are smiling," she snapped. "It is most certainly true. Anyway, she is certainly old enough to be married."

Her surreptitious glance at Mary made Mary grit her teeth and remember her morning reading about practicing patience.

"I cannot help but feel a mite envious."

That was hardly a surprise.

"But anyway." Joanna tossed her hair over her shoulder. "That is beside the point. Father, it is only right that Emily should know whether Adam Edgerton will be better."

"She and her parents can always apply to me," he said mildly.

"But I wanted to give her some encouragement today! Surely you can see, Father, that if he is not to recover, then it would be best for her to know so she can make alternative arrangements."

"What alternative arrangements would that be?" Mary tilted her head.

"Would you wish to be married to a blind man?"

Mary's mouth fell open. "Are you implying she wishes to end the betrothal if he is blind?"

Joanna tossed her head. "Isn't that what you would do, should you ever be so fortunate as to find a man willing to offer you marriage?"

"Not if I loved him."

"But how would he ever be able to provide? A farmer cannot farm if he is blind. What would happen to the Edgerton farm if Adam cannot see? Where would Emily live? How would they ever be able to manage? No, it is simply ridiculous to think she would be expected to marry him simply because she had promised to do so when he was in full health before." She turned to their father. "And this is why it is imperative to know if he will ever get better."

Father exchanged a glance with Mary across the dinner table, the flickering candlelight sending eerie shadows across his face. "I'm sorry, Joanna, but these types of conditions can never be precisely determined."

"But Emily is beside herself! Apparently, she was told he might not recover his sight."

"Who told her that?"

Joanna shrugged. "I think it was the Edgertons' cook, Mrs. Parr."

"She would certainly know, with all her medical knowledge." Mary focused her gaze on her plate.

"For someone who acts so high and mighty, you surely have a sharp tongue in your head," Joanna snapped. "I'm simply concerned about my friend, that is all."

"Listening to Mrs. Parr's advice is not always helpful," Father said, in a tone that raised Mary's eyes to meet the concern in his face. "It is a terrible situation, but I do not believe it to be without hope. His fever has come down, and I intend to visit again soon to ascertain the damage to his eyes."

"Poor Emily," Joanna moaned. "I could not fathom being married to a blind man."

"He is not blind."

"How would you know? Truly, Mary, you may have helped some people before, but it doesn't mean you know everything."

Mary's brows rose. She had never heard such venom in her sister's voice before.

"Joanna, dear. I don't think it is precisely kind to speak to your sister so," Mama interpolated.

"Mary cannot know for certain, that is true," Father said.

What? Mary swallowed a protest as her sister threw her a smirk.

"As I said before, none of us truly know the situation. But you still should not speak to her in that way."

Joanna's sneer took on an edge of chagrin, and she dropped her gaze, a faint flush highlighting her cheeks.

"I do believe God can heal most miraculously, Father." *Remember the Gosper twins,* she longed to say. The two children who had sickened most mysteriously then recovered after she had laid her hands on their brows and prayed. She'd often wondered since what would have happened if she had not obeyed that internal nudge.

"And I agree, my dear, and yes, we have seen God do most wonderful things. But that does not mean we can simply expect Him always to answer our prayers the way we see fit."

Mary opened her mouth to protest, but her father held up a hand.

"No, my dear, I am not veering to pragmatism at the expense of faith. We see in the Gospels that Jesus is willing to heal, but sometimes I think we can discount God's purposes by focusing on the here-and-now answers, while our heavenly Father might see a greater good can occur by an answer that's delayed. Or His response might even be a no. It does not mean that we stop praying, nor does it mean He does not love us or that He is not in control. God works all circumstances together for our good. Our challenge is to trust Him when it does not seem to go our way."

The words penetrated deep into Mary's soul. What if God's purpose was *not* to heal Adam? What a struggle to continue to trust God that would be.

Joanna sighed. At Father's swift look she sought to cover it with a cough, the attempt unsuccessful, judging from his raised brows. "So, when do you plan to see him, Father?"

"I hope to do so tomorrow. His fever has abated, it is true, but I suspect it will recur."

Joanna looked disappointed. "That is not very helpful."

"I'm afraid it is all we can offer. Besides our prayers."

Her sister glanced at the ceiling for a moment, as if she doubted the value of any prayers.

And the rest of the dinner continued in strained silence.

❧

A noise startled Adam from restless sleep. He listened carefully, but whatever it was died away. The room filled with deep stillness, save for the undercurrent of fear pulsing in his ears. The doctor was due today, and some questions over the future might finally be answered.

The questions had hung heavy over him during a week that had passed immeasurably slowly. He remained abed, his body having decided to settle in a place between chills and heat, his head losing a little of the ache each day. He was able to stay conscious for longer, able to hear the conversations around him and grasp those details counted most pertinent.

Bracken had left, apologizing for his departure but needing to return to his family near York. His absence sucked away the levity Adam desperately craved, the reminder that life was still worth living despite his parents'—and his own—ever-deepening gloom.

His parents remained despondent. They'd spoken to the doctor several days ago when they had supposed him asleep, and even now that conversation continued to play through his mind.

"But his eyes, Doctor. Tell me, will he be able to see?"

"I'm sorry, Anne, but I am not gifted with prophetic knowledge. It is something only God knows."

"Yes, yes, but can you not hazard your best guess?"

"Again, I am sorry. I should not wish to offer you hope that may prove to be false or dampen hopes for a miracle."

"You think a miracle will be necessary." Father's voice had been flat, resigned. "That says enough."

"But he is to be married!" Mother wailed. "Oh, poor Emily. I know how much she esteems him. Do you think she would wish to go ahead? Oh, what is to be done about the wedding?"

"What is to be done about the farm?" Father said heavily. "My son, my only son, my only hope. I cannot believe God would be so cruel as to do this."

"You must not give up hope yet."

Adam's lips twitched grimly at the memory. Precisely when should they give up hope? When should he?

If he was blind . . .

Blind. He dared to dwell on that for a moment. The word seemed impossible. Foreign. Ridiculous.

He was not a blind man. Blind men were old, like Mr. Crowdey, or strangers to be pitied, like the poor folk who lived in dilapidated parts of London and begged for coin and scraps. He was not like that. He was young, he would be strong again, he had family, funds, access to skilled medical practitioners. He wasn't to be pitied.

But if he really *was* blind . . .

He allowed his thoughts to venture beyond the constraints of denial, to imagine what life might be like should this prove impossibly true.

Darkness. Deep and utter darkness. No light. No sight of loved ones' faces. No knowledge of approaching danger. Adrift in a world of profound darkness. Forever.

A shuddery breath released at the pitiful person he would be.

Wretched. Useless. Deficient.

He was not that man. He was *not* that man!

He'd always thought he cared little for what others might think, but his heart writhed that he might be pitied if he could not see.

If he could not see.

If he could not see?

Fear—that ever-present shadow on his soul these days—swelled within his chest, rising up his throat to clog his nose, threatening to leak in a most unmanly way from those very places he had been told were problematic.

What if he *was* blind?

How could he live in this darkness for perpetuity? *Would* he be able to live in this darkness forever? His lips twisted. What was the alternative? To destroy one's life was a sin, was it not? Something only the most weak and vulnerable and deprived of reason did. He was not like that.

Yet.

But Father was correct. What would happen to the farm, to the future of their family?

Mother was right to be anxious, too. What would this mean for dear, sweet Emily? Her maidenly shyness had prevented her visit thus far—such maidenly shyness that also meant she'd scarcely shown much warmth on their prior encounters.

But was it right to force her to adhere to such a commitment? Regardless of his sight, he was not the man he was before the war.

What kind of man would demand she keep her word? It was not as if anything had been signed; a mere understanding, that was all they shared. Would it be a relief to her, to find someone else who was whole?

A shiver rippled through him. Fears seemed to encamp around him, seeking new ways to torture and torment. Fears about his health, his future, what this would all mean about his family. He could pray, but God felt so very distant . . .

"Mr. Edgerton?"

He jerked, mentally blinking, his mind slowly returning from the fog as he forced his thoughts to focus on the present. "Who is it? Who's there?"

"It's Dr. Bloomfield. I'm here with your father and mother to see how you are feeling today."

"Much the same."

A hand grasped his left wrist, fingers pressed against his pulse. "Hmm. The headaches?"

"Remain."

"I see."

That made one of them.

"Adam," the doctor said, "I want to take the bandages off today."

What? His pulse hammered louder. He'd known this would happen someday soon, but suddenly it felt too soon. His future would be determined too quickly. If it wasn't as he hoped, then he didn't want to know—

"Son?" Father's voice. "How would you feel about that?"

He sucked in a breath. Exhaled. "I suppose it is time we learned the truth."

"If you are sure?"

No. "Yes."

"Then let us begin." Cool hands touched his head, but today there was no scent of lavender, nothing to suggest the doctor's daughter was nearby. Not that he would ask about her; that would be very strange. But he could not deny that the touch of her fingers had seen a decrease in pain, and the sound of her voice had brought a soothing to his soul.

He shook his head, eliciting a concerned enquiry from the doctor.

"I am fine," he rasped, refocusing his attention.

"I'm here beside you," his mother said. She clasped his hand, small fingers intertwined with his large rough ones.

Adam gripped it tightly, like a scared child, as the bandages around his head were unwound slowly. His heart beat faster and he internally braced. Oh, *please God*, let his eyesight be restored. Let him be strong enough to bear whatever the outcome might be.

The pressure released, and the skin of his forehead and temples felt fresh air.

"Keep your eyes closed, that's it. I want to examine the stitches. Yes, they seem to have healed nicely."

Please, God, please.

Fingers prodded, tugging gently at his temples. "The gash here appears to have come together well. The skin is much improved from when I last saw it."

"That's good, isn't it?" Father said.

"Yes. But I'm afraid it's no guarantee that his eyesight will be as it should be."

The tiny arrow of hope shot up at the good report quickly plummeted.

"Now, Adam," said the doctor, "I know this may be a little distressing, so I want you to do this slowly. You may experience a strange sensation, you may feel ill, or your vision may be blurry. Just gradually open your eyes."

Adam's eyelids lifted slowly as per the doctor's request. Darkness. Utter darkness. He lifted his hands, reaffirmed the bandages had gone and that his eyelids were indeed open. No. *Dear God!* No!

"What can you see?"

His throat closed in. "I . . ." *No, God, no,* his soul screamed.

"Adam?" His mother's voice, her fingers, were tight.

He swallowed. "I . . . can see . . . nothing."

"Nothing?" Father repeated, anxiety ridging his voice.

"Try again," the doctor encouraged. "It may take some time for your eyes to adjust, especially as they've been bound for so long."

Adam blinked. Rubbed his eyes. Rubbed his eyes harder. Still nothing. "I can't see anything."

"Not even indistinct shapes?"

He narrowed his gaze, wrinkling his brow in concentration.

"Don't strain yourself now."

The whirling in his head suggested it was too late for that. He swallowed nausea. "Is the room dark?"

"Not at all," his mother cried. "Oh, Adam, the curtains are drawn back, the fire is blazing, it's the brightest room in the house."

Well, it wasn't to him.

"Adam?" His father again. "Can you see anything? Anything at all?"

"No."

"No shapes, no shadows?" the doctor persisted.

"No." His voice was hoarse. He could see nothing. *Nothing.* Something cold, something that tasted like despair, swept through his soul. "I'm blind, then."

"Blind? No, of course not, son."

"How would you know, Father? You're not a doctor." Adam heard the note of hysteria in his voice and breathed deeply to push the panic down.

"Doctor? Tell me this isn't so!" Mother's voice broke. "Tell me my son will be able to see again."

Dr. Bloomfield did not answer.

"Bloomfield? You cannot mean to suggest that this is permanent. Surely something can be done."

"I . . . I wish I had some better news. I'm sorry, but I cannot offer a definite prognosis. Adam's sight may return in time or, I'm very sorry to say, it may not. These things are in God's hands."

God, why haven't you healed me? Adam drew in a deep lungful of air. "So, you *are* saying I'm blind?"

"It does appear that way for the moment," the doctor said in his gruff, blunt way. "But I must emphasize it is for the *moment*. It may not remain the case."

A tiny spark of hope ignited. "There's a chance I may recover my sight?"

"With time, yes."

"Oh, thank goodness!" Mother squeezed Adam's hand. "You will get better, I'm sure."

"Aye, that is what we shall believe for," Father said. "I cannot allow the thought that my son can no longer see."

"Refusal to believe is not, however, conditional to it being true," the doctor said gently. "I'm afraid this is a case where only time will tell."

"How much time do you think?" Mother asked.

"A few days, weeks, months. It is hard to know." Apology laced the doctor's voice.

"But we don't have months. We hoped to have the wedding soon."

Wedding? What a farce. "No . . . wedding," Adam rasped.

"I beg your pardon?"

Adam coughed, fire ripping across his lungs. "Don't want Emily to feel . . . obliged."

"But you and she are sweethearts," his mother said, voice pitching higher.

Somehow he summoned strength to say, "I cannot ask her to tie her life to mine until we know for certain how things stand." He dragged in a breath, forced courage to continue. "And as we may never know for certain, it seems unfair to ask her to wait. It's best to simply quit things now and be done with it all."

"Oh, but Adam, my dear, you cannot mean to suggest—"

"Mother, I insist." He squeezed her hand and let go.

"Adam, I don't think you're thinking clearly—"

"I had best leave," the doctor spoke gruffly.

"But Doctor, can you not give a slightly more defined time frame?" Mother asked. "I cannot speak to dear Emily and her parents when we have no fixed date of recovery."

The doctor cleared his throat. "I'm afraid, my dear Mrs. Edgerton, that recovery is in the hands of the Lord, and He allows such things to occur as suits His plans and purposes."

"But, but—"

"Leave it, Anne," Father said brusquely.

Smooth fingers touched his arm. "I'm sorry this isn't the outcome you wished," Dr. Bloomfield said.

Adam nodded, not trusting himself to speak. Wretched emotion clutched his chest.

"I will visit again in a few days. I have left a salve that may ease any eye irritation, for use as necessary. In the meantime rest as much as possible, and if there is any change whatsoever, any unbearable headaches, anything at all, please send for me straightaway."

The pause suggested Adam should speak. But he had nothing he could say. He nodded again.

"Edgerton, Anne, I shall see myself out."

"I'll come with you," Father said. "Must see what Davis is doing. I fear we'll have to rely on him far more than we ever anticipated."

Old John Davis. Adam's lip curled. Father's aged chief laborer made a minimal effort as it was. How laughable to think his efforts would improve under a blind farmer, if take on the farm Adam did.

But if he didn't, what would he do? His soldier's pay was but basic; he could scarcely support himself, let alone a wife and family, on such a pittance.

The swirl of worries increased in his head, rushing round and round. Nausea attached to the headache thumping in his head, and he wanted to expel the pain, end the uncertainty, find a solution.

Oh God, what do I do? What do I do?

His mother's weeping filled his ears.

While he longed to offer comfort, he had so little emotional energy left to give. *God, help me. Help me! I've got nothing.* Misery burned at the back of his eyes. *I am nothing.*

Despair chased him to sleep.

Chapter 7

Something stole into her consciousness, requesting attention, begging her to wake. What was it? A sound. A woman crying. Mary pushed up on her elbows, ears straining. There! The sound came again. She pushed off the covers, pulled on a wrap, and stole to where the cries continued.

"Susan?" She twisted the door handle and pushed the door, but it caught on the latch and refused to open farther. "Susan? Are you well?" Foolish question. "Please come open the door." She tried to peer inside, but the room was too dark. "Open the door now, Susan," she said, putting steel into her voice.

"Oh!" A creaking sound came, then the door unlatched. "Oh, miss, I didn't mean to disturb you." Tears streaked her face.

"It's no matter." Mary gently rubbed Susan's shoulder. "But please, what has upset you so?"

"Oh, I was just having another bad dream."

Mary wrapped an arm around Susan's frame and encouraged her to move back to bed. "You are safe now."

"Yes, but what about the future?" In the dim light of the dying fire, Susan's eyes glistened. "No man will ever want to marry me."

"Shh, shh. Don't say that. You cannot know the future."

"I know every man will look at me and think that I'm nothing but soiled."

"Should you ascribe such prejudice to all men? There are many good-hearted ones who would appreciate you for your kind heart and bonny looks."

Susan shuddered out another breath. "If that is the truth, then why haven't you wed?"

Mary winced. It was far too late in the night to have to pretend such comments did not hurt. "I suspect marriage is not part of God's plan for me. And I am content." Mostly. "I try to remember to pray for contentment when people hint that I've been left on the shelf, or that I should wear a cap, or other such things."

"Oh, miss, I did not mean to say—"

"Hush now, I am not offended. I know that my heavenly Father has good plans for me, as He does for you, too. Besides, both you and I are most fortunate in that we have fathers who care for us, and will doubtless do all they can to ensure our futures are provided for." Thank God for that. "But such an outcome is highly unlikely for you, seeing as you are so young and pretty after all."

"You really think so?"

"I do. Now, it's time to go back to sleep." Mary smiled. "Tomorrow I'm afraid I shall have to enlist your help in making bandages. Papa is quite particular, and there is always more work than one person can manage. That is, if you don't mind."

"Yes, miss."

"Good night, then."

"'Night, miss."

Mary closed the door, remaining behind as the door latch was shoved into place and the floorboards squeaked several times. Then silence. She spent a few minutes praying, then returned to her own bedchamber.

But Susan's questions refused sleep.

Why had Mary remained unsought? The looking glass had never pretended to be much of a friend, but neither did it suggest she was a hag. Many people had expressed appreciation for her involvement in the community, had spoken kindly of her attempts to show compassion, but whatever quality kindled a young man's heart to affection had eluded her. What *was* it that made a man notice a woman in that way? One's face or form could pique a man's interest, but what stoked it? Men were not that superficial, after all.

Another minute of fruitless soul-searching, and she deliberately pushed it from her mind. It did not do to dwell on such matters; doing so only led to lowered spirits and envy that did not benefit her professed state of contentment. Instead she turned the concern raised by Susan's fears into breathed prayers.

"Heavenly Father, please comfort Susan at this time. Give her sweet sleep and pleasant dreams. Help her to seek You and find strength and peace in You. May her shame be covered over, and grant her a sweetheart who will love and protect her. Please bring healing to her pain. And Lord, please ensure the man responsible for this attack is quickly found. Amen."

Her whispers filled the room, easing her heart, and she lay back in her bed, pulled the covers up to her chin, and closed her eyes.

Sleep still refused to come.

A new strain of sadness stole in, something dark and unsettling. What pain people lived with. Poor Susan. Emily. Adam. Her heart pained for him. How horrible it must be, to not only be reeling from the challenges of ill-health at this time, but also be wondering about his future with the girl he loved, all because of a *possible* blindness.

Poor man. If Mary loved someone, she would certainly not stop doing so because of such a challenge. There was a reason the marriage service included promises to love through sickness and in health, for better and for worse. Marriage was not a promise of rainbows and starshine. Indeed, for most married people, it seemed more like hard work. Even Mother and Papa had their moments of sharp words and long-suffering and gritted teeth. Such a thing was hardly surprising. Years of observation demonstrated that marriage involved the melding of two distinct personalities into one household, two wills into that which made compromise and forgiveness necessary. Her lips twitched. It was probably due to her practical-minded view of marriage that she had never, and would never, be considered a potential object of romance.

And with that cheering thought, she rolled over and willed herself to sleep.

After a morning spent distracting Susan by teaching her how to roll bandages, Mary moved to the still room. Here, glistening bottles filled with all manner of herbs and potions and ointments awaited further attention. Papa's special medicines were kept in his study's safe under lock and key—they were expensive and, thus, must be guarded—but here, the old ways were found in glowing bottles of liquids and powders.

Wintergreen for wounds, knotgrass for worms, fig milk for boils, water fern for bruises. Each treatment required its own particular formula, which meant allocating part of each week to preparing the cures. Not every person would have use for such methods—indeed, the Carstairs would simply sneer at such medieval practices, as she had once heard his lordship call them—but they had their uses, and in fact proved quite successful in complementing Papa's more modern medicines, even if it was mainly to ease the minds of those mistrusting of nontraditional means.

She pulled down a bottle labeled *For Consumption or a Cough* and eyed the contents. The level was a little low, and it would be prudent to ensure they had enough for upcoming weeks, when the increase of pollen in the air meant sneezes and sniffles were bound to increase.

The old, large recipe book held instructions for all sorts of concoctions, but this was one she knew by heart. A pint of oil of turpentine, four ounces of flower of brimstone, and an ounce and a half of the ashes of gold, prepared in the heated sand that allowed the vessel to have an even temperature.

She performed the actions, retrieving the ingredients as necessary. Such a syrup might seem expensive, but for people like Mr. Crowdey, it was what they were used to. No matter of scientific explanations or modern medicines would he accept. Perhaps it was that he enjoyed all the sugar this traditional elixir demanded, with which she could not argue. Seven drops on a moist spoonful of sugar morning and evening for three days, before waiting three days, then repeating the dosage, all while avoiding cheese and other kinds of medications.

Sometimes the simple act of taking the medicine gave as much relief as any of the ingredients, although she'd spied in Father's science and medical books many references to a vast array of herbs and spices that were considered to have healing qualities. Regardless, God was the ultimate Healer, as she often reminded people, and irrespective of what medicines they used, trust should not be in medicine alone.

After finishing the cough concoction, she moved to make a tincture for toothache. Letty Jamieson had complained of aching teeth, and the remedy wasn't hard to make. She retrieved the dried root of pellitory, the pungency wrinkling her nose. After quickly cutting off a small section, she replaced the larger portion in its compartment in the wooden case and drew the mortar and pestle near. The smaller section she ground firmly, crushing each piece until eventually it resembled powder. Added directly to the tooth, or rubbed along the gum, it would ease the throbbing and provide respite from the fear of having teeth pulled.

When this was completed, she eyed the rest of the preparations. It seemed Father's special eye salve was missing, which meant he was likely using it on Adam and would soon require more. She reached for the dried herb of eyebright, the juice of which dropped into eyes had proved to aid infirmities that caused dimness of sight. Father favored a paste made of the powder of dried eyebright mixed with fennel and crushed bilberries, which, when mixed with hog's grease, made a strong-smelling salve which eased inflammation and had previously helped those struggling with their sight. She followed the directions and scraped her mixture into the small container Papa preferred such things be placed in, as it had a lid to keep contaminants out.

She was cleaning up when the door opened, and her father appeared. "I wondered who was in here. I saw your mother and sister in the kitchen rolling bandages with young Susan." He sighed.

"Oh, Papa, you look exhausted. Please, sit down, rest awhile. I'll ask Ellen to make you some food and a cup of tea."

He shook his head and slumped into the chair in the corner of the room. "I'm not hungry, just a little weary, that is all."

"Well, no wonder. What time did you get back this morning?"

"I snatched a few hours of sleep." He yawned, rubbed his hand across his face.

"Ellen mentioned you went to see the Crokers this morning. How are Sally and her babe?"

"Mother and child are both well, but it appears now little Betsy has sickened. She has a bad cold and, what with Sally's attention on the new child, I'm afraid there's less time for those other wee mites."

"Would it help if I visited?"

"If you can make the time, then yes."

"I will tomorrow."

"You are a good girl."

She allowed herself a moment to savor his approval, then asked, "Father, there was something else I wished to speak with you about. Has there been any word about the man responsible for Susan's attack?"

He sighed again, which became a groan. "I'm afraid not. The trouble is Mr. Payne is unconvinced that there even was an attacker, even despite my reporting of the results."

"How can he? Did he not see how scared she was?"

"He appears to think Susan a girl of loose morals who invited the man in."

Mary drew a sharp breath.

"I know. Inconceivable. But there you have it."

"Mr. Oakley must be furious."

"Truth be told I rather wonder if he's half-inclined to disbelieve Susan's story also."

"But it's not a story. It really happened."

"I know that, you know that, but mayhap for Susan's sake it's better if this is hushed over."

"But then the man gets away with it! That is wrong, Father, and you know it."

He glanced at her. "Are you going to speak to the magistrate? Do you truly want Susan's reputation smeared, and her chance at marriage quashed?"

He sounded like Susan herself. "But what about the good men who would be willing to overlook such things?"

His lips pursed. "You are not naïve. I wish I could say I agree, but with there being so many more young ladies than young men these days,

I suspect most young sirs will not wish to align themselves with a girl believed to have been less than virtuous."

Her chest grew tight. "This is so unfair."

"Yes, it is," he said, with a gruff tone that always signified constrained emotion. "Believe me, I wish I had a better answer."

"What if he strikes again?"

"We shall have to pray he does not."

Mary bit her lip. Was praying for protection truly all the solution they could offer? What about taking some form of preventative action? "What does this mean for poor Susan?"

He exhaled heavily. "Susan is not your responsibility, Mary. She will soon return home, and she and her father can best work out what happens next."

"But she will feel ashamed."

"I don't believe everyone knows."

"Knows of what?" Joanna's voice came from the door.

Mary looked up to face her sister.

Joanna's brow lowered. "What doesn't everyone know?"

"We were simply speaking about Susan."

"I'm afraid you will be disappointed to hear most people in the village do know." Her lips pursed, her brow wrinkled, and her expression held sadness. "Poor thing."

Joanna's rare articulation of sympathy softened Mary's heart. "Mr. Payne does not believe her and thinks her possessing of loose morals."

Joanna nodded. "I'm afraid that's also what I heard." She turned to their father. "Can you make him see reason? Anyone with half an eye could see how distraught she has been. Even if she did know the man, he obviously did not treat her as he ought."

Her own sister did not believe Susan innocent? The warmth she had felt towards Joanna at the rare moment of sympathetic accord cooled.

"I can speak to him again, but I'm afraid he'll be as close-eared as before." He chuckled suddenly. "I cannot believe you two. Your mother would have a fit if she knew you were speaking of such matters with me."

"Not for the first time," Mary reminded him gently.

His expression grew a little shamefaced, he muttered about finding some papers, and exited the room.

Joanna sighed. "It does not seem fair, does it?"

"An extremely unfortunate situation." Mary had as good as promised Susan no one would ever know. Now to discover that in fact most people did know . . . Had she made things worse by offering such a promise?

"I wonder if Father would be more inclined to action if it was his daughter involved."

"Joanna! You cannot say such a thing."

"Why not? It's the truth, is it not?"

"It . . . it is disloyal to suggest Papa would not do his utmost to protect everyone in this village."

"Do you think Mr. Payne would believe us?"

Mary studied her sister. "Why do you harp on about this?" Concern niggled. "You . . . you have not ever been attacked, have you?"

Joanna laughed carelessly. "Of course not. It is simply that I have strong doubts about whether a magistrate gives equal attention to all those who come under his jurisdiction."

Mary slowly nodded. Not for the first time had she this thought, too.

"Have you noticed his son? Charles always has such a nasty look in his eyes, as if he's plotting some nefarious deed."

"Joanna, you really shouldn't speak like so."

"No?" Her sister's brows rose. "You do not like to speak poorly of anyone, but I prefer to speak the truth. And the truth is that Charles looks like just the sort of person who might wish a girl harm."

"The truth is that Charles is in possession of a rather unfortunate squint."

Joanna chuckled. "That, too." Her expression hardened. "But if you had heard the way he spoke to me at the assembly a fortnight ago . . ."

"What?" Mary grasped her sister's arm. "Did Charles threaten you?"

"No. Of course not."

But Joanna's refusal to meet Mary's eyes did not convince of truth. "What did he say?"

"Nothing worth all this bother."

"Tell me, Joanna, what did he say?"

"Oh, very well! He said it was rude of me to decline his invitation to dance, and that one day he'd show me exactly what I was missing."

Mary blinked. "He said that?" Concern tightened her chest. "Oh, Joanna, please be careful."

"Don't look at me like that. And please don't start saying it's my fault because I refused both Joseph Beecham and Charles Payne that night."

"I would never—"

"I simply didn't care to dance with either man." Joanna shrugged. "Now, I really don't want to hear another of your lectures about how right he was to be affronted."

"I am sorry you think that of me. His words were uncalled for. I have no wish to scold you."

Joanna sniffed. "That would be a first."

Mary suppressed the desire to continue sparring and eyed her sister seriously. "What do you think he meant by saying such a thing?"

"At the time I thought he was just speaking nonsense. But now I think upon it, and given what happened to Susan, I can't help but view it in a more sinister light."

Mary pressed her forehead, willing the dull pain to go away. She could not help but hear such words in a sinister context, also. Could the magistrate's son truly be the villain? If so, it certainly explained Mr. Payne's reluctance to investigate the matter thoroughly and his willingness to blame the victim rather than seek the culprit's capture. But what could be done? *Heavenly Father, protect us.*

"Mary? I declare you truly can be most vexing. I do not like to waste my breath talking to someone who clearly cannot be bothered to listen."

"Forgive me. I was just thinking."

"You think far too much sometimes."

A reluctant smile escaped. "You would prefer me to be doing, correct?"

"You do a lot of that as well. No, what I'd prefer is for you to pay attention to your wonderful sister."

"And be at your beck and call?"

"We have a maid for that." Joanna looped her arm through Mary's. "Now, let's leave this sad conversation and go find Ellen. I want to know what is for dinner."

"Adam?"

"What is it, Mother?"

"It's very dark in here. Would you like me to open the curtains?"

"It makes no difference to me," he grumbled.

There came a sound of curtains being opened, of his mother's sigh—a sound he was fast starting to hate.

"How are you feeling today?"

"My head hurts." His heart hurt. His hopes were damaged beyond repair.

"Shall I fetch the doctor?"

"No. He'd only insist on giving me more vile concoctions that do no good."

"I'm sure they must help in some way, else why would they be given?"

He bit back a caustic answer.

Her footsteps drew closer, then a hand touched his forehead. "You do feel a little warm . . ."

He closed his eyes. Opened them again. It truly made no difference. Unbelievable.

"Would it help for Miss Hardy to visit?"

"Not today." Not ever. Except, as a man of honor, he knew he'd have to speak to her one day soon. But not today. He already felt so wretched.

"Would you like something to eat?"

And be fed like a baby? "No, thank you. I'm not hungry."

"But you're wasting away. I can have Mrs. Parr make up a nourishing bone broth for you—"

"I'm not hungry, Mother."

Another sigh. "Would you like me to read to you?"

A spark flickered. He wasn't usually one for much book reading, but then—his lips twisted—there was nothing usual about this situation. "Yes, please."

"Oh, good!"

She sounded relieved at having finally found something he was pleased for her to do, and guilt writhed that he had made her life so hard.

"What would you like me to read?"

Another decision? The thump in his head worsened. "Anything."

"Hmm. Let me see. I'll be back in a moment."

Her footsteps receded, leaving him in blessed relief. He should have just told her to let him rest, but his thoughts churned too much for him to ever find real sleep.

"I have a selection. How about the farmer's almanac?"

Was she joking? "Thank you, no."

"I was given a novel by dear Emily's mother, but I must say some of the content is rather lurid for my taste."

"Then it certainly won't suit mine."

"There is the Bible," she said doubtfully.

"Very well."

"You are sure?"

"Yes." He probably could do with hearing the Scriptures more.

There came a sound like flicking pages.

"Start at the beginning," he muttered.

A few more flicked pages. "In the beginning—"

"That's what I said."

"—God created the heavens and the earth."

Oh. He lay there, feeling a half-wit, listening as his mother read about the history of creation, the world's first people, the fall of man, the flood, and God's promises to Abram. His mother's voice was nearly hoarse when he finally directed her to stop, but these reminders of an ancient promise settled a kind of assurance on his soul. And as the thumping in his head finally eased to allow him to drift to sleep, he wondered if the God who formed the world from darkness might be able to breathe new life and make Adam whole.

Chapter 8

The next day Mary was returning from her visit to the Crokers when she spied Mrs. Edgerton, face wan, talking with—or rather listening to—Emily and her mother. She nodded courteously and moved to pass by, but Emily broke off from the conversation and hurried to clutch Mary's arm.

"Please say you'll come with me."

"I beg your pardon?"

"Come with me to the Edgertons'." She lowered her voice. "I cannot go there by myself. I cannot bear the thought of seeing him so injured, and Mama is insistent I do."

"And Mrs. Edgerton?"

"Oh, she's very quiet. She does not seem quite well herself, I think."

"This has been a big shock for the entire family."

"Yes." Emily sighed, then glanced up at Mary again. "Will you come?"

"I'm sorry, but I have errands—"

"Oh, *please* say yes! Going without you is unthinkable."

Suspecting this line of conversation had the potential to run on in a similar vein for quite some time, Mary acquiesced and allowed herself to be drawn back to the older ladies, who both wore worried looks.

"Good afternoon," she greeted them both, before turning to Mrs. Edgerton. "And how is Mr. Edgerton?"

"You ask after Adam?" At Mary's nod, Mrs. Edgerton's eyes filled with tears. "He cannot see."

Mary's heart gave a violent twist. She swallowed. "I am deeply sorry."

"He's very low in his spirits, very low indeed." Mrs. Edgerton's voice wobbled.

Mary gently touched her arm. "I'm sure that is only to be expected. It must be extremely hard to come to terms with the loss of sight."

"Oh, it is. He's started to say the most nonsensical things." She tossed an anxious glance at Emily.

Just what nonsensical things had Adam said?

Mrs. Edgerton dabbed at her eyes with a handkerchief. "Which is why I know that if he were to just see dear Emily here, it would only boost his spirits."

Emily's face fell. "But if he cannot actually see—"

"I'm sure Mrs. Edgerton is right." Mary nodded quickly. "A visit from someone he cares about must be a new focus for him and would likely cheer him."

Emily stared at her, eyes wide as if unable to believe Mary was pushing her to do such a thing as go visit her intended.

Mary hardened her heart. It was only right that Emily visit the man to whom she had once pledged her devotion. And it was only right that she face the facts of what the future might hold.

"Would you come with us, Mary?" Mrs. Edgerton asked, her pleading expression making it very hard to refuse. "Even if it's only to keep dear Emily company. It will do us all good to have your cheerful presence for a little while."

"Of course, if you wish it."

"If Miss Bloomfield is available to go, then I might be able to visit the milliner's after all," said Emily's mother with an air of relief, glancing at her daughter. "You don't mind, do you dear?"

"No, Mama."

Mary willed her expression to remain neutral, and her brows not to rise. Millinery above her daughter's heartbreak?

"I'll be sure to send them both back in the gig."

"Much obliged, Mrs. Edgerton." Mrs. Hardy patted her daughter on the shoulder, smiled at Mary, and toddled off to the milliner's.

Mrs. Edgerton beckoned to Emily and Mary to join her in the gig, which proved quite a squeeze, as Emily insisted Mary take the middle seat. A snap of the reins and they were heading up the steep hill to the Edgerton farm.

Far below them Windermere glistened, the green hills crisscrossed with grey stone walls seeming more a landscape painting than reality.

Mary exhaled, glorying in the view that gave respite from silent tension. "We are truly fortunate to live in such a lovely place. The view of the lake from up here is quite beautiful."

"And something my poor Adam will never see again," Mrs. Edgerton said in a broken voice.

Oh dear. How insensitive must she appear. Mary bit her lip.

Emily whispered in Mary's ear, "It is so dreadfully easy to utter the wrong thing. I scarcely know what to say, for if you can say such a heartless thing, then I have no chance!"

Mary willed her countenance to impassivity. "You will manage, I'm sure. Your love for him will ensure you think of him and his feelings above your own."

Emily drew in a sharp, broken breath that drew Mrs. Edgerton's notice.

"Oh, I know this is very hard for you too, my dear." She reached across to pat Emily's arm. "But we must be brave, for dear Adam's sake."

The gig drew into the Edgerton yard, and Mrs. Edgerton handed the reins to a laborer and stepped down, hurrying inside as if she'd forgotten her guests.

Mary shot Emily a wry look and followed.

Emily grabbed her arm. "I can't do it! I can't go in there."

"Please, Emily, think of him. I'm sure he'd expect to see you, that he wants to see you."

"But that's just it. He'll *never* see me, will he? He is blind."

"Do you think he has forgotten exactly how beautiful you are? I'm sure he remembers all the reasons why he chose you to marry in the first place."

"You think so?" For the first time there was a note of hope in Emily's voice.

"Please, for his sake. Go inside and remind him that you love him, that he has friends who care."

"Emily?" Mrs. Edgerton reappeared. "Oh, forgive me, I was so distracted. Come inside and I'll show you to his room."

Emily clutched Mary's arm.

Mary glanced at Mrs. Edgerton, who gave an impatient-looking nod, as if she couldn't understand Emily's reluctance.

They walked into the dim hallway and followed Mrs. Edgerton to the room Mary had visited before, remaining in the doorway while Mrs. Edgerton approached the bed. A fire glowed in the hearth, but the curtains were drawn. At least the smells of illness had been expunged.

Mrs. Edgerton touched her son's arm.

Emily's nails dug into Mary's arms, eliciting a wince.

The figure on the bed moved. "Who is it?"

"You have a visitor, my love," his mother said. "Well, two actually. Emily has come to visit you, and Miss Bloomfield is here also."

"Emily?"

Mary's wry amusement at the clumsy introduction died at the desperate note in his voice, the sudden sweet smile that illuminated his face. Oh, she shouldn't be here. This felt suddenly too private, her presence too intrusive.

"Emily is here?"

Emily gave an inarticulate cry, and Mary wrapped an arm around her. "Go to him," she murmured.

"I cannot," she whispered. "It's simply too awful. He might look so sick and dreadful, nothing like what I remember. I don't want to—"

"You must." Mary gently propelled her forwards.

"Oh, Emily, I knew you would come," he said, face tilted slightly away, facing the window and not the woman by Mary's side. He held out a hand as if for Emily to clasp.

She looked at Mary with tear-soaked eyes and shook her head.

"Go!" she muttered, nearly shoving the younger girl towards him.

Emily stumbled forwards to clasp his hand and murmured a broken greeting.

Mary's heart twisted and she took a step back.

"Oh, Adam! Oh. Oh, no," Emily murmured, with an audibly shaky breath. "I'm so sorry."

"There, there. These things happen." He caressed her hand.

How gallant he was. Mary bit her lip at the sudden sting of tears.

Mrs. Edgerton studied the pair soberly, then turned, caught Mary's eye, and nodded to the hall.

Mary obeyed the silent summons and met her in the drawing room.

"She's taking this very hard," Mrs. Edgerton said softly. "I did not realize just how much he meant to her."

Mary pressed her lips together.

"I'm sorry, my dear. I did not mean to upset you, too."

Mary touched her hostess's sleeve. "You need not concern yourself with me. I am simply glad he is restored to you, which must be such a relief, especially as so many families cannot boast the same."

Mrs. Edgerton sighed, a tear trickling down to her chin. "I am thankful, although I cannot help but wish he was whole."

"Such a feeling is only natural." Mary wrapped the older woman in a light hug. "But here, with family and those keen to see him well, he is in the best place to find that."

Mrs. Edgerton sniffed loudly and shook her head. "But what if he never recovers? What if he's never the same? What future has he got? What future can he offer that dear, sweet girl?"

"God will make a way. He loves you all and He will direct your paths."

"But you cannot know—"

A loud sob came from the room, then a rush of pink flew past the door and down the hall to outside.

"Emily?" Mary called, hurrying after her down the steps.

Emily held a hand to her heaving chest, the other splayed on her forehead, as she gulped in fresh air. "I cannot do this. I feel sick when I look at him."

"Emily," Mary cautioned, tilting her head as Mrs. Edgerton approached.

"Oh, my dear." Mrs. Edgerton clasped Emily in a motherly hug. "It is so hard to see him like that, I know."

"I . . . I—" Emily's frantic eyes caught Mary's as Mary raised her brows. "Y-yes."

"I expect after the initial shock, Emily will soon feel more the thing, won't you, Emily dear?" Mary said, with a warning look.

"Y-yes." Emily dabbed at her nose. "It was the shock."

Mrs. Edgerton sighed. "I know you care for him very much. Perhaps it's best if you return home now and rest, gather your strength. I fear it will be a long road ahead of us."

"Oh, yes," Emily instantly agreed. "I must go home. I must leave now. Thank you, Mrs. Edgerton. I . . . I wish there was more that I could do."

"There, there," Mrs. Edgerton said, in a soothing manner reminiscent of her son. "Do not worry your pretty little self. He will recover."

"I'm sure he will," Emily said in a piteous manner that allowed for plenty of doubt.

Judging it was best they depart now, Mary motioned to the gig and nearby laborer. "Might we borrow Mr. Lovett for a few minutes for our return?"

"Of course." Mrs. Edgerton embraced Emily and then pressed Mary's hands warmly. "Thank you for coming, my dears."

"You're welcome. If ever you need anything, please don't hesitate to let us know."

"Goodbye," Emily murmured.

They were handed into the gig, and Mr. Lovett drove slowly away.

Emily was silent on the journey, which was unsurprising. There was a great deal to consider for everyone concerned. Was Emily courageous enough to weather such a storm? It was one thing to say yes to a proposal from a handsome soldier about to head to war, quite another to say yes to a broken farmer's son, with no future assured.

They reached the village, and Emily insisted on following Mary inside the Bloomfield residence. "Perhaps Joanna will be back."

Joanna *was* back, and Mary thought she could escape, but Emily caught her hand as she was making her excuses. "Please stay."

"Shall I make some tea?"

"I don't care for tea. I don't think I'll ever be able to eat or drink again!" Emily turned to Joanna. "You should have seen him, he looked so pitiful and pale. He didn't even know where to look when I spoke to him."

Joanna nodded sympathetically.

"It was dreadful. I had no idea what to say. Adam is nothing like he was before, nothing at all."

Joanna exchanged a look with Mary.

"Oh, Mary, you understand, don't you? I cannot marry him. I simply cannot. What future has a blind man got?"

"I'm sure he has many years ahead of him—"

"No! I don't mean that! However will he provide?"

Mary stayed silent, heart cringing at what was truly being revealed. Did Emily truly not care for the heroic man?

"Do you wish to end things between you?" Joanna asked.

"But what if he recovers? Then I would have left the most handsome man in the neighborhood for naught."

The one she'd just announced looked pitiful? The one whom she'd said made her feel ill? For whom she'd expressed little regret save in how it affected her? Disgust swept through Mary's soul. "If you do not love him anymore—"

"Oh, I do not think that is quite so." Emily dabbed at her eyes with the edge of a pink handkerchief. "But I cannot love him *quite* so much as before."

Even Joanna looked a little startled at this proclamation.

The injustice of it all swelled within Mary and finally burst out. "If you truly cannot envisage yourself married to a blind man, then I'm sure you will find that he is honorable enough to allow you to withdraw, should you wish." The echo of her own words wrenched within. She had seen the hope in Adam's features when he'd learned Emily had come to call. But if such hope was misplaced and the angel he imagined was simply that—an illusion—then wasn't it better for this to be nipped in the bud now, rather than have his hopes bloom, only to wither and fade?

Besides, Emily's eyes had lit up. "You truly think so?"

Mary nodded, avoiding Joanna's open-mouthed stare.

"Oh, you have given me hope!"

Mary tried to smile, but it seemed more like a grimace. Was this how Judas felt, betraying his close friend? Only it wasn't as if either Emily or Adam Edgerton were her close friends, something that Joanna's narrowed gaze seemed to imply.

"I best go." Emily stood, then gave Mary an impetuous hug. "Thank you so much for coming today. And for your advice. I never would have thought I could manage today, but your encouragement has helped so much."

"I'm glad," Mary murmured into Emily's lacy froth of sleeve, still unwilling to meet her sister's glare. "Let us know how you get on."

"I will. Goodbye." With a little wave of her fingers, Emily hurried from the room, leaving Mary to face Joanna's raised brows.

"I cannot believe you just said that."

"What?"

"Don't try to play innocent with me. You don't want her to marry Adam."

"No, I don't think I do."

Joanna's mouth fell open. "You dare admit it?"

Mary drew in a steadying breath. "Would you want someone to marry you who had to be dragged inside to even say hello?"

Joanna blinked. "She was reluctant to see him?"

"Oh, Jo, you should have heard her. 'I can't see him. I can't do this. I feel sick when I look at him.' How is such a girl going to cope should he never regain his sight?"

"But she loves him."

"Does she? Really? Or is she in love with the idea of being loved by a handsome hero?"

"You sound almost bitter."

"I'm not bitter. Truly I am not. But I cannot help but feel this is so very wrong. You heard her before. You know how reluctant she's been. Why encourage her to continue with this attachment? She's not what Adam needs right now."

"No, but—" Her sister's eyes enlarged, then narrowed. "But neither are you."

"Me? I have no interest in him."

"Are you sure? Because it certainly seems as if you do."

"You are mistaken. I cannot believe that you would even think such of me!" Mary exhaled, willing the heat in her chest to subside. "I feel very sorry for him, and for Emily, as I can understand this is a situation she never envisaged, and the shock of it all is likely overwhelming her right now."

"After some time she will adjust to it and be the wife he needs."

"Do you really believe that could be true?"

Joanna's gaze slipped, her brow furrowed.

"Breaking the engagement would be most difficult and emotional, but I believe it very likely needs to be done."

"What needs to be done?" Mama wandered into the kitchen and bestowed pecks of affection on their heads.

"Mary thinks Adam Edgerton would be better off without Emily as his wife."

"Hmm." Their mother's gaze bounced between them. "And so he might well be. Emily Hardy can be something of a flighty thing."

"Mama!" Joanna protested.

"Come now, you must admit she is hardly the sort of girl one could depend upon to nurse one through an illness, let alone take on the role of nursemaid for life."

"I don't think he will be as bad as that," Mary murmured.

"Of course Nurse Mary wouldn't think so." Joanna threw another glance at the ceiling.

Mary held her peace. For a second, at least. "It's just that he has been very healthy, and I cannot imagine he will be content to stay indoors for the rest of his days. Perhaps one day he might want to run the farm and wish to work there."

"A blind man working the farm? You are full of nonsense. How could that ever be?"

Mary shrugged. A quiet certainty filled her. God, who did miracles, would draw this situation to good somehow.

Chapter 9

"Emily, I am sorry, but I must break our engagement."

Adam winced. That sounded rather too bald.

"Emily, I am terribly sorry, but I fear it only best to release you from any sense of obligation you might feel towards me."

His lip curled. Might as well call him a wet-goose and be done with it.

"Emily . . ."

His mind blanked. Was there any point to practicing his speech? Preparation might be important, or so his former commanding officers used to say, but it allowed little room for following the nuances of conversational tone, nuances he would very much have to rely on now that he had no visual cues to guide.

Emily and her parents were expected within the hour. His request to see her again had been met with caution from his mother and reluctance from his father, although he'd sensed that reluctance was mixed with a little relief. His mother had said Emily was in tears after the first visit, had needed Miss Bloomfield's arm for support as she'd gone home, and that another visit might only worsen things. His father was none too pleased once hearing Adam's plan either, so sure was he that Adam was simply being hasty.

But Adam could not put this off any longer. Her previous visit, where he'd been the one to do nearly all of the talking to his near-silent betrothed, had only confirmed what he already suspected. Each day he'd woken this past week knowing it must be done, going to sleep wishing it had been done, and pleading with God for His help with an answer. Hopefully Emily would hear his heart, not just his words. He had no desire to hurt her, but neither could he allow her to hold on to false hope.

For he was blind. He would not see. He would not improve. A type of certainty had entered his soul. Regardless of what others might say, regardless of the evil concoctions he was forced to drink or have smeared across his eyes, he would never see again. Never.

Moroseness settled on him, weighting him in his chair. He'd requested Father to help him to sit upright, certain Emily's mother would consider Adam being in bed rather beyond the proprieties that would permit her to allow him a private word with Emily. This, though Emily had seen him thus before. Although being abed might be beneficial in enhancing his invalid status, thus eliciting Emily's desire to break the engagement the sooner. Too late now.

God, help me, help us, with this. Thy will be done.

A knock came. "Adam, they're here," his father said.

He nodded, lifting his chin, bracing himself. He wished not for her pity, but if it helped him in these next few minutes . . .

A murmur of voices echoed in the hall, then his father's voice came again. "Adam wishes to have a private word with Emily, if that is convenient."

A higher, softer voice murmured something that sounded like protest. Adam frowned.

A deeper rumble—Emily's father, perhaps?

Then the door squeaked open, and Father said, "Emily, here is Adam."

A gasp let him know she had seen him. "Hello, Emily," he managed, forcing his lips up in a semblance of a smile.

A footstep, another one, another. "Hello," her shy voice came.

Oh, she was a sweet thing. He was cruel to do this, but it was best for her sake.

"How are you?" he enquired.

"Oh! I am quite well, thank you. How . . . how are you?"

His lips pulled to one side. At least she was talking to him now. "I've been better." He did not bother to hide the wryness in his tone.

"Did . . . it hurt? I mean, when your eyes were damaged, did it hurt?"

"It hurt a little." Like the blazes. "My eyes feel as though they are slowly improving."

"Oh! You can see? Adam, that's wonderful! I didn't know! Oh, this changes everything."

It did? But wait . . . "Emily, forgive me, I did not mean to suggest my eyesight has returned. It is the pain that is slowly alleviating, that is all."

"Oh." Crushing disappointment filled that one word. "Oh, poor Adam."

He forced his lips to remain up in a garish attempt at conciliation. Who knew pity could feel so painful?

"I . . . I am so terribly sorry." Another movement of air, the faint scent of roses, suggested she had drawn a step closer. "Your father said you wanted to speak with me. What . . . did you wish to speak about?"

"You. Me. Us." He winced. How harsh that sounded. He really should have—

"Oh, I'm so glad! You cannot know how relieved I am for you to raise this. Mama said I really should not speak to you about such things—she said I'd be labelled unfeeling, or worse, a jilt—"

A jilt?

"—but I knew you would understand how things should be. It is simply too much for one to bear."

His throat tightened. "Too much for whom to bear?" His voice sounded like a strangled cat.

"I *knew* you would see reason and agree we should break our attachment. You need to spend time concentrating on getting better, and not be planning weddings and the like."

Break their attachment? He coughed, then swallowed a self-mocking bubble of hysteria. So, he hadn't needed to toil over his words, after all. "Emily, I—"

"No, truly, it is best this way. I . . . I cannot help but admit to now feeling a little shame when I remember the kisses you were kind enough to bestow on me."

He'd *bestowed* them? She made it sound as if she hadn't been a willing participant. He remembered things far differently.

"I know it was terribly forward of me to behave so shamelessly when you left for the war, but you must forgive me and put it down to youthful ignorance."

He must, must he?

"Oh, I just knew you would understand. You are *such* a good man, after all."

Just not good enough for her to see her way to being married to him.

A savage kind of pain clawed at him. He clenched his fists, willing himself not to show emotion. How hard it was to know that others could read his emotions and he be ignorant of theirs. He drew in a deep breath, mind whirling at how this interview had turned jiggardy-jaggerdy so quickly.

"Is . . . ?" He cleared his throat, willing his voice to regain a degree of normalcy. "Is this truly what you want?"

"Oh, yes! That is, I truly would prefer not for you to be in this terrible situation—"

Something they agreed on at least.

"—but I do believe it best, especially given the circumstances . . ." Her voice trailed off, yet her words still held conviction.

He coughed again. "Forgive an injured man's befuddled brain, but I wish to understand things clearly. This is a permanent break, yes? You have no wish to marry me anymore." Her breath caught, and he winced at the ungentlemanly sound of his words. War had obviously stolen more than just his sight.

"I . . . I might be persuaded to think otherwise should your eyesight be restored."

An unbidden, cold fury surged. "You might, might you?"

"I beg your pardon?"

"Seemed you needed little persuasion before." He gritted his teeth. "Or was that just your father who was keener for this match than his daughter?"

She gasped.

He didn't need to see to know what her face was saying.

"You, sir, are being very rude."

"No, I'm just suddenly seeing things more clearly now." He snorted at the irony. At the sound of her crying, remorse bit. He gentled his tone. "Forgive me. That was unkind. I am sorry."

"I am sorry about it all, too," she said in a small voice.

He groped back the self-pity wanting to overwhelm him and forced a note of cheer into his tone. "I shall endeavor to inform the reverend immediately."

A muffled whimper might have been acquiescence. He was too shaken to enquire otherwise. He needed this interview to conclude as soon as possible.

"Now, can we agree to part as friends?" He held out a hand.

She touched his fingers briefly. "Goodbye, Mr. Edgerton."

This was it? Their engagement was broken? His own desire had been to have the same result but in a far different manner. His heart felt torn apart. He managed to mutter, "Goodbye, Miss Hardy."

There came sounds of departure, the murmur of voices, the closing of a door.

How had it come to this? *God?*

The utter absurdity of being on the receiving end of his own planned rejection. A desperate kind of chuckle escaped. Perhaps God answered prayers after all.

"Adam?" His mother's voice. "Is it over?"

"Yes."

"Oh, but are you certain you want to end things?"

"Yes, Mother. I am sure." He had no wish to remain betrothed to someone who clearly wished otherwise.

"And if your eyesight returns?"

"Then I'll be able to see."

"But what will you do then? Win Emily back?"

"Probably return to the war."

"What? You cannot mean it. You need not give Napoleon another chance to kill you. Besides, then you could make Emily wish to marry you again."

"Again?" His laughter sounded bitter. "I have no wish to marry a woman whose affection seems dependent on my health. There will be no wedding, Mama. Not now, not ever."

A sob.

He stifled a spurt of impatience. Why must women be so emotional? It wasn't as if Mother or Emily were the ones sitting here unable to see. "I am sorry you are disappointed."

"Oh, Adam, I wish I knew what to say."

Goodbye would be a start. *God, forgive me.* "Mother, I really wish to be alone now."

"Oh, but—"

"I really wish to be alone!"

She gave a muffled cry which rent his heart in two, and the shuffling of feet and door closing suggested she had taken the hint and left him to his pitiful self.

He listened, senses sharp, for any sound of breathing, any sign someone else remained with him still, but no sound of breath met his ears but his own. He slumped in the chair, propped his head into his hands, and bent over his knees.

He was a failure. As a soldier. As a suitor. As a farmer. As a son.

"God, help me," his voice rasped, as wretched tears clogged his useless eyes.

⁂

Mary twisted open the door and moved into the kitchen. The house was silent, as if mourning the loss of Susan Oakley, who had returned to her farm, and all the potential ramifications of such a move. Regret knotted Mary's heart that such a plan had been deemed necessary. She knew the reasons why it had been thought so, but could not help but feel a sense of failure, failure only exacerbated by the reproachful look in Susan's dark eyes as Mary farewelled her at the Oakley farm door.

But what else was she to do? Father was right. It was a situation Mr. Oakley had to take up with the magistrate. It was not Mary's place to do so. But still, restlessness ate at her, a kind of yearning for something more, for provision to be made for those who might find themselves in similar unfortunate positions, and for the vile and wicked perpetrator to face certain, dreadful justice.

And now the house felt too quiet, too still, almost accusing of her failure to keep her word.

She dropped into the kitchen's stiff-backed wooden chair, thankful no servants were near to witness her exhaustion. A yawn escaped, testament to last night's efforts at the Crokers. Poor Betsy. She was not at all well. However, her screams at the suggestion of leaving her mother caused all to think it best to leave her at home, at least for one more night. If Betsy was not showing signs of improvement by the morning, then she would be their newest charge.

Mary scrubbed a weary hand over her face. All she wanted was to sleep. But there was a fresh batch of bread to make; today was Ellen's half day. And with the potential of Betsy's staying with them, perhaps Mary should make something sweet to tempt a young girl's appetite. She had appreciated the currant buns . . .

Another door banged, and there came the sound of voices, of feet.

"Mary? Mama?"

"In here, Joanna," Mary called. She tried to push herself up, but weariness claimed her. Oh well, it was only Joanna.

The door opened and in strode Joanna. Followed by a weeping Emily.

"Emily? Oh, my dear, what has happened?" Mary rose and placed an arm around her shoulders. "Please come sit down."

Joanna glanced around the kitchen, as if the space was foreign to her and she hadn't sat at the kitchen table a hundred times before. "Why are you in here?"

"I . . ." She shrugged. It was too hard to explain.

Joanna joined her at the table, tugging Emily's hand to join her. "Sit. Tell Mary. She can be quite good at listening."

"Yes, Emily, do make yourself comfortable here by the fire. Can I make you tea? I've often found a nice warm cup of tea to help."

Emily sniffed and managed a barely audible "Yes, please."

Mary busied herself with heating the water. Her heart thudded painfully. Clearly Emily was upset—did it have something to do with Adam Edgerton? Had he worsened?

As calmly as she could, she steeped the tea, poured it in a cup, added milk and sugar carved from the sugarloaf, and stirred it in.

Mary patted Emily's arm. "Now, drink that up, and try to relax."

Emily nodded and obeyed, as Joanna cast Mary a wide-eyed look that implied this was a story worth waiting for. Mary made small talk, chatting about inconsequential things in an effort to help Emily calm.

Her efforts did not seem appreciated by Joanna. "For goodness' sake, Mary, we haven't come to talk about the weather!"

Mary glanced at Emily, who sipped the last of her tea. "Are you feeling a little better now?"

Emily nodded, although her large eyes remained filled with tears.

Oh dear. Mary needed to tread very carefully. "Would you care to tell me what has happened?"

"Can you believe it?" Joanna interrupted. "He has ended the engagement!"

Mary gasped. "Adam ended it? I thought—"

Joanna sighed dramatically. "Really, Mary, you might have more delicacy than to refer to Mr. Edgerton in such a familiar way. It's not as if *you* were ever engaged to him."

Mary glanced apologetically at Emily. "You must excuse me. As he was such good friends with my brother, I never saw any reason but to call him by his given name, especially when we spent much time rambling together when we were younger. I assure you, I speak your Mr. Edgerton's Christian name only from years of thinking him as a brother."

For some reason this seemed to devastate Emily all the more. Her face crumpled. "He . . . he is not *my* Mr. Edgerton anymore."

Mary bit her lip. "I'm so very sorry." How confusing. Was this not what Emily had said she wanted? Why was she not at least accepting if not overjoyed?

"It is too bad of him," Joanna said. "I've never heard of anything more dishonorable in all my life!"

Obviously Susan's case made a case for a man's far greater dishonor. Mary kept her first response barred behind her teeth. She turned to Emily, whose bottom lip wobbled dangerously. "What has happened?"

"He . . . he doesn't love me anymore."

"Oh, I'm sure that cannot be true."

"It is." A tear tracked down her cheek.

Mary handed Emily a clean, freshly pressed handkerchief. But . . . "Forgive me, but I was given to understand from earlier that you were not disagreeable to the idea of revising your agreement."

"Postponing things. Not ending them."

"Oh, my dear. I am so very sorry." Her insides knotted in the echo of her words. Had she been precipitate in advising Emily to end things, and underestimated the true nature of Emily's affections? "Perhaps there might be a way to reconcile—"

"No. Not after the things he said."

A short recounting followed of all the beastly things Mr. Edgerton— it was *not* Adam now—had said, concluding with Emily's dramatic statement: "So, you can see, if someone can make such allegations about my father, then I cannot love him, and have no interest in being with him whatsoever!"

"Ah." Mary exchanged another glance with Joanna, who shrugged helplessly. At least her sister was shrewd enough to not be blind to the caprices of her friend.

"Come now, Emily." Joanna patted her hand. "If you are glad to have your engagement at an end, then why allow this to upset you?"

"Oh, but you do not understand! Neither of you can, for neither of you have ever been betrothed." Emily tipped her head and studied Mary. "You have never been betrothed, have you, Mary?"

Heart stinging, she could not speak for a moment. Perhaps grief made Emily's remark callous and cruel.

"My mother is beside herself. Mr. Edgerton is considered quite the best catch in the district—well, he *was*—and I was considered by all our neighbors to be so very fortunate. And now to know that he is blind, well, I cannot conceive of marrying into that situation, can you?"

"Indeed not," Joanna said reassuringly.

Mary said nothing. She could not conceive of marriage to anyone.

"But then, what if his eyesight is restored? Mother and Father fear I'm making a big mistake."

"Pardon me, but I thought you said it was Ad—I mean, Mr. Edgerton who ended things."

"Yes, well, I . . ." Emily's eyes lowered.

Ah. The girl was perhaps not quite the victim she made herself out to be. The swell of sympathy that had lessened at Emily's selfish comments dropped another degree.

"Mary, do you think there is a way for their pledge to be restored, should Mr. Edgerton's eyesight return?" Joanna asked in a hushed voice.

A spark of indignation flared. The chit only wanted Adam if he was whole? "Forgive me, Emily, but I thought you said earlier you did not love him."

"Did I?" Her eyes opened wide. "You misunderstood me. I do not think I said that precisely. I perhaps meant to say it was difficult to love somebody in that situation."

"Do you love him?" Mary asked in as casual a tone as she could muster.

"Of course!"

"Why?"

"Mary," Joanna muttered, with an undertone of warning.

"I do not precisely see why this is your business, but I love many things about him."

Mary's brows rose as she invited explanation.

"He is handsome, of course—or he was, anyway—and he's brave, and he will inherit the farm—although I have to wonder if he still will, given his current condition, for how could a blind man ever be a farmer? But if he should recover, oh, what shall I do? Tell me, have I made a mistake in agreeing to end things? I cannot help but fear I have. Oh, I am such a wretch."

No argument there.

"Mary, tell me, please. Should I do whatever I can to win him back?"

She swallowed. God forgive her, but Adam did not deserve a self-focused girl like Emily. He needed someone with a care for him, not for the status and accoutrements he might bring his wife.

"Mary?" Joanna said. "Do you have any advice?"

"I . . ." She licked her bottom lip. "I do not think such a thing wise."

"I beg your pardon?"

"Emily." She touched her hand. "I wonder if it might be for the best if you asked your mother if you could visit your aunt in York. A period away from the vicinity might prove helpful in giving time and space to heal. It seems, from what you have said, there is no guarantee that Mr. Edgerton's eyesight will ever return. If you are simply holding on to that hope for the chance at a reunion, then it might quite prove a waste of time."

"Mary!"

She ignored her sister's gasp and pressed on. Her conscience would not allow this to be unsaid. "If, however, you are prepared to marry him as he is, blind, with no thought of a cure, then perhaps you could return to him and beg his forgiveness for being hasty, and . . . and look for the qualities in him that might engender your respect and admiration. I do not think a man would like to be appreciated simply because of his lack of infirmity."

"I did not mean that!" Emily exclaimed, cheeks flushed, before glancing away.

"Mary, you are distressing her."

She ignored her sister, kept her focus on their guest. "I am sorry if what I say upsets you, Emily. I only seek what will benefit you both. If you cannot bear the idea of being married to a blind man, then surely it is better not to foster thoughts otherwise."

Emily was silent for a long moment. Then her gaze returned to Mary. "Perhaps your idea about seeing my aunt is a wise one. I shall ask Mother to write to her at once." She shivered. "I cannot bear to think of what others will say. They will label me an unfeeling jilt."

Very true.

"You could save face by saying these trying circumstances have meant matters needed to be postponed," Joanna suggested.

Except that was not entirely true. Mary frowned.

"Thank you, Joanna, Mary." Emily pushed back her chair and rose with purpose. "I see you are both true friends."

Mary managed a hollow smile, as Joanna offered further sympathies before guiding Emily away.

The door closed, and she sank her head into her hands, heartsore. Had she advised correctly? Oh, what a sad, sad situation. For Emily. Adam. Mr. and Mrs. Edgerton.

She bowed her head and began to pray.

Chapter 10

The heart was a strange country, filled with odd fancies, twists and turns. Adam barely knew himself these past days. The concern he'd felt at being a noose around Emily's neck had lessened following her visit, but the lightness he'd initially felt at the end of their engagement had quickly sunk into heavy spirits.

He'd started snapping at his mother, hating her way of treating him like a child, insisting on dressing him, on reading to him, on feeding him—a process that had led him to suppress more than one curse as food slopped over his skin, as if he were an unkempt beggar. And the despair of his father was an emotion Adam desperately wanted not to indulge in. Misery wormed its way inside, shadowing his heart, stealing away his notice of what was good. Thoughts of a hopeless future begged attention. What would he do? What could he do? Was he destined to be housebound forever? Here he was, barely in his thirty-first year and he was blind.

Blind.

The idea still seemed ludicrous. Overwhelming. At times he placed his hands to his face, fingertips touching his eyelashes, unable to believe his eyelids truly were open. Other times he wished he could claw his eyeballs out, as if the violence of such an action might truly legitimize his condition. How could a man simply have sickened, then be left without sight? The body was a very strange thing.

His life was a very strange thing.

A noise came from without. His ears pricked—his hearing sharper now—as he tensed, waiting for whomever had opened the room to identify themselves. "Yes?"

"It's the doctor, Adam," his mother said, "here to speak with you." His mother ushered Dr. Bloomfield inside. A chair leg scraped, then creaked as someone sat.

"Doctor."

"Adam." There was a pause. "It's quite dark in here."

"Really? I wouldn't know."

Silence. Apparently the good doctor did not find Adam amusing. Well, that made two of them.

"I came to see how you are."

"Alive."

"Yes, that is something to be thankful for."

Was it? The darkness seemed to have penetrated his bones.

"Have you had any more headaches?"

"No." Only when he strained too hard, as he foolishly willed his eyes to see.

"You must continue to be careful, to not push yourself too much, but I think it is probably time for you to start moving about."

"What?"

His question was echoed a second later by his mother, who must have entered the room.

How he *hated* not knowing who was here, feeling as vulnerable as a newborn.

"There's no need for a healthy young man to be bedbound all his days."

"Healthy?" Adam nearly laughed.

"Your lungs and shoulder seem to have improved, and your legs work, don't they?"

"Yes."

"Then perhaps it is time for you to make an effort to move. If you stay in bed too long, bedsores will eventuate."

"Wonderful."

"Adam," his mother interrupted. "Please don't be so—"

"Forgive me, Dr. Bloomfield, I have not been feeling like myself for some time now."

"For about six months, I suspect," the doctor said gravely.

A reluctant chuckle pushed up and out, and he blinked in the darkness. "True."

"I know there is still a lot of adjusting to do, but I assure you that a future is still indeed possible."

"Really?" A spurt of anger lent strength for Adam to push up in the bed. "Do you happen to know of someone willing to employ a blind man? Or perhaps you know a young lady who would be willing to take on an invalid like me?"

There was a pause, then a cleared throat. "I heard that you have recently parted with Miss Hardy."

"Or she did with me," Adam said, unable to hide the bitterness. "I barely know what happened."

"My poor boy!" Mother's whimpering sigh grated his nerves.

"Mother, please leave me to discuss things with Dr. Bloomfield." He fought to keep his tone polite.

"Oh, but—"

"Please go."

"But, Adam—"

"Anne," the doctor said, "I'm afraid I have certain matters to discuss with your son that may make you feel somewhat squeamish."

"In that case, I'll leave you two, then."

Adam waited until he heard footsteps fade and the sound of a door close. "Has she left?"

"Yes."

Finally. "She hovers over me all the time, treats me as though I'm an infant." He exhaled heavily. "I find I can be short-tempered."

"Most understandable, on both your parts."

Adam grunted. "Which squeamish things did you wish to speak with me about?"

"Oh, nothing squeamish."

"What?"

"No, I simply figured you might enjoy the peace."

A real smile tugged at his lips. "Thank you."

"But I do strongly believe it is important for you to learn to move about and be independent. No good will come of you lying here, day after day, feeling sorry for yourself."

"I beg your pardon?"

"Do you want me to repeat that?"

Well . . . "No."

"Forgive my bluntness, but I have known you since you were a boy. Adam . . ."

He felt a touch on his shoulder.

"You are not someone who was born to lie about and be bored."

"I wasn't born to be blind, either."

A gravelly chuckle. "True. But while there seems to be little we can do about the one, there is much we can do about the other."

"So, you want me to stop my self-pitying ways and start living, is that it?"

"Yes."

Another snort, this time tinged with amusement, erupted from Adam's throat. "Ever tactful."

"I leave the tact to my wife and my eldest daughter."

Miss Bloomfield. "Mary." Try as he might, he still could not really remember much about her. Hardly surprising, when his thoughts had been full of Emily, with her golden hair, sky-blue eyes, perfect pink lips, form so soft and pliable and—

"Adam?"

He reined in his thoughts. "Yes?"

"Start by getting up and moving around the house. By getting to know this room and learning to do things for yourself."

"I cannot see Mother agreeing to this. She thinks I'm as helpless as a child."

"Are you?"

"Of course not."

"Then don't give her reason to think so. Prove otherwise."

The challenge tugged at his soul. Perhaps this would be a way to stop the cosseting, to stop the fussing that made him feel even less of a man than he already was.

"You need to do this for your parents, as well as for yourself. If they can see you can attain a measure of independence, then perhaps they will regain some optimism. Your father has seemed very bleak of late."

And Mother had barely stopped crying. Adam's upper lip curled, half with impatience, half with desperate hope. "Very well. How do you propose this happens?"

"Slowly. You may well find yourself encountering dizzy spells as your sense of balance tries to adjust to the lack of sight."

His mouth tightened. Wonderful.

"I will speak to your mother and see if your room can be rearranged so that you can more easily move around. You will need to be sure to replace clothes, shoes, objects in exactly the same space to help you remember where they are."

"You wish me to dress myself as well?"

"I was not aware you had a valet."

Another reluctant smile begged for release. "You have a very dry sense of humor, sir."

"So my wife tells me. Now, I will speak to your mother about this, but before I do, I wish to know you will cooperate. There will need to be many adjustments, and it will take time and much hard work. I'm afraid it will be both frustrating and quite tiring at times. Remember to take things one day at a time. If you want to be free, then I'm afraid this is how it has to be. Otherwise, you may wither away on that bed until you die."

"Thank you, Doctor. Has anyone ever told you your sickbed manner can do with some work?"

"Mary tells me that all the time. Now, are we agreed? I feel I must warn you I will be forced to give you more of these delicious concoctions until you agree."

"Agree that you will torture me until I start to live? I suppose."

"Good. I shall fetch your mother, and we'll explain things to her." The chair creaked, footsteps, then the door whisked open.

He frowned. The doctor certainly could work on his sympathy. He wondered if he was similarly gruffly spoken at home.

"Adam?" His mother's voice, her footsteps as she padded near. His arm was touched. "Are you feeling well?"

"Yes, Mother," he said, stifling fresh impatience.

"Then what is this Dr. Bloomfield speaks of, that you are wanting to be more independent?"

His lips tightened. God bless Bloomfield.

"Well, he *is* a man of enough years to do so," the doctor said.

"Yes, but he is injured."

"Mama." Perhaps the old name would soften her heart. "I appreciate all you have done, and I do not want you to grow weary in helping me in every way."

"But I must!"

"You must *not*, Anne," Dr. Bloomfield said, in a softer tone. "You need to ensure that you're not growing so tired yourself by constantly running around looking after Adam here that *you* get sick. Then where would we be, hmm?"

"I need to look after him."

"No, Adam needs to learn to look after himself. He will grow quite capable of doing certain tasks given the opportunity. But he must be given that opportunity. If he does not, there is every likelihood that he will grow more depressed, then sicken, weaken, and die."

Mother gasped. "You cannot be so cruel as to say such things."

"I cannot be so cruel as to not believe such things, ma'am. Now, if you truly love your son, then you will need to let him try to do tasks for himself."

"But what if he fails?"

"Then he'll learn how to do things better next time."

"But what can he do?"

"I still remember how to dress myself, Mother." Adam pushed his lips into something approaching a smile.

"And he will learn how to wash and shave himself, and feed himself, and move around the house. I suspect one day he'll even be able to ride a horse."

"What?"

"Really?" A flicker of interest crossed his chest. Perhaps his life wasn't going to be so completely hopeless after all.

"You must start with the small tasks. Which is why I want you to assist him with these things while allowing him the opportunity to learn what it is to be independent again."

Adam could have cheered.

"Anne, I know you love your son, so please, love him by encouraging him in this."

A sniff denoted tears. "Very well. If this is what Adam wants."

"Adam?" the doctor asked.

"It is." And in his heart, he felt that flicker of animation once again.

"Mary, Mary, wait!"

She waited for Susan at the market's edge, conscious that as she did so, a number of villagers eyed Miss Oakley askance. Indignation roiled within, but Mary was careful to show none of it as she greeted Susan with the warmest smile she could summon. "Hello. How are you today?"

"Miss Bloomfield, I must speak to you most urgently."

"Of course. Would you like to come to my house?"

Susan nodded and moved close to Mary's side, matching her strides. Unease stirred within. What had Susan so concerned?

Once they settled in the drawing room—Mama was out visiting with Joanna—Susan's pale face and gnawed fingernails demanded Mary learn the truth at once. "What is it?"

"Oh, miss, it was the new calves that did it."

Mary blinked. "I beg your pardon?"

Susan nibbled the end of her fingernail. "How . . . how do I know if . . . if that man has made me . . ." She blushed.

"Oh! Oh, my dear." Mary's cheeks heated as she struggled for what to say. If only Father were here. Or Mother. "I . . . I believe it takes a few weeks before one can truly know."

"A few weeks?"

"Yes." She coughed. "One must have enough time to, ah, ascertain whether the monthly cycle has been affected."

Susan's eyes grew huge. "I see."

"When was your last monthly?"

Susan bit her lip. "Several weeks ago."

Fear pressed Mary's heart. She sought to cover it with a smile. "I am sure you should not worry. Both Father and Mrs. Liddell have mentioned how hard it is for some people to fall pregnant." But not all. Hence Sally Croker's six children.

"'Scuse me, Miss Bloomfield, but I don't rightly think that you can be sure. What if I am? What will I do?"

Dear God, give me the right words to say. She clasped Susan's hand. "We shall pray and ask God for wisdom and not borrow trouble from tomorrow. I'm sure He will provide the answers as the time comes. But you should not worry, not until you know for sure."

"And then I should worry?" Susan tightened her grip. "Da would kill me. He can barely look at me as it is. If he didn't need me to cook and clean, I'm sure he'd have me sent away or cast off to the poorhouse."

"Why, Susan, surely your father loves you. He likely just struggles with how to show it since the loss of your mother."

"No." Susan shook her head. "Not every father is like yours."

Mary squeezed her hand. "You can always stay here again if you need to."

"Really?"

Mary nodded, even as she wondered about her impetuous invitation. Father hadn't been keen for Susan to remain before. What would he say if she needed to return? *God, please help us, direct our paths.* At least for the moment, without any surety of the situation, Susan would not be ostracized due to a baby.

After a few minutes more chatter about all manner of things, Susan got up and was in the midst of her farewell when a rapping came from the front door.

Mary opened the door to see Mr. Oakley, gaze piercing as he eyed his daughter in the hall.

"They told me my Susan was 'ere. Best get home, lass. Leave Miss Bloomfield be."

Susan paled and threw Mary an anxious look. "Mary and I were just chatting about . . . about—"

"The new calves," Mary supplied.

"Calves?" Mr. Oakley scratched his head. "I dunno why you'd be talking 'bout such things. I be figgering those dogs of yourn need settlin'."

"Da wants to sell some of the dogs," Susan murmured. "We have more than we need."

"I'm sure you will have many takers. They are such beauties."

"Aye, and a better temperament you'll never meet."

"I can believe that," Mary said. "I will speak to Father and see if there is anyone he knows who needs such an animal."

"I'm not giving them away for free, mind."

"I'll be sure he knows."

Susan and her father departed, leaving Mary to a few moments of ease and contemplation. How she wished she could do more. If Susan was pregnant, what would her future be? Would she have to go away to have the child, only to be forced to give it away? Father had mentioned homes for unwed mothers, but surely it need not come to that. And if Susan were not pregnant, perhaps one day a young man might be inclined to overlook the shadows of the past and offer her the protection of his name.

Mary clenched her fists. As for the man responsible for Susan's fear and suffering—*God, let there be justice!*

She spent the next few minutes praying, then lifted her head as Joanna's voice pierced the quiet. How much easier it was to care for those who lived afar than to practice love for those at home. *God, forgive me. Help me love her, too.*

"Mary?" Joanna called again.

"In here."

The door opened and Joanna hurried in. "Oh, good. Have you heard the news?"

"I suspect not, judging from your sparkling eyes."

"It is not exactly wonderful, but interesting nonetheless." Joanna slumped into a seat. "Emily is to go visit her aunt in York next week!"

"So soon?"

"She says it's not soon enough. She thinks everyone now believes she is a flirt, and she's finding it very hard to manage."

"She will find a change of scene refreshing."

Joanna nodded, then glanced away, before picking at a loose thread on her sleeve.

Mary waited. This pensive Joanna was one she'd rarely seen.

Finally Joanna glanced at Mary again and offered a wry smile. "I know I was hard on you before, when you suggested Emily leave the village, but I agree it would be best. Mama wanted to visit Mrs. Endicott, and permitted me to walk home with Emily, when . . ."

"When what?"

"Oh, nothing. It was just a number of gentlemen made less than flattering remarks as they passed by on the road."

"Really? Who might they be?"

"Charles Payne and his friends."

"Not Joseph Beecham?" Perhaps Joanna's eyes would be open to the kind of man she had spurned at the assembly when he was compared to a rogue.

"No." Joanna's face took on a rosy hue. "Actually, Mr. Beecham must have seen us from his father's shop. He proved to be rather more gentlemanly and provided escort for us, which was quite surprising but very welcome."

"One's station in life does not determine his degree of courtesy."

"No." Joanna looked thoughtful. "I, er, saw Susan earlier. Is she well?"

"Yes, thank goodness."

Joanna raised a brow but enquired no further.

Mary hastened to change the subject. "And are you well? I imagine this news about Emily leaving is not easy for you."

"I'm pleased for her, but sometimes it does seem as if everyone is leaving while I am stuck here."

Mary patted her sister's hand. "It is not the worst place in the world one might live."

"I suppose not." Joanna heaved an exaggerated sigh that led to a chuckle, a sound Mary hadn't heard in quite some time. "Do you think Mama would allow us to take Emily on a picnic? One more time beside the lake, before she has to leave?"

"That's a wonderful idea. I believe we should propose it tonight."

"Well, not tonight," Joanna said, with a glinting smile. "It would be rather too chilly tonight for a picnic."

Mary laughed, her heart lighter. Yes, a picnic would be just the thing.

Chapter 11

Today would be the day to enact courage. Adam sighed, drew back the bedcovers, and swung his legs onto the floor. After a moment, he placed a hand on the side of the mattress and slowly pushed his way to stand. His legs felt as weak as twigs, and his head hurt like the blazes, but he focused through the dizziness and took a tentative step away.

One sliding step. Two. He could do this. He might be blind, but he was walking!

He stretched his arms in front, fingers waving through the air in a vain attempt to ascertain his surroundings, heart hammering with nerves.

Another step. Another. He could do this! *Thank You, God.*

He banged his toe into something and tried to stop, but momentum kept his body moving. Air rushed past his head in terrifying haste as he fell, arms flailing, unsure of which way was up. He tumbled to the floor and smashed his jaw. Pain billowed through his face, wave after wave of throbbing hurt, and he swore.

The crash brought his mother rushing in with cries of "Adam! What has happened?"

"I fell."

"What were you doing up? If you wanted something, you only needed to call." Her hands grasped his upper arms, but her feeble tugs could not lift him.

He pushed to all fours, then, shifting his hand around, found the edge of the bed and used that to help himself rise.

"My dear, you must get back into bed. You are obviously not fit enough for this."

"No, Mother. Dr. Bloomfield is the expert, and he thinks I must try."

"But you will hurt yourself."

"Yes." He gritted his teeth and wrenched himself upright again. "But I'd rather try than waste away and die."

"Oh, my dear."

He could hear the tears threatening to spill and felt a familiar spurt of irritation. Then knew guilt for feeling such a thing. "Mother . . ." He gentled his tone. "You remember the doctor thinks it important that I try."

"Yes."

"He said it would not be easy."

"Yes, but I am your mother, so I'm an expert on you, and I don't want to see you hurt."

His lips lifted. "Then it's good you did not see all the scrapes and bruises of our time in war."

Her hand grasped his arm.

He swallowed his protest and allowed her to guide him to a chair. There would be plenty of time to let her adjust to his new condition. His smile faded. The rest of his life, in fact.

A few hours later Adam sat, head propped in hands, elbows leaning on his knees as his mother continued her readings from Genesis. He *was* thankful for her, and tried to express this in his clumsy way, but she merely patted his arm and assured him that she knew he never meant to sound cross. Which was true. But her easy forgiveness knotted shame within.

Some days he felt full of shame, his hours seemingly woven together by the weft of remorse and the warp of pain. He longed to return to his previous life, when he knew his place, pictured his future. Now, it was as if he floated in a world of the unknown, save for these twin threads that crossed through his days.

A sound came from outside.

His mother broke off reading, as the knocking came again. "Oh, that's right. Mrs. Parr is in the village. I'll need to see who that is."

Perhaps he'd have a visitor. That would make a change. Save for an awkward visit from Alby Jamieson, whose stuttered thanks had quickly subsided into painful embarrassment, he'd barely had a caller. He didn't mind; it saved him from uncomfortable conversations and the reminder that he was somehow less than what people expected. And it protected him from the unfair advantage their sight allowed. How he hated that they could see him while he still felt so exposed.

Steps came back down the hallway. "Adam," his mother said, "you have a visitor. It's—"

"Who?"

"—Bloomfield."

"My favorite person," Adam murmured, sitting up in his seat, pasting on a smile.

"Really?" A soft voice—most definitely *not* the doctor's—said.

"Who is this?" He smelled a faint trace of lavender.

"It's Mary Bloomfield, sir."

"*Miss* Bloomfield." Oh. He'd misheard his mother. "Hello."

"Father asked me to give you a fresh batch of the eyebright poultice."

"Because the last batch worked so well." He grimaced.

There was a pause, then . . . "Apparently something has worked well if you are sitting up in a chair instead of lying in a bed."

His cheeks warmed. "Forgive me. That was rude."

"Yes."

What?

"But you are forgiven."

He could almost hear the rest of her sentence humming on her tongue. "Forgiven, because 'we pity your sad situation'?"

"I do not hold that position."

"I beg your pardon?"

"I do not pity you."

"No?" Had he truly said that aloud? Was he going mad?

"No, sir, I do not pity you."

"Then you are the only one."

"Although, if you insist on feeling sorry for yourself, I may have to change my mind."

Her censure stung. "As if I care about your opinion," he retorted.

"Adam!" his mother exclaimed.

Wait—she was still here?

"Apologize to Miss Bloomfield."

"There is no apology necessary, ma'am." Miss Bloomfield's voice was quiet. "Please forgive my unruly tongue. I've been told I can be overly forthright."

Adam cleared his throat. "Miss Bloomfield, I *am* sorry."

"You're forgiven." A pause. "That is a nasty looking bruise on your jaw."

"I had a little misstep."

"My father mentioned you are to work on walking."

He nodded.

"He'll be pleased to know you've made an effort. Well, goodbye, then," Miss Bloomfield said.

To Adam or to his mother? This conversation was enough to make him dizzy.

"Goodbye, Mary," his mother said. "Thank you for calling."

"And here is his medicine."

"Yes, I'll be sure to see he has some."

Adam's lip curled. "Wonderful."

"He seems to be looking forward to it." Their visitor sounded as if she suppressed laughter in her voice. "Goodbye, Mr. Edgerton. I hope you enjoy."

He schooled his features to impassivity, and inclined his head, but had no idea if she even saw him, let alone whether he was nodding in the right direction. He clenched his fists. How he *hated* this infirmity.

"Adam, I cannot believe you were so rude," his mother said a few moments later, after she had shown Miss Bloomfield out the door.

How many times must a man apologize?

"You know she was only on an errand for her father."

"I think she was laughing at me," he grumbled.

"I do not think so. Why, Mary Bloomfield is almost as much of a saint as her father," his mother protested.

"A very blunt-spoken saint, like her father." Which he'd found surprising. He'd always thought her meeker than that. And yet she was the one apologizing for having an unruly tongue?

Miss Bloomfield was a puzzle indeed.

⟡

Her unruly tongue!

Mary hurried from the Edgerton farm, careful not to look behind her. Her cheeks must still be bright red. What a terrible person she had been, exchanging banter—like Joanna might with her suitors!—with a man who had no way to escape her presence.

The poor man. Her heart softened. She had uttered an untruth in there—*forgive me, Lord*—as she did pity Adam Edgerton. Nobody with an ounce of compassion could remain unmoved by his condition. But she was surprised and encouraged to see how much he had improved since her last visit, especially that he now could sit up in a chair. Father had mentioned the circumstances of his last visit, how he'd needed to convince both son and mother as to the benefits of learning independence. She had determined to foster that during her errand today but hadn't realized just how close encouragement could run to tease. It wasn't as if Adam was her brother, after all, no matter what she had said to Emily Hardy.

She dragged in a long breath. He certainly was *not* like her brother. Her second thought upon entering the room—a thought that had come right on the tail of the first—was how much better looking he appeared than she remembered, even with that dark bruise on his jawline. Quite handsome, in fact, with that dark hair flopping over his brow, and those strong brows and firm chin and lips. She'd even been conscious of a tiny tug of attraction, which was definitely *not* something that she'd ever admit to a living soul, and which had prompted her to hide such thoughts behind a mask of levity. What would Emily say if she ever found out? What a faithless friend Mary was.

Though when was the last time she'd ever felt the slightest interest in a young man? Had she ever? Oh dear, she was as bad as Joanna and her friends, fixing interest on a handsome face without learning the character that truly made the man. Was she truly that shallow? She frowned, trying to suppress her unruly thoughts as well.

"Miss Bloomfield."

"Oh!" She drew to a start. "Mr. Edgerton, hello."

The farmer doffed his hat, eying her. "You seem a mite preoccupied." He jerked a thumb back at the farmhouse. "Been visiting my boy?"

"Yes. That is, not really." Oh dear, he must think her a fool. "I came on behalf of my father and delivered some medicine."

"Much as I respect your father, I don't rightly see how any medicine will set Adam to seeing again."

"No . . ." She hesitated. "But surely anything is worth trying rather than not. We all need hope in this world."

He nodded, glanced away at a sheep-dotted field. "You think he's looking better?"

Thank goodness he was looking away. Her cheeks heated again. "I—" She swallowed to steady her voice. "He seems much improved from last time. He was even sitting up in a chair," she added.

"Aye, the doctor told him he needed to." His mouth turned downward. "This be such a bad business I scarce know which way is up."

She remained silent. What could she say to help his pain? *Lord, comfort him.*

He released a long breath. "Did the missus tell you we've been missing sheep?"

"No."

"Doesn't surprise me. All she thinks about these days is . . ." He shook his head. "And rightly so, I suppose."

"I hope the sheep will be found soon."

He gave a bitter laugh. "Oh, I suspect they'll be long gone now. Someone's dinner, or joined someone's flock."

"That's dreadful! Has the local magistrate been informed?"

"What's he going to do? Payne might be the magistrate, but if he can't even keep his own scamp of a son in check, how can anyone trust him to do what's right when it doesn't affect him?"

How could he, indeed? "Surely there's something that can be done. Do you need more shepherds, or sheep dogs, or—?"

"Old Jock grew sick last winter and moved away. His place is empty now." He gestured to a small stone structure on a distant fell. "As for dogs, we have enough, though the missus says she wouldn't mind one for the house, seeing as we be gone for most of the day."

That reminded her . . . "I understand the Oakleys have some pups for sale."

"Aye. They be fine dogs." He peered at her suddenly, the weathered countenance revealing facial features so like his son's her breath suspended. "You be careful, Miss. There be bad people in this world. If you're going to be walking up this way alone, then maybe you should get a dog, too."

Her chest knotted. Was his concern based on Charles Payne or the sheep stealers? "Thank you, sir."

He nodded, touched his forehead, muttered a farewell, and trudged away.

Later that night she kept her father company as he ate his dinner after returning late from tending to Mr. Pendle, who had sickened rather suddenly.

"He may never play the flute again. But he is long in years, and that's what gets us all in the end."

"He will be missed," Mary said.

Her father nodded, chewing his mouthful of mutton pie.

Poor Mr. Pendle. What would happen to his small holding and his sheep? "Father, have you heard anything about missing sheep?"

His brows pinched as he swallowed his dinner before looking up at her. "Why do you ask?"

"Mr. Edgerton mentioned some of his had gone missing. Said it might be good for me to get a dog for when I pay my calls."

"That might be for the best."

The drop of fear from her earlier conversation with Adam's father swelled and spread. "What do you know?"

He gazed at her steadily for a moment, then said in a low voice, "This is not something I wish your sister or mother to know. You, I think, can handle the truth."

"Father, you're starting to scare me."

"Good."

She blinked.

"You need to take care. There are desperate people out there who do not always obey the laws of the land."

"Who?"

"There has been talk in the village that there are some returned soldiers in the area who are desperate for food and will take whatever they can get." He eyed her significantly.

"Surely not!" She knew her eyes were wide. "You don't mean they were responsible for the attack on Susan?"

"We cannot know as yet. But we do know a few vagabonds dressed as soldiers have been spotted not too far from the Edgerton farm, up near Upton Pike."

"I don't understand. Why would they have come? There is little to gain from thieving around here. Surely there is more opportunity in a city such as London."

"It's warmer these days, and London is always crowded with the poor and never pleasant in the summer months. Maybe they think that, in a part of England that holds fewer people, they are less likely to be troubled and can hide away in the hills."

"But why has nothing been said? If people knew, then surely they would take precautions and not travel afar."

"It's been thought best not to panic people."

"Who thought best?"

"Lord Carstairs and Mr. Payne."

Those considered to be authorities in these parts. "I don't understand. Such a decision seems foolishness to me. What if someone else is unprepared and is attacked?"

He muttered something under his breath. "You best not concern yourself. Simply keep to the village and paths for the meanwhile."

Her breath caught. "Joanna and Emily Hardy have planned a picnic for tomorrow."

"Really? Why did I not know this?"

"You have been so busy. It was only decided yesterday."

"Where? When?"

"I believe they mentioned the lake, at around noon, but that may have changed. Joanna was hopeful that some of the young gentlemen who are their friends might be able to come. Oh, and I'm sure they invited Mama, and Mrs. Hardy. It's meant to be a kind of farewell picnic before Emily moves away."

"Because she's broken the engagement with young Adam." He muttered something else under his breath.

"I beg your pardon?"

"They would never have suited. He's a man and she's but an empty-headed girl."

"Father." She should protest, shouldn't she? "She is young, that is all."

"And vain, and foolish, and has scarcely known a day's hard work in her life, thanks to her overindulgent parents. She'd scarcely be able to take on the responsibilities of a farm, let alone care for someone like young Adam needs."

"It would be very challenging to find someone who can meet all of Adam's needs."

"Hmph." He shoved in another piece of mutton pie, watching her carefully as he chewed. "How did he seem today?"

"Better. He was sitting upright in a chair when I was there."

"He needs to get out and about, get some fresh air into him. It won't do him any good being stuck in that dark room."

"I don't think he cares too much about the darkness of the room."

Her father's mouth twitched. "Saucy lass."

"I've learned from the best."

Father took a gulp of wine and lowered the glass, its contents ruby red in the candlelight. "About that dog. I do think it would be helpful for you to have a companion."

"Susan Oakley mentioned they had some new pups."

He nodded thoughtfully. "They'd do. Although a pup wasn't quite what I had in mind. Something older, steadier. That's what you need." He glanced at his plate. "That's what young Adam needs too."

Her breath hitched. No. He didn't mean what she'd thought. He couldn't. Her foolish imagination ran too quickly along certain lines. "You're feeling a little tired, aren't you, Papa?"

He grunted, but lines of weariness etched his face.

Poor Papa, with his constant visits and broken sleep as he tended the many sick and ailing. Thank goodness it was nearly summer, and the colds and conditions brought with winter would not need to be faced for some months yet. Father might get the rest he so desperately needed.

This conversation needed to be steered away from dangerous currents. "You know, I agree with you."

Father's shaggy brows lifted.

"The person who really should get a dog is Adam."

He opened his mouth as if to protest.

"Don't you think that would be helpful? I was picturing his situation. A dog could give warning that someone approached him." She smiled. "A clever enough dog might even be able to be trained to help in some ways."

He rested his elbow on the table, chin in hand. "I once heard about a man from Carlisle who had a dog that was trained to fetch his boots. You mean something like that?"

"Perhaps. Poor Mrs. Edgerton looked so weary. If there was some way of alleviating some of her concern, then I think it good to try."

"You might have the right of it." His expression grew thoughtful. "That reminds me of something else. Mr. Crowdey has a stick he uses to ensure his path is clear. Perhaps we should investigate getting something for young Adam."

She nodded, although she couldn't see the virile younger Mr. Edgerton holding a stick like old Mr. Crowdey. "Do you really think he'd use one?"

"One day, perhaps. I'll make some enquiries." He pushed back his chair. "Now, I'm off to bed to catch what sleep I can before the Bennett baby is born."

"Isn't Mrs. Liddell going?"

He shook his head. "They won't have anything to do with her, such religious people that they are, too busy judging what they know nowt about. Says her herbs and potions are witchcraft."

She smiled. "They must think I am a witch, too."

"That's enough out of you, young lady. I suggest you go to sleep, too, else you'll be too tired for picnics and the like, and the young gentlemen who might attend."

"I don't think they'd miss me."

"Then they're fools." He moved to clasp her shoulder. "You, my dear, are leagues out of their world, so I wouldn't let it trouble you."

She nodded, her vision blurry in the swift rush of tears. Father was not often prone to commendation. But neither could she allow his words to nestle too close to her heart. For if her father thought all the young gentlemen of the district were not good enough, then how would she ever meet one who was?

And a deeper, more secret part wondered whether any young gentleman might ever consider Mary good enough for him.

Chapter 12

Somewhere from outside came birdsong and the distant bleat of sheep. Yesterday he'd asked Meggie if she'd leave the window open a crack, and the past night's cool air seemed to have blown away most of his room's mustiness, its freshness a reminder of time spent out of doors, the sights he'd seen, the places he'd been, the experiences he would never have again.

Adam gritted his teeth. How easily melancholy could steal across his soul. He'd always despised those who pitied themselves, and here he was, bemoaning his losses, just like the doctor's daughter had challenged him on. He exhaled loudly, seeking to forget her, as the guilt at his careless words again rose.

He swung his feet from the bed, feeling carefully with his stockinged toes to ensure nothing lay there that might lead to another tumble to the floor. He stood, then moved with tentative steps and outstretched hands to where he judged the chair to be. A moment later he sank into it, gladness at his small victory releasing in a tight smile.

"Adam, you are up."

"Good morning, Mother." When would she learn he preferred people to knock instead of walking in? It would serve her right if he was undressed.

"How did you sleep?"

"Well enough. And you?"

"Oh, I don't think I've slept properly since your return, my mind is so full of worries."

Compassion stirred his heart, chasing away the earlier impatience. His mother loved him, and so many of her worries concerned him. "I am sorry my situation has caused you so much pain."

"I know I should not be gloomy. As Miss Bloomfield says, we are blessed to have you return, when so many families never have that privilege."

The spark of irritation at that name—was she always to be in the right?—faded in surprise. "That is true."

He *was* thankful to be alive. He'd witnessed too many deaths in combat, too many men whose words and hopes and dreams had been felled by a bullet, or insidious sickness, or misadventure, like the unfortunate lad who'd slipped overboard when they'd boarded the boats to return to English shores. Poor lad, thinking he was heading home, only to reach a watery grave.

His mother sighed. "I find it hard to remember to be thankful. I suppose I'm out of the habit."

"I agree it is not easy, Mama. I'd do well to remember it, too."

She squeezed his hand.

The action strengthened the bonds of affection he felt to her. "I am thankful for you."

"Oh, Adam." Her voice seemed muffled. Then she pressed a kiss to the top of his head. "I am just so thankful you are here, and you are safe."

He rose and awkwardly pulled her into a hug, resting her head against his chest, trying to show her he was still strong, even though at times he appeared so weak.

She sighed, and drew away, gently pushing him back into his chair. "I forgot how tall you are."

"I forgot how short you are," he teased, as in the manner of years gone by.

She chuckled, and the weighty emotion of earlier was broken. His mother chattered on about assorted village matters—all manner of things that held little interest, but in his new desire for accord, he stifled his impatience until she mentioned something about hearing of a village picnic being held "because, did you know, dear Emily is leaving?"

Emotion stabbed. Adam suppressed it, answering his mother as colorlessly as he could. "Is she?"

"Apparently she is going to stay with an aunt in York."

He nodded, affecting disinterest, but the pain in his heart still felt raw. Her rejection might have forestalled his own, but that didn't lessen the hurt. What would his future look like? Forever black and devoid of a life's companion?

"I cannot like it," Mother said, with another sigh. "Who will she know there?"

"Perhaps we should ask Teddy Bracken to pay her a call."

"Perhaps." She was silent for a long moment. "Adam, are you sure this breaking of your engagement is for the best?"

"It is best for her. That is all that matters."

"And what about you? What is best for you?"

He heard the note of anguish in her voice and reached out a hand, felt her fingers clasp his. "Mother, at this point, what is best for me is being here with you. Certainly not with a young lady who wishes to be elsewhere."

He could not blame them, either one. Mother was only looking out for his best interest; Emily was only looking out for hers. He frowned. Why did that thought seem so harsh? Best to change the subject.

He let go of her fingers and carefully maneuvered to stand again, swaying slightly as he attempted to balance by himself. "I want to dress myself today."

"Oh." There came an unsuccessfully suppressed sigh. "Of course."

"Thank you, Mother. Dr. Bloomfield was right in insisting I try to be more self-reliant. I prefer this sense of independence, illusion though it may be."

"It is not easy to let you attempt some of these things," his mother confessed, "but I am trying."

"And so am I. Very trying, I'm sure."

She chuckled. "I will lay a fresh shirt and trousers for you on the bed."

There came a faint whine as the wooden drawers were dragged open, the whisper of garments being lifted and being placed.

"Thank you, Mother."

No more the fancy coats, neckcloths, and breeches expected of a soldier. He was now a humble farmer's son again, and his clothing must be as simple as he could manage—as simple as his ancestry determined.

He moved to the bed and shrugged out of his nightshirt, dropping it onto where he thought must be the bed. He felt around and touched a freshly laundered cotton shirt and slowly dragged it over his head, managing to get his left arm in.

"That's it."

He jumped, his mother's voice startling him. She was still here?

"Now the other arm."

He clenched his teeth, and managed not to respond, even as he tugged the sleeve down and fumbled tying the ribbon at his chest. Ever the spectacle unaware of observation. Well, if his mother insisted on staying in the room, she'd know what to expect.

He felt around, met the texture of heavier woolen fabric, and swiftly assessed that it was the trousers he wanted.

"Adam, they're—"

"Don't tell me, Mother. I need to learn for myself."

Ah. Further exploration revealed he'd discovered the legs. Feeling farther, he bent to slip one leg in then—without wobbling too much—the next. He drew them up and felt immeasurably proud to achieve something that once was so routine. But they seemed a little tight and uncomfortable, and the front flap had disappeared.

"Do you want me to mention that they appear to be on backwards?" Mother queried.

"No." Cheeks heating—thank goodness it was only Mother and not the doctor's daughter—he sank back on the bed and peeled them off. Clearly this dressing of oneself would require some assistance at the start.

For the next few minutes, he bit his tongue innumerable times as his mother clucked about him, issuing instruction and advice as he sought to learn by touch just what he ought wear. The selection of a waistcoat took a number of attempts, his efforts to button it correctly took more.

Listening to her many varied suggestions made him long for peace, for the calm he remembered in a woman not so very long ago. He frowned.

"Adam?" His mother paused in her ministrations. "Have you a headache?"

"No. I just recalled something."

"You mustn't let the Emily situation trouble you," she said, patting his knee as she handed him a fresh woolen stocking. "I think it best we resolve to speak no more of her, don't you agree? Even if it is such a shame—but, no more."

Please God, no more, he agreed.

He managed to pull on both stockings without mishap, then was questioned about footwear. Boots, half boots, shoes? Really, this getting dressed business was exhausting.

"Half boots, I think."

"Black or brown?"

What colors did he already wear? Biscuit trousers? Blue waistcoat? "Black will do."

There came a shuffling noise, and the sound of two boots thudding to the floor.

"Now, slide your left foot in here—no, your *other* left foot. There."

He dragged on his other half boot, then, following her instructions, struggled into his topcoat, before feeling about for the nearby chair, into which he sank with a sigh.

He closed his useless eyes, rubbed at the pain sprouting between his brows.

"You have a headache, don't you, son?"

"It will pass."

"Shall I get some more of Dr. Bloomfield's tonic?"

"Please don't. It is vile." *And please leave*, he wanted to add, but she'd be crushed, so he refrained. However, he couldn't stand this persistent fussing, this never-ending fretful bustle. He wanted peace, just a moment's quiet. He wanted—

"Oh! You have another visitor."

Anything except that.

"It's Dr. and Mrs. Bloomfield."

Wonderful. At least it wasn't Miss Bloomfield, with whom he'd had that somewhat unnerving encounter yesterday. And at least he was dressed. And sitting upright. And—

"Good morning, Mr. Edgerton."

"Good morning, sir. Hello, Mrs. Bloomfield."

There was a moment's pause, then, "It is Miss Bloomfield, sir. Mary."

The faintest trace of lavender stole into his awareness. "I thought— oh, never mind." He heard the rudeness in his reply, and bit back a soul-deep sigh. What was it about Mary Bloomfield that got under his skin? And for that matter, why had he misheard his mother—again? Was his hearing going, too?

"Mary mentioned that you were moving about a little more," Dr. Bloomfield said.

"Trying to. Following doctor's orders."

"Good, good."

"He dressed himself today," Mother said proudly, as if he were a child barely out of leading strings.

Adam winced.

"I imagine that was not easy," Miss Bloomfield's voice dripped with sympathy.

Well, didn't exactly drip. In fact, she sounded more interested than overly sympathetic. He pushed away the confusing resentment to admit, "It was harder than I expected."

"These things will get easier with time," the doctor said. "Now, we have come with both a gift and a proposal."

Adam stiffened.

"Now, now, no need to look like that. This isn't anything unpleasant, I assure you. I take it you've been none too fond of some of my other offerings, eh?"

"I don't understand."

"He means both the eye salve and the elixir," Miss Bloomfield said softly. "Both are on your night table and appear to be untouched."

Oh. That. "I, er, have had no need for the elixir thus far."

"I wouldn't blame you for not tasting it, even if you had," the soft voice continued in a conspiratorial tone. "I'm fairly sure it tastes like the insides of muddied boots after rain."

A small smile escaped. "Have you had this misfortune of being on the receiving end of said elixir?"

"I have not had the pleasure, but I have smelled it, and you have my deepest sympathies, sir."

He could hear the smile in her voice. What might she look like now that she was older? His memories seemed so vague, nothing but a shadow of the realities he was now forced to brave.

A throat cleared, and Adam turned to that direction.

"About that gift," the doctor said. "I have here something you might find of assistance as you learn to navigate your way. I remembered back to my training about the benefits many found from using a special stick, something that helps you ascertain whether there are obstacles in the way. I hope, as time goes on, you will find such a thing useful."

"Thank you," he muttered. A long, light object was passed into his palms, and he drew his hand along it, only to encounter a splinter, which elicited a hiss of pain.

"Oh."

A moment later Adam's hand was snatched up, and cool fingers plucked at the offending particle, then the pain was gone.

"I'm afraid it's still rather rough. I know the Jamieson lad was keen to make it somewhat smoother, so with your permission, I might ask him to do so."

"Of course."

"It's important to have something that is both lightweight and that matches your height," Miss Bloomfield said, "so I suspected Mr. Crowdey's old stick was never going to be quite right."

So, the stick was really his *entrée* to decrepitude. Wonderful.

"But you can use it for the meantime, until another more appropriate is made," the doctor added.

"Thank you."

"Now, about that proposal. We—though really it was Mary's idea—wondered about whether you might consider having a dog."

"A dog?" Mother asked. "Well, Mr. Edgerton has a number of dogs working the farm already, so I—"

"This would be more of a companion dog. A creature to keep Adam company, when you were busy."

"Or might provide a degree of warning, should someone come inside," Miss Bloomfield added. "He might even be trained to fetch or assist around the house."

"A dog." Adam thought about it for a moment. A dog that warned when others approached? That could be quite helpful, provided it did not go racing after mice, or chase his mother's cat, or harass the sheep.

He offered these as mild objections—no sense letting people think he was a puppet and inclined to follow their every whim—which were each met with staunch justifications.

A dog. The more he thought about it, the more the idea seemed to hold merit. "I used to have a dog many years ago."

"Bear."

"Yes," he said, surprised Miss Bloomfield knew his dog's name.

"Bear used to follow you and Robert everywhere, did he not?"

He blinked. "That dog was a very good chum, yes." He hadn't thought about Bear in years. Certainly not during the war. But Bear had been an intrepid fellow adventurer, accompanying himself and Rob on escapades to the tops of forbidden peaks, even proving so plucky that he'd willingly escorted them on a boat ride or three. Bear had eventually grown too old and stiff for such adventures, and he'd died, and been buried beside the farm's Peak Rock, in the month before Adam had joined up with the militia.

"I don't know what my husband would think of this." Mother's voice intruded through his memories.

"He thinks it a fine idea, provided a new dog knows its place is here and not with the sheep," Dr. Bloomfield said.

"We saw him on our way up," Miss Bloomfield said, "and he sounded rather keen. I believe it would prove of great benefit."

Oh she did, did she?

"Well!" His mother didn't sound so enthralled. "What say you, Adam?"

He stifled the irritation at Miss Bloomfield's presumption and slowly answered. "Provided it be the right kind of dog, and not too young and foolish, then I rather think a canine companion could be very welcome."

"Excellent!" the doctor said. "I believe you will find this helpful for your future plans."

"Plans?" Mother interrupted. "What plans?"

"I have no plans yet, Mother."

"Save to regain a degree of independence." The doctor sounded hopeful. "And at this stage, that is probably all the plans one needs. Well, I am glad then. If you don't mind, I would recommend that you allow my Mary here to find the right sort of animal for you."

"Father," she said quietly. "I have no wish to . . ." Her voice dropped to hurried whispers, but he could not determine the words, save for her apparent displeasure at her father's request. Did this mean he disconcerted her, too?

"It's important to ensure the dog has the right kind of temperament, which can take time."

A pause, long enough to make him wonder if he was being addressed, ended with Miss Bloomfield's soft-spoken "Of course."

"Well, thank you, Doctor, and Miss Bloomfield. You have proved very thoughtful, very thoughtful, indeed," Mother said.

"Yes, er, thank you," he echoed weakly, like a child needing to be prompted with his lines. "Most considerate." He heard a sound like that of a smothered chuckle and frowned.

"Goodbye, Adam," Dr. Bloomfield said.

"I shall endeavor to find another Bear-like creature for you," that cool, low voice said.

Bear-like? "Oh, er, thank you. I am much obliged."

"Of course."

Of course? He barely heard their farewells and exit as he puzzled out his strange reaction to Miss Bloomfield. He wasn't used to being so introspective, but the loss of his sight seemed to have sent his thoughts inward, honing all his senses and increasing the volume of his thoughts. His experiences with young women had not been abundant—war and godly principles had seen to that—but he could scarcely remember when he'd last encountered someone who roused such varying emotions as peace and irritation at the same time.

He liked her voice—soothing and calm. He liked that funny burble in her throat that suggested suppressed laughter, even though he suspected it might be at his expense. But neither explained the way that, when in her company, he felt somewhat defenseless and vulnerable. The feeling goaded him to the audacity of his soldiering days, when he so easily veered to either impertinence or that forthright quality some had lauded as heroic.

Miss Bloomfield seemed to be quite a managing kind of thing, someone who always knew what was best, despite having few qualifications to justify her opinions. In some ways she reminded him of those armed forces superiors who bought their commissions without ever having trained as a soldier, yet thought their understanding so advanced they lectured those more battle-hardened on the rudiments of war. The spurt of resentment grew. Perhaps if she married, she'd be less inclined to interfere, although he couldn't imagine what kind of man would be willing to put up with her meddlesome ways.

The front door closed, then footsteps trod back in.

"Mother, do you think Miss Bloomfield dislikes me, or does the fact that she's unwed at her age mean she dislikes all men in general?"

There was a lengthy pause, a cessation of all sound.

Why wasn't Mother answering? Unless . . .

"I assure you, Mr. Edgerton," came the soft voice, "I've never disliked you."

Until now. He could almost hear her unsaid words. His stomach roiled, heat tingled across his face. "Miss Bloomfield, I did not know—"

"Evidently."

"Forgive me, I've not been myself."

"That is apparent." The words were clipped, stiff. "The Adam I once knew would never have been so unkind."

Remorse bit, weighing more heavily on his chest. "Miss Bloomfield, I am sorry."

"And I am leaving. I simply returned to collect my gloves. Goodbye."

A quick, firm tread, and the door once again squeaked open and then closed with a firm bump.

The nerve of him!

Mary blinked back tears as she hurried to join her father in the gig. She should never have come today. Should never have allowed herself to feel sorry for him.

"Mary?" Father eyed her. "Are you well?"

She drew in a steadying breath, pasted on a smile. "Quite well." She turned to Mrs. Edgerton, who had come to see them off. "I hope you will get the chance to rest soon."

"And when will that be?" She groaned. "I be that tired, what with looking after Adam and helping Mr. Edgerton run the farm. And Mrs. Parr told me just this morning that she needs to help her sister in Rydal and will be gone for some weeks. Meggie is a good-natured girl, but hardly here enough to make a difference. A rest simply isn't feasible, I'm afraid."

"Hmm." Father's brows lowered in thought. "Perhaps Mary here might be able to come and relieve you at times."

What? "Father, I'm not sure that is the best idea."

"Oh, Mary, would you?" Mrs. Edgerton's weary eyes lit. "I'd be that grateful."

"Forgive me," Mary hastened to say, "but I suspect there would be some people who would question whether I would best be suited for this role. A young lady in the company of a young man, presumably without a chaperone?"

"Oh, nobody thinks of you in that way," Mrs. Edgerton said.

Heart stinging, Mary pressed her lips together and glanced at her father with raised brows.

"Mrs. Edgerton is right," he said.

She gasped.

He avoided her eyes, turning and studying the far hills and distant glitter of lake. "In fact, I can think of no one more suitable for the role.

After all, you are experienced with caring for those with illness, and have such a way with people."

Oh yes, and that last was proved by her most recent interaction with the invalid in question. "I do not think he would like it." She glanced apologetically at Mrs. Edgerton.

"Whatever makes you say such a thing? Now I think about it, he's always had a soft spot for you—"

He had?

"—being so patient when you used to follow him and your brother over hill and dale."

Mary cringed. Now it sounded as if she'd been enamored with him for years!

"Not that I'd let that bother you any. People know that you're not one who is inclined to marry."

So not only did her father and the woman standing in front of her believe this, but this was the general assumption of the village? Something the Edgertons had talked about before? A shudder rippled up her spine.

"Oh, Mary, you're looking rather pale. Have I spoken out of turn?"

Yes, she longed to say. *Yes, you have spoken out of turn.* She looked Mrs. Edgerton in the eye. With a stiff voice, she quietly said, "There is a difference between being unwilling and having opportunity, Mrs. Edgerton." She pressed wobbling lips together and looked away.

"Oh, Miss Bloomfield, Mary, I didn't mean—"

"Can we please go?" she said under her breath, nudging her father.

"You'll have to excuse us." Father slapped the reins. "I must return to the cottage infirmary and my next appointment."

Mary summoned a stiff smile and managed to nod in Mrs. Edgerton's direction before the gig carried them over bumpy trails down to the village.

"I'm sorry if that sounded harsh," Father said.

She exhaled. Father rarely apologized—so like a man—but she would forgive him.

"But Mrs. Edgerton can be a little one-eyed in her attentions."

Wait. Father wasn't apologizing for his own bluntness? Should she ask him, or let it lie—and likely fester? "Father . . ."

"Hmm?"

"Did . . . did you really mean to suggest nobody thinks I wish to marry?"

"What? Of course not. But it is hardly the sort of thing one can talk about, is it? And the fact of the matter is that there are very few men I'd consider worthy of you."

Somewhat reassured, she said more steadily, "But I do not think Adam would be pleased for me to undertake that role."

"Why?"

She told him of what Adam had said, which made him laugh.

"It is not a laughing matter, Father."

"Oh, I think you'll find it will be. Poor lad. No, he'll need someone who won't keep pandering to his every mood, which is why I believe you'll do most excellently."

"Because he thinks I despise him?"

"Do you care for him?" He gave her one of those quick, shrewd looks that seemed to peer into her soul.

"Of course not."

"Then what does it matter what he or anyone else thinks?"

"But the villagers—"

"Know you have nursed many a patient over time. And if they choose to think dishonorably about an honorable situation, then Mrs. Edgerton and I shall simply set the record straight."

There appeared no way to withdraw, and that she'd best resign herself to the fact. She drew in a long breath, then released it slowly. She was going to have to care for the man she now disliked, who seemed to hold her in aversion, too.

Chapter 13

Mary paused at the Edgerton farmhouse door, the scent of fresh baked items drifting to her nose. She gathered up her courage, her compassion, and knocked on the heavy wooden door. If she was trying to live God's way, then she really needed to work on being quicker to forgive, to not hold on to resentment, and to remember to treat others as she'd like to be treated. *God, forgive me. Help me do better.*

The door swung open and revealed Mrs. Edgerton. "Miss Bloomfield! We had wondered if you'd forgotten all about us."

"No." Mary smiled at Mrs. Edgerton and worked to ensure her voice held no edge. "I have been a little busy these past days." Busy with making herbal medicines, with her visits, with comforting her sister after Emily's departure the previous day.

"Oh, I know all about being busy, I be that weary. Well, it is good to have you finally return. Adam has been very down today, and I'm at my wit's end."

Poor woman. Mary followed her inside. The pique from days earlier dissipated, like dew in summer sun.

"Yes, come in, set your basket just there."

"I've brought some currant buns." She held the basket out to her.

"How thoughtful. I've barely had time to bake, and only the essentials. It will be good to have something a little different for a change."

Perhaps Mary should drop a hint in the reverend's ear that baked goods would be welcomed here.

"Adam is in his room." She gestured to the bedchamber and went inside. "Adam? Miss Bloomfield is here."

There came a murmur she did not quite hear, although she recognized the flat tone.

She hesitated, then drew in her spine. He had apologized, after all. "Good afternoon," she said, in as bright a voice as she could muster.

"Is it?" His voice, his demeanor held dejection. He sat at a small table, a teacup by his restless hand, patches of brown liquid on the table.

"Adam, you've spilled the tea." Mrs. Edgerton hurried to her son, drew out her handkerchief, and began wiping up the mess.

Mary watched, lips pressed together. No wonder Mrs. Edgerton complained of feeling weary if she attended to every little thing.

Mrs. Edgerton sighed. "Would you like a cup of tea, Miss Bloomfield?"

Seeing her exhaustion, Mary was tempted to decline, when a thought struck her. "Yes, please."

"I'll be back in a moment. Please, take a seat."

The only available chair was at the small table where Adam sat, so she gingerly removed a stained man's shirt and placed it on the back of the chair. Poor Mrs. Edgerton. How much more work this must mean for her.

She examined the man seated before her. He wore an odd assortment of mismatched clothes, as if a child had dressed in the dark. Compassion unfurled within. Of course. That was his life now.

"Miss Bloomfield? Are you there?" He spoke with his face tilted away, facing the door and not herself.

Her eyes filled. Poor man. How could she have taken offense?

"I . . ." She swallowed. "I am here, sir."

At once his head followed the sound of her voice, and it was as if he was looking at her again. Except he wasn't, of course. Her heart tugged.

"Mother said you might visit."

"I hope you do not mind."

"It makes a change. Your father seems to be the only other person who bothers."

"Nobody else has called?"

"Alby Jamieson visited. Once was enough for him." He laughed, a sound that held more than an edge of bitterness. "No one knows what to say to a blind man."

"Likely, people don't want to say the wrong thing."

His lips pressed together, and she could almost feel the weight of despair clinging to him.

What could she say to alleviate some of his gloom? *God, help me.* "It *is* peculiar," she suddenly felt compelled to say.

"What is?"

"Well, it's not as if you are deaf. Now if you were deaf and blind, that would indeed make a visit rather hard to undertake."

His lips pulled to one side, as if he was amused.

She blinked and glanced away. Really, she was spending far too much time looking at his lips. But whenever she looked at his eyes, so dark, so hooded, so blank, she found she *had* to look away.

"Do you mean to try to cheer me?"

"I'm not sure if that's entirely possible."

"And why not?"

"I mean, one can try to cheer another, but there needs to be some degree of effort exerted by the other party in his determination to be cheered. Otherwise, it is extremely hard work for all concerned. Or so that is my experience, anyway."

"Your experience is as the one giving cheer, I suppose?"

"Yes. Although I've had my moments being the other, also."

Before he could enquire further, she proceeded to tell him a story about an elderly patient at the infirmary who refused to eat until Mary had threatened to spill porridge from a very great height into the person's mouth.

"You didn't."

"I did." At her father's suggestion, when, at her wit's end, she had gone and asked what she should do. "Best decide if you are determined to remain miserable, and if so, please let me know at once, so I'll know if I am wasting my time here or not."

He stared at her.

Or at least in her direction, she realized, heart twisting a little. Was it so very cruel to say such things in an effort to be kind?

"Otherwise you'll be unkind to me?"

"What is this I hear?" Mrs. Edgerton's entry to the room had gone unheard, given that the door had remained open the entire time. "Mary? You're not being unkind, are you?"

"Of course she isn't," Adam said wearily, forestalling Mary's impulse to apologize. "She's simply warning me that she won't have me acting so blue-deviled."

Mrs. Edgerton's expression eased. "Mary, here is your tea." She placed a cup and a plate with currant buns on the table.

"Thank you."

Mrs. Edgerton nodded, and looked around as if wondering if she should sit down.

Mary glanced at Adam. He had tensed again. Mary held out the shirt. "I wondered, ma'am, if you might want this."

"Well, I don't really, but I suppose I should." Mrs. Edgerton sighed. "It seems a never-ending round of things to do. And look, Adam's sleeve is now stained, too."

His jaw clenched, as if he was holding back a retort.

"Thank you for the tea, Mrs. Edgerton."

The subtle directive seemed to work, and Mrs. Edgerton bustled out, with an "I best get on with things, then."

The room grew silent again. Just what should Mary do? Clearly, Adam needed help. Equally clearly, he resented any attempts to do so. *What do I do?* She eyed her tea, then the man seated opposite. "Did you drink all your tea before?"

He shrugged. "Not much."

She pushed the cup and saucer towards him, until it bumped his restless fingers. "Then have this."

"What?" He slid fingers over the sturdy porcelain. He had nice fingers, long and slender. "This is yours, is it not?"

"I find I'm not terribly thirsty and would much rather you have it."

"Feeling sorry for me, are you?"

"No. I just want to see how you can manage such things as eating and drinking."

He frowned, then inhaled audibly. "What's that I smell?"

"A currant bun. Would you like some?" She pushed the plate towards him.

He tentatively reached out, shaky fingers moving near the plate, bumping against the cup, which spilled tea into the saucer.

A hiss escaped. "Clumsy clod-pole."

"It's to your right."

He moved a fraction in that direction, then grasped the still-warm bun.

"I should warn you that it is a little sticky on top."

"I don't care." He lifted it and inhaled, a tiny smile curving his lips, before he broke it apart savagely and devoured it.

She watched him, heart twisting once again. The man ate as if he hadn't eaten in days. "You like that, then?"

He stopped, pressed the remaining portion in, and swallowed. Cleared his throat. "I must seem most ungentlemanly to you."

"Not ungentlemanly. Just hungry."

He gave a bark of laughter devoid of humor. "I've told Mother I need to eat by myself. But anytime I do I seem to spill more than I consume."

"Which is only natural."

He shook his head. "I get so frustrated, it's a wonder that she still feeds me."

"I imagine there is a lot of adjusting needed from everyone. Go on, have a sip of tea."

His hands tentatively tapped the table, moving to the cup and saucer. He grasped it, the tiny cup looking monstrously small in his large hands. He completed the action and placed the teacup back in its receptacle with a loud clatter. "Sorry," he mumbled.

"What for?" She smiled. "I enjoy the sight of such a large man holding a dainty cup."

"You're laughing at me again."

"Again? No, not at all. I do find certain aspects of this rather fascinating."

"You are fascinated by the most peculiar things, then."

"But don't you think it interesting how much we rely on sight? I'm sure, if I were to close my eyes, I would not do nearly as well as you."

"You are being condescending now."

"You think so? Here. I'm going to take the cup." She drew it forwards, placed it in front of her, and closed her eyes. "I've now shut my eyes, and I'm having a sip." She lifted the cup and tentatively sipped, noting the small spark of fear as she returned it to the table. What if the cup fell and broke? What if she spilled hot tea on herself? She felt around with her fingers, then placed it slowly down on the table, the tension giving way to ease. She opened her eyes. "There."

"Did you just drink my tea?"

"Well, it *was* my tea to begin with."

His lips pulled to one side again. "You, Miss Bloomfield, are a very unusual woman."

"So I've been told."

But the activity had given her new insight as to his troubles. What would it be like to always have that moment of hesitation, of doubt, of worry about where things should go, of what he might walk into? Clearly she would need to give this more thought.

⁓

Upon her return home, she spent the rest of the day practicing her usual routine with her eyes closed as much as possible. Mother was horrified, Joanna was amused, but Father understood, even when Mary had dropped her glass at the dinner table.

"Do you really mean to spend the rest of the evening with your eyes shut?" Joanna asked, after their parents had retired that night.

"I'm trying to understand what it would be like, in order to understand what might be necessary for Adam to live a normal life."

"Normal?" Joanna scoffed. "He can't be normal. He's blind."

"But he is strong, and courageous. And he has never been considered a fool. In fact, I seem to recall Robert often talked about Adam's clever brain, and his knowledge of all sorts of things."

Joanna's silence grew so pronounced Mary had to open her eyes to see if her sister was still seated at the table. "Don't allow yourself to admire him too much."

"What?"

"Just remember who he was promised to, and how he left her. He's hardly likely to fall in love with you after Emily."

Her sister's words, foolish as they were—if she only knew how much Adam Edgerton disliked Mary—still carried the power to sting. "I have no interest in him, save as a patient of Father's."

"I've never seen you go to such extraordinary lengths for one of Father's patients before." Joanna sniffed.

"I've never encountered anyone who was blind like this before."

"Hmph," came Joanna's inelegant response.

Mary ignored her sister's remarks and soon excused herself. Closing her eyes, she clutched the handrail, made her way up the stairs, and felt along the wall until she reached the second door, her bedchamber. She felt for the handle and twisted it, then stumbled her way inside. In her efforts to move about by touch, she'd forgotten it needed a slight lift and push, and misremembered the whereabouts of the rug that always seemed to catch her foot.

She inched her way to her bed and sat down, eyes still closed. This was exhausting. No wonder Adam was always tired, with those deep shadows underscoring his eyes. There was so much to remember, and her nerves were snapping—and this only after half a day's pretense that she was blind!

A resurgence of compassion mingled with that stubborn tug of appeal that had persisted even after his rudeness in recent days, after lying dormant for years.

Mary undressed in the dark and hurried into her nightgown. Thank goodness no one could read her heart or mind! She must be very tired indeed to mistake compassion for fascination, to allow emotions to entangle her heart. How foolish she was being, as silly as one of Joanna's latest fancies. This was *not* what she should do.

She didn't want to misread things, nor engender feelings that were not right, so she lay on her bed in her likely misbuttoned nightgown, eyes kept shut in the dark, and found herself praying for wisdom as to what to do. *Please, God, guard my heart.*

Fingers were remarkable things. Able to grasp, to gesture, to sense hot and cold. Able to guide a blind man's steps from his bedchamber through the hall.

"Oh, Mr. Adam!" Meggie's voice. "Whatever are you doing?"

"Looking for the dining room."

"Here, let me help you."

"No. I need to learn to find it for myself." His fingers trailed along the wall, bumping the pictures, likely setting them askew. One benefit of being tall was, with his arm outstretched, he was less likely to encounter the usual detritus adorning small tables and the like. Finally, his fingers slid round the cool stone to a doorway. A moment's triumph! He turned to where he sensed Meggie remained standing. "Here?"

"Aye." A pause. "You are sure that you don't wish for help?"

Oh, the uncertainty in her voice. "Thank you, I'm sure."

"In that case, I'd be grateful if you tell your ma when she returns that the master's lunch is ready. I'm going to check on the chickens."

"I'll tell her."

She farewelled him, leaving him to absorb the silence of the house.

Finally. A few moments to be alone. He could be free, free to make mistakes, free to fall down if need be, and free from interference from well-meaning women.

He inched his way along the wall, thinking, calculating the measurements of where things might be. How strange that a place he'd known all his life needed to be relearned. He reached out, bumped into a chair, felt around the wooden top rail, and drew the seat out with a loud scrape before sitting heavily into it. There. His personal challenge for the day, completed. He savored his victory.

A door opened. "Adam?" his mother called.

"In here."

"You're in the dining room?"

"Yes."

"But why?"

"Because I wanted to come in here."

"You're sitting here in the dark."

His lips drew sideways. "The dark doesn't bother me."

"Well, it bothers me. Don't you feel cold?"

Well, yes, now she mentioned it.

There came a rasp of curtains being opened, and a sense of warmth pervading the room.

"It's a glorious day today," she said brightly.

"Is it?" He dredged up some enthusiasm to try to match hers. "And how was your trip to the village?"

She chattered on about various people with their various little problems before exclaiming, "I almost forgot! You have a letter."

His lips tightened. Wonderful. Reading letters was yet another thing he needed others to assist with. "Who is it from?"

"Edward Bracken."

"Well, how is he?"

There came a sound of unfolding paper.

He waited impatiently in the long moments that followed. "Can you just read it, please? Aloud?"

His mother sighed. "I'm sorry. I started to read it for myself."

"And yet it is addressed to me, is it not?"

"Yes, well, that may be so, but how can—?"

"Just read it aloud, now please, Mother."

She murmured an apology. "Mr. Bracken writes and sends you his greetings, hopes you are feeling better. He wants you to know that he has arrived safely—"

"Is that really what he wrote?" Adam's voice grew louder. "Please, Mama, all I'm asking is that you simply read the letter aloud as it was written, without commentary, without your personal interpretation."

There was a silence broken only by the release of a very long sigh, a sound that once again wound guilt around his irritation.

Oh, how far thankfulness seemed to be from him these days.

"Very well," his mother said. "Edward writes: *Dear Adam, I trust you are feeling more the thing, and are able to find something of a new way of life now that you are at home. I'm very glad to have been able to be of service, so put that out of your mind. I'm at home myself now, in York, and happened to bump into a friend of my mother's who told me of a Miss Hardy who is soon to visit and stay for a long duration. I don't suppose this is your Miss Hardy of whom you spoke so well? If so, I can only conclude that things have come to an end between you two, and if that is so, then you have my heartfelt condolences."* She paused. *"I'm so sorry."*

Emily. His heart grew heavy with regret. If only . . .

"Adam. Do you want me to keep reading?"

He was barely aware she'd spoken, so mired was he in past reflections. "Is there more?"

"Not much. Just good wishes for your future health, and a request for you to keep in touch."

"As if I can write legibly now."

"You could barely write legibly before."

A chuckle broke past his self-pity. "Thank you."

"If you wanted to respond, we could write for you. Or Miss Bloomfield could."

"I don't think we'll be seeing her here again."

"Why? Were you rude to her again?"

Again? Oh, that's right. He'd told her about his misfortunate words when thinking the room visitor was his mother. "I don't think I was rude last time. If I was, it wasn't intentional."

"At times it's rather hard to know when you are intending to be rude or not."

He reached across and felt for her hand, squeezed her fingers gently. "I'm sorry, Mama. I am such a wretched son."

"Not a wretch." She sighed again, igniting that persistent spark of irritation at the sound. "I know this is not easy."

"No."

"And it's probably good you are learning to do things for yourself, though it is hard to not want to dress you."

"I am not a child, Mother."

"You'll always be my child," she said softly.

His heart stirred. With the ever-present guilt, most likely.

"Mary is happy to visit."

"Is she, though? I rather thought she visited under protest."

"Well, it's not as if she has a lot of other things to do. Who knows? Perhaps if you were to spend enough time with her, you might find she is someone you could learn to live with."

"You mean marry her?" His nose wrinkled.

"She would make someone a fine wife one day. And heaven knows she must be keen to see herself married and running a household of her own."

"That may be the case, but it certainly won't be with me." A new thought struck. "Is that why you think she agreed to help me?"

"Well, not exactly. But it can't hurt that you are quite fine to look at, and able to offer a snug house and farm one day."

If he ever learned to manage it. He sighed and was uncomfortably aware just how much like his mother he sounded. "I have no interest in her. And if you think she's only here to try and throw her cap at me, then I wish you to disabuse her of such a notion."

And he would ensure the next time she called to behave in a way considered gentlemanly, but that in no way gave rise to any softer feelings in a woman's breast.

There came a sound from without. His ears pricked and his nerves tensed. Dear heavens, he hoped it wasn't Miss Bloomfield, hearing him speak ill of her again. "Who is it?"

"Only your father." Relief shaded his mother's voice. Perhaps she'd been worried they'd been overheard, too.

The door scraped open, and the clomp of heavy boots and stale smell of sweat suggested it was indeed his father who had arrived.

He tested his theory with a "Father."

"Son." There was a double pat on his shoulder, then the sound of a chair scraping out, and the *thud thud* that was likely two boots hitting the floor.

Liquid was poured—he was getting better at discerning things now—and a rasp as something was pushed across the table.

He inhaled. Smelled like another of those sticky buns.

"Surprised to see you sitting in here," his father eventually said.

"He's trying to do things as he used to," Mother spoke for him.

There was a sound like a snort, then a loud breath released. "S'pose we have to start sometime."

Except it felt as if he'd started this process to normalcy a while ago. "How is the farm?"

"Another two sheep missing." Something plonked on the table, sending the crockery a-clatter. "I need to speak with Payne again, but I don't think it'll do any good."

"Still nothing?" Mother asked.

"Davis says he's seen nowt. It's gettin' that I scarcely know who to believe. Someone around here must know something."

Frustration balled within his chest. If only he could see! He unclenched his hands, exhaled slowly. *God, let the culprits be found.*

He drew up short. Where had that prayer come from? He'd barely acknowledged God this past week. *Sorry, Lord.* Would God listen to him even if Adam struggled to believe?

"At least tomorrow is Sunday," Mother said.

"You think the thieves will have a day of rest?" His father's tone dripped with heavy sarcasm. "Maybe they'll be in church."

"Adam? Do you want to come too?"

"Where?"

"To service."

Adam frowned. And have everyone look at him and he be unable to know their thoughts? "No, thank you. I can barely make it from one room to the next, let alone ever think of going anywhere."

"I'm sure it won't always feel that way."

Adam held his objection behind his teeth.

"Well, I best serve the meal," Mother said.

For an instant he was transported back to a simpler time, when he'd been a small lad in short coats trailing his father around the farm. The sounds, the scent of dinner being prepared, the quiet conversation as his family shared about their day. A strange longing for that welled inside. How he wanted that for himself one day, wanted the family—the wife—that would make such a thing possible. *Dear God, if there is any way . . .*

Chapter 14

Mary escaped the church service, breathing in the fresh air, wishing the breeze might blow away the cobwebs which crept across her brain. The service, which consisted of the usual hymns and a sermon based on First Samuel, had dulled her to lethargy. It seemed Mr. Ponsonby was more inclined to sneer at King Saul than attempt to enlighten anyone about why Saul had not trusted God. Where was the talk of faith in God? Where was the belief God might actually intervene in people's lives and surprise with His miraculous power? How could someone be a minister of God and not believe God could actually minister?

She exhaled, turning in the tiny churchyard towards where the water sparkled in the valley down below. Seeing it brought an ease to her heart, caused the rushing of her pulse to slow. Perhaps she should not be so quick to judge Mr. Ponsonby. Perhaps he did believe God still healed but was reluctant to say so from the pulpit. She could not know the workings of another person's heart. Mary smiled wryly to herself. She scarcely knew the workings of her own heart! But recent times had proved just how vulnerable she was to prejudice and ill-conceived perceptions, and she truly wanted God to help her see more clearly.

For some reason that last thought circled her contemplations back to Adam Edgerton. She lifted her eyes to the hill where the Edgerton farm brooded. He hadn't been in church today, though he had not missed much. She winced. *Forgive me, Father.*

Mr. and Mrs. Edgerton had attended the service but made quick apologies that they must away. However, they hadn't left before Father captured their attention and talked quickly. They'd nodded, then escaped. What had Father said?

"Oh, Mary, here you are."

She turned, heart dipping at the drab figure with slumped shoulders standing before her. She summoned a smile and forced brightness to her voice. "Hello, Susan. How are you today?"

"As best as can be expected."

"Any, er, sign that things might be better than expected?"

"If you mean have I had my courses, then no." Susan's lips compressed, her eyes filled with tears.

Oh no. Mary moved closer, clasped Susan's arm. "Please don't worry. Whatever happens, God is with you."

"Are you sure?"

The bleakness in Susan's face and question stole Mary's breath. It was a moment before she could speak. "Of course He is with you. He loves you."

"I'm not so sure. There is little good that I see."

"Oh, Susan." Mary wrapped her in a gentle hug. "Please try. I know that it is easy to grow disheartened, to only see what is challenging or sad, but God wants us to remember that there is good, also."

"Like what?"

"Like His promises. Like that view." She pointed to the lake. "Why, even the wonderful friends you have," she dared jest, pointing to herself.

Susan gave a wan smile.

"Now, I wanted to ask you about your pups. Would it be possible to come see them and visit you soon?"

"Of course. You could come this afternoon if you wished."

"That would be perfect."

⸺⁂⸺

A few hours later, Mary sat surrounded by tumbling balls of black-and-white fur. She laughed, pleased to see Susan's expression much brighter than it had been this morning. "Oh, they are too sweet!"

Susan stroked the docile mother, a collie. "They are certainly a handful."

"How old are they?"

"About six weeks, so nearly ready to go to new homes."

Mary clutched a particularly wriggly creature to her chest, tilting her head away as he tried to lick her face. "You are such a friendly boy, aren't you?" She glanced at Susan, then back at the pup. "Whatever dog we choose for Adam must be sweet-tempered and calm. It probably won't be you, then."

"I imagine you'll be wanting something older than a pup."

"Yes, there are enough challenges without the need to train a dog, also."

Susan's brow knit. "I still don't understand why you think a dog might be able to help Mr. Edgerton."

"Have you not heard of the children's alphabet verse: 'A was an archer, and shot at a frog, B was a blind man and led by a dog'? Obviously, such a thing has been done before."

"Well, yes. But I'm not sure that simply leading a blind man will be enough."

"Perhaps. Perhaps not. But I can't help but pray a companion dog might provide some comfort for young Mr. Edgerton rather than not. Especially if he is trained."

"Who, the dog or Mr. Edgerton?" Susan actually smiled.

"Both, I should think!"

They laughed, which seemed to excite the pups into greater licking frenzy.

After a time Susan sighed. "I am not sure if these little fellows will be quite the thing. But I shall keep an ear out in case I hear of one more suitable."

"It should not matter if it's a few weeks away. Poor Mr. Edgerton does not seem to be in the mood for anything at this stage."

Susan looked at her curiously. "Is it true you are going to see him regularly?"

"Well, not exactly regularly, but I've been asked to help him, yes."

"Oh, I just wondered."

"Wondered what?"

"Oh, nothing. But I suppose it's easier without Emily Hardy here now."

"I'm sorry, but I don't take your meaning."

Susan looked a little awkward. "I just meant that Emily would not like you spending all this time with her beau."

Mary straightened, placed the pup gently on the ground. "I'm not swooning over him, or indulging in picnics and quoting poetry, if that's what you mean."

"No, no. It seems funny that you're taking such an interest in someone like that."

"I didn't realize caring for one's neighbor construed interest of a romantical nature," she said. "I was asked to, remember? By his own mother."

"Oh, Miss Bloomfield, forgive me. I did not mean to give offense."

Mary exhaled, summoned up a smile. "And I did not mean to be touchy. It's just that Joanna has made similar observations, and I cannot seem to convince her, either."

"You are not enamored of him?"

"No." She paused. *No!* "And I'd appreciate it if you tell any you might hear speculating on the matter that it is simply an act of caring for one's neighbor, as requested by Mr. and Mrs. Edgerton."

"I will." Susan nodded meekly.

But Mary knew this would not be the last time such an aspersion would be made.

⁓

Conscious of the village talk, it was not without some reluctance that Mary next visited the Edgerton farm. But gossip should not be reason enough to keep her from the role Father had requested of her. When she murmured something of what Susan had said, Father had simply looked at her incredulously and said, "If you let such things stop you from doing good, then you're not the daughter I thought you were."

Chagrined by his disapproval, and conscious of her recent experiment of what life must be like without sight, she had endeavored to visit at the next available opportunity. But now her walk to the Edgerton farm was delayed by the sight of the reverend and Mrs. Endicott outside the church. Her heart sank. Mrs. Endicott was one of Amberley's greatest gossips.

She peered at Mary with her brows raised. "Miss Bloomfield."

"Good afternoon, Mrs. Endicott. Hello, Mr. Ponsonby."

"I understand you are helping Adam Edgerton." The large-bosomed lady frowned.

"At his parents' and my father's request, yes."

"You should be careful," Mrs. Endicott said, spectacles balancing dangerously at the end of her long nose. "A young lady always needs to be mindful of her reputation."

"You are so right." Mary nodded. "I must confess the thought of visiting was not mine—I'm afraid I'm not so saintly minded as to originate such an idea myself—but when both the village doctor and the patient's mother are insistent, well, it would be unchristian to refuse to help, do you not agree?"

They both looked a little startled by this but nodded anyway.

"Tell me," Mary continued, "for I have been thinking on this very issue of protecting my reputation, Mrs. Endicott. What more do you think I should do? I only ever visit when Mrs. Edgerton is in the house. Even then, she is either in the room or the next and only a call away, as are her servants. And as poor Mr. Edgerton is still rather weak and literally learning how to manage things, it is not as if he's in any place to cause a person harm. Not that I think he would do so anyway, for he has always been quite gentlemanly in his notions, even when he was young. But I would dearly love to know what more you think I should do in order to still the gossips' tongues and prevent unsavory speculation."

Mrs. Endicott clucked. "Well, he has been a soldier, dear, and we all know soldiers aren't always nice in their notions as to what constitutes proper behavior."

Mary studied her for a lengthy moment. "Do you hold such truths about all soldiers, or just this one in particular? You might recall that my brother currently serves in the King's armed forces whilst undergoing very trying conditions in Spain."

The woman's cheeks mottled, and she hastily begged Mary's pardon.

Mary accepted this with a nod. "It seems most peculiar to me that prior to his arrival Mr. Edgerton was lauded as a hero, and there were all sorts of plans for picnics and balls and things to celebrate his return. Now, scarcely a soul goes to visit him, as if the village is ashamed of what he is. Do you understand why this might be, Mr. Ponsonby? I fear I do not comprehend such things."

"That is odd," Mr. Ponsonby said, his frown smoothing to geniality. "Miss Bloomfield, you are right. It is quite mean-spirited for people to consider your assistance as anything less than what it is: charity."

She winced inside, knowing how those words would be loathed by the person she was trying to help.

"And it is small-minded indeed for people to gossip about such things."

"Indeed." Mary lowered her eyes, hoping she looked as meek as Mrs. Endicott seemed to think she needed to feel. "I would hate for people to gossip about me, especially, as you can see, it being so unfounded." She raised her face, as if a suddenly wonderful idea had struck her. "I know! Perhaps if either of you were to accompany me, then all would be seen to be well." She smiled brightly. "It is not as if people would ever gossip about either of you, seeing as you can stand here talking to each other safe in the knowledge that your reputations will survive."

Their eyes widened, and they took a step apart.

"If either of you would be so kind as to accompany me today, I'm sure I will be safe from the work of idle tongues."

"I, er, I'm afraid I have a sermon to write."

"Oh, that's a shame." She turned to Mrs. Endicott. "Perhaps you might accompany me."

"Oh! Well, I would, if I had more notice, but I'm rather busy myself."

Yes, so busy she had time for a lengthy chat with the reverend.

"I'm afraid Mrs. Edgerton might be waiting on me. Poor woman, she's so tired with all the extra demands this terrible deed has inflicted on her family. Why, she's been so busy she's scarcely had time to bake, which is why I made this apple cake today. You know, Mr. Ponsonby, if you wanted to encourage charity among your congregation, you might ask a few of the more capable bakers to make Mr. Edgerton a nice cake. Such a tribute to a famous war hero would only be right and just, would you not agree?"

He nodded. "That's a wonderful idea, Miss Bloomfield. Perhaps I will accompany you one day soon."

"That would be good." Her smile sagged at the notion of sharing a visit with Mr. Ponsonby and she hitched it up. "You must excuse me. I am expected. Good day."

They echoed her goodbye and she hastened away, a tumble of emotion churning in her soul. She was glad to have said what she had— words seeming to pour unaided from her mouth for once. But why did the reverend's offer of future accompaniment trouble her? Did she merely wish to avoid his company, or any company at all? She bit her lip and hurried on.

⚬⚬⚬

"Good afternoon, Mr. Edgerton."

Adam had caught the trace of lavender as the bedchamber's floors creaked when she stepped inside. "Good afternoon, Miss Bloomfield." He sniffed. He smelled something else. "What is that you have with you?"

A rustling of paper, then the scent of yeast and—apples?

"It is an apple cake, sir. I hope you like it."

"Did you make it?"

"Yes."

"Then I'm sure to enjoy it, especially if you bake as capably as you do everything else."

There was silence for a moment, enough to make him wonder if his words had been misconstrued. He hadn't meant to sound resentful; rather, he'd endeavored to be friendly. To be *friendly*, that was all. Friendly, yet still aloof, to not encourage a young lady's interest— though he could scarcely see why any young lady should choose to fix her interest on a blind man such as he.

"I will give it to your mother." Her voice was strained.

He'd upset her. Being unable to see, unable to read a person's face and take his cues from them, made even the art of conversation more challenging.

There came the sound of departure and muffled voices, and he took the moment to check his buttons were fastened as they ought. This dressing of oneself without vision had led to some interesting choices of attire of late, according to his mother.

There came the sound of Miss Bloomfield's return, along with the clink of crockery. "I have brought tea."

"Thank you." Was he destined to have his insides stained with tea? It seemed all he was deemed fit for, like an elderly lady with her dozen cats and slice of cake and tea.

"I saw Mr. Ponsonby earlier," she said, as liquid was poured. "Here's your cup."

Who? Oh, the pompous little reverend of the church. "How is he?"

"Apparently he is thinking of visiting you soon."

"Wonderful."

A ripple of low laughter stole through the room. "Now, now. When he does visit, you must behave, and be sure to tell him how much you loathe these visits of mine."

"What? Why?"

"Apparently there are some in the village who think my visits here are nothing short of scandalous. Of course, I tried to set both him and Mrs. Endicott straight, but I'm not sure how successful I was, even despite my saying such visits derived from mere 'charity.'"

Charity? The word hammered into his bones. She had no thought of him, then. Well, good. He felt around for his cup, took a sip. Almost choked.

"Mr. Edgerton? Are you all right?"

He exhaled. "Forgive me. That was rather hot." Scalding hot, in fact. If she weren't here, he'd hang his tongue out like a dog to cool it down.

"Oh! I'm so sorry, I should have thought—Here. Have some cake. Perhaps it will cool your mouth."

He felt a plate pushed into his hand, and, after a moment of gingerly testing its dimensions, he broke off a bit with his fingers, inhaled the warm, spiced-apple scent, ate—and felt as if he'd died and gone to heaven. One mouthful quickly turned to two, to three, and he was suddenly feeling around on his plate for any more.

"Did you enjoy that?"

"Not really," he mumbled past crumbs. "But I thought it only good manners to attempt to eat it."

That little chuckle in her throat . . . he couldn't help but smile.

"Your attempt was most noble."

"I have moments of selflessness, it is true."

Another smothered gurgle.

His heart eased further. These moments of banter made him feel almost close to normal.

"I did feel it only fair to warn you that you may find yourself the recipient of a visit from Mr. Ponsonby sometime soon."

This abrupt reversion to the previous topic made him struggle for a moment, before he inclined his head, even as he felt his smile fade. He wasn't keen for these times to be altered by another's presence. It had taken time, but today he'd felt almost comfortable with Miss Bloomfield's company. She might be a little unorthodox in her conversation and have a tendency to be a trifle overbearing in her ways, but she didn't push too hard. Somehow, she possessed the ability to make him feel safe.

"If you prefer, I can tell him you're not ready for visitors just yet."

"Oh, but we can't have your reputation suffer," he said, his tone harsher than he intended.

There came another long pause.

He felt another pang of regret. He was about to apologize when she cleared her throat.

"I see your stick has been replaced."

He reached out a hand, felt the smooth grip at the end, experienced a moment's reassurance. "Alby Jamieson made it." As a kind of penance, he suspected. If Adam hadn't dashed out to save the man, Adam would likely not have been shot in the shoulder, thus necessitating time in the hospital where the mysterious sickness had claimed his sight.

"Less splinter-laden?"

"He did a good job sanding any slivers away. It's longer, too, and lighter. Although I haven't had much cause to use it yet."

"You'll have time."

He grunted. Time was all he had these days.

"Speaking of Albert Jamieson, I was hoping you might be able to tell me more of your soldiering life."

"Why ever would you want to know about that?"

"I realized that there has been such a focus on your injury that we never really learned about what you did in Spain. And one can't really be deemed a hero unless one does something heroic."

Can't really be deemed . . . ? "Sometimes, Miss Bloomfield, you appear most impertinent."

"That *is* strange," she said in a most bland way.

He found himself wanting to smile. For all her managing ways, she did have a dry sense of humor he appreciated.

"So, would you please?"

"What do you want to know?"

"Your usual routines, what you ate, what you saw. I'd love to know about some of what you did that was considered as worthy of a medal."

"Truly?"

"Truly."

Very well, then. He settled back in his chair and described his time in the peninsula, the craggy, dry slopes, the tents that proved their accommodations, the hares that constituted their stews. It had been a rough life, a tough life, and one that now seemed more cautionary tale than real. Had that really been his experience for the past four long years? He seemed to be describing a different man, a different existence, than that which he knew now.

As he talked he grew conscious that her questions seemed to probe beneath, that she was somehow reminding him of who he'd once been, that those qualities that had enabled him to help Stamford and Balfour save a dozen men still existed somewhere within.

"And the episode that was in the releases?"

"I couldn't say."

"You mentioned something about Captain Balfour."

"He was my captain. A good man." A Christian man. "He's the one who saw me sent out as quickly as could be when I grew sick. He and Captain Stamford, whose connections made sure I was treated by the best in London, before I was released to come here."

"God bless them both."

"Aye." Awareness grew of her sympathy, of the way her understanding seemed to tug memories from his soul, other memories he did not want to pursue.

"Thank you for sharing," she said softly. "Robert doesn't write often, and it's very helpful to get a glimpse into what his life must be like, though I suspect sharing such things is not easy."

Of course. That was why she was interested. He was a fool to think it was simply because she cared about him. Hadn't she told him as much? That she couldn't afford to be seen to care?

"Your life as a soldiering man must have been somewhat stripped down to the basics, yes?"

"Yes."

"Would . . . would it be helpful, then, if your room was arranged a little more? So that whatever you needed, you could find close to hand?"

"I don't know what you are asking."

"What did you have to do before you'd go out to the battle? What was your routine?"

"You mean like pull on boots and things?"

"Yes. You see, if during war you must have had those items close to hand in order to be able to move out quickly, then it would make sense that those items you use regularly would be placed close to hand here, too. It need not be a struggle to remember where things are. You should simply put your hand to find them, and there they are."

Why had she spent so much time in reflection about him? He wasn't sure he appreciated it. "You are all consideration," he finally managed.

"Oh no. Not at all." A pause. "I'm simply doing what Father asked."

Ah, of course. The doctor. "How is your family?" He supposed he should be polite, and not let these conversations be so one-sided after all. And if he did, he might protect himself from her uncanny insights into his soul.

"Father is well, although he always looks a little tired to me. He never complains, though. Mother, on the other hand . . ." She sighed. "Joanna, my younger sister, although I don't know if you remember her very well—"

"She was . . . one of Emily's friends, yes?"

"Oh, so you do remember her. She's a couple of years younger than Miss Hardy, which makes her ten years younger than me. She seems to enjoy turning the heads of young men, although I personally think her manner is just a trifle too free and easy."

He remembered another young lady whose manner had been deemed rather free and easy, back when he'd been deemed rather a catch. His lips twisted. As if he could ever be considered that again.

"Mr. Edgerton?"

He sighed. "I suppose you should call me Adam. Whenever you say Mr. Edgerton, I expect to see my father. Or not, as the case may be," he said, with an attempt at ghoulish humor.

"Very well, Adam. I shall call you such unless in public. And you may call me Miss Bloomfield."

He chuckled at this, waiting for her to give permission that he might call her *Mary*, but she did not.

His laughter grew. This was the first time since the incident had happened that he had laughed. Perhaps the world was not so dark a place after all.

There came a sound of rushing feet, then his mother's voice. "Adam? Miss Bloomfield?"

He chuckled again.

"What is this? Why are you laughing? Why is he laughing?"

"I truly couldn't say," Miss Bloomfield replied.

"It's nothing, Mother." She had never understood his slightly skewed sense of humor. Not many people had. But perhaps Miss Mary Bloomfield might.

"I was suggesting to your son that it might be best if he could consider exactly where in his room he would like items to be placed to ensure they can be found quickly. Much like when he was away, and soldier's quarters meant things needed to be easily at hand."

"Adam? You've been talking about your time away?"

"Yes," he admitted. Today's conversation had been the first time he'd spoken of such things. He'd barely talked to his own parents about his war experiences. Guilt at this realization lifted a smidgen at another revelation. Today's conversation had brought a small amount of healing. Perhaps his injury need not define his entire existence after all.

Chapter 15

"Who's a beautiful boy, then?" Mary stroked the dark head before bending to press a kiss between the dog's ears. "He's adorable."

"He's such a lovely natured boy." Susan Oakley rubbed his white chest affectionately. "And has a way of somehow knowing what one needs."

"But you don't know why he has been returned?"

Susan shook her head. "I suppose the Paynes did not appreciate him like we do."

"What is his name?"

"Frank."

"Frank? How unusual."

"That's what I be thinkin'," Mr. Oakley said. "Right unnatural to call a dog anything."

"You'd call all dogs *Dog*, wouldn't you?" Susan said, humor tweaking her lips.

"Aye." He shrugged good-naturedly.

Susan rubbed the wriggling dog's stomach. "It is what the Paynes named him, and so he answers to it now. I like to call him Frankie."

"And you think he will be helpful for the Edgertons?"

"Aye," Mr. Oakley said. "These dogs be known as water dogs, imported from Newfoundland, and used by fishermen both there and here. They be strong, good-natured, and not afeared of water. I admit I first thought it a strange idea, but I can see a companion dog might help young Edgerton."

"And be a friend," Susan said, as the dog licked her face. "So eager to please, aren't you, Frankie?"

"Eager to please sounds just like what Adam will need." Mary nodded. "Hopefully he'll enjoy your company more than others from recent times."

Admittedly her last visit had gone considerably better than she'd expected—Mrs. Edgerton had even taken Mary aside afterwards and thanked her, with tears in her eyes, for helping her son find something to smile about. Mary had been surprised by her voluble thanks, a condition not altogether unconnected to the surprise in how Adam had responded to her queries about the war. He'd seemed happy enough to relive the time, to remember who he'd once been, to not be thought of as a victim. She'd wondered whether stirring up such memories might make him wish for those days again but had sensed a degree of acceptance and appreciation that what once had been had not been forgotten altogether.

She'd said as much to her father last night at dinner, and he'd been agreeably surprised. "He needs to remember what he's capable of, especially if he's ever going to have any chance of running that farm."

"Running the farm?" Joanna scoffed. "Blind people can't do such things."

"Why not?" Father had asked. "Have you never heard of Blind Jack?"

Therein followed a story about a man from Yorkshire, John Metcalf, who, though blinded by smallpox at a young age, grew to become an accomplished fiddler, athlete, and road builder, who was responsible for over a hundred miles of northern England's turnpike roads.

"A blind man building roads? That is make-believe."

"I've travelled those roads myself, and he's been honored for some years in Knaresborough. It's quite true, I assure you, Joanna."

"How impressive he must be," Mama said.

"I believe he died just on a year ago. But yes, he certainly possessed a courageous heart and a strong back, and was unafraid of what he could not see."

"You should share that with Mr. Edgerton, Father."

"Perhaps." A twinkle lit his eye. "He might hear it better coming from a friend, however."

A friend? The pointed look he gave her had sent her to study her plate, aware of her heart's rapid tattoo. She did not exactly consider Adam Edgerton a friend. He was a patient, and there was little of the interest from his side that designated friendship as far as she was concerned. Though he *had* asked about her family during their last visit, so perhaps friendship in their future was not a hopeless prospect after all.

"Mary?"

She blinked, returning her attention to Susan, whose enquiring look suggested she now awaited the answer to a question. "Forgive me. My mind was wandering. What did you say?"

"I wanted to know when you thought you might wish to take Frankie."

"Soon," she promised, rising and dusting off her skirts. "Mr. Edgerton will need some more practice with basic walking before we introduce a dog. Even if the dog is as sweet as dear Frankie here."

Mr. Oakley nodded and ambled away.

Mary took Susan aside. "How have you been feeling?"

"Well enough, I suppose." Susan frowned. "Why do you ask?"

Oh dear. She really didn't want to spoil today's good mood with enquiries into the sordid past, but it was for Susan's benefit. "Have you any more, ah, indications, about any possible repercussions of the incident from several weeks ago?"

Susan shook her head and glanced away, holding the dog to her chest like a shield. "I . . . I don't want to talk about it at all."

Mary nodded, patted Susan's arm, and made her farewell. That seemed a conversation best left for another day.

She made her way farther up the hill, the bend in the road offering glimpses of Windermere gleaming over yonder. The air held a kind of shimmering quality, what older folks called "glisky," which seemed to fill the day with a hopeful kind of promise.

Perhaps Susan was without child, and she and all the village could one day forget the nightmare that happened on the Oakley farm. Perhaps Adam Edgerton would be able to find a sense of happiness and purpose again. Perhaps God might even perform a miracle and heal him! Wouldn't that be marvelous? That thought hastened her steps to the farmhouse door.

A few minutes later she was being ushered inside to where Adam sat at the table in his room. The furniture appeared straightened, with less clutter.

"I see you have altered things in here."

"That makes one of us."

She tried again. "I hope the new room arrangement is making things a little easier for you."

He shrugged.

She bit her lip. He seemed rather morose today. "I was thinking that perhaps you might like to go outside."

His head jerked up. "Where?"

"Outside. It's a beautiful day."

"Is it? I wouldn't know."

"I suspect you'll enjoy being out of doors. There is a fresh breeze that feels most invigorating."

"Are you always this infernally cheerful?" he grumbled.

"No. I suppose some people just bring it out of me."

His lips twitched, and he lumbered to his feet.

She was startled again at how much taller he was than she.

He stretched out a hand. "Where are you?"

"Here." She clasped his hand in hers, and gently squeezed. "Now, I'm going to let go, but I want you to walk to the door."

"But—"

"You've done this before, have you not?"

His nose wrinkled and he released her hand. His gait remained steady as he moved to the doorway.

She backed away, offering quiet encouragement as he followed her voice through the hall, his fingertips touching the wall.

"You're very persistent, aren't you?"

"I try. Now, we're almost to the front door. Ready to venture outside?"

Was he ready? No. But would he do it? What choice did this stubborn little lass give him?

"Adam? Are you ready to go outside?"

No. "Yes." He slid a foot forward, then bumped his head. "What's that?"

"The front door."

"Why didn't you tell me it was closed?" He rubbed his brow.

"I did, so no complaining. You must not have paid attention."

Oh, he'd paid attention, just more to the soothing quality of her voice than to all her instructions.

"You should probably learn to unbolt the door, so your mother need not always do so."

Adam exhaled but obeyed, for she was right. These recent weeks had shown that his mother had been under a great deal of pressure. It was time he contributed to taking some of the load from her shoulders. Answering the door was the least that he could do.

He felt around for the locks and latches, and spent the next few minutes practicing opening the door, to varying effect. He supposed it would look amusing to a stranger, seeing the number of times Miss Bloomfield knocked, the door opened, then closed, then she waited as he struggled to remember the process once more.

"Are we done yet?" he finally asked, rubbing his knuckles where they'd been scraped by the metal bolt an unfortunate number of times.

"I think so. You'll remember how to open the door next time?"

"Yes, Miss Bloomfield," he intoned, like a schoolboy.

"Very well. We'll do it just once more." With that, she shut the door with a loud thump, loud enough that his mother hurried up to ask just what was going on.

"The latest of Miss Bloomfield's lessons, Mama. Nothing to worry about."

"But what are you doing?"

He heard the knock, stayed his mother's efforts, and showed her by swift movements that he could answer the door. "Yes, Miss Bloomfield?"

Their visitor laughed, the sound adding light to his heart.

Or maybe that was caused by the scent of meadows carried on the fresh breeze. He drew in a deep breath and took a careful step down to the stone flagging, suspended breath releasing as he completed the

action safely. Three steps forwards and he was on the gravel of the
yard. He stood, drawing in the sunshiny fresh air, feeling the caress
of warmth on his face, hearing the faraway call of birds, the bleat of
sheep.

It was heavenly.

Adam gingerly slid his foot forward, then the next, trying to follow
where Mary's voice led.

"That's it, well done."

Somehow he didn't mind the congratulations today. It felt like a feat
worth celebrating.

"How are you feeling?"

"Fine."

"Do you notice a difference between day and night? Any lightening
of the darkness?"

"It's still the same," he admitted. "Not like before when I could see,
when I'd close my eyes during the day and still have a sense of brightness beyond my eyelids."

"Do you notice the difference between being inside and out?"

"I notice the change in temperature, and how the air moves. Things
feel more alive." Surprising but true. "There is more to smell and hear
and feel." He took a long moment to do just that, drinking in all that
his senses could receive. He had missed this, missed feeling part of this
world, feeling alive. Something within urged him forwards. He'd spent
too long in a cold, dark cave. "Where are we going next?"

"It's probably best to just refamiliarize you with the yard."

"Lead on."

With a careful slide of steps and by following Mary's voice, he was
soon able to negotiate the path from the house to the road. But the rush
of sensations—the scents, the breeze, the sounds—grew overwhelming.
He'd soon need to sit.

"Are you tired, Adam?"

How did she always know what he felt? "A little."

"Here, hold my arm."

He heard the swish of her skirts and noticed the movement in the air
as she stood beside him.

She grasped his hand and shifted it to her arm, just above the elbow. "As I walk, you will feel the pull towards the direction I'm going."

Holding on to her felt a tad ridiculous, but it helped steady him, to allow his feet to move without worrying as much about the obstacles in his way.

They walked on a little longer, with only the occasional "there is a large stone" or "here comes a tuft of grass" to break the silence.

His arm, bending as it did at this angle, grew tight, and he had to call a halt to proceedings.

"What is it? Are you in pain?"

"I'm sorry, it's just this position is a little uncomfortable."

"Oh, I should have realized, especially as you are so tall. Perhaps if you held on to my shoulder instead, that might prove easier."

It *was* easier, feeling the way her body shifted slightly, the movements in her muscles giving indication as to what lay ahead. From the slender bones under his fingers, it seemed she was quite petite. Hopefully his greater weight was not unpleasantly heavy for her.

She did not seem to mind. Instead, she described what was around them—the sparrows twittering on the fence, the red rosebud on his mother's rosebush—the sights ones that he recalled along with sweet memories.

"You are very good to help me in this way."

"I'm glad to help."

His heart softened. What a generous-hearted lass she was.

"Mind, here is a fence post."

He held out a hand, grasped the rough, textured wood. "So, we are at the end of the garden, then?" He quickly calculated from his memory. "About twenty yards from the door?"

"Exactly so!"

He smiled at her enthusiasm. But really, he was doing rather well. Upon Miss Bloomfield's observation to this effect, he simply said, "It's not as if I've never seen them before."

"True. In fact, you're doing so well, I think you should try with your stick."

"Really?"

"If you're not too tired, that is."

He shrugged, and she seemed to take that as acquiescence, removing his hand from her shoulder and explaining she would return in just a moment. He savored the solitude, the way the air caressed his face, but was not sorry when Mary returned and slid his stick into his hand.

"Here you go."

"Thank you." He felt around for her. "You won't walk with me?"

"Try by yourself."

He followed her instructions, waving the stick back and forth to ascertain obstacles, gradually growing in confidence.

"You're doing very well," she called.

"You're quite the encourager, aren't you?"

"I try."

He smiled at the mischief lining her modest answer.

"It probably helps that you are tall."

"Do you not encourage short people?"

"What? Oh." She chuckled. "No, I'm referring to how well you move around. Being tall helps because you need fewer steps to get places. I find that I'm scurrying along like a mouse."

"You make me sound like a giant."

"You're not too tall," she hastened to say.

"Not too tall for what?"

"That I can't keep up."

He realized afresh just how much time she devoted to assisting him, time she might have spent elsewhere, with others or for her own amusement. Gratitude ballooned within. "Miss Bloomfield?"

"Yes?"

He stretched out a hand in the direction of her voice, then realized he still held the stick, something brought home by its abrupt halt and her sudden gasp.

"Oh, no! Did I hit you? I'm so sorry!"

"I'm sure I shall mend."

"Can you walk? Should you sit down?"

"Your wild stick swinging simply caught my arm. I shall be perfectly fine shortly. It just stings a little."

"I truly am very sorry." Regret kneaded inside. "Miss Bloomfield?"

"Yes?"

"I truly have no wish to hurt you, and I'm sorry that today, and on previous occasions, I have been less than careful with both my actions and words." He swallowed. "I know you have sacrificed time"—and God forbid, even her reputation!—"to assist me, and I want you to know I appreciate it."

Her small fingers gently clasped his, then released them in a pat. "I'm glad."

That was it? She was merely glad? His heart grew heavy, weighted by the condescension in her reply. He might like to think he could resume some of his old activities, but it was a fool's hope. He would always be blind. Always be pitied. Always be patronized.

"Would you like to continue walking?"

"I'm really rather tired." So very tired of being pitied, of being so pitiful.

And as he'd hoped, his mention of weariness swiftly brought their outside venture—and her visit—to a close.

Chapter 16

Mary pressed the wriggling bundle in her arms against her chest as she walked along the muddied road towards the Edgerton farm. It had been over a week since her last visit; Father had required her assistance in the infirmary, then Mother had requested Mary accompany her on a short trip to Ecclerigg to visit a cousin. She didn't like to admit she would have preferred to visit the Edgertons. It was exciting to see how much progress Adam was making with his walking, with his confidence. Although he still left her confused, one minute joking as if they might be friends, the next retreating into a stern silence she dared not break. Did he dislike her still?

No. She lifted her chin. Such thoughts were silly. He was sure to appreciate her visit today.

Anticipation swelled. How she hoped Adam would like this new surprise. If he'd kept practicing the walking since her last visit, that would definitely help with what she would deliver today.

Her boots crunched across the gravel to the white farmhouse. Today her mission was to introduce Frankie to the Edgerton household and see if there was any connection between potential master and animal. If not, she had every intention of taking the dog to be her companion. She smiled down at him. Frankie really was a dear, sweet thing.

She lifted a hand and knocked.

Mrs. Edgerton answered the door. "Hello, Miss Bloomfield. And who do we have here?"

"This is Frankie." Mary held out the mid-sized dog.

"Frankie? What a peculiar name."

"It is rather. But he is a very sweet-natured animal. I'm hopeful Mr. Edgerton will think so, anyway."

"Adam? Oh, it's hard to know just what he thinks these days, one day down in the dumps, the next almost like he was before. He got something of a cold after that walk outside the other day, and he's not quite himself, I'm afraid."

"I'm sorry to hear that." Her stomach tensed. Had the walk outside been a bad idea after all?

"Never mind. Come inside. You know where he is. I'll bring some tea in shortly."

Mary thanked her and moved to the room, unsurprised to see Adam sitting at the table. Judging from his posture, today seemed to be one of his dejected days. She pressed her lips together, then called a cheery "Good day," and gingerly took her seat, placing the dog on the floor.

Frankie immediately went to sniff in the corners of the room.

"How are you, Adam?"

He shrugged, barely lifting his head to acknowledge her.

Oh dear. It seemed a very bad day. "How has the walking been going?"

"It hasn't." His voice was raspy.

She forced cheer into her voice. "I brought you a gift today."

"Thank you," he said, without a spark of animation.

"I think you will truly thank me once you see what it is."

"See?" His laugh held bitterness. "I think you forget to whom you speak."

She paused. He obviously was feeling very discouraged. But was pandering to his loss helping any? It didn't seem so. "It's something that may encourage you to get out a little more, give you a feeling of independence."

"Is it cake?"

"I beg your pardon?"

"Is your gift a cake?"

"Why do you ask?"

"We seem to have been inundated with various cakes of late."

Oh. Mr. Ponsonby must have passed on her message after all. How glad she—

"They've not been very good, some of them. Not like your apple cake, anyway."

She almost reminded him about the limited choices of beggars but refrained.

At that moment, little Frank padded up to Adam's booted foot.

"I say, what *have* you brought?" Adam shifted his boot, but not before Frank had released a thin trickle of—

"Oh my goodness! Frankie, stop that." She hurried to scoop up the dog.

"Who? Who is Frankie?"

Oh dear. This was not such a good idea after all. She held out the dog to his enquiring touch. "This is Frank. He's a young water dog who has not quite remembered his manners."

Adam made a face. "My foot is wet."

"Yes. I'm sorry."

He coughed. "I gather that was the dog's fault."

Laughter bubbled up. "Mr. Edgerton! You put me to the blush."

His lips pushed to one side. "A watering dog, did you say?"

She knew a moment's desire to laugh again, so bit her lip savagely, wondering how to clean the puddle. This was *not* the way to garner Mrs. Edgerton's support.

"Is there much of a mess?"

"I'm afraid so. Here, hold him, and I'll attempt to clean it up." She placed the dog into his arms, where it instantly licked his face.

Adam jerked back. "Why, you are a friendly fellow, aren't you?" The dog gave a short bark, as if in agreement, and Adam smiled. "But you're going to have to learn some manners, especially around Miss Bloomfield. She does not take kindly to untamed beasts."

"Indeed, she does not," she muttered, vainly mopping at the floor with her handkerchief.

"Is he trained? Obviously he's not trained in all things."

She ignored that barb. "The Oakleys say he is able to fetch." She sat

back on her haunches. "But I believe he will prove quite useful in many ways."

A cloud passed over his features. "Oh, you do, do you? Well, what is the latest plan for my recovery from the ever-knowledgeable Miss Bloomfield?"

Her heart stung. She pressed her lips together to stop the quaver, and eventually managed to say in as mild a voice as she could manage, "Do you find my presence here distasteful?" So much for thinking they might one day be friends.

"I find *my* presence here distasteful." He shifted away and put the dog down, a look of despair crossing his features as he thrust his head into his hands.

"I can leave if you prefer. And I can take the dog."

"Leave the dog," he said roughly.

Her throat closed. "Very well, then." It was foolishness to take his words and manner personally. He must be suffering, and pain and grief were talking, but still, his words hurt. She gathered her reticule and rose.

"Miss Bloomfield?" Mrs. Edgerton said, arriving with the tea. "You are not leaving so soon, are you?"

"I'm afraid so," she said, glad her voice had steadied. "I'm sorry to be here such a short time, but I have some errands to take care of, some people I must see."

"But I thought you were staying. I made tea—"

"Thank you. I am sorry if I've disappointed you." Her breath caught. "I hope little Frank enjoys his new home." She reached down and smoothed the black fur between the dog's ears.

Adam pushed a hand through his hair. "Miss Bloomfield, I . . . I am sorry."

"Adam?" His mother looked between them both. "What have you been saying?"

Mary affixed a tight smile to her face and shook her head. Let him explain himself to his mother. "I'll see myself out. Goodbye, Mr. Edgerton."

"Miss Bloomfield, Mary, wait."

But she could not. Her bottom lip trembled, her eyes filled with a rush of tears. She needed to get away before she broke down and admitted the tiny arrow of hope she'd so foolishly dared to entertain was indeed sheer folly. He, like every other man, had no use for her, or wish for her to be in his presence.

⁓

"Adam, I demand to know what you said that chased Miss Bloomfield away. She looked as if she was about to cry!"

Guilt twisted through his stomach. "I was rude."

"I can tell that," she replied tartly.

"She was talking about some scheme with the dog here, and I, and I . . ." He shook his head, and something that felt awfully like tears gathered in his eyes. His stupid, stupid eyes. Why did they not work when he needed them to, and work like this when he didn't want them to? He exhaled, ducked his head, tried to cover the moisture leaking onto his face.

"Oh, Adam." His mother's voice trembled, which proved his undoing as tears fell.

He angrily swiped them away, but they insisted on escaping, more and more of them as emotion ballooned, refusing to be suppressed a second longer. He bent his head lower. His mother stroked his head, then pulled him closer, and he cried against her chest in a way he hadn't since he was a child.

He cried for his lost vision, he cried for his lost future, he cried for the lost friendship he'd not realized he'd wanted until now. He despised himself as much for breaking down as for his despair. But the emotions refused to be silent, and he knew himself to be fragmenting, jerky sob by jerky sob, so very far away from the hero people once assumed him to be. How utterly wretched was he.

"I hate this, Mama," he eventually managed to say in a broken whisper. "I hate who I'm becoming. Forever bitter, hurting people, saying things I don't mean. I *hate* this misery."

"Shh, shh." She patted him gently, stroking his head.

If only his fellow soldiers could see him now. "How pathetic I am." He pulled away, wiping underneath his eyes with his fingers.

A piece of soft cloth was pressed into his hand. A handkerchief?

He felt the stitched edges and lifted it to his nose. The scent of violets met him. His mother's handkerchief. Wonderful. Was he turning into a lass? He wiped his face and blew his nose. "I'm sorry," he muttered. It was unmanly to cry. But somehow the action felt cleansing, too.

His mother kissed his cheek, stroked his head once more, then patted his shoulder. "Do you feel better now?"

If by better she meant not quite as wretched as before, then, "Aye."

The dog emitted a short bark, and Adam lifted his head. "Is someone there?" God forbid his father see his son had crumpled like a baby.

"I can't see anyone," his mother said, then sighed. "Except the dog."

"Frank." He cleared his throat, attempting a semblance of self-control. "What does he look like?" He clicked his fingers. "Here, boy."

"Well, he's got a black coat, with white markings down the front, as if he's wearing a white vest. Oh, and four white paws, and he's white around his jowls."

A wet nose pushed into his hand.

Adam gently rubbed between his ears.

The dog pushed into the affection and moaned happily.

He drew the dog onto his lap, pulled him close to his chest, and smelled his dog scent. "Hello, Frank."

A sudden lick on the chin.

"It's a very odd name." His mother clicked disapproval. "Do you think you might change it?"

"Perhaps. But maybe, no. I knew a Francis in the army who was known as Frank. He thought Francis sounded too much like a girl." He rubbed the dog's chest, garnering another lick in response. "And I suppose if you're anything like Miss Bloomfield, who is never shy of speaking bluntly, then Frank might be appropriate." His ear was licked twice in a row, and he finally smiled.

A knock sounded at the front door.

His mother exclaimed and hurried to answer it.

Adam's heart caught. Was that Miss Bloomfield returned, so he could make amends? He quickly blew his nose again and wiped his face, hoping his expression seemed contrite, that his eyes and nose were not too red.

"Adam, you have a visitor."

"Miss Bloomfield, you must forgive me, I—"

"It's the reverend, Mr. Ponsonby."

Oh. No. "Er, hello." He thrust out a hand, which was eventually shaken, then he heard his mother ask the reverend if he'd like tea, which he accepted.

Hopefully he'd also accept some of the interminable number of cakes they'd received this past week. None of them had tasted nearly as good as—

"I passed Miss Bloomfield in the yard," the reverend said. "She seemed to be in a hurry."

In the yard? Surely he meant the road. Otherwise she would have had ample opportunity to—no. She wouldn't have heard him, would she? She didn't witness him break down like a wee bairn?

"She has been very kind in coming," his mother said. "Such a busy young lady, too. Always helping others."

"Which is why I felt it time to visit," the reverend said. "I would not have you think the church is backwards in coming forwards to help those in need."

Which is why it had taken weeks for the reverend to make this visit. "Of course not," Adam muttered.

"I see you are sitting up," the reverend said slowly, loudly, as if talking to a deaf or slow person.

What was he supposed to reply? "Yes."

"That is good."

Did he mean to sound so patronizing, as if he thought Adam an imbecile?

"And you have a little friend."

He had one little friend. The other he'd apparently chased away with his tongue. "This is Frank. From the Oakleys, so I'm told."

"I see." There was a pause.

Frank let out a low growl.

"He does not seem a very friendly chap."

"He's only very recently arrived, so he's still getting used to things."

"I see. Well, I wished to see if there is anything we can do. I trust the cakes have been satisfactory?"

"Oh, yes, wonderful," enthused Mother. "I don't know how people knew we enjoyed such things."

"We live to serve," the reverend said in a way that Adam supposed was meant to sound humble but sounded rather pompous instead. "And you are recovering well?"

"I don't know if recovery is possible from being blinded," Adam said.

"Of course not," the reverend replied with a low titter. "I suppose I meant how are you now?"

But Adam couldn't answer. Wasn't a reverend supposed to believe that God could answer prayer? Hadn't Jesus healed people long ago? Perhaps Adam should start believing that God could heal him, instead of blaming Him for this condition.

"Adam?" his mother said. "The reverend wants to know how you are now."

"I am as best as can be expected." He swallowed, then dared ask, "Tell me, Mr. Ponsonby, do you believe that God can do miracles?"

There was a cough, then, "Well, of course we see God has proved His miraculous power time and again in the Bible."

"Yes, but do you believe He still can do them today?"

"We read in the Scriptures that God is the same yesterday, today, and forever, so I believe it *is* possible." The way he said it sounded more like doubt than faith. "Do I believe He will? Well, I am not God, so how can I answer that appropriately?"

How indeed. Still, Adam's heart had latched on to hope and he wanted to be sure. "Do you think God could heal me? That is what I need to know."

"Could heal you, yes. Will heal you, no."

He felt as though cold water had been dashed across his face. "Right, then." He'd known it had been foolish to hope.

The doctors in Spain had been wary of offering false hope, the doctors in London, too. Even Dr. Bloomfield with his Edinburgh training had deemed it best for Adam to forget any chance of having restored vision and think about making changes for the future.

He sat for the remainder of the visit answering questions mechanically, willing his features to appear pleasant, even as he itched for the man to leave.

And later, after pleading a headache and refusing dinner, he lay on his bed, head burrowed in the dog's back, as new tears silently seeped into its fur.

Chapter 17

That look on his face. *Dear God.* That look on his face.

Mary turned in her bed, sleep refusing to come. How could she sleep, after she'd accidentally witnessed that terribly sad and private moment between mother and son? *Oh, dear Lord, please comfort him.*

Her gaze traced the shifting shadows on the ceiling, the branches of the apple trees skeletal in the dark. She'd never seen a grown man cry before. Save once, when old Mr. Ellis had lost his wife of forty years and tears had trickled down his face as Mary held his hand in sympathy.

But she'd never seen a young man weep, never someone whom she'd thought life and war and death had toughened to be stoic, to be steady, to be brave. Poor, dear Adam.

In that moment when she'd come to apologize for her quick temper and seen him sobbing in his mother's arms, she'd known he'd never forgive her should he learn she'd seen him in such a state of brokenness. Her heart wrenched anew. *Dear God, please help him.* She'd determined to keep on praying, keep on helping as best she could. Obviously, he'd thought her methods thus far overbearing and unwelcome. She must think of another way.

She rolled over.

A cough came from her parents' room.

Dear God, please heal Father. He'd looked rather pulled of late. *Dear God, please comfort Adam.*

Her prayer mocked her. Did she not believe God could heal Adam? "Dear God, please heal him," she finally dared pray aloud.

What if God did not? Was it wrong to request it, if healing Adam wasn't God's will? Who could ever ascertain what God's will was, anyway? Mr. Ponsonby seemed more inclined to follow church doctrine than believe the Bible. But surely in this modern age God could still work His age-old powers?

Her mind whirred, refusing sleep. She exhaled.

Lord, forgive me for being upset today. I'm sorry. Help me to remember not to take things personally. It wasn't necessarily Mary that Adam was upset with, although she should probably take heed to how she spoke and acted. "Give me wisdom. And help me sleep."

And she closed her eyes, prayers continuing, until exhaustion pulled her under.

◦◦◦∞◦◦◦

The next day she emerged heavy-eyed, heavy-headed, feeling out of sorts. The reflection in the looking glass had almost made her turn tail and head straight back to bed. Almost. But not quite. Father had coughed a few more times last night, and she was disinclined to add to his workload. Not if she could help alleviate some of his duties.

"My dear!" Mother exclaimed, as Mary stumbled into the kitchen for a cup of tea. "You do not look at all the thing."

"I rarely do," she mumbled, and Joanna snorted in amusement.

"Joanna, *dear*," Mother murmured.

Mary exchanged amused glances with her sister, then slumped into a chair and glanced around. Her sister had already changed into a walking dress. "It seems I have slept in."

"Are you feeling well?"

"Just a little weary." And heartsore. "But nothing to signify."

"Then we should pick some lavender today, so we can dry it and make more of those pretty scented sachets you like so well." Mother placed Mary's breakfast in front of her.

Was Mother including both her daughters for this expedition, or just her youngest? Mary sipped her tea, then said, "I might visit Susan Oakley later—"

A knock came at the door.

"I wonder who that can be?" Mother patted down her hair and moved into the hall as Joanna moved to the small window, half-obscured by a white cotton curtain.

Her indrawn breath drew Mary's notice.

"Who is it?"

"You'll never guess! They came here! And in his condition! Oh my!"

Mary rolled her eyes and propped a hand under her chin. Must her sister always be so dramatic? "Who is it, Joanna?"

Wide-eyed, she turned and hissed, "The Edgertons!"

Mary blinked. "The parents?"

"*And* the son."

"Adam Edgerton is here? Quick, let me see." She nudged her sister out of the way to ascertain that it was, in fact, true. "He's here," she whispered.

"Yes. How strange."

"How wonderful."

Her sister turned to eye her askance. "How so?"

"I don't believe he's even left the house since his return, so the fact that he came here is quite extraordinary."

Joanna peered through the curtain again. "He doesn't look quite like a blind man at this range. In fact," she said, as they watched him being helped down from the gig by his father, "if one didn't know better, one could almost consider him your suitor."

Mary pinched her sister. "Don't be unkind. He doesn't even like me."

"Hmph. Well, he is quite tall and still handsome. After all, Emily would not have countenanced anyone who was not. Though he's always seemed a bit too old for my liking."

"Let's hope he's not come to pay a call on you, then."

Joanna chuckled. "Now who is being unkind?"

Mary smiled, her earlier weariness gone as she patted her hair and straightened her gown.

A moment later, Mother requested their attendance in the small drawing room.

Her pulse accelerated. So, this wasn't a mere doctor's consultation after all.

"Good morning." She curtsied as she entered, the action repeated by her sister as she followed. They took the seats opposite their guests, and Mary couldn't help but notice how large Adam seemed in this graceful space. He sat, awkwardly stuffed into a too-small chair, his attire neat, his expression pensive.

"We are just waiting for your father to return," Mother said by way of explanation.

"Has little Frank been behaving himself?" Mary asked, hoping to ease the conversation.

"Frank?" Joanna tilted her head quizzically.

"Oh, the little dog has been getting under everyone's feet." Mrs. Edgerton moaned. "He even managed to trip up poor Adam here."

"Oh, no!" Regret churned within, as Mary desperately looked for signs of injury.

"It was my own fault." Adam shook his head. "I forgot he was there and nearly squashed him, poor chap. I don't think he's quite forgiven me."

"I'm so sorry."

"Why? Did you train him to trip me up? If so, then perhaps you should be sorry, for my knee took rather a beating, but if not, then I can only blame myself. I cannot blame the little fellow simply because he's with someone who obviously cannot see where he's going."

It took her a second to realize he was making a joke, that the bitterness of yesterday had quite passed away. Her breath drew inward, and she met Mrs. Edgerton's eyes.

Mrs. Edgerton inclined her head, as if in silent agreement.

Her husband spoke. "I don't quite know what we'll do with the dog if he doesn't start behaving."

"I hope to keep him." Adam gave a tolerable impression of looking at Mary, his face turned in her direction. "It was most comforting to know there was a friendly creature there last night."

"I'm so glad."

"I, er, wondered if I might be permitted to have a word with Miss Bloomfield, please."

Mother glanced at her, eyebrows raised, but said nothing other than, "I was hoping to pick some lavender with Joanna this morning. Perhaps, Anne, you and Mr. Edgerton might care to join us for a moment, seeing as my husband has obviously been delayed."

"Of course." Mrs. Edgerton shot Mary a quick look, then followed Mother and the others into the hall.

Mary turned to face Adam, whose face wore none of the ravages of the grief she'd witnessed yesterday. "You wished to have a word, sir?"

He cleared his throat. "I . . . I asked my parents—actually, I insisted that my parents drive me here today to give opportunity for me to offer my deepest apologies. I am sorry for how I spoke to you yesterday. It was uncalled for, it was ungentlemanly, and I have no excuses. I am sorry."

A knot within her heart eased. "You are forgiven."

"Really? Because the more I thought about it, the more I realized just how helpful you have been, and I would hate for you to think I'm unappreciative or that I haven't realized just how much you have sacrificed your time to help an old wretch like me."

"I've been glad to help." Then honesty burst out. "Mostly."

A small smile crossed his lips. "One of the things I find most refreshing about you, Miss Bloomfield, is this most disarming way you have of speaking bluntly. I cannot abide mendacity."

"Nor can I."

He seemed to stare at her for a moment. "Then may I trust that when you spoke of forgiveness just now, you truly meant it?"

"I truly meant it." And she had.

His face broke out into a most attractive smile. "I do not deserve such forbearance, I know, but I am thankful. And I do hope you will care to return to the farm and explain a little more about what you thought little Frank might be able to do."

"I will return. And as to the other, well, I do not want you to think I'm presumptuous—"

"Miss Bloomfield, can we please agree to speak openly and honestly with one another? If I find your manner encroaching, then I shall tell you. If you think I'm being blue-deviled, then simply tell me. I . . ." He swallowed. "I regard you as someone I might dare to call a friend. If you don't think that is too presumptuous."

Her eyes filled, and it took a moment before she could swallow the ball of emotion filling her throat. "I am happy to agree."

"To speak honestly, or to my claiming you as a friend?"

"Both," she said softly.

"Good." He gave another of those warm smiles she had so rarely seen, something that caused an interesting twinge in her upper torso. "May I count on seeing you again soon?"

She chuckled at his little joke. How good he had regained his sense of humor! "You may."

"Excellent. I rather wonder if some of my misery was due to my lacking a daily dose of Miss Bloomfield's medicine."

"My medicine?"

"Yes. You are a tonic, equal parts sweet and astringent, and excellent for bucking up one's spirits."

Heat filled her cheeks. Surely he was joking . . .

He turned his head. "Is that your father approaching?"

She strained to hear, then saw her father's figure pass the window. "You have excellent hearing, sir."

"It seems to be compensating for other things. My sense of smell has improved of late as well. I can tell when you—" He abruptly broke off and turned to the door as it opened.

"Mary? Oh, Adam, hello."

"Dr. Bloomfield." Adam held out a hand which was shaken by a very surprised-looking Father.

"I did not expect to see you here." Father glanced at Mary with raised brows before settling into the round-backed chair.

"I insisted my parents drive me, as I wanted to speak to you about something." He shifted his head, acknowledging Mary. "And your daughter also."

For a moment Father looked quite startled, but for what reason? "Very well," he said slowly. "I'm listening."

"It is about my sight."

Father's shoulders relaxed.

Mary studied him. What had he expected Adam to say?

"I was wondering if you have any new predictions as to whether I could ever expect to regain some vision."

Father sighed. "I'm afraid, from everything I've studied and read about such conditions, it seems most unlikely."

Adam nodded, lips flattened. "I suspected as much. But . . ." He hesitated. "Do you not think that—forgive me, but I'm curious to know your opinion as both a man of faith and a man of science—do you not think that such things can be healed in a miraculous manner?"

Mary's jaw sagged. Did Adam believe God healed even today?

Her father tugged on his collar. "God can heal in the most unexpected ways. Will He do so in your case? I do not know. But I do know that faith in Him and His promises is very important to maintain, for if we lose that, then it can be hard to remember the point of living."

"I know."

Father shot Mary a look.

"I know I have been a little too inclined to self-pity of late." Adam's visage held another of those wry facial expressions. "Your poor daughter has been quite patient in dealing with someone who has been too quick to wallow in pain. I'm very thankful that you sent her to me, sir."

"Well, that's good then," Father said in his gruff voice. "Mary is a good lass."

She caught her father's gaze and smiled. "I suspect Mr. Edgerton has shown a great deal of his own forbearance towards someone who has been rather too inclined to think she knows best."

"We make a good pair, then."

Father coughed and raised his brows as Mary attempted to hide a blush.

"I meant—"

"I know what you meant, Adam."

He seemed to relax, leaning back against his chair. "So, you do not think I should expect a miracle?"

"You can pray," Father said slowly, "but remember, God's will prevails, and we need to keep on trusting Him, even if we do not receive the answers the way we might hope."

Adam nodded but did not seem overly disappointed in Father's answer.

She was about to offer tea when the door opened, and Mother returned with Joanna and their guests.

"You've returned," Mother said to Father. "We've been waiting in the garden."

"So I see." Father motioned to the basket she carried filled with lavender stalks.

"So I smell." Adam's mouth curved to one side.

Mary chuckled, and his head turned her direction, his smile growing. Joanna cleared her throat and stared at Mary.

Adam turned back to her father. "Have you heard anything more from Robert? I often wonder how he and the other men are getting on."

There followed a conversation, chiefly steered by Mother, about the challenges and pitfalls of the English mail system during a time of war. Watching Adam's face closely, Mary caught flickers of amusement as he listened to the mothers converse about their sons' inability to write little more than what their commanding officers directed, and that this, combined with their illegible scrawl, proved just how hopeless the younger generation seemed to be these days with their mode of communication.

"What say you, Mr. Edgerton?" Mary asked slyly. "Care to defend yourself?"

"Do you refer to me or my father?" Adam asked, with a slight smile.

"I refer to the younger, of course."

"Then I must insist on your calling me by my Christian name."

"Well, *Adam*, what have you to say about your decided lack of letter writing?"

"Only that if we had the luxury of both time and paper for writing whatever and whenever we might choose, then one might suppose Napoleon would never see defeat."

"Are you suggesting that you actually enjoy writing?"

"I certainly did not mean to imply that," he countered, amusement crossing his lips. "Only that it was never my intention to let loved ones live in fear about how we might be getting on."

"It's always been hard enough to decipher his scrawl, noways," his father grumbled.

"And now he has a perfect excuse for it," Mary said.

The room fell into stunned silence.

Then Adam laughed, and his parents exhaled and smiled, and her parents and Joanna looked at her in astonishment.

"Mary, *dear*," her mother said in the greatest agitation.

But Mary did not mind the mild rebuke. She'd made him laugh. And that was all that mattered.

Although later, when the Edgertons had left and her parents had resumed their duties, Joanna sidled up to her. "Are you sure there are no warmer feelings between you?"

"Between whom?" Mary feigned ignorance.

"You and *Adam*." Joanna emphasized his name as Mary had done earlier. "You could barely keep your eyes off him earlier."

"I was pleased to see him smile, that's all."

"Really?" Joanna studied her with a mistrustful glint in her eye.

"Of course! Why, you do not harbor suspicions of your sister and a blind man, do you?"

"He really *is* quite handsome when he smiles," Joanna said thoughtfully.

"Such things do not concern me."

"Yes, but you may find that they concern him."

"What do you mean?"

"Only that if you do not want a blind man for a suitor, then you best be careful he doesn't grow too attached to you."

"What nonsense."

"I mean it," Joanna insisted. "For some reason he seems to find your company appealing—"

Mary snorted. "Thank you, sister."

"—and it wouldn't do for you to secure his affections if you have no wish to further them."

"Such talk is nonsense. He's still pining after Emily."

"Yes, and she is so much younger and better looking than you."

"Thank you again, Joanna."

"Not that looks would mean anything to him now. You could look like a hag and he wouldn't know, would he?"

"I suppose it's good he cannot see my face and must rely on my sweet temperament and kind words, then," Mary said acidly.

"Oh, I did not mean to offend you."

Mary raised her brows.

"No, I didn't! I just wanted you to be aware of what could happen."

"Thank you, dearest sister. I appreciate your concern."

And while she did appreciate her sister's clumsy attempt to show concern, such talk was mere foolishness, so she pushed it to one side and ignored it. It had been so *good* to see Adam laugh, after all.

Chapter 18

Within three days of Frank's arrival he quickly proved himself a valuable member of the household, not only providing company and enlivening the farmhouse with his antics, but also serving as an apt hunter of rodents, or so Adam's mother said. These past weeks had seen the dog learn to obey, to fetch as had been suggested, the bond between Adam and Frank growing closer every day.

Miss Bloomfield also continued to prove needful, the tension of the past seemingly lost in a new accord. Such advice as the rearrangement of his items in his room had indeed shown benefit—he was increasingly confident and quicker in getting dressed—and little Frank's presence had proved a boon as well. Adam knew himself indebted to her, and although she pushed him with challenges he'd rather ignore, he was glad that someone like her was helping him attain the mobility and independence he sometimes forgot he desired. Like now.

"Mr. Edgerton—"

"Adam," he growled. "How many times must I tell you?"

"Adam," the sweet voice continued, "I was thinking—"

Oh, how he was starting to fear that phrase.

"—now that little Frankie is obeying so well, would you not like to explore beyond the confines of the house again? It is such a beautiful day."

As if he could appreciate any day's beauty. He pushed the bitterness down and released an exaggerated sigh. "I really don't think young Frank likes to be called Frankie. I'm sure he thinks it quite unmasculine."

Miss Bloomfield gave that funny burbling sound again, like smothered laughter, that always made him smile.

"I think you're laughing at me again, Miss Bloomfield."

"Oh no. I'm simply enjoying the vagaries of the day."

"Hmm." Well, he supposed going outside again wouldn't kill him. He'd actually enjoyed the short trip to the village to visit the Bloomfields, the fresh air and sun touching his skin. He stood, heard the rustle of her skirts that suggested she now stood too. "Are we going outside or not?"

"We are."

He felt for his stick, glad she ignored his tendency towards abruptness, glad they'd had the chance to commit to forthright speaking. It reminded him of his long-ago walks with Robert, when he hadn't needed to guard his tongue and could say whatever came into his head without fear of causing upset. "Come on then, Frank. Best we obey Miss Bloomfield before we get into trouble."

Judging from the way Frank's little toenails clicked, the dog was as much in awe of Mary as Adam was.

He swallowed a smile after remembering his way to the hall without needing Mary's instructions and, better yet, how to unlock the front door as he'd practiced. He stood on the front step, breathing in the freshness of the day, relishing the sigh of the wind in the trees, the warming breeze on his skin, and hearing the yap as Frank scampered away, his footfalls fading in the gravel.

"Frankie!" Miss Bloomfield called. "Oh dear. I'm afraid he's seen your mother's ducks and is chasing them away."

"He might need to be on a leash."

"Yes. Oh, no! Excuse me."

Before he could ask her what was wrong, she hurried away, calling out the dog's name in accents of ever-increasing agitation. "Put it down now! Now!"

Adam gingerly slid his foot forwards, then the next, using the stick to ensure his path was clear as he swung it from side to side in front of him, following where her voice led.

"Frankie, you are such a naughty thing! However will you be trusted if you do the wrong thing?" She made a noise of irritation. "Down. Now."

Something dropped with a raucous quacking protest and scuttled away, complaining loudly.

"At least the fowl still seems to be alive," Adam offered.

"No thanks to Frankie." She sighed. "I shall have to apologize to your mother. Again. I hope she did not see."

"I wouldn't worry about it. She's used to dogs. And Frank isn't the first dog that's tried to have duck for dinner."

"Very well, then."

He smiled at the note of dejection in her voice. "He has proved a good little fellow. I do enjoy having someone there to keep me company at night." He realized how that sounded, and added hastily, "I mean, it is good to not feel completely alone. Forever in the dark."

"I can understand," she said softly.

And in that moment, he knew she truly understood. Unexpected warmth enveloped him, drawing his steps to a standstill, and hastening him to say, "Where are we going today?"

"It's probably best to let Frankie become a bit more used to the out-of-doors, so perhaps familiarizing him with the garden might be best before we visit the barn and all the excitement to be found there."

He could just imagine Frank's delight upon meeting the cows. "Lead on."

Through following Frank's bark and Mary's voice, he was soon able to negotiate the house garden and approximate the fences and road. Apart from a few mishaps between stick and dog—who seemed to think the stick some kind of toy—Adam managed well.

"He needs a leash."

Adam turned to where his father's voice came from. "Does he refer to me or the dog?" he asked Mary in a low voice.

"I'm fairly certain he means the dog," she murmured back, before saying more loudly, "You refer to Frankie?"

"Aye. That dog is a young scamp. Needs good training."

"He's just a little excitable and should outgrow that," Mary said. "Obviously takes after his master," she added in an aside.

Adam snorted, lightness flaring through his chest. He quite enjoyed these outlandish things Miss Mary Bloomfield said, though he'd never admit it.

"There's an old leather strap in the barn that should work," Father said. "Come on, then."

Mary's small hand gently clasped Adam's fingers, and she steered him towards the barn, a place scented with cows and sheep and sweat. A place he used to love to visit when but a young boy.

"Here 'tis," his father said. "Now, Dog, this here is a collar, it fits around your neck like that, and the lead connects here. Adam."

He felt a leather strap pushed into his hand. "Thank you."

"'Tis nowt," his father replied gruffly. "Now get on, show that dog who is master."

Adam felt a pat on his shoulder, heard his father mutter an "Aye" to Miss Bloomfield's farewell, then felt his arm nearly tugged from his shoulder by a yapping tearaway.

"Frank!"

The dog quieted enough to allow him to catch Mary's smothered laughter. "What's so amusing?" he grouched.

"Have you ever noticed how your father never says Frankie's name? He only calls him 'Dog' or 'the pup there' or some such thing."

"I had not, but will be sure to notice in the future." She was an observant thing. For all her plainspoken comments, what else did she notice that she kept locked up inside? Like what she really thought about him, and what she would say if—God forbid—she'd seen him fall apart on the day of Frank's delivery.

He allowed himself to be persuaded forwards by Frank's insistent tugging. "Oh, you rascal."

"Frankie seems most persistent."

"He has some good qualities." Glad for the change in subject that steered his thoughts away from heavier things, he hurried to talk about a mouse Frank had captured in the larder. "I know Mother is not always terribly fond of having to deal with some of the chores associated with Frank, but I wonder if such incidents have reconciled her to the idea."

"I'm sure they would."

They walked on a little longer, his thoughts returning to his earlier musings. She was so patient, so forbearing. "Why do you do this?"

"Walk with you and the dog?"

He cleared his throat. "Why do you bother to take such a lot of time for me?" He couldn't very well see Emily doing the same. His heart skidded. Comparing Emily and Mary? Miss Bloomfield hopefully did not regard their friendship more warmly than she ought. Perhaps he should be more circumspect in his dealings with her.

"Father asked me to. He was busy, and your mother was quite overwhelmed."

"I am very grateful."

"Well, I'm certainly gaining that impression. If you weren't, I should cease coming, and then where would you be?"

"Lost." Adrift in darkness.

"Exactly. So I'm afraid you shall need to put up with my company a little longer."

"But surely you have other duties to attend to—"

She drew in a hasty breath.

"Not that I'm wanting to be rid of you," he added.

"It's a good thing I don't take offense easily, is it not?"

His lips twitched. "It's a good thing we both agreed to speak honestly," he reminded her.

"Hmm. Well, you may think my company tedious, but in fact I'm only here for a couple of hours each day. And, even then, it's not every day. I spend my other time helping Father at the infirmary, or helping Mother with the household, or doing errands in the village."

"You're always busy."

"I prefer it that way."

They kept walking.

"Have you . . ." He swallowed. An awkward topic, but she had proved herself willing to talk openly about most subjects. "Have you no prospects?"

She coughed, and for a moment he was sure he'd offended her despite choosing his words so carefully. "When we agreed to speak honestly, I did not think you would choose to be quite so direct."

"Forgive me," he said humbly. "I did not suspect you of being missish."

"Very well." She gave an exaggerated sigh. "By prospects, do you refer to the matrimonial kind? If so, then no. I am resigned to being an old maid."

"But you are kind, and rather—" *sweet*. He swallowed.

"Rather what, sir?"

"Rather good to people," he finished awkwardly.

"I'm afraid those qualities don't tend to be what most young gentlemen deem important."

"Then they are fools."

She said nothing, and they continued to walk, when a startling thought made him stop suddenly. "Do you mind if we return? I'm afraid my head has begun to ache."

"Oh, of course!" She touched his arm, and gently steered him back, as the dog whined and tugged him on.

He made his way inside, made his farewells, assuring her he had no need for the doctor, and let the peace of his room surround him once more.

His talk of fools . . .

Had she not responded, because he—like every other man—had never appreciated her good qualities until now?

"Why has Miss Bloomfield never married?" he asked his parents that night at dinner.

"I suppose someone has to ask her," Father responded.

"She must be nearly my age." Adam thought back. How many years younger had Robert said she'd been?

"Nine-and-twenty," his mother confirmed. Then sighed. "I do not wonder at it much myself. She was never as pretty as . . . as that younger sister of hers."

Never as pretty as Emily, he could almost hear her say.

"She might have had offers. If she hasn't, I don't think it's because there's been no interest." Mother took a quick breath. "I'm sure some of the elderly widowers wouldn't mind having her cheering presence around the place."

His stomach turned. "That sounds rather desperate and depressing."

"Is it? Surely it's natural for a man to be well-disposed to a woman who is kind and sweet-tempered, willing to help whenever asked. I wouldn't be surprised if Mr. Ponsonby had considered her a candidate for his own new wife."

"She'd never have him," he said, thinking of her previous comments.

"She has always been a little particular with her requirements." A pause. "Is there some reason for your asking?"

"No. Just thinking."

His father's silverware clinked on his plate. "You will need to consider marriage one day, son. You could do a lot worse than a young lady like Mary Bloomfield."

What? He shook his head. "I don't think so."

"Well, there will come a day. I cannot keep this farm running forever by myself, and when I'm too old, then what will you do? No, marriage is necessary. And marriage to the right sort of woman is important. A flighty young lady will not manage to work at a farm."

"Do you mean a flighty young lady like Emily?" They now attacked his former choice? "I thought you liked her. I thought you wanted us to wed."

"I do. I did. But she's grown up in ease, which is not a life we can offer here, is it?"

No. But, "You never said anything before."

"It wasn't a problem then. You could see before," his father said softly.

Except, when he'd had his vision, it seemed he hadn't seen very clearly at all.

⚜

Whispers of conversation rippled down the pews, and Mary was sorely tempted to join the others to peek over her shoulder, but was spared by Joanna's whisper, "It's Adam Edgerton!"

Oh. She sat back with a small smile.

"He's looking quite well."

She was about to agree—recent days in the sun had renewed his tanned countenance—but any comment of that kind would only reinforce her sister's suspicions that Mary was slightly enamored by him. Which was absurd. She willed her features to impassivity and offered a slight shrug as she focused on the altar.

Mr. Ponsonby moved to the front and introduced the first hymn. She followed as best she could—she had never held any pretensions to musicality—and tried to engage her heart as he prayed his prayers. But soon her mind insisted on moving beyond the rote phrases to something more personal.

Heavenly Father, thank You for today, for the chance to worship You, for the other believers in this place. Thank You that Adam is here. Help him to feel comfortable, and for people to be kind.

"In the name of our Lord Jesus Christ. Amen," Mr. Ponsonby intoned.

"Amen."

The liturgy continued, but she was hard pressed to focus, save to glory in God's ability to soften hearts and turn them to Himself. Her prayers continued, for the future of Susan Oakley, for the health of the Croker family and dear overworked Papa, as she pleaded the life-giving power of Jesus over their lives. Mr. Ponsonby spoke about sheep and goats, referencing the story of Jacob and Laban, which made her wonder again about his choice of texts and their relevance for today. Mr. Ponsonby might think her rapt in his sermon, so still was she. Joanna apparently spent most of the service thinking about her gowns, or how best to dampen a young suitor's aspirations without seeming either the coquette or too shy—she'd admitted to such things once during a dinner after services, much to Mama's horror. How many other congregation members questioned if this information was supposed to have current relevance and be of any practical application, resulting in personal transformation?

Such thoughts are not what a young lady should dwell on, she could almost hear Mama say, but the distractions would not desist, try as she might to maintain attention.

Following the closing hymn and benediction, she joined the others in the aisle awaiting Mr. Ponsonby's handshake.

"He doesn't look as though he's blind," Mr. Beecham murmured, in a huddle with several men in front of Joanna and herself.

"If you didn't know, you'd hardly know," came the draper's somewhat cryptic reply.

"I hear he's been seeing a lot of Mary Bloomfield," mused a third voice.

She stiffened. Then, catching her sister's affronted expression, gently shook her head.

The procession inched forwards. The number of people and her stature meant she could barely see beyond the coats of the men in front and Joanna's dark-green pelisse.

"I've heard she's been up at the farm quite a lot."

"Aye, setting her cap for him, they say."

Enough was enough! Mary cleared her throat, opened her mouth, retort ready.

Joanna suddenly leaned forwards and said, "Good morning, gentlemen."

They turned, their mouths falling open.

"Oh, Miss Joanna, and Miss Bloomfield! We didn't see you there," Mr. Beecham said.

"I did not think you had." Mary offered an overly sweet smile. "Forgive me, but I could not help but overhear your concerns for poor Mr. Edgerton and his parents."

The men's faces varied between shades of pink and puce.

"I, er, that is, we, ah—"

"My sister has been most magnanimous in giving up her time to assist Mrs. Edgerton in caring for her blind son," Joanna said in a low, tight voice. "How dare you cast aspersions otherwise? Do you not think we should be considerate of our neighbors, and show compassion where we can?"

"Well, of course." Mr. Beecham shot an uneasy look to the man at his side.

"Then does she, or anyone else, need your permission or approval before daring to visit an injured man?" Joanna demanded.

"It's just not the done thing for a young lady, Miss Joanna."

Mary's ire rose. "I assure you—"

"Do you question Miss Bloomfield's honor and integrity, or mine?" a deep voice asked.

She stilled, not daring to look up at the tall figure beside her.

"Forgive us, sir, but—"

"They know not what they do," she murmured.

A quick peek revealed Adam's ever-mobile mouth twisting to one side before settling into sternness. "Please refrain from such foolish speculation. It does no one any good. Good day." He turned, spoke quietly to his parents, and, grasping his arms, they carefully exited the pew from the other side.

"Well!"

"Well."

"Well," whispered Joanna. "That's three holes in the ground. And three mouths shut for the moment." She looked delighted. "Fancy Adam Edgerton standing up for you. If he's not careful, there really will be rumors circling about you two."

"Don't be foolish. As I keep telling you, he's only a patient for whom Father wants me to care."

Fortunately the line shifted forwards, and she was soon released to the churchyard and the fresh air. But the concerns the villagers had raised refused to dissipate and filled her with wariness for her visit the next day.

Chapter 19

The arrival the following day of the doctor lacked the attendance of the daughter.

"Mary?" Dr. Bloomfield said, when questioned partway through his examination. "She asked me to pass on her apologies, but she felt it necessary to visit a friend. Poor lass," he muttered, almost as an aside.

"Oh." The anticipation he'd felt in hoping to laugh about the silly comments of yesterday fell strangely flat. "I hope you don't mean by that remark that your daughter is unhappy."

"Mary? No. Well, she was a little dispirited after services yesterday, but then she has no great opinion of Mr. Ponsonby's intellect, so that is nothing to wonder at."

Adam knew himself a fool to think her absence today had anything to do with him.

"It's good to see you are getting more mobile. I do like this little chap here." The doctor's voice came from lower. "Are you taking good care of your master?"

There came a bark.

Oh. Dr. Bloomfield was talking to the dog.

"Yes, I should think so." The doctor coughed, begged pardon, then said, "I hope you will continue to go on long walks."

Adam cleared his throat. "Are you speaking to me or young Frank still?"

The doctor gave a hoarse chuckle. "You, of course. Although I suspect young—Frank, did you say?—would enjoy a long walk, too. Such things are helpful to regain strength and stamina. I expect I'll see you heading up Upton Pike before too long."

"Forgive me, Doctor, but are you mad?"

"Indeed no."

"Your faith in my ability might be a trifle misplaced, sir."

"Oh, I don't think so. You have a walking companion in this little fellow, and it's not as if you were ever an indoors kind of man. I still remember the treks you and Robert made all those years ago. You visited Upton Pike many times, did you not? Such things will hold you in good stead now."

"Perhaps." This doctor seemed to hold vast reservoirs of faith. "How is Robert these days? Have you received another letter yet?"

"Finding his work a challenge, yet fulfilling. I'm sure I don't need to tell you just how busy those working in the field hospitals can be."

"They saved my life." And had stolen it, too, in a way. But that last thought held less pain today.

"I will write, and let Robert know how you are getting on, if you like. He'd be pleased to know how well you are doing."

"That would be kind."

"Now, have you had any more headaches? Mary mentioned you felt a little unwell last week."

She had? The pinprick to his heart at that name soon subsided to unease. What else had she mentioned about him to her father?

"Adam? Have you had more headaches? Have you been unwell?"

Apart from this strange lethargy when his daughter was not in the room? "I find I still grow weary fairly easily, but the headaches seemed to have subsided for the most part."

"Good, good. Well, I expect Mary will be able to visit again on the morrow, so you need not fret. You must make the most of this good weather before the rains come again."

"Yes, I suppose I should."

The doctor advised that Adam continue—or even begin—use of the special salve and eyebright syrup, and made some further suggestions in the manner of his daughter before taking his leave. Adam pushed his head into his hands. Just how true was his accusation of fretting over Mary's absence? What else had the doctor seen that Adam seemed to be missing?

⟡

The next morning saw the arrival of a much quieter Miss Bloomfield, who for once had no suggestions about what he should do. The quietness had even seemed to summon his mother into the room, who suggested Miss Bloomfield might like to read to him.

"Would you wish that, Adam?" Her voice was too quiet, missing its usual spunk.

"Yes." He wasn't used to this moroseness. Anything had to be better than these half-hearted attempts at conversation. "Wherever Mother was up to before."

"The thirtieth chapter of Genesis," his mother said.

"Mrs. Edgerton?" Meggie's voice. "Oh, I didn't mean to disturb—"

"I'm coming now," his mother said, and the squeak of floorboards announced her departure.

There came a sound of rippling pages, then Mary cleared her throat gently. "It seems this passage is what we heard on Sunday. Do . . . do you really want to hear it?"

He murmured affirmation, and her clear voice began to read. He closed his eyes and listened to the account of Jacob and Laban, and Jacob's plan concerning speckled and spotted sheep. Her voice was soothing, her presence restful, he loved to hear her speak.

"Adam? You're not falling asleep, are you?"

He opened his eyes. "Of course not. Whatever gave you that idea?"

There was no corresponding sound of amusement as he'd hoped.

He tried again. "I cannot understand some Scriptures," he confessed. "My mother has been reading through Genesis, as you may have gathered, and we were discussing whether God still speaks to people in dreams."

No answer.

"Miss Bloomfield? Do you have an opinion?"

"On dreams? Well, I believe that it is possible. You may not recall Mr. and Mrs. Gillis—"

"The former grocer and his wife?"

"Yes. She had a dream that her husband would die. The next day he fell off a ladder, and quickly succumbed to his injuries. I remember her telling me about that dream, and both of us thought it was more than mere coincidence. Though I doubt Mr. Ponsonby would agree."

"You have the right of it, there. But just because we don't understand how or why doesn't mean God can't work in wondrous ways." He paused, then dared ask the question that haunted his dreams. "Do you . . . do you think God might be willing to heal my sight?"

An intake of breath.

His hope trembled on a precipice.

"Oh, Adam. I wish I could pray for you and be assured you would see, but I'm not God."

"Would . . . would you pray for me?"

"I haven't stopped since I first heard of your condition," she said quietly.

His chest, his throat, grew tight. "Would you mind praying now?" His voice seemed hollow, what volume there was sounding like wind over stones.

"Of course."

He closed his eyes, as her fingers were laid softly on his arm, and in the silence that followed came a strange heat, followed by inexplicable peace. His heart thudded loudly. His pulse rushed in his ears. Did this mean God had healed him?

Hoping against hope, he opened his eyes.

Nothing.

He knew a savage pain of disappointment and pressed his lips together. *God, why?*

"I'm so sorry, Adam."

He jerked a nod. "I am, too."

Her small fingers wrapped around his hand and lightly squeezed, and again he felt that curious peace. He sucked in a deep breath and released it slowly.

"I wish I could pray and we'd know it guaranteed healing, but I'm afraid God's ways are above ours, and can't always be understood," she said softly.

He cleared the boulder in his throat. "You don't fault my lack of faith?"

"I am not God. But even Jesus did not heal all of the sick people he encountered."

"But he commended the faith of those he did heal," he objected.

"Yes." She gently squeezed again. "Sometimes I wonder if trusting in God even despite a lack of seeming answers might be the faith God is really looking for."

Perhaps it was. Trusting God seemed to be about pushing away the confines of the easy and explained, to a daring place where one *needed* God in a deep, profound way. To walk by faith, and not by sight. His lips twisted.

How ironic.

His thoughts tracked back to what she'd previously read. "I have to admit, I don't fully understand how all Jacob's trickery works. I suppose God is somehow honoring Jacob's faith in the face of Laban's treachery."

"I suppose." A pause. "I gather you're happy to be finished with today's reading."

"Yes. Thank you." Nothing more was said, allowing him to hear her quiet breathing. Was she still pondering his questions? "Forgive me, Miss Bloomfield, but have my questions upset you?"

"No, sir. Not at all."

"Have I done something to offend you?"

"Why do you ask?"

"Simply that you are so quiet, and I am unused to it."

"Oh. Was there something you wished to talk about?"

Apart from clearing up the little matter of the church gossips? "Not especially." Silence filled the room, save for Frank's snuffling explorations, as Adam struggled as to whether he should own his concern, both to what had been said and her reaction. "I, er . . ." How to say this without sounding vain and presumptuous? "I hope you were not too concerned about the incident at the church."

"You mean the silly talk from Mr. Beecham and his friends? I had quite forgotten it."

"I thought—never mind."

"You thought?" she prompted.

"I thought that perhaps you were reluctant to return here, and that is what has you preoccupied today."

"Please forgive me. I . . . I have been a little shaken by some news."

"Is there something I can assist with?"

"Only if you can find the scoundrel who did this," she muttered, almost under her breath.

"I beg your pardon?"

"Tell me." Her voice reverted to her usual decided tones. "Should a man be forced to own the consequences of his actions?"

"Of course."

"Then how can one convince someone that such a person must be held to account?"

"I'm afraid I do not understand."

She exhaled. "I know I'm not making much sense. It's not my secret to tell. Only it has upset me very much, and I wish I knew what I could do to help."

"I'm sorry."

"I am too," she murmured. Then touched his hand. "Forgive me. I have been glum."

He coughed, then added shyly, "You shall be in my prayers."

"Thank you." Her voice held a mix of gratification and surprise.

"And I am glad you are not concerned about the gossip."

"I must confess I do not relish being the subject of gossip, but I have little wish to let other people's ill-mannered thinking stop what I enjoy."

"You enjoy coming here?" His heart warmed towards her.

"This is a good thing to do, the right thing to do."

A strange kind of disappointment crossed his chest. "At least you are motivated by noble reasons."

"Certainly not the ignoble ones some might suggest," she retorted.

He smiled at this show of fire. "So, you take little pleasure in these visits."

"No! Sir, it really seems that you are determined to make me sound a fool."

"I would never think you a fool, Miss Bloomfield. Far from it."

"Hmph. I won't deny that it is not unpleasant to spend time with someone who is more quick-witted than he likes to appear—"

"Miss Bloomfield!"

"—and I certainly don't mean to suggest that I am glad you cannot see, for that grieves me deeply. No, forgive me for regarding this in a personal way, but I find coming here a respite for the other situations that are rather less hope filled."

"You think my situation hopeful?"

"Yes, oh, yes! Have you not realized the great progress you have made in these past months? At first there was concern that you might not even survive, and now to see that you are managing all sorts of things some never thought possible."

"Some like me."

"Not just you. I suspect he may not say it, but your father is quite proud."

He was?

"He watches you sometimes, a little smile on his face, as if he cannot believe you are doing so well. Your mother, too. So, it has been quite a blessing for me to come here and know my feeble efforts have made a small difference."

"Feeble efforts, indeed. You are a veritable harsh taskmaster, Miss Bloomfield."

She chuckled. "I'm glad you can jest about it now."

"What it must be to have such faith to see the impossible. Your father holds that ability, too. Yesterday he was telling me that he believes I should start thinking about going for a walk to one of the peaks."

"He mentioned that last night."

"It's one thing to be advised to do so, but quite another to do it."

"I know. So, I am prepared—at great personal sacrifice—to offer you my assistance to traverse Upton Pike."

"Are you serious? That is a full day's hike in itself."

"Ah, I suspected you might feel timid."

"Timid? I simply am aware that my limitations mean such things are impossible."

"Impossible is rather a faithless word, isn't it? Improbable, perhaps, but nothing is ever truly impossible for those who believe. Excuse me for a moment."

He heard the rustle of skirts and light tread as she departed. "Methinks Miss Bloomfield is rather too much the optimist," he said to Frank, who lay upon his feet.

Frank gave a short bark, and Adam smiled.

There came a sound of return and he shot to his feet.

"Oh, you do not need to get up for me," Miss Bloomfield said. "Now, your mother has given us some supplies, and I've assured her we shall return in time for tea."

"Return from where? We're not walking to Upton Pike?"

"Indeed no. That would be too ambitious for today, even for me. But I assure you one day you'll be walking the peaks again. I thought instead we might visit Peak Rock, if you feel like it."

He suppressed a tremble of fear, covering it with a smile. "Because you don't want to be too ambitious?"

"Exactly." Mirth echoed in her voice. "Now, have you your greatcoat? A hat? The sun is out but there is a slight breeze."

"You are quite the indomitable." He moved to where he'd laid out his hat and coat, pleased to find them both there.

"That makes us a good pair, as I have it on good authority you displayed similar qualities in Spain. You have everything you need? Excellent. Let's proceed."

With a command to Frank, and clutching his stick in his hand, Adam followed her voice and exited the house, and they were soon on their way on the road. It was part lesson, as he continued to negotiate the differing challenges of walking with the stick versus learning to train and trust the dog. And it was part respite, as he drank in the fresh air and remembered walks like this from before.

As they walked she described the views, and he could see in his mind's eye the peaks and valleys, the fells and trees, the lakes and villages, the rocks and sheep. It was a route he had travelled many times years ago, a path worn to dirt and relatively smooth. Apart from a few stumbles, where he'd needed her steadying arm or shoulder, he felt immeasurably proud of himself to reach the crest of the hill. He stood, pleasure filling his chest, his soul.

They moved to a hillside clearing and paused by the great rock that gave this place its name. He held out a hand, touched the gritty texture. "Bear is buried here."

"Just three steps to your right."

He moved with care, unwilling to disturb the grave of one he'd considered a great friend. "Here?"

"Yes."

He crouched, hand outstretched, until he found the first of the smooth stones he'd laid in memory of his dog. They covered the burial spot, just as they had when he'd placed them here ten years ago. "He was a faithful companion."

"He was very loyal." Her soft voice held understanding.

After a final pat, he pushed upright and stepped back from the memories, conscious of Frank's barks. "Young Frank will prove to possess a similar disposition, perhaps."

"I believe he will."

Something warm rushed through his chest as he marveled at this woman who displayed such consideration. Had he ever felt this degree of tenderness from a woman before? Towards a woman before?

Emily fell a distant second.

Startled at his thoughts, he took a step away, slipping on a loose stone. "I'm all right," he quickly assured her.

"I know."

In her words he felt renewed confidence, as if one day he could actually be all right, even if God chose not to heal him. That he was not the broken blind man he'd once thought was all he could ever be. Was that truly how Mary saw him? Someone who could possess a future? He did not sense the pity anymore. Not from her anyway.

"Just don't take many more steps farther forwards, else you'll be back in bed."

Because he'd be lying injured. "I remember. It's a long way down."

"But quite spectacular."

"Yes." He drew in deep breaths of the freshening air. There, as he stood tall, with the breeze buffeting him, the distant calls and caws of birds drifting on the wind, he had a glimpse of the past, when he'd stood in a similar pose, gazing out on the peaceful valley and lake far below. He closed his eyes, felt the cool touch his eyelids.

Beautiful. What a beautiful scene.

"I recall Robert saying how anything felt possible when standing here," she said.

Possibilities. His world had some now. And it was all due to Miss Bloomfield.

How good she was to him. How thoughtful she proved to be. Tenderness wrapped around his heart. *God, bless her.*

Gratitude swelled within. How thankful he was. That his life was spared. That he had his health. That he could walk. That he had family, friends, Miss Bloomfield. "Thank You."

Peace stole into his heart, in this moment that felt hushed, and almost holy.

She moved beside him. "God is very good."

"Yes." How did she know his thoughts? He drew in another breath. Paused. Listened intently to a high melodic sound. "Do you hear that?"

"What—oh, the singing?"

"Is anyone else around?"

A pause. "No."

A shiver prickled his spine. "It sounds like an angelic chorus."

"Perhaps it is," she whispered.

The high melody lingered, then faded on the breeze, the moment of awed reverence casting a tingle through his soul.

"How glorious," she murmured.

"Indeed." How wonderful. How humbling.

"I wouldn't blame angels for singing here. This is a little piece of heaven, after all."

A little piece of heaven. A trace of lavender lifted, alluring. He swallowed. He drank in a steadying deep breath, slowly exhaled. "It's going to rain soon."

"How do you—oh, I see." She described the banking clouds on the other end of the fells.

"I can smell it in the air, as if there's a heaviness."

She inhaled. "I can smell it now, too."

"We should return."

"Yes. I think Frank has had enough adventures for the day."

The descent was more challenging, his legs protesting the forward motion that made balancing rather hard.

Miss Bloomfield took the dog's leash and handed him the long stick, encouraging him to check what obstacles might be in the way. "It might help you balance a little better, too."

But he found the rush of movement rather daunting, the stick's flimsy nature feeding fear that he might fall. "Could we stop for a moment?"

"Certainly."

"I don't want to use the stick on the descent," he confessed. "Would you mind if I clasped your shoulder?"

A pause. "Very well. Here." She grasped his hand, placed it on her shoulder.

"Thank you," he muttered. At least there was no one around to see their situation. This was not at all the thing.

But her movements—the way she braced or slowed or dipped—gave him greater confidence as to where to place his feet, what kind of terrain they covered.

"I should have thought of this before."

"It helps." He explained what he could sense through her movements. "You've proved very stable."

"No one has ever accused me of being fickle."

"A good quality, indeed." He smiled, enjoying this return to banter.

She tensed and inhaled sharply.

"What is it?"

"There are two men approaching whom I don't recognize," she murmured, "but judging from their appearance, they look like tramps. Please, hold the stick like you might use it for walking. And please, let me hold your arm, and pretend we're courting."

He nodded, dropping his hand from her shoulder as protectiveness surged within. Were these the men Father had mentioned a few days ago?

Mary clutched his arm with extra pressure, and the sounds of low voices and footfalls warned the men were nearing.

"Good day, sir, miss," an unfamiliar voice said.

Adam dipped his chin, conscious Miss Bloomfield had not slowed. "Good day."

"Would this 'ere be the way to Amberley?"

"Yes," Miss Bloomfield said.

"That be a fine-looking dog there."

"Oh, please, do not touch him," she continued. "He has a tendency to bite."

"Aw, he looks like he'd nae hurt a flea."

Adam gathered by the growl that Frank had taken exception to the men. They'd best be leaving. "Excuse us." He slung an arm around her shoulders, and gently propelled her forwards.

She whispered, "They're going now."

He stumbled on a slippery rock. "Blast."

She steadied him, slipping her arm around his back. "Try to stay upright," she murmured. "They're still looking."

He bowed his head and drew her nearer, regret surging that he was next to useless should something happen and he need to protect her. "I'm sorry."

Her forehead touched his, and he drew in the scent of lavender in the warm space between them. He positioned his hands behind her shoulders, holding her in a near embrace. A moment passed, another. He was conscious of his rushing pulse, of her slender form, of the way her breath caressed his chin.

"They're turning, they're walking on." She exhaled. "I do not like the look of them."

"What do they look like?"

"Both medium in height, so shorter than you, and rather emaciated looking. One of them had a scar on his cheek, while the other seemed to have a limp. Perhaps they are former soldiers."

"Perhaps." He felt a swell of compassion. "But what concerned you?"

She released an unsteady breath. "It was the way they looked at me, then at you, and then decided that they would not try whatever they intended to do." She released him, and the air grew cool between them. "I know I sound mistrustful, but I'm not used to seeing strangers here. And these strangers seemed rather . . ."

"Strange."

"Exactly! Oh, I'm so thankful you are here, Adam."

"I am, too." And he was. Perhaps he could not do as much as what he used to, but his size and bulk still seemed to count for something. "Come, we should head back now."

"Yes."

The sound of feet treading over stones suggested she'd fallen in with his suggestion and was going on ahead. "Miss Bloomfield," he called.

"Oh, dear! I'm sorry. For a moment I forgot."

His chest filled with new warmth. To have her forget he was blind could only be a good thing, could it not? It suggested he might be more than the object of pity.

He sensed by the way the air moved, the way her skirts rustled, when she drew near. Again she placed his hand upon her shoulder, and they continued their strange descent. But something seemed to have shifted between them, something . . . tender. He was conscious anew of her small frame, that his much larger size must be placing a burden on her, but she never complained, and her, such a little thing . . .

His stomach knotted. Imagine if she'd been up here alone. Imagine what those men might do to an unprotected woman. He'd known of unscrupulous, unprincipled men who did not hesitate to take advantage where they could. Protectiveness rose again. "I trust you will not visit up this way again alone. I would hate for something to happen to you."

"I assure you I am not in the habit of taking long walks by myself."

"Except when you visit the farm."

"Except for then," she agreed.

"Still, even then you should be careful."

"Why Mr. Edgerton, you sound as if you care. Are you worried that you might miss me?" she said, reverting back to her former playful tone.

He swallowed. Should he share what Father had said? "There have been reports of sheep going missing, and I wonder if you just saw the culprits."

"Your father himself once warned me of such a thing," she added in a thoughtful tone. "That might account for the . . ."

"Account for what?"

"Now I think about it, one of the men looked as if his sleeve had blood on it."

"And you didn't mention this before?" He picked up his pace, nearly tripped over another stone. "You best get home immediately and alert the magistrate. If they are sheep thieves, then you are in danger."

"As are you. For they would never think that you cannot see."

He shook his head, stumbling down the road, boots sliding as if his feet were determined to find every uneven section of path. "We should never have come."

"Oh, yes, we should have."

"What?"

"For if they were the thieves, then at least they know they've been seen, and are unlikely to visit here again."

He laughed, despite himself. "You, my dear Miss Bloomfield, have a most unusual perspective for a young lady."

"That might be because I'm not such a young lady."

He shook his head, reaching out to clutch her arm, to steady both his balance and her personal misconceptions. "You do yourself a great disservice talking such nonsense."

"Most people would consider it nothing but the truth." As if determined to close the subject, she hurried on. "Now, I wonder, has my father ever told you about a man called Blind Jack?"

"Who?"

For the remainder of the walk home he listened to tales that seemed most improbable about a blind man from Yorkshire whose spirit refused to let him settle to be less than anything God had made him to be. Tales about a man who rode horses, who swam rivers, who even went hunting, and who had married and fathered four children.

"That sounds most unlikely."

"Father assures me it's true." And she proceeded to tell about this John Metcalf's audacious business schemes, and how he grew to know the land so well he was responsible for building roads that still criss-crossed Yorkshire's north.

"But how?"

"I don't know. I can only imagine it was his knowledge of the land and understanding of the earth that helped, along with the assistance of trustworthy sighted men."

"Am I to gather from this that you want me to be encouraged?" He exhaled. "I know Father would be terribly disappointed if the farm need one day be sold because of his useless son."

"You're hardly useless, Adam."

"No?"

"No."

The quiet confidence in that word trickled hope into his heart, and made him feel taller, stronger somehow.

"I'm sure you can do anything you put your mind to, with God's help. Even farming."

He remembered her words later that night—they seemed to have clung, limpet-like, to his soul and fueled faith in his dreams. He might not be able to do things he once could, but surely God would give him what he needed for what was still to come. But how could he farm, what could he—with all his weakness—bring?

"I have so little, Lord," he muttered in the darkness.

Frank whined and curled up on the bed beside him.

Adam cuddled him close. "I'm sorry, Frankie. I should remember God's blessings, shouldn't I? Like you, like my parents, like Miss Bloomfield."

He spent a moment praying for her, that she might not feel fearful from the day's events, that whatever had concerned her before would not worry her, but she would have pleasant dreams. "Lord, I do thank You, but I'm only too aware I cannot do things in my own strength. But I'm willing to do whatever You want me to do. So please reveal Your plan to me."

And he closed his eyes, and dreamed about the farm, and his father, and lost lambs, and Jacob, Laban, and colored sheep, and that moment when he'd been *sure* he'd heard angelic song, and how he could sense the rain, and the warm sensation of holding Miss Mary Bloomfield in his arms today.

Chapter 20

Had that been an illusion, or had it really happened?

Mary yawned and rubbed her eyes, blinking in the dimness of the morning. Somehow she was going to have to get more sleep. The weight of the past days had intruded upon her dreams. Such wild, fantastical dreams of soldiers, heroes, angels, fells, and sheep. For the first time, she'd even dreamt about being a bride, finding love, finding a husband and home of her own—such foolish, *foolish* dreams! She smiled wryly. God certainly had not been speaking to her through last night's dream.

She sat up and drew the bedclothes to her neck, huddling in their warmth. What an odd day yesterday had turned out to be, full of the unexpected. She certainly could not think of young Mr. Edgerton as "poor Adam" anymore. He seemed a very different man, walking with greater ease, almost as she remembered from many years ago. But it was more than that. He held a new kind of empathy, of consideration and kindness. At times he seemed to be concerned for her, as if he truly did regard her as a friend. And then in that moment when she'd spied those men, he'd pretended to be something rather more than just a friend . . .

Her heart had pounded. She'd inhaled his scent. Dared to enjoy his strong arms about her.

Oh, foolish, foolish girl. She groaned, shook her head at herself, and hurriedly dressed in the dawn. No good could come of this. None. She was a walking contradiction. Purporting to be but a nurse—as she'd declared on Sunday—yet secretly savoring the time spent with him.

A cringe rippled through her soul. Had Joanna's long-ago accusation been correct, and Mary had encouraged Emily to leave Adam because Mary wanted him for herself?

Oh, foolish, foolish girl. Did this make her a hypocrite? Saying one thing, doing another. Oh, it was likely best she stay away, to not stir up emotions, to focus on what was real rather than a foolish infatuation.

And those men—who were they? Were they responsible for the missing sheep? Had they been the cause of poor Susan's shame?

She'd mentioned it to the magistrate upon her return yesterday, thankful to find him as he left the vestry meeting, but when she explained her concerns, Mr. Payne had virtually laughed in her face. "You cannot blame every stranger for misdeeds, Miss Bloomfield."

"I do not. But I must question why they were in that place that is unknown except to locals." She'd eyed him. "Why, do you suspect a local for such crimes?"

He'd reddened, and said she wouldn't understand, being a woman, after all. And she'd bitten her tongue, and saved her complaint for her father, and determined to think on it some more. For if not those men, then who? And why did Susan not reveal anything further about her baby's father?

For a child she would bear, so she had whispered tearfully on Monday. It had been over six weeks since her last menses, and it seemed there could be only one cause.

"But I will not have it," she'd said forcefully. "I will not!"

"But Susan—"

"No. I will pray and ask God to take it away." She clutched her stomach. "It is not right, it is not fair!"

"I know, but God is still with you here."

"No." She'd shaken her head vehemently. "How can He be? If God cared, then He wouldn't have let that happen to me."

"Your father—"

"Doesn't believe me."

"But surely my father's words—"

"He doesn't care." Tears had streaked down her face. "What am I going to do? Oh, I wish I was like Emily Hardy and had an aunt in York or someplace where I could go and hide until I knew what to do. But instead, I must show my face and pretend all is well, until one day I'll be so big that everyone will know and there will be no way to escape the truth."

"Oh, dearest Susan!"

But Susan would not allow Mary to embrace her, would not listen to reason.

Mary had poured out her concerns to her parents—thankfully Joanna was elsewhere—but neither had anything to offer.

"What do I do?"

"We must pray and ask God for wisdom."

"Could we not send her to Aunt Margaret in Lancaster?" she asked Mother.

"She would scarcely have the room, my dear."

"Let alone the inclination to help," Father muttered.

"But surely there must be something we can do."

He'd shaken his head sorrowfully. "I have made enquiries, but . . ."

Mother's eyes had gleamed with tears. "I know this is hard, but you cannot take all things so personally."

That had been Monday, and she'd needed a day to regain her equilibrium. Of course, yesterday's trek to Peak Rock had resulted in its own set of challenges, not least of which was the meeting of those strange men, and all that encounter had led to.

And those moments close to Adam that caused her senses to flutter anew—

No. This was ridiculous. The sooner she resumed her regular duties, the better it would be. For everybody.

She quickly breakfasted and attended to her tasks, the time in the still room providing sufficient distraction through the concentration demanded to mix the medicines. Every stray thought of whimsical fantasy she instantly suppressed, then asked God's forgiveness and busied herself with prayers. Prayers for Father, for her mother, for Joanna, for her brother. She didn't want to pray for Adam—well, she might want to, but thought it best she did not focus her thoughts his way—so she prayed for his parents, for Emily, for poor Susan.

A prompting came to visit her.

She frowned. "Very well, I'll visit her."

Her words echoed in the empty still room, the heaviness of her heart momentarily lifting at the questions some might raise about her answering God in this way.

After a quick break for bread and cheese, she was glad to find the gig was free, which meant she could travel more quickly to the Oakley farm. The urge to visit had grown more pronounced.

"Good day, Miss Bloomfield," Mr. Oakley called as she entered the yard. "How be that dog for young Edgerton?"

"Frank has proved to be exactly what is needed."

He shook his head. "I never understood why the magistrate gave 'im back. But it's good he's got a fine home now."

She nodded. "Is Susan here?"

His face shadowed. "Aye, she is."

"She did not seem very happy when I spoke to her two days ago."

"It be a bad business."

"But not one of her making," she said gently.

"Aye. But . . ." He glanced down. Heaved in a breath. "I cannae help but wish her mother was still alive. She would know better what to do."

Doubtless that was true. Mrs. Oakley had been a kindhearted woman with a strong dose of practical judgment. Her death three years ago had left both husband and daughter in this state of half-existence. Mary's heart grew softer still. What comfort could she offer in the magnitude of such grief? "You're both in my prayers."

He jerked a thumb at the farmhouse. "She's inside."

"I'll go see her."

He nodded, moved away, but not before despair clouded his face.

Dear heavenly Father, help this family. She moved to the front door but startled when it swung open to reveal Hannah Liddell. "Oh, hello."

"Miss Bloomfield."

Mary caught a glimpse of Susan's scared-looking face beyond. "Susan?"

"I be going now." And with a thin smile, Mrs. Liddell walked away.

"Susan?" Mary moved inside to the warm kitchen. "How are you today?"

"Better. Well, better than the other day."

"I'm so glad to hear it." She placed her reticule on the wooden table and noticed a small bottle of golden liquid. "What was Mrs. Liddell doing here?"

"She, er, wanted to give me a tonic."

"A tonic? Is this it?" Mary picked up the golden bottle.

"Aye."

"And what is this tonic to treat?"

"Oh, it's nothing." Susan snatched the bottle from Mary's hand. "Would you like a cup of tea?" she asked with what seemed like forced cheer.

"Yes, please."

"Then you best have a seat."

Mary drew out a soot-stained chair. Unease continued to prickle within. "I'm sorry that you have not been well."

"Not been well? Oh! Oh, well, you know I have been worried. Mrs. Liddell just said this was something that would . . . that would make me calm-like."

"I see." Except she didn't. She rubbed her forehead, swallowed a yawn.

"What brought you here today?" Susan turned her back to Mary, busying herself with cups and tea preparations, judging from the clank and clatter.

"I simply wanted to see how you were getting on. I was concerned about you after our conversation on Monday."

"That was good of you."

There came a sound of liquid pouring.

Mary peered at Susan. Something definitely was not right. "You know, I would have been more than happy to have made a special calming mixture for you."

"Thank you, miss, but I don't think you'd make the right sort." Susan's head tilted. She gulped. Coughed.

The right sort? "What did Hannah say was in the mixture?"

"Some herbs, some special extracts."

Mary slid out her chair. "Did she mention exactly what they were?"

"No. Just said it would make things better."

"I see." Alarm pounded within, and she hurried to Susan's side. "Have you just had some of this mixture?"

"Yes," Susan whispered, turning to face her. Her eyes were large, pupils dilated.

"Susan." Horror curdled. "Was this a mixture to get rid of the baby?"

"It's not a baby. Not yet, anyway."

Oh, dear God! Mary grasped her hands. "Susan, you didn't."

"I had to," she breathed.

"No. No, we would have found a way."

"Mrs. Liddell said it doesn't matter, that until the quickening it is not a baby anyway."

"Oh, Susan." Sorrow for the poor lost girl, for the poor lost child, grew heavier within. Tears pricked. She swallowed.

Susan coughed, her face suddenly rather pale. "I don't feel very well."

"I'm not surprised." Mary wrapped an arm around her shoulders. If Susan had taken what Mary suspected Mrs. Liddell had prepared, then she was bound to grow extremely uncomfortable. "Here, let's get you into bed."

"I don't want to stay here," Susan cried, shrugging away. "I hate this place, I hate feeling unsafe."

Mary drew in a deep breath. Perhaps if she were to get Susan back to the infirmary, then Father could see to her more quickly. "Would you care to come back with me? I could take you now, if you like."

"Oh, please, would you? Even after—oh, I feel so ill." She groaned, her weight suddenly so heavy that Mary had to lower her into a chair.

"Mr. Oakley!" Mary called.

Susan retched and clutched her insides.

Mary snatched a large mixing bowl and thrust it in Susan's lap. "Mr. Oakley!" She rushed outside. "Mr. Oakley!"

He appeared at the barn door, wiping his hands. "What is it?"

"It's Susan. She's dreadfully unwell, and I want to take her back with me so Father can see her."

"What's happened?"

"Mrs. Liddell gave her a special potion."

His eyes widened, and he hurried inside, groaning as he looked at his daughter. "Oh, Susan, what 'ave you done?"

"What has Mrs. Liddell done, more like," Mary muttered, wrapping an arm around Susan's shoulders and supporting her to rise. "I know you probably need to take care of your animals, Mr. Oakley, so I'll take her to the infirmary. Father can look after her there. But she'll need some clothes."

"It might be better if I drive you both."

She glanced at Susan's increasing pallor. "Yes, that might be best. We should hurry."

He glanced at Susan, slumped against Mary, and moved as if to take her.

"Get the gig ready," Mary directed. "We'll be quicker—"

"We'll be quicker this way." With surprising speed, he picked up his daughter and carried her outside, giving Mary only enough time to seize her reticule and the bottle which Susan had partly hidden behind a crock of eggs.

She rushed outside to the readied gig, where Susan sat gasping, almost doubled over in pain. "Oh, it hurts!"

Mary squeezed onto the seat, Mr. Oakley snapped the reins, and they soon were speeding to the infirmary. "We'll be there soon," she soothed, smoothing Susan's hair from her brow, "and Father will be able to assist."

"Oh, miss, I feel awful."

"I know. But soon you'll feel better." *Please God, heal her. Protect the child from the poison.*

Such prayers filled her heart on what seemed an uncomfortably long drive, Susan shuddering at every bump, her groans adding to the turmoil in Mary's heart.

They managed to pass into the outskirts of the village without attracting too much attention, and she thanked God that Joanna and her mother were in the kitchen. They rushed out as soon as they saw Mr. Oakley was driving.

"Mrs. Liddell gave Susan a tonic." Mary raised her eyebrows at Mama. "We need to get Father here right now. Do you know where he might be?"

"I believe he was visiting Mrs. Payne, so I'll go there directly."

"Please."

"What can I do?" Joanna asked, eyes wide.

"Help us to get Susan into a bed, and someone needs to find Mrs. Liddell so we can learn exactly what she gave Susan."

Joanna—bless her—caught a slumping Susan round the shoulders, and together with Mr. Oakley's help, they brought her up to the bedchamber Susan had occupied before.

"Mr. Oakley, please find Mrs. Liddell."

"What's she done to my girl?"

"That's what we want to know. Please, go now," Mary said more sharply.

He nodded and escaped.

"Did Mrs. Liddell poison her?"

"I don't think she meant to," Mary said. But the baby . . .

Susan gave another sharp cry, a gasp riddled with pain. "She said it would restore my menses. Oh, I feel terrible."

"I know." Mary positioned the sickroom's bowl as Susan retched and then vomited up her stomach contents.

"Oh, that's disgusting." Joanna backed away.

Mary's pulse accelerated. What should she do? *Lord, what do I do?* "Joanna, boil some water, would you?"

"Anything to get away," Joanna muttered.

Mary drew Susan to lie on the bed. She had never seen such a violent reaction. "Susan."

Her face was pasty white.

"Susan!"

Susan's head rolled to one side, and she vomited again.

What were the herbs Father used to expel poison? Marigolds? No, that was for fever. Ragwort? No, that was indigestion. Oh, why couldn't she think! "Dear God, please help!"

"Mary?" Mother hastened to her side. "I have sent someone for your father. Oh, Mary, whatever shall we do?"

"We need some hot water and ginger. Perhaps that can calm her."

"Of course. I'll be right back."

Susan gasped. "I did not know, I did not mean to do it—oh!" She clutched at her midsection. "Oh, it hurts, it hurts!" She sobbed, her wails like scratches on a slate that shivered under the skin.

The sound of hurrying footsteps was followed by Father's entry. "What's happened?"

"Mrs. Liddell," Mary said quickly. "She gave her herbs and spices to bring on—" She couldn't finish the words.

"Get me sage and tansy now."

Mary rushed downstairs to the still room, searched through the medicine drawers, found the bottles, and returned to find Susan huddled on the bed.

"She's not responding." He placed a hand on Susan's forehead. "Her brow is hot."

"She was fine but half an hour ago."

"It's fast acting." Grimness lined Father's brow. "I wish we knew what exactly was in Liddell's evil brew."

"What do we do?"

"Has she eaten anything?"

"Not since I've been with her."

"Then get her some bread. If she eats that, the poison may be absorbed."

Mary hurried to get some bread, and met Mr. Oakley rushing in. "Oh, sir, please, go see your daughter. She's up there!" She pointed to the stairs.

At that moment Susan screamed, and his face paled. "Dear God."

"Go, sir! She needs you." Even if only to give a chance to say goodbye.

Had Mary done wrong in sending him to find Mrs. Liddell? What if she'd merely stolen time from his daughter whilst she was still alive?

As he thumped up the steps, Mary moved to the kitchen and found the bread and hastened back. She thrust the heel of bread at her father. "Here." She supported Susan's shoulders as he tried to force a piece in, but Susan refused to swallow.

"Take it, girl, take it."

"Susan," her father cried. "Eat it, please."

Susan slumped against Mary, her breath raspy, wavery. "I'm sorry, I didn't mean—"

"I suspect she would have had pennyroyal and rue," Father said, "so we need white lilies and masterwort."

Joanna rushed in, a kettle in her toweled hands. "Here is hot water."

"Good. Now let's see if she can drink it." Father tilted a cup to Susan's lips, but the liquid simply dribbled out as her movements grew stiff and jerky. "No, Susan, you must have it."

Susan's heavily lidded gaze slid from Mary to her father. "I'm sorry."

"Please, Susie, for the sake of your mother, don't—"

She groaned loudly, once, twice, thrice, then slumped back in the bed, limbs eerily still.

"No, no, no," Mary cried. "Susan, you must get better!"

Susan's father exhaled heavily, tears dripping down his face, as Father grabbed Susan's wrist and searched for a pulse.

"Susan?" Father called out. "Susan, wake up."

But Susan made no response, her eyes gazing at the ceiling in a fixed, unmoving stare.

"Dear God, help us," Mary whispered, putting her hands on Susan's other wrist. "Heal her."

But there was no response. No answering heat.

Mary stared in horror at the still form, her soul anguished, not wanting to believe.

God had apparently decided Susan's earthly life must cease.

Chapter 21

The wind atop Edgely Hill threatened to steal his cap and breath, reminding him of that last encounter with Miss Bloomfield near Peak Rock. His spirits dipped. She had not returned for several days now. Had he offended her? He shook his head at his digression, forced his thoughts back to the present. Adam reached down and picked up a handful of earth, smelled it, and turned to where he assumed John Davis stood. "This seems rather dry."

"Aye," the aged laborer said. "It be the winds. They dry out the earth."

"So this stretch of land is fairly useless for growing crops."

"Ever since the line of trees were slashed two years ago, it gets that dusty now."

"I cannot imagine the sheep like it, either." The wind ripped through his clothes. How would such conditions affect the sheep? "Did we lose much stock this year because of it?"

"Not as much as might be supposed, given it was a hard winter, you remember."

"I recall people saying something to that effect, but I was in a London hospital for much of that time, and not always aware of the weather."

"Well, it's right good to see you back 'ere where you belong."

Adam managed a polite smile. He still didn't feel as though he belonged. He'd always had a yearning for adventure, a desire for life beyond the dull confines of the farm. That had seen him leave ten years ago and join the local militia, before the toll of war brought his unit to Walcheren and then the peninsula. His visits home had proved far between and few, the chief benefit of the latter years being the time to charm and court Emily for a future that had always been rather hazy. But those days were done. His options had narrowed to the here and now.

He knew laborers such as John considered "the young master" with no small amount of suspicion. He'd never concerned himself with such things before. But now, with other avenues closed to him, it behooved him to care for the land, which meant learning it. Which meant spending time with those who needed to teach him, despite a measure of disdain in their voices.

His lips twitched. So much for once being considered something of a hero. But at least by standing here in a windblown field and attempting to learn something about the lands his family had farmed for generations, he was trying to fit in. Trying to belong.

"Master Adam?"

"Forgive me. You were saying?"

"The windbreak. Or the lack of one. It seems we'll need to replace it."

"Have you spoken to my father about this?"

"Aye. He says he'll get to it when he has half a chance."

"Good."

Except it wasn't good. From his forays through the farm these past days, it seemed evident from the state of the fields and barns—and from what the laborers said openly when Father wasn't around—that things had not been good, had not been properly managed, for years. Was this what had happened while he'd been chasing Spaniards and the French? Had his family's legacy crumbled to dust because he'd never taken an interest?

He had so much work ahead of him.

They continued with the rounds of field inspection, his mind ever ticking. Slash the gorse to encourage grass for feed. Spread manure to improve the soil. Develop more dams to store water. Fix the broken stone walls. In his mind's eye, he had a rough idea of the size of the fields and the general lay of the land. It wasn't completely foreign. And with the benefit of more good workers and his father's help, he might one day develop an affinity for this.

He grew conscious John was still talking, and, guiltily, he forced himself to listen. ". . . they must be counted as lost."

He must be talking about the missing sheep. "How many sheep in total?"

"P'raps four, mebbe five."

"Is there anywhere they may have gone to be lost, or is it likely they were stolen?"

"We've looked up fells and vales and found nowt, so it seems most likely they were taken."

Adam released a breath of frustration. "Do these thieves not realize they can be hung?"

"Mebbe they dinnae care. They have to be caught first."

"Who do you think responsible? I can't see any farmers doing so, can you?"

"No. Wouldn't be locals. Your father is too well-respected, and, er, since the, er . . ." His voice trailed away.

"Since what?"

"Since your, er, return the villagers have been quite keen to support your family. It cannae be locals doing this."

"So it is thieves."

"Aye. That's my best guess."

"What can we do?"

"Apart from keep the sheep closer afield, I don't rightly know."

"That cannot be all." He thought hard. He'd seen some sheep in places like Spain. What had they done to prevent theft? *God, what do we do?*

A memory sparked. What had he heard read to him not so very long ago?

"What if we dyed them?"

"Killed them? I cannae see your da being overfond of that idea."

"I mean mark them with dye, with paint."

"Paint?"

"Aye." He chuckled inwardly at his lapse into the local brogue. How his fellow soldiers would laugh. "It likely would be gone when the time comes for shearing, and would let others know which are our sheep, no matter where they be."

"But the low numbers suggest it's only a few used for meat."

"Then if they are found with our marked sheep, there is no excuse, is there? These thieves cannot pretend that our sheep are theirs and would have a hard time explaining things to the magistrate."

"Aye, that they would."

"Then you agree this is a plan?"

"Mebbe even a good one."

Adam's lips tweaked into a half-smile. "Then let us investigate what can be done. I shall speak to my father about it."

"Verra good. And you be sure you be wanting to fix that stone wall by Prior's Field?"

"If you get me the stones, yes. I'll attend to it tomorrow."

"I be thinkin' we'll need more laborers."

"I be thinking you're right."

Adam held out a hand that was grasped, then, with a nod goodbye for old John, he commanded Frankie to direct him home. A tug on the leash suggested he was obeyed; he could only trust it was where he wanted to go. But that was his life now. Trust that Frankie knew the way home. Trust that God would guide his steps. Trust that Adam's family, the farm, and his future would be safe in God's hands. "Lord, lead me."

His mind whirred with new plans. There were some things he could do, after all, not the least of which involved the repair of some of the stone walls which John had mentioned today. It had not been quite so many years since he'd helped his father do so; he could no doubt learn it again. The building of stone walls required a sense of the size and weight of stones as much as judging how things could be fit together. If John sourced the stones, then Adam could save Father's energy by rebuilding the walls. Anything he could do to help in these matters would be better than simply staying at home, bored, waiting for Mary Bloomfield to visit him again.

He walked on, long stick in one hand, the dog lead in the other, knowing a sense of accomplishment for once. And an underlying sense of gratitude to Miss Bloomfield for inspiring him with that story about Blind Jack.

Frank started barking and by the smooth, leveled ground he knew he was close to home.

"Adam, there you be." His father's voice. "Your mother is inside, quite distressed."

"What's happened?"

His father's voice lowered. "There was an incident in the village a few days ago. You remember Susan Oakley?"

Barely. She was but a child when he left.

"She died."

"What? How?"

"I'll let your mother tell you."

His father patted his upper arm, and Adam made his way to the house. A careful reconnaissance of his surrounds later, he soon got his bearings and grasped for the door. He stumbled inside to the hallway, which felt cool. "Mother?"

"In here." Her voice was quavery. "In the drawing room."

With fingers tracing the walls, he guided himself to the doorway. "Mother?"

"Oh, Adam."

He inched his way inside, collided with her outstretched hand, which she used to tug at him.

"Come, sit down here beside me. I need to speak with you."

"Father mentioned something had happened in the village."

"You know how we've been wondering about why Miss Bloomfield hasn't come to visit these past days? It's Susan Oakley. Remember her? Her family had all the dogs. Miss Bloomfield has cared for her for the last weeks, since a truly unfortunate event befell the girl. And now she's passed away."

His heart panged. Poor Mary. "That is sad. And rather sudden. How did she die?"

"Nobody knows. Or nobody is talking about it, anyway. I tried to visit the Bloomfields today, but there was no response at the door, and the rest of the villagers know little more. Mr. Oakley is beside himself. Susan was all he had, as he lost his wife three years ago."

"People don't just die. Especially not young people."

"That's what is so strange about it. If the Bloomfields could only share about what happened, then people would likely not be so upset. But they're proving quite tight-lipped."

"Did you see Miss Bloomfield?"

"Only for a moment. I caught a glimpse of her in the kitchen, and she seemed so upset, poor lass."

His heart wrenched again. "She always tries to help others."

"It's so terrible. And—oh, I almost forgot! That witch Mrs. Liddell seems to have disappeared."

"What?"

"Nobody can find her anywhere. The magistrate went to that hovel she called a home to question her, but when he arrived the cottage appeared abandoned."

"She's hardly able to disappear into thin air."

"Well, she's disappeared somewhere," his mother said tartly. "People in the village are wondering if she poisoned young Susan."

"Why would she do that?"

"Nobody knows."

"That is most terrible." Poor Susan, poor Mr. Oakley. Poor Miss Bloomfield. "We should go and see her."

"Miss Oakley? It's too late."

"No, Miss Bloomfield."

"But why?"

How to explain this tugging in his heart? "She must be devastated, and if there's some mystery over why this has happened, it must be difficult to cope with all the gossip and speculation."

"She has her parents to support her."

But that wasn't quite the same as someone she might regard as a friend. "Still, I want to see her. To offer what support I can."

There was a pause. Then, "Very well. Perhaps your father can take you down later."

But when Adam asked, his father was not receptive, insisting that Adam's time would be better spent in consideration of the future of the farm.

"I have been doing so, Father. I spent the day walking around the fields with John today. Together"—he didn't think his father would be receptive to thinking it was simply Adam's ill-informed opinions on display—"we have come up with a number of strategies to see our way forward."

"And I suppose you're going to tell me what these might be."

"We think it's important to shift the sheep to the fields closer to the house."

"But there's less pasture here. The top fields are where we've always had them over summer."

"But we haven't had cases of sheep being stolen in the past, have we?"

"Well, no. But I'm sure that's just a few."

"John thinks it could be nearly half a dozen that we've lost."

"Half a dozen?"

"I think we're best to get them all in and count them."

"Oh, you do, do you?"

"Father, I know I'm no expert, but I do believe it's important for the future of the farm that I am able to help make decisions. Not that I want to take over—"

"How could a blind man do that?" his father questioned.

"—but if you do not want your father's land sold, then this is important to consider."

His father said nothing for a long moment. Then he sighed. "Very well. Move 'em in."

"Thank you. We'll do so tomorrow." He wanted to ask Father about the paint marking as well, but thought it more prudent to wait until he had a chance to speak to some of the other local farmers about such matters. Perhaps their support might prove of benefit—for the sake of their own sheep, as well as his father's.

"Is it possible to be driven into town now?" He couldn't explain this desire to see her, save that he sensed Miss Bloomfield might appreciate his support at this time.

"Not presently. I have those dratted stone walls to fix, and a thousand things beside."

His disappointment receded in the truth of that statement. "I told John I'd help him with the stone walls tomorrow."

"And just how are you going to manage that?"

"I remember helping you in the past."

"Seems you'll have a very busy day, between counting sheep and rebuilding walls," his father said, not without sarcasm.

"It seems so," Adam said, willing mildness to his tone and expression.

It was another two days before he was finally able to find time for his visit to Miss Bloomfield. Days of sheep mustering and stone wall reconstruction had left him wearied and bruised and sore, but with a sense of accomplishment, too. John had been taken aback at Adam's assistance with the walls, but it had proved surprisingly less difficult than one might first assume. John had marked out which sections needed attention by placing piles of stones on the ground, so Adam ascertained the weakest parts by running his hands over the walls, his height and strength proving beneficial for this. Then it was simply a matter of using the stones from the ground and adjusting them until he sensed they were lodged firmly into place. It had left him with aching shoulders and scraped fingers, and he suspected John had bit back more than a few laughs watching Adam's fumbles. But it was good to have the physical distraction from other worries and disquieting concerns. And heartening to have finished this section of wall along Prior's Field, in addition to the satisfaction of hearing John's approval.

Yet despite his endeavors, his heart for the pain of others had not receded. His frustration had only mounted, as he realized just how one-sided this friendship had been. Miss Bloomfield had proved a steady support to him, and in her hour of need, he had offered nothing. The Sabbath was tomorrow and he suspected conversation would not be easily managed at the church service. He needed to speak to her now.

He moved to the barn, where a whistling and sounds of leather unclipping suggested Mr. Lovett was unhooking the bridle and reins. "Abe? Are you here?"

"Aye, lad."

"Would you drive me into the village?"

"What, now?"

"I have urgent business there that Father is unable to attend to." Unwilling, perhaps, rather than unable. "I'd like your assistance."

"Well, it just so happens that Ned and I were heading there ourselves. You best jump in."

His smile grew wry. "I'm afraid these days I don't tend to jump anywhere."

"Ah, I was forgetting. Come closer and I'll talk you through it."

Adam felt for the side of the gig.

"That's it, lad. Up you get."

He carefully hauled himself up and settled onto the seat, feeling that same sense of accomplishment from earlier.

There came a sound of reins jostling, then, "Walk on, Ned," and with a sudden jerk that almost toppled Adam from his seat, they were off.

"Thank you for doing this, Abe."

"I should have realized afore now that you might be wishin' to do such a thing. But sometimes it's hard to remember that you be blind, looking as healthy as you do."

"You really think so?"

"Aye. There be some that are blind and its obvious, with the whiteness across the eyes and all, but yours are just as brown as ever. And it seems you're getting much better at sensing where people be at, so it's not as if you are staring off into the distance."

That was something at least. Perhaps others might one day think him as somewhat normal.

For a moment there was nothing, save the *clip-clop* of Ned's hooves, the swish of his tail, and the mournful moan of the wind. Adam shivered, drew his collar up, and pulled his coat more tightly around him.

"Walk on, Ned."

The horse nickered, as if in response. Was it really true what Mary had said, about this Blind Jack fellow? How had he ever learned to ride a horse? Mind you, a week or two ago Adam had barely dared believe he might actually have some sort of future with the farm—might have any future at all. Perhaps one day he *would* dare to ride a horse again.

With lots of help. On a very docile horse. What was it Dr. Bloomfield had said? One day at a time.

"It's good to see you taking an interest in things again, lad."

"It's good to feel like I can be interested in things again. For a long time life felt very dark," he admitted, lips lifting at the irony.

"I imagine a hero on the battlefront might feel that way about being back on the farm."

"It's not what I once dreamed, that is true."

"We all remember you as the lad with a need to see the world."

"It's a good thing I had the opportunity to see what I could while I could still see."

Abe gave a wheezy chuckle. "You might've lost your vision, lad, but you've still kept your sense of humor."

Adam shrugged.

There was a pause. "I can't help but wonder if the ability to laugh might be more valuable than one's sight in the end."

"Says the man who can see," Adam said dryly.

Abe wheezed again. "You do my heart good, lad. You've been doing your da's heart good, also. He was that worried about you, you know."

Adam's throat tightened. "I know."

"Ah, don't sound so glum. It's only that he cares for you so. You should have heard him boastin' about his son when those reports came back about you saving young Alby Jamieson. Proud as Punch, your da was. And I wouldn't be surprised if you continue to show him just what a fine lad you be as you work out your way forwards with the farm now."

"I fear that will take a long time."

"Then he'll have to come around to it. There be a lot you'll need to learn, and a lot he'll have to accept."

That was true.

"I don't suppose you'd be wanting to take the reins?"

"Me?"

"You don't think there be anyone else here, do you, lad?"

Well, no. He hoped not, anyway.

"If you want to do this in the future yourself, you'll find it easier if you've had some practice."

"A blind man driving a cart?"

"Ned here knows the way," Abe said stoutly, "and it's not as if you haven't ridden this road a hundred times before. There be more challenging things, I be thinkin'."

Adam's thought reverted again to Miss Bloomfield's descriptions of Blind Jack and all that he had been able to do. Hunting? Diving? Surely driving a cart was child's play in comparison. "Give them here, then."

He felt the reins being handed to him, then gradually focused on the sway, the rhythm as the horse led the cart along the road. He recognized that turn, as did Ned, suggested by his slackening pace.

"That's it," Abe encouraged. "Now, we be coming to the bend near the Oakley farm. You'll want to take this slow."

Adam nodded, his ears straining for any sign of approaching persons or transports.

"That's it, keep it steady. Ah, Ned's a good horse."

"He's certainly passed this way many times before." Thank goodness. It seemed preposterous to think Adam was actually driving.

"Next, we'll have you riding on horseback."

Adam snorted, but suddenly it didn't seem so impossible. If he could manage a horse and cart, then it wasn't so far-fetched to think he might one day manage a horse, especially one that knew his way around the farm.

How indebted he was to Miss Bloomfield for inspiring him to live again. He needed to tell her, to show her, to offer his support.

He snapped the reins. "Walk on, Ned."

"Take it easy, lad," Abe cautioned.

Adam had no choice, as it seemed Ned refused to pay attention to the gentle nudge of the reins, his pace ever steady. Ah well. Patience was a virtue, or so people said.

Within a few minutes they had reached the village outskirts. Abe accompanied this observation with the comment that "there be that many people looking at ye, lad."

"I suppose blindness has the benefit of never being made self-conscious by other people's stares."

Abe chuckled, and directed Adam to turn the cart towards the Bloomfield residence as requested. "Here we are."

Adam gently pulled, and the cart came to a halt. "Now what do we do?"

"You get down and go in and talk. I'll be but a few minutes, then will return here."

"Very well." Following Abe's instructions, he cautiously descended the cart and made his way to the door. There'd be time enough to learn the other aspects of driving blind, on a day when his head wasn't consumed with more important things. For now he simply wished to speak to Miss Bloomfield.

But he was destined for disappointment when his knock was answered by her mother, who said she was away on some errands for Mr. Oakley, helping the grieving man as she could.

"Was there something in particular you wished to speak to her about?"

"I heard she was quite distressed, and wished to offer my condolences."

"That is very kind of you, sir. I'll be sure to let her know."

He heard the lilt in Mrs. Bloomfield's voice that suggested she wanted to close the conversation, and asked hurriedly, "*Is* she very distressed?"

"Oh," her mother said, voice catching, "Mary is that worried, fretting about everything, and hardly ever sleeping. She's exhausted but refuses to rest. I can't help but feel she somehow thinks this is her fault."

"How would Susan's death be her fault?"

"Oh, don't mind my foolish tongue. You don't need to be concerned about such matters, not with everything else you have going on. I just wish Mary could get away, to clear her head."

A thought struck. "Do you think she would be inclined to a visit to Upton Pike?"

"Perhaps. Yes, something like that might help." Her voice had brightened. "I know she has always enjoyed tramping, and that is such a good way to blow the cobwebs away."

"Would she care to accompany me, then?" He smiled. "I know I'm not an ideal companion, but I appreciate her company. She can view it as yet more helping, if that makes it more palatable."

"I can ask her later tonight, and she can give you her answer tomorrow at the funeral."

It seemed that would have to suffice. He thanked and farewelled her, and slowly moved to where he could hear Ned's soft nickering. "Abe?"

"Here, lad."

After feeling the position of the cart, he gingerly hoisted himself into the seat. "We best get on. Seems Miss Bloomfield has other matters to attend to and is unlikely to be released for some time yet."

"If that's what you wish."

"Thank you."

His companion steered their course around the sharp bend—Adam knew he'd be hard pressed to manage such things any time soon—and within a time that seemed half their outward journey, they were home.

"You're here?" his father called.

"So you can see," Adam said with no small amount of dryness.

"I'm glad. There'll be a big storm coming soon."

Adam tilted his head and sniffed the wind. "I can smell it."

"Did you see Miss Bloomfield?"

"She was busy."

"Too busy for you? That's unusual."

"I'm sure I do not feature in her every thought."

"That may be so, but I'm sure you feature in some."

Adam shrugged and walked past his father. He didn't need such comments to pierce the confidence that risked rapidly deflating.

"Adam?"

He halted.

"What did you want with her anyway?"

He turned back to face—he hoped—his father. "I felt she needed a friend, as she's just lost one."

"Hmm. You need to be careful you don't go giving people ideas."

"Honestly, Father, I simply want to be a listening ear, especially when she's done so much for me."

"That's you being honest, is it?"

"Yes," he said evenly. When nothing more was said, he turned to leave.

"Adam?"

He halted his steps.

"I'm glad you're back and mending, and happy you be taking an interest in the farm. But be careful not to push things."

"You mean with the farm work? I assure you I feel strong—"

"It's not your strength I have a problem with, but—"

"My plans for the farm, then, is that it? I know I don't know much, but I am trying to learn."

"Aye, you're trying, all right," his father muttered. "Be careful with *other* things."

Other things?

"Unless, of course, those other things be things you want after all."

Chapter 22

Stained glass glowed in the morning sun, trapping Mary's attention as she waited for the service to begin. The picture of their Savior, holding a lamb, shepherd's crook in hand, had been gifted by the Carstairs family and deemed most appropriate for this congregation. Although there had been questions raised as to why the sheep did not hold the black faces most often seen in the sheep of these parts.

Jesus, the Good Shepherd. Did He hold dear Susan now? Despair yawned before Mary, and she mentally tiptoed back to the assurance of the cross. God still loved the broken. He'd still forgive those broken in heart, in mind, who knew not what they did. Wouldn't He?

She felt broken inside. Guilt, an ever-present friend these days, murmured her to sleep, echoed through the shadows of each day. Why had she not known? Why had she not sought help faster? Why had poor, dear Susan drunk the potion?

Had Susan been victim to an unfortunate brew that was meant to take only the child's life? Father seemed to believe that Mrs. Liddell's remedy had either been concocted in the wrong quantities or Susan had taken too much.

Or had Susan sought to go against all the Scriptures and end her life? Mary could not be sure. Father hadn't seen the despair in poor Susan's eyes, but Mary had.

Mary had woken with the question heavy on her heart, but a tiny measure of relief lived there, too. Mr. Ponsonby had graciously allowed

Susan's funeral to be conducted in the church, and the grave next to Susan's mother was prepared for her. He had been persuaded by Father—and surprisingly, Mr. Payne—that Susan be remembered as if there were no whispers about her life or death.

"Take poison with the intention to commit self-murder? Don't be ridiculous, man." Father had gone on to report that Mr. Ponsonby had wanted his assurance that he would not be burying someone in sacred ground who was not in right standing with the Lord. "I had to remind him that young Susan had taken communion here not two weeks ago, and that she was someone whom God loved, and she should be remembered as such, to which Payne agreed."

Thank God Susan would not be left to rot in a pauper's grave, as would likely have happened if she had been completely friendless. As it was, Father reported that an anonymous donation had been made for a memorial stone, something which had caused Mary to question whether he was the mystery benefactor, which he'd denied.

"Mysterious, indeed. I hope that such actions will help Mr. Oakley feel his daughter was loved and respected."

Father had sighed. "I don't know if such gestures will ever help heal the sorrows of that unfortunate man, but we will continue to pray for him."

Mary had barely ceased her prayers, futile though they seemed.

Following the service, they would have to face the church congregation, the enquiring faces teasing to know the true facts of what had happened. The problem was they had no facts of which they could be certain. Everything was swathed in the mists of wretched possibilities, and a dread no one wanted to entertain.

In past days she and her parents and sister had spoken with deliberate obtuseness, had sought to conceal the truth as best they could. Mr. Oakley was still lost in the fog of denial, something she'd witnessed firsthand yesterday at the farm, when he kept gesturing to Susan's room, asking when she was to return. The quarantine of shock was something none of them were keen to draw him from. Who could comprehend the loss of a child—and by this means?

Mary shuddered and fixed her attention to the pulpit.

But the reverend's words seem to come from a place very far away as she struggled to understand this terrible incident in light of her understanding of God. Why had God allowed this to happen? Surely He could have prevented Susan from drinking the potion, or from drinking quite so much of it. Surely He could have intervened at the last, and performed a miracle to demonstrate His awesome power.

Yet He hadn't. It was as if He didn't care. That did not accord with what she knew of God.

A sudden desire to leave made her half push to her feet, before her sister's urgent tug at her gown pulled her down again.

"You cannot leave now," Joanna whispered.

But Mary had to. She had to escape. She had to be away from the all-seeing eyes and the gossip and speculation. She had to escape the heavy pall of grief that weighed her down. She had to be *away*.

After the recessional hymn they were finally freed to follow the coffin to the small cemetery outside. The ground was muddied, the result of last night's rains. Mary wiped her eyes and moved with her sister to offer a shrunken Mr. Oakley their condolences and Mary's assurance that she would be willing to assist in whatever was needed in upcoming days.

This was met with a blank gaze and jerk of the head, as if Mr. Oakley had barely heard, and fired fresh determination that she would visit again soon.

"What a lonely man," Joanna murmured. "It must be so dreadful to have lost both wife and child."

"Yes." Following the burial, Mary glanced up from the gravesite and, through brimming eyes, noticed Adam Edgerton standing behind the most unexpected sight of Charles Payne. She ducked her head and, when the last prayer was prayed and the mourners scattered, she did not follow, but instead moved quickly to the yew trees behind the church building. She looked out across the steep valley to the lake glinting below. "Heavenly Father, help me."

The weight of unspent grief ached in her eyes. So weary. She was so very weary.

A strand of hair pulled loose from her chignon, wisping brown strands across her eyes. Oh, how she yearned to leave, to have a simpler life, to not feel this ever-present burden of responsibility and grief . . .

"Miss Bloomfield."

She jumped, turned, and was guiltily grateful that young Mr. Edgerton was unable to see her startled fright. "Hello."

"They told me you were here."

"Which must be why you found me." She winced at the too-glib comment. Oh, what was she doing bandying words with a young man while Susan was not yet cold in her grave?

His lips eased from pleasant humor to something that pulled them down. "I . . . I can leave if you prefer."

"No! I'm sorry. I didn't mean—oh, I'm glad to see you again."

For a moment, he seemed to truly see her, as his eyes seemed to study her, his expression intense.

Breath suspended, and she wondered for a second if this hapsly-rapsly pattering in her pulse was what Emily had once felt when this handsome man gazed at her.

Then sadness crossed his features. "I was very sorry to hear about young Susan."

She nodded, but he could not see her, so she managed to swallow the large rock in her throat to whisper, "Me, too."

He took a step closer, his hat in his hands. "I have missed you."

The backs of her eyes burned. She had missed him, too.

"I thought you might like to know that I have spent the past few days visiting around the farm." He proceeded to tell her about fixing walls and planning fields. That he had even managed to drive the cart yesterday.

A strain of gladness stole through her heart. "I'm so pleased."

"I thought you might be. After all, it was you who inspired me to dare to dream."

She managed a smile but shook her head. "It was simply you choosing to assist your own recovery."

"Regardless, I am thankful."

Mary bowed her head, suddenly unable to look at the man before her. Standing in the dappled light of the yew tree, with his dark hair and eyes, he seemed so strong yet so humble, willing to acknowledge her small efforts.

"I was hoping," he said, "that you might consider taking another walk with me. I spoke to your mother about it yesterday, and she seemed to think it a good idea."

"You spoke to my mother? She didn't mention it." She peeked up, noticed his face fall. "But that might be because when I returned, I was so weary from helping"—she swallowed—"poor Mr. Oakley that I barely spoke to anyone before I went to bed."

"How is he?"

"Not well. He's struggling a great deal."

"I cannot blame him."

"No." Her eyes grew wet with tears. It was suddenly hard to breathe.

"Miss Bloomfield." His hand reached for her. She touched his fingers, which closed over hers. "Please, do not let yourself be troubled."

"I cannot help it," she whispered. "Susan came to me for help, and I could not help her."

"She is with God now."

"Is she?" The church taught that those who committed self-murder would not be in paradise, but would a loving Father turn His back on one of His daughters? "I don't know what to think anymore."

"Please don't distress yourself." His grip tightened. "I know what it is to worry, to long for answers that cannot be satisfied. But you do know that God loves His children."

His tenderness curled around her heart, drawing fresh moisture to her eyes.

"Would you consider my invitation?" He lifted her hand slightly. "I suspect my father would prefer to do without my so-called assistance for a day or two, and so I recognize the need to be away."

Away. The word called to her. Oh, if only she could have a day of distraction, when she need not think, need not feel this tremendous guilt.

"Miss Bloomfield?"

She nodded, then recognizing the utter futility of such an action, murmured, "Yes."

Oh, why had she agreed to this? She exhaled, her breath expelling in a long and steady stream, which she desperately tried to keep quiet. How unfit she was. But admit such a thing to him? Never.

"Did you say something?" Adam asked.

"No." She had to conserve her breath. "Save I should never have agreed to this."

He chuckled and drew her onwards, his hand gripping the dog leash tight.

She was surprised at how well he negotiated the path. Today he seemed so much more confident, so much more like the bold yet kind boy she remembered trailing all those years ago, that she could even recognize the soldier he'd once been.

Though the burning in her lungs wasn't quite what she'd like, after yesterday's funeral she was *so* happy to be out, relieved to be elsewhere, to be able to focus on the meres and fells and enjoy being away.

Adam was proving very thoughtful. He hadn't pushed by asking questions, hadn't probed the sadness that swelled and subsided so unexpectedly. Yet she sensed in him compassion, that he understood she could not yet speak, a trait that demonstrated him as caring, patient, kind.

"And what can you see now?"

She stopped and gently pressed his arm. He stopped too, and as he called to Frank to heel, she used the moment to steal a few surreptitious breaths as she surveyed the view. "From this part of the track we can see Windermere glittering in the sun like a blue diamond with the river curling into it below. On either side are forests of dark trees and fields of brightest emerald green. To the right are tiny specks that are sheep, and to the left hills steeply rise to their craggy tops of stone. It is beautiful."

"Yes."

This was said in such a heartfelt manner she had to ask. "Do you remember?"

He nodded.

"And ahead of us are large boulders, including one shaped like—"

"A hat!"

"That's right." A smile peeked out, the first in what felt like forever. He was as excited as a child. "Come, we best press on."

She readjusted his angle so he was back on the track, and they continued walking. "We pass quite close to Hat Rock now. In fact it is right . . . here."

His hands stretched to touch it as they passed.

She again felt a shiver of memory from many years ago when he used to perform the exact same action. Who knew then all that would befall them?

"My memory is a little rusty, but I find that the scents of the grass and heather, and the feel of the path, bring back a sense of what things looked like. The same happens when I move about the farm."

"Yesterday you sounded as if your father is not entirely enamored of your schemes."

"I don't understand why," he grumbled, still not out of breath. "It's not as if a soldier with over a decade's experience can't be expected to know about farms, too."

A chuckle escaped. "It does seem *most* unreasonable."

"I'm so glad you understand. You really are quite an understanding thing."

Her chest constricted, and she knew herself to be a fool. How tired was she? He was just being kind. Only a fool would read anything more into it. "We are nearing the top of Upton Pike, just passing the old shepherd's hut on our left now."

The shepherd's hut was a broken-down thing made of stone, with a damaged door and tumbled-in roof.

Frank barked, straining at the leash.

"He does not seem to like that place."

"No." The hut did look a little threatening, with the glassless windows like empty eyes and the moan of the wind whistling through. "It looks rather run-down, it's roof and door caved in as if no one has lived there for years. We best keep on going."

"How much farther do you think?"

"Do you feel these rocks, like steps?" She waited as he cautiously tested with his booted foot, then nodded. "There's only another fifty yards or so until the top."

"Oh, good." He exhaled heavily.

"Why? Are you feeling weary?" Perhaps she wasn't as unhealthy as she thought.

"No. But the exhilaration might be wearing off a little."

A fresh bout of amusement released, chased by a pang of guilt. She really shouldn't be laughing, not with poor Susan dead.

"Miss Bloomfield, forgive me, but I cannot help but notice that your laughter does not seem very mirth-filled."

"How can it be, considering?"

He paused, and she stumbled to a stop beside him. He reached out a hand, somehow clasped her arm. "You cannot hold yourself responsible for other people's actions."

"But I do."

He nodded, and again it seemed his eyes could peer into her soul. "I understand."

"How?"

"War is complex and never leads to a simple resolution." He gently squeezed her arm. "You are not alone with holding regrets."

She inhaled sharply, eyes burning with tears. She blinked them back, kept her lips firmly compressed, and eased her arm from his grip. His tender understanding was simply that. No need to look for hope-filled possibilities where none existed.

"Now, how far?"

She swallowed. "I would say about twenty yards."

"Good. I'm growing anxious to reach the top."

As was she. Ellen had packed some food—apples, bread and cheese, and slices of cake—but the path had taken much longer than Mary had anticipated. Or maybe that was simply the emotion dogging her steps.

Frank scampered up the last of the hill, tugging his owner behind him, forcing Adam to steady himself on her shoulder a few times.

She did not mind. She liked his nearness. She enjoyed his company. She liked him.

Oh dear. No. She *liked* him.

She swallowed and took a moment to answer his request about whether they'd reached the summit. This was not as it ought to be. He was supposed to simply be a friend—technically, her brother's friend. And she could not have a future with a blind man.

Could she?

Now she sounded like Emily—Emily, whom she had virtually encouraged to run away because she could not envisage such a future! Oh, how wretched Mary was, indeed.

"Dear God, help me," she whispered. The sound was lost in the wind. How could she have been so blind to this? She groaned.

The sound seemed to reach his ears, for he turned. "Miss Bloomfield? Are you quite well?"

"Yes," she managed, in a voice most unlike hers.

"You sound a little tired."

She exhaled, willed her voice to lose its squeak, her heartbeat to resume a walking pace. "I'm quite well, thank you. We are almost at the top, just another step, and—now, yes, now we're here. Put your hand out, and you will feel the cairn." He grasped the stones of the ancient pile. "Stand still and feel as though you're on top of the world."

For a moment he closed his eyes, seeming to absorb the freshness of the breeze against his skin, the breeze that toyed with his hair, ruffling it across his brow.

How solid he looked, how strong he appeared. How had she ever thought him weak?

But how could she ever think he offered a future?

She shook her head at herself, suddenly not caring about the dramatic scene below. Was she as prejudiced as those who thought a blind man needed to be locked up in a special home? She did not like to think so. But perhaps she was, after all.

The weight of her ruminations pushed her to slump down upon a rocky seat.

"Mary?"

"I'm sitting down here." She forced brightness into her voice. "Do you want something to eat?"

"I'm famished." He slid his feet gingerly as he moved to join her on the rocky outcrop next to the cairn that served as the backrest of their seat.

She distributed the bread and cheese, the fruit and cake, careful not to touch his hands, and the next moments were filled with the sensations of eating and hearing his murmur of appreciation for her thoughtfulness in supplying the apple cake.

"I have discovered a taste for such delightful things."

"You're welcome." Pleasure warmed her chest. She was glad he liked her cake. Glad he liked her—

No. She was a fool to think he meant more than just the cake.

"What can you see now?" he asked her.

She refocused her attention on the stunning scene before her and described the ribbon of lake glimmering between green hills. "We can see farther here. If it were a clearer day, we might even see the silver eye of Levers Water. But there are clouds."

From this vast height she could see the clouds that would obscure the sun for those in the valley.

But it didn't mean the sun wasn't still shining. She exhaled. There were always clouds. She did not think happiness could ever remain wholly untainted by clouds. But did that suppose there could not be happy times once more?

God *was* good. The evidence lay in jeweled tones before her. She had seen His faithfulness time and again. Just because the sun might feel hidden for a time did not mean it was not there. God's goodness did not fade away simply because she did not perceive it. Circumstances were not a faithful prism through which to see God's love. God's love, like the sun, always remained.

Mary closed her eyes. *Lord, please forgive me for my doubts. Help me trust You.*

"What are you thinking about so deeply?"

She startled, eyes flying open, then realized afresh he did not know she'd been sitting with her eyes closed. Breath escaped silently. How relaxing that could be—she need never be wondering if he approved her looks.

"Miss Bloomfield?"

She pressed cool hands to hot cheeks. Oh, how she needed to get these thoughts under control. "I was, er, oh, nothing."

"I wonder if it is truly possible to think of nothing," he mused. "Surely the intention to think about nothing means it is indeed something that one now thinks about."

"You are a philosopher, I see."

"Not at all. The merest fribble."

"A fribble is the last thing I would consider you, sir."

"And what exactly *would* you consider me, Miss Bloomfield?"

Handsome. Patient. Courageous. Kind. Someone with whom she could see a future should God wish to grant her a personal miracle. She could say none of this, of course. "A friend."

"That is better than a cantankerous patient." He shifted a fraction closer. "If you do regard me as a friend, won't you tell me what has worried you these past days?"

She swallowed. "You mean more than just Susan's death?"

"I suppose I do."

"I . . . I don't want to gossip."

"And I'm not asking you to. But if you think it would help to share some of what troubles you, then I've been told I'm good at listening."

Emotion caught in her throat. "You are very kind."

"I am, yes, that is true."

She chuckled, and the sound broke the tension, and her reserve, and she shared her concerns about the potion, her guilt, her failures, that nothing seemed to assuage.

"You blame yourself?"

"Yes."

"Because you made Susan drink that poison."

"Well, no, of course not."

"You made the poison."

"No."

"You didn't do anything to help her."

Her throat constricted. "No! I did everything I could to help her."

"So why do you blame yourself?"

"I wish I could have done more," she whispered.

He grasped her hand, squeezed it gently. "Your father couldn't save her, Mary. Your father with extensive medical training."

"I know."

"God didn't save her."

"I wish He had."

"But you are not God. I remember you telling me not so very long ago that God's ways are higher than ours. And if God chose not to save her, how could you do more than He?"

She nodded and tightened her grip in response. "Here atop this mountain, so close to the heavens, I am reminded of that, also. People down in the village may only see clouds, but the sun still keeps shining above the clouds and rain. It reminds me that God's love is always present."

"Exactly. I would like to hear God's reasons for why I cannot see, but I suspect I'll never know. Should I spend the rest of my life asking why? That only leads to frustration and tears, I know."

Tenderness crossed her heart as she recalled his weeping in his mother's arms. Oh, how she knew that, too.

"I am still learning, but I want to keep on trusting God, even though my faith feels weak. But just because I'm weak today does not mean I can't believe God for outrageous things tomorrow."

A chuckle broke free. "And what outrageous things might they be?"

He turned to face her, his smile a little crooked. "That would be telling."

Her heart swelled and she was forced to look away. Forced to swallow twice before she trusted her voice to speak. "I suppose you want to be as outrageous as Blind Jack, and learn to ride and hunt and fish and such."

"I don't think the fishing would be too hard, provided I don't take someone's eye out with a poor throw of the line."

"That would be unfortunate. But fishing would be manageable, especially with such a good doggie as Frankie." She stroked the dog's head, which had pushed between them. "He is trained for helping with such things, so I believe."

"Is he?"

"I believe that's what Susan said."

Susan. The moroseness stealing over her was cut short by Frank's licking of her cheek. "Oh, you are not a gentleman!" She wiped her face with a handkerchief.

"I'm not—? Oh, you mean Frank is not."

A chuckle escaped. "You know very well what I mean, sir."

"Adam. But you can call me 'sir' if you prefer."

"You are a jokester, sir—Adam."

"Sir Adam? Now that has a certain ring about it."

She laughed and released his hand to push to her feet. "I think it's time we go."

He scrambled upright, and she was confronted by his nearness. She need only tilt back her head, and he bend his down, and she would know what Emily knew about Adam's kiss.

"Oh!" She stepped back.

"Miss Bloomfield? Are you quite all right?"

No, she was quite possibly all wrong.

"We best head back." She dusted off her skirts and collected the remains of their meal. "It's getting cool now."

"There's a storm brewing," he said. "I can smell it."

Beyond the cairn, the angry grey clouds in the distance foretold a summer storm that so swiftly ravaged this area. "We best hurry."

He nodded, and with a sharp command to Frank, carefully made his way back along the path. After a short time, he begged the use of her shoulder, which he leaned on as they slowly descended. "I feel as though I am crushing you."

"Here." She grasped his hand. But this time she did not place his hand on her shoulder. She simply held it in her own, gently squeezing and steering him into different directions as they negotiated the path.

For the next few minutes, she walked beside him, all the while casting anxious looks at the clouds banking overhead. "I'm not sure we'll be able to miss the rain," she admitted. "I'm sorry, I should have paid more attention."

"You had your mind on other things."

"I know, and I'm sorry, I should have—"

"No, it was as it ought be. Besides, a little rain never killed anyone, did it?"

She winced, and he seemed to notice the echo of his words.

"I didn't mean that to sound quite so trite."

"I know. I'm not that sensitive, I assure you."

"Truly?" he asked, smiling a little.

"Did you figure me a weakling?"

"Not at all."

Frank was getting restless, leaping ahead, pulling the lead this way and that, as if the wind harassed him.

"Someone is more anxious than us to be home."

A drop of water pelted her cheek, another, and the wind picked up as the skies turned ominously black.

"Adam, I'm very sorry but I suspect we're in for a downpour."

"Now I'm the one who is sorry. I should have told you before. As soon as I smelled it."

"How talented you are."

"Not quite talented enough. If I had more skill I might have realized—" He slipped on some scree, and the shift of momentum made her slide sideways.

She regained her footing on the slippery step. "We're almost there," she panted.

"Almost where?"

"To the shepherd's hut. Perhaps we can shelter there until this deluge passes."

"How much farther?"

"Perhaps thirty feet." She huffed. "Just down these steps—oh!"

Her foot slipped on the rain-slicked rock, and she let go of his hand, her legs twisting in the dog leash as Frank gave a sudden yelp. She caught a glimpse of rock and earth, a glimpse of Adam's panicked face. Then she fell, screaming, tumbling into a rock and crashing into—

Darkness.

Chapter 23

Panic seized his chest. "Miss Bloomfield?" Rain-laden wind lashed at his face, threatening to tear at his clothes. "Mary?"

She'd been beside him one minute, lost the next.

"Miss Bloomfield?"

Frank whined.

Adam crouched, leaning forwards, feeling with his hands. Where was she?

The wind grew in its intensity, threatening to topple him. He clutched Frank's leash, drew him near.

The dog whimpered into his chest.

"Mary?" He couldn't see. Couldn't see! The darkness held an ominous weight. He was being pummeled from every side, as if something unearthly sought to destroy him. But he would not give in.

Adam pushed to his feet, and slowly, carefully, clambered down the slippery rock step to the next. "Mary!" he bellowed, trying to be heard above the wind. Maybe he'd find her, stumble over her foot or something.

He inched forwards, sliding one foot in front of the other.

Frank was barking now. Had he found something?

There came a sudden jerk, and Adam hurtled to his knees, then groaned at the impact. "Where is she?"

Frank's excited yelping drew him to one side.

Adam looped the leash around his wrist—he could not afford to lose the dog, also—and started crawling, feeling carefully in the mud and stones. "Lord God, help me find her." He reached out, hands extended in a desperate search, then felt a hard object, softer than a rock, and discovered her boot, a leg, a sodden gown. He scrambled beside her, felt along her side to her shoulder, then leaned in close to where he judged her face might be. "Miss Bloomfield?"

No response.

"Mary?" he yelled.

Nothing. Nothing except the wind and the rain and the barking of Frank. And the desperation pouring through his veins.

He reached out, touched her face. There was no response. It was too hard to tell if she breathed or not, so he dragged her upright as if in a casual embrace. "Mary?"

Still no response. Fear drummed in his heart. He had to get her out of here. The darkness was so intense, so cold, so furious. He needed to find that shepherd's hut. How far had she said it was? Thirty feet? How close would it be now? Twenty? But dare he do so, completely blind, when he might tumble off the edge of the mountain to the rocks far below?

"God, what do I do?" His screech sounded like that of a young lass.

Frank tugged, and Adam hugged Mary close, trying to shelter her as much as he could from the elements. Perhaps they both might die here, on a lonely mountaintop. He shoved down that foolish thought. If Napoleon's forces had not succeeded in killing him, then no summer storm was going to. There was probably someone on their way right now to come rescue them. There was probably someone right now who was praying for them. There was probably—

He shuddered violently, the rain saturating his neck. It was folly to stay out in the cold and wet. He had to get them out of here.

Adam pushed to one knee and her frame shifted in his arms. He couldn't drop her, couldn't let whatever injuries she'd sustained be worsened by another fall. What should he do? "God, thank You for showing me where she was. Now help me keep her safe, please."

Another jerk at the lead, and Adam was tugged forwards, his burden sopping, weighty in his arms. He gingerly rose, and half-carrying, half-dragging her, slid one booted foot slowly forwards. It felt smoother here, like the worn path they'd trodden on their ascent.

Fear spiked. Unless it was a rock leading them over the edge. "God, I need to see!"

There was no flash of lightning, no miraculous deliverance of scales from his eyes enabling sight, but a sense of peace stole underneath the frantic fear. Assurance strengthened. This path *was* the right one. He moved forwards, the barking Frank still in the lead, Mary's motionless body in his arms.

How much farther? Ten yards? Twenty paces? Thirty of his little sliding steps? Another movement. Another inch down. Where had she said the hut was located? Near the base of the rocky shelf that constituted steps, which must make it a few yards to his right.

"Where is the hut, boy?"

Frank tugged at the lead, pulling to the right.

Adam slid careful foot after careful foot, elbows splayed as much as he could without dropping his cargo, in the hopes of discovering a wall or the edge of the doorway.

His shoulder hit something hard.

He swallowed an oath, realizing that they must now be . . . "Here." He carefully lowered Mary to the ground, then felt in front of him, inching his way along the stone wall until he came to a door. He pushed.

The door itself seemed to fall in.

Yes, Mary had described the hut's dilapidated condition. He reached into the space. At least the rain wasn't pelting down here. He moved back outside, drew Mary up and in, stumbling his way inside as he tripped over her wet, useless cloak. He fell hard, hurting his knees, but doing his best to protect her from further harm. "Mary? We'll be safe here."

Frank's barking bounced off the walls, hurting his ears.

"Quiet, Frank!" he ordered.

The dog subsided into whining, with the occasional yelp.

Adam flexed his fingers, blew warmth onto his frozen joints, and felt for his precious burden. "Mary? Can you hear me?"

She still didn't stir.

But at least the space was a fraction quieter. Drier, too, although there was an odd smell. He ignored it, focused on trying to get a response. He carefully felt for her throat, for the pulse.

There. A slight beat met his fingertips.

"Thank You, God." He exhaled. "Mary? Wake up, please. Please."

She remained in her slumber, so he continued his careful examination. There was the slightest exhalation from her nose. *Thank God.* No bumps on her forehead. *Thank God.* He felt around the back of her head and encountered something sticky and wet.

Wet he could ascribe to the rain, but the stickiness could only be blood. *Dear God, let her be all right.*

He drew out a handkerchief—had he used it today? It scarcely mattered; she'd need something to hold the blood in. Memories of wartime resurfaced, the need to keep the wounded warm, to prevent shock, to stop blood loss. He shifted on the floor, moving so his back was against the hut's internal wall. He laid Mary down, called Frank to her side to warm her, and dredged up strength to inch, hand outstretched, through the hut.

Surely there was a fireplace here somewhere. From the vestiges of memory, he recalled a chimney—a shepherd would have required something to heat the structure during the long, frozen winters. Careful reconnaissance, aided by his superior sense of smell, led him to bump his head against a thin strip of wood—a mantelpiece?—underneath which lay an enclosure in the wall, where his frozen fingers encountered warm coals.

Hadn't this hut been abandoned for years? He shook his head, shoved that surprise to one side, and refocused on the task ahead. He needed to find wood, then light a fire. Was there even wood here? He grimaced, continuing his slow exploration. As if he could expect—

But wait. That *was* wood. A small pile, doubtlessly abandoned years ago. At least it would be well-seasoned. He picked up some kindling, placed it on the coals. A splinter dug into him, and he gritted his teeth. When he reached up along the mantelpiece where he'd bumped his head, he found a metal box.

A tinderbox? He tried to slide open the lid.

It wouldn't budge.

He used as much force as he had left and wrested it open. Found the tinder, lit the spark. He bent to where the grate was and placed the flame to the small pieces of wood—or hoped he did—and prayed it would light.

Behind him Frank had ceased his awful whine. The wind had dropped, too, leaving only the heavy pounding of the rain, some of which he could feel invading the space, helped along by angry gusts of wind.

"Come on, light," he begged the kindling.

Something crackled beneath his fingers, and a spurt of heat touched his hand, causing him to snatch back his fingers from the fire. He exhaled. "Thank You, God. Keep us safe."

He waited a moment, warming his hands over the flame, then searched for the other pieces of wood he'd detected before. "Come on. Where is more?"

There. He found one piece, then another, and carefully deposited them on the still-burning flames. He then committed the fire to God. It would hardly last for hours—how could it, given he had no way to see?—but if the fire could warm the room a few precious degrees, Mary might just be kept warm enough.

He crawled back to where he'd left her, found her lying unmoved. "Mary?" he whispered, lips close to her ear.

Still nothing.

"I'm going to take you closer to the fire. Not very romantic, but I hope it will suffice."

Where had that sprung from?

He shook his head and dragged her closer, until he was propped against the hearth, feeling the warmth of flames on his right side. He drew her nearer and tucked her under his right shoulder, his arm around her waist. God forbid anyone ever saw them like this, but he'd need to know if her breathing changed. That was all. The nearer proximity meant he noticed when she began shivering.

He unclasped his greatcoat, drew it from his back, and spread it over her, tucking in the ends as best he could under her legs.

Frank whined again, then pushed closer, settling onto Adam's out-stretched legs, the dog's weight no burden due to his welcome warmth.

"Mary, I wish you'd wake up."

But her response remained the same.

He kissed her forehead, rested his cheek against her hair, and thanked God for His protection, until exhaustion dragged him to sleep.

An indefinable essence caught her senses, tantalizing, teasing her to remember. What was it? Something that had always reminded her of warmth, of tenderness, of hope. She lifted heavy eyelids, and shivered, suddenly conscious of a great feeling of cold, dimness, and a thundering thumping in her head. Where—? What—?

Mary turned her head slightly, realized the heavy thumping emanated from a broad chest . . . A broad chest her hand rested upon. Who—?

Oh no. What had happened? What had she done?

She groaned, the sound loud in the stillness of the . . . cottage? She blinked. This didn't look like any cottage she'd ever visited. Where was she? And who was she with?

A tilt of her head and she saw the shadowed whiskers of a firm chin, the dark brows that slashed across a dirt-smudged face. Adam Edgerton held her in his arms, her cheek pressed to his wide chest. *Oh my.*

She tried to wriggle free, but his clasp remained strong still, so she gave up the effort, then realized his coat was over her front and aching legs. Why?

Oh, she smelled so dirty, sweat-soaked, tinged with soot. Her eyes opened wider as she took in her surrounds. Dull light inched past broken shutters, revealing a room of dilapidated furniture, a pallet in the corner. Why hadn't he gone there? Of course. He couldn't see. Then why hadn't she?

She touched her aching head. Oh, how it hurt. What did she last remember? Seeing a beautiful vista, wishing Adam could see it, too. Then a dark cloud destroyed everything.

A groan escaped from near her ear. Adam stirred, blinking long dark lashes as he stared unseeingly at her. "Mary?"

His voice was raspy, and for one shocking moment she imagined what it would be like to wake in the morning to hear him speak her name like that again. Never mind what was happening now.

"Mary, can you hear me?"

"Y-yes." Her voice sounded hoarse. She coughed, the action seeming to trigger a paroxysm of hunger. "Are you all right?"

He closed his eyes, lifting a hand to smother—rather unsuccessfully—a yawn. "I'm so weary."

"My head really aches." She scrubbed a hand over her face, felt the strands of damp, limp hair straggling across her face and down her neck. She touched her scalp and winced, then ran her fingers through her hair in an attempt to smooth it down and pin it up. But she had no pins. "I must look like a drowned rat."

"You look fine to me."

His words, mumbled with the edge of a smile, pressed the bruise in her soul. Of course he'd say something like that. She shook her head at her foolish emotion. What did it matter what she looked like? Such a predicament meant there was little need to be genteel after all. "What happened?"

"We were caught in a fierce storm, and you slipped and must have bumped your head."

She reached up, felt a new throbbing at the back, along with a dirty handkerchief. She pulled it away, examined it. "Is this yours?"

"Yes."

"What is that color?"

"I expect it is blood."

She shuddered. "My blood?"

"I'm afraid so. I did my best to help."

"No wonder my head aches so."

"No wonder," he said softly, and her heart grew suddenly sore.

How tender he was with her. "I still don't understand. Where are we?"

"As far as I know, this is the old shepherd's hut."

"It's so cold." Another shiver wracked her frame.

He lifted his arm, drew her closer. "I'm sorry the fire went out."

"The fire? What fire?" She shifted her head. "Oh."

There lay the remains of charred wood, a tiny glowing ember giving weight to his claim. "You lit a fire?"

"Tried to. I don't know how successful it was."

"It caught." She shifted from under the weight of his arm. "Here, let me see if I can light it again." It took a moment for her vision to clear, for the blur to sharpen, then she reached across to the small stack of wood and placed a few twigs and sticks on the not-quite-dead ashes. "Come on, burn," she whispered, then blew on it carefully.

Nothing.

She sighed. "I was never very good at lighting fires." She shook her head. "That's why it's amazing that you—" She bit off the rest of what she was about to say.

"That I could light it?" he asked. "Consider it one of the many miracles God did for us last night."

"Is it morning? Have we been out all night?"

"I believe so."

Oh no. Everyone must be so worried about her! And about him. And—oh! She gasped as the impropriety of their situation suddenly gained purchase.

"What is it?"

"Everyone will think—oh!" Oh no. "Why didn't my parents suggest a chaperone? Everyone will think the worst!"

"I doubt that. Everyone knows you have been kind enough to visit and help me, often for hours on end. This has just proved to be a little longer than expected."

Yes. Overnight. She cringed. "We should . . . we should probably try to return, now it's not raining."

"Yes." He shifted, winced. "Cramp."

"You poor thing." She lightly prodded a sleeping Frank. "Frank? Wakey, wakey."

The dog rolled over, ignoring her, his canine snores unabated.

"He doesn't sound as if he's ready to obey."

"But the longer we stay here—"

"You need not worry. People will likely assume you stayed at my parents' to avoid the storm. There can be no impropriety in that."

"But that isn't what happened. What if Father has someone out searching for us now?"

"Your father is a sensible man. Do not worry over the unknown."

His calmness soothed, and the frantic pace of her heart eased. "Thank you."

"For what?"

"For reminding me to not worry."

"You're welcome." His smile reached the corners of her soul.

She breathed in, caught a tinge of the aroma that had scented her dreams. Something earthy, with a hint of mint? She leaned closer to him, sniffed again. Even with the extra tang of manly sweat, she liked his scent.

His lips twitched and mortification streamed through her.

She scrambled up and away, staggering as dizziness swamped her senses, and her legs buckled in protesting pins and needles. She gasped.

"Mary? Are you injured?"

"'Tis nothing. I shall be right in just a moment." She glanced around, waiting for the pain to subside.

The hut, which had previously appeared empty, seemed to hold traces of recent inhabitation. The pallet, spare wood, a lantern.

"Those men," she whispered.

"Which men?"

"Those men we saw that day on our walk. I suspect they've been living here."

"What can you see?"

"There are chairs placed next to a makeshift table, and two plates. Oh, Adam, what if they're returning? What if they're coming now?" Panic squeezed her chest. "What if we're still here when they return?"

He chuckled. "Remember that no worrying thing?"

"Apparently not." She forced a deep breath and made her shoulders relax.

"If they return, then we'll simply ask them why they're hiding here. On land that doesn't belong to them."

"But what if they fight you, or attack you, or—" attacked her, like poor Susan had been?

"I'll protect you." He promised with such conviction she could not help but feel assured.

"I still think we should leave as soon as possible."

"And avoid the potential for gossipmongers?" He gave a wry smile.

And avoid lots of potential for evil consequences. "Here, let me help you up." She grasped his hand, tugged, and nearly collapsed. He was so large and heavy.

A noise most wild and unruly roared through the space. "Forgive me, my stomach is unmannerly," he apologized. "I don't suppose our ruffians have left anything to eat?"

She examined the space. "Nothing. Except . . . oh." Her eyes widened as she finally identified the source of the strange odor. In the corner of the hut were the remains of a sheep. "Oh, no."

"What is it?"

"I do believe we've found your stolen sheep. One of them, anyway." Panic reared again. "Now we really *should* leave, for if they return and find us here, then know that we know—oh, it cannot be good!"

"I'll alert Father as soon as we get home."

"But don't send him up here alone. Tell him to gather other men. To go to the magistrate." How she'd hate for Mr. Edgerton to be embroiled in a fight he could not win.

After ensuring they had left no evidence of their stay behind, she clutched Adam's arm, and together they made their way outside, Frank leading the way on his leash. The wind held traces of moisture and buffeted them, threatening to steal away their coats as it had already stolen their hats. Her hair whipped in her eyes, lashing her skin, and their progress on the descent was much slower than before.

Thick fog meant she could barely see ahead, but at least there was no real rain. The mud clinging to their boots was thick and treacly, sucking at their every footstep. Coupled with empty bellies and her thumping headache, it seemed exhaustion was but a step away. She pushed on, past the stinging burn in her legs, past the desire to sit down, past the desire to cry. This was torturous. She never wanted to walk this path again.

"How are you feeling?" he asked.

"Wonderful," she said in a flat tone.

He chuckled, and the sound lifted her heart for just a moment. "This mud is not making things any easier, is it?"

"No."

"I'm sorry this simple walk has turned into such an adventure."

What could she say to such solicitude? *I'm sorry, too?* She said nothing.

"Miss Bloomfield—"

"You might as well call me Mary."

"Well, that's one good thing that's come of this, I suppose." He grinned.

Her heart clenched. Oh, how she loved when his handsome features lit up.

"I hope you will forgive me for jeopardizing your reputation."

"For what? There is nothing to forgive. Things happen unexpectedly at times."

"True." He patted her arm. "You are more understanding than some."

She didn't dare ask of whom he meant. Frank barked, and she lifted her gaze beyond the path to see distant figures. "Shush, Frank!"

"What is it?"

"There are people coming. Oh, I hope it isn't—"

"The soldiers."

She nodded.

The shapes took on more distinct forms.

"Wait, it looks as if it's your father. And mine also." She released her breath in a big rush. "Oh, how glad I am." Her pace picked up, but she was halted by his hand.

"Promise you won't hold this against me."

"Of course not," she exclaimed. Oh, how she longed to be in her own house, in her own bed—

"It's simply that I . . . I do not want this misadventure to cause your visits to cease."

"It shan't." Honesty compelled her to say, "That is, I shall be happy to visit until . . . until the day you are married, sir. I cannot envisage a wife being happy with my visits to you."

"That would put a strange complexion on things, indeed. But I wouldn't worry. I can't see anyone wishing to marry a blind man like me, so your visits can continue."

Her heart sank a little, as his words reinforced the musings of last night. He seemed to have little thought of her beyond her nursing ability, which was probably just as it ought be. But in a secret chamber of her soul it seemed a hard thing to have to forsake this promising friendship with a man who seemed to understand her as few others did. She exhaled, affixed a smile, and hurried forth to meet her father, his embrace, and his worried exclamations.

Chapter 24

Mary's words continued to echo through his mind over the next day, and the next. Did she really think him eligible for marriage? Perhaps his recent actions had given hope that his life was not so hopeless as he'd once thought. He could do things. He could—with a great deal of trustworthy assistance—run a farm. He could still interact with others. Life would never be the same as before the war, before his blindness, but perhaps he could carve out a new version of what his life might look like.

What his life "looked like." His lips curved to one side. Well, he might never actually see what things looked like, but he could gain an understanding of things. And maybe that was enough. Anyway, wasn't he supposed to live by faith and not by sight? Perhaps this was simply a demonstrable example of how to act with nothing in plain view: hoping, believing, trusting.

That might work with the farm, but should he hope for more than that? He wished he could speak to Mary again and know her thoughts.

He had so many things to consider, not least of which was the contents of a letter from Captain Balfour his mother had read to him earlier. He appreciated his former superior's concern, knew the man's Christian faith motivated his compassion. But what was the right answer to the question he had posed? Should he help the men? His mother had been concerned. What would the villagers say? What should he reply? Mary would likely know an answer both compassionate and wise.

"Adam? The doctor is here."

"Thank you, Mother."

Soon came the tread of Dr. Bloomfield.

Only one footfall, one visitor. Disappointment crashed. "Good morning, Doctor. Just yourself today?"

"Mary needed to stay home, since she's been plagued with headaches and a cold since your little misadventure."

"How is her head wound?"

"Improving. She told me she's indebted to you for your assistance. You have my thanks," he added gruffly.

"I'll continue praying that she feels better soon."

"Thank you. And you? How have you been keeping, Adam?"

"Very well, sir. Although my mother tells me I slept most of the day away."

"'Tis only to be expected after such an episode."

"Father was telling me the lake has risen by five inches."

"Yes. There's a fear of flooding in some of the lower-lying villages. You were fortunate to find shelter where you did."

"God provided."

"So it seems." There came a pause. "It's about your time there of which I wished to speak."

He could hear the strain in Dr. Bloomfield's voice. This did not sound promising. "Yes, sir?"

"I understand from Mary that she slipped and hit her head, and you managed somehow to drag her inside the shepherd's hut."

"I wished I could have done more, but there's nothing like that kind of situation to realize the limitations of having no sight."

"And yet you managed this feat, something which would be regarded as most heroic."

"It was nothing. I'm just glad we were kept safe."

"Something we all thank God for. But . . ." The doctor cleared his throat. "You do understand what this means?"

"Forgive me for being obtuse. What does what mean?"

The doctor exhaled. "My wife was most insistent I come and speak about this to you today. Already there are rumors circulating in the village about your absence and that of my daughter's. I know you have no thought of her, but I'm afraid that people will see things otherwise, and assume . . ."

And assume Adam and Mary had been engaged in activities most damning for a woman's virtue and reputation. His chest grew taut. "I had hoped that word of our circumstances would not spread. And at the least, I thought people would be more generously minded than that."

"Yes, well, Mrs. Endicott saw Mary return and enquired of my younger daughter, and I'm afraid Joanna was not precisely discreet."

He swallowed. "And now you think I should make Mary an offer."

"She is my daughter, and a maiden, and her reputation must be protected."

"I see."

"I understand it's not ideal, and I don't mean to force your hand, but I find that there is no other way. Unless, of course, you have made further plans with Miss Hardy, after all."

Emily? He'd barely thought on her in weeks. "I have not."

"Then, please consider your actions towards my daughter."

"Sir, you must know that nothing of a dishonorable nature occurred. I would never treat a woman so, and especially not"—he almost said Mary—"not Miss Bloomfield."

"I know that, but there are still many who will question a young man and young woman being alone overnight. Now, I know this is not what you have wanted—"

Why did he keep saying that, as though he thought Mary a substandard prize?

"—but I have discussed things with your father, and he agrees."

"What? Why is he not here?" Adam sat up straighter. "Please understand that I do recognize your reasoning, and have no desire to besmirch your daughter's name. She has proved a kind companion, someone I can depend upon in many ways, but I do not like to think she is compelled by these circumstances to accept an offer she has little wish for."

The doctor paused a lengthy moment. "Do you know how many offers Mary has received for her hand?"

He dreaded knowing the answer. "No."

Another pause. "None."

His heart softened. What was wrong with the men of this world to ignore a woman who possessed such a beautiful soul?

His stomach churned. What had been wrong with him?

The doctor cleared his throat. "I say this because I do not think she would turn you down."

How strange this seemed, as if this were happening to another man. "But sir, you cannot be desirous of a blind son-in-law."

"I am desirous of a son-in-law who cares for my daughter. But if you will not, then I shall likely have to send her away."

"When she's done nothing wrong?"

"Exactly. Where is the justice in that?"

The world seemed to be turning. He felt dizzy and rather strange. "I will speak to her on the morrow," he said stiffly. When he'd determined just what to say.

"Thank you. I will take my leave of you."

Adam ignored his farewell, thoughts churning. *Dear God*, what had just happened? Perhaps he should have realized that the consequences of staying out all night were more severe for Mary, but people ought to show more charity. Hadn't people known that they had taken walks by themselves before? Nobody had insisted on chaperonage before. Was the lack of chaperones Mary's choice, or a lack of foresight on his part?

He rubbed his forehead. And why was he so reluctant to propose to Mary, anyway? He thought her kind and sweet, and he liked her voice and enjoyed her laugh. He'd come to think of her as a friend. But was that enough for which to get leg-shackled? Or was it simply the doctor's somewhat clumsy mode of delivery, the thought that social obligations had forced his hand to rush something that with more time might have naturally occurred?

And what was this about Father having had agreed? Mother, too, that probably meant.

He exhaled a shaky breath. Regardless, it seemed he would be riveted far sooner than he expected.

"What did you say?" Mary pushed higher against the bed's headboard and stared at her stepmother, whose face could not hide her dismay. "Father actually spoke to Adam and told him he must marry me?" Oh, the shame! She could hide in her bedchamber for the rest of her days!

"It was deemed best—"

"By whom? Not by me!"

"I know marriage to a blind man is not what you dreamed about—"

"I never dreamed about marriage, Mama. Not like Joanna did." *Or Emily*, a voice murmured in her head. "And Adam being blind matters little to me."

"He will never see your children," Mother said mournfully. "Never see his bride."

"Well, his bride will certainly not be me," Mary snapped. "I cannot believe you told him he must propose."

"I cannot believe you did not expect something like this."

"Where was all the concern when we were partaking in long walks? You never insisted on a chaperone then."

"There wasn't talk in the village then."

"And now there is talk in the village and you think I should accept a man who doesn't want to marry me simply because of these unknown villagers' idle tongues?"

"Well, not exactly anonymous."

"Who, then?" Mary challenged.

"Mrs. Endicott said something to your sister, and Mr. Ponsonby dropped by earlier, hinting it would be a very good thing."

"And you care what he thinks?"

"He is a man of the cloth, dear."

"Whose opinion we've always held in low regard until now."

"Perhaps we were not right to always question him."

"No, we were right," Mary insisted. "He seems to believe a different gospel to the one in the Bible, and I cannot agree that we should take his opinion on anything."

"But your reputation—"

"Mother, you have not concerned yourself with my reputation for many a year. I have visited farms and people of all ages and in all sorts of conditions, and seen many a thing most people might label as indelicate, but that's never been a problem before."

"That was your father's doing. Looking back, we were a little lenient."

Mary drew in a long breath, released it slowly. Her head ached powerfully. "I cannot believe you are insisting Adam does this."

"He does not seem averse."

The note of uncertainty in her mother's voice only raised Mary's hackles again—and cinched her throat tight. He didn't want to marry her. But foolish hope longed to hear her mother's denial. "Really? Or will he simply be harangued into agreeing?"

"Mary, it's most unlike you to respond in such a way."

"Forgive me, Mother, but I dislike being told a young man has had his arm twisted in order to propose to me."

"I don't believe it was twisted," Mother said, a furrow between her brows.

Mary released a huff of impatience, flattening her lips to withhold her choler. How dare they do this? Require Adam to propose? Now she'd never know if— Her eyes filled with tears.

"Oh, dear one, I certainly didn't mean to upset you." Her mother wrapped Mary in a hug. "We thought you'd like to be married, to have a home of your own, children."

A tear escaped, and she pulled back. "Do you want to be rid of me?"

"No! Not at all. We just want you to be happy and fulfilled." Mother's eyes sheened. "Your father and I won't be here forever."

"I know, and I don't want to seem ungrateful, but I hate the thought of marrying to oblige other people's expectations." *And not because he loved me.*

"If it's any comfort, he said he depended on you."

How romantic.

"And I'm sure in time you could grow closer in your affections."

How reassuring. "Mother, I understand you have the best of intentions, and have no desire to be saddled with a daughter whose reputation is beyond repair, but I do not wish to marry him. Not like this. Not because everyone assumes we must."

"Then you'd give some thought to marrying him if you knew his affections were already engaged?"

"That's the problem. They already were engaged . . . by Emily Hardy years ago."

"My dear, that is not so—"

"And how would any of this appear to Emily?" Fresh conviction shook her. "I . . . I encouraged Emily to go away, Mama. I did not think she could ever manage life with a blind husband, and I advised her to live with her aunt for a time. How she would hate me, thinking, as she surely would, that I had stolen away her husband-to-be."

"Oh, Mary, I'm sure she wouldn't think such a thing."

"I'm sure she would. If our positions were reversed"—she gave a bitter laugh at the thought—"I suspect I'd think exactly that."

"You cannot know for sure."

She shrugged. "I wish I could speak with her and explain, but that cannot be, can it? Regardless, it doesn't change the fact that Adam was betrothed to her for four years, and now he's been back for only a few months and you think he's had a change of heart. I certainly cannot see any evidence if he has."

"Why, when he—"

"Mother, he doesn't care for me in that way." And never would. A savage, jealous pang crossed her chest. Emily had known his affection. Had known his kiss. She dug her fingers into her forehead, willing away the pain.

"Adam cares for you."

"But not enough, Mother, and that's all I have to say. I have a headache, and would prefer to rest now, please."

"But what shall I say if he comes to request your hand?"

"Offer Joanna's instead. He seems to have liked girls of her age in the past." She turned away, waiting until her mother closed the door and her footsteps faded, and then collapsed into her bed and allowed her disappointments and sorrows to seep onto the pillow.

Chapter 25

Adam picked up the stone, weighed it in his hand, felt for the hole in the wall, and placed it firmly in. There came no sound of shifting or, worse yet, falling, so he judged it a good fit. This drystone wall bounding the lane had only needed a few sections mended. He felt along for the next gap and repeated his action, his mind on the interview from yesterday.

His efforts to meet with Mary had proved doomed. It seemed her time on Upton Pike had either given her a perpetual headache or a fear of him. What else could her reluctance to see him be? He couldn't very well force his way upstairs at the Bloomfields and demand she speak with him. It appeared her initial disinclination regarding marriage had mirrored his. He'd been forced to speak with her sister, whose efforts to entertain him in the drawing room had fallen flat. Until Joanna had mentioned a recent letter from Miss Hardy.

"She asked after you, sir, and wants you to know you're in her prayers."

"How kind." He found he didn't care.

"Isn't it?" Joanna's voice seemed to lack conviction. "I am glad she's been enjoying York."

He was about to make his excuses and leave when she'd spoken again.

"I was thinking about Emily recently and wondered how she would have coped if you'd married her soon after proposing."

He'd drawn in a breath at the impertinence. Then allowed her words to soak into his brain. How would Emily have coped four years ago when she was but seventeen, pretty as a picture, and he'd begged her father for the right to marry her immediately?

"She's too young," her father had said.

And even though Adam and Emily had pleaded, her father had remained resolute. And been proved right. For while the past four years of war and death and loss had seasoned Adam, naïve, innocent Emily had scarcely changed. Would perhaps never change and mature into the woman he needed—no, that he *wanted*—now.

"She wouldn't have coped well, would she?" he'd finally said.

"No." Joanna's voice was thoughtful. "Emily is most amiable, but I wonder how she would have managed as a soldier's wife."

"Or as a farmer's wife." The only life he could offer now.

"Traipsing over hill and dale is not exactly her style."

His lips twitched at the image of dainty Emily holding up her skirts, trying to avoid mud or sheep manure. "No."

"I can't imagine Emily ever closing her eyes to imagine what life would be like to be blind."

"I beg your pardon?"

"Or trying to eat dinner with her eyes shut, or getting dressed without sight or help. Such a funny thing." Joanna gave a throaty chuckle reminiscent of her sister's, then gasped. "Of course, I didn't mean to suggest that it would be funny if she really *was* blind."

"Of course not," he said dryly.

"No, truly. But I cannot imagine Emily ever doing those things."

"Excuse me, but of whom do you speak? Who pretended to be blind?"

"Why Mary, of course. When she first went to help you. She would practice her normal routine with her eyes closed, so she could understand how you might feel."

His chest seemed to constrict. "She did that for me?"

"Of course she did. You should have heard her, she was forever 'Adam this' or 'Adam that,' and it was all we could do to make her talk about anything else."

Oh. Dearest Mary.

"She wouldn't want me to tell you this—"

"Then you best not tell me."

"—but I suspect she's had an infatuation for you for ages."

What? "She never hinted anything of the sort."

"Of course she didn't. She would never want to cause trouble for someone *you* had an infatuation for."

Someone like Emily. He'd groaned. "I've been so blind."

"For years, it seems," the saucy miss had said.

How could he have not known? How could he have missed the one whose presence seemed to fill his world with light? Forget his blindness; she brought laughter and joy and hope into his heart. Had Emily ever done so? Or were her radiant looks all he'd ever really noticed?

His groan now carried on the cool air, seeming to excite Frank, whose padding footfalls raced as he enquired with a bark. "I've been a fool," he muttered.

Frank yapped as if in agreement.

"Thank you, Frankie. You are indeed a true friend."

A true friend.

The words seemed to echo on the wind. Mary Bloomfield had proved herself, time and again, to be his true friend. Through her honesty. Through her help. Through her gentle persistence. She was someone he could trust. Someone he could be his natural self with. Someone he cared for in such a deep way his heart would shrivel if she ever went away.

She was someone that he loved.

His heart, his skin, it seemed his very soul tingled. He released a deep breath. What should he do? Mary seemed determined to avoid him. Even Joanna had been unable to persuade her to join them. Would Mary attend church on the morrow or miss that, too? Perhaps he'd need to employ her parents to advise him.

He picked up another rock, weighed it in his hands.

Frank started yapping again.

Rocks moved as multiple steps approached. "Excuse me."

He tensed, looked up to where the voice came. "Yes?"

A man's throat was cleared. "Would you happen to be Lieutenant Edgerton?"

Adam straightened, called the dog to heel. That voice. A fragment of memory begged to be recalled. "Yes. How can I help you?"

"Me name's Conway, and this is Gilroy."

"Sir," a second voice said.

"We was told you might 'ave work for us."

Were these the two soldiers Mary had been startled by? The ones they presumed had stolen Edgerton sheep? Had they realized he could not see them? "Who told you that?"

A cough. "Captain Balfour, sir. Said you might take pity on returned soldiers who haven't a place to sleep."

Ah. So these were some of the men Daniel Balfour had suggested in his recent letter for whom Adam might find employment. God bless him, he thought wryly. Adam seemed to be surrounded by those who wished for him to show compassion. "I'm not sure what you want from me."

"Just some work, a roof over our heads."

"How long have you been staying in these parts?" Perhaps, if they admitted to their actions, he could be persuaded.

"We, er, arrived a few weeks ago."

"And said nothing to me then? Why not?"

Another cough. "We, er, wanted to see if there be alternatives. We didn't want to presume, none."

"And we 'eard you'd been a mite unwell."

A mite? Adam swallowed wry amusement and nodded. "And where have you been staying?"

"I, that is, we, well, we don't want to get in no trouble, sir, but we found an old hut not too far away and stayed there a few nights."

"Ah. Did you shelter there the night of the big storm?"

"No. We was in the village, then, and 'ad to find a barn that didn't leak."

Adam nodded slowly. "And did you happen to find a few stray sheep there as well?"

"Beg pardon, sir?"

"Were there a number of sheep that you found in the shepherd's hut?"

"Well, no . . ."

"Oh, come on, Harry. Tell 'im the truth," the second voice said. "If yer asking did we kill a sheep, then yes, we did, sir, and we be sorry."

"You know that's a hanging offense, don't you?"

"Aye. We know we did wrong, but we was that 'ungry."

"Why didn't you ask for food at a house?"

"I dunno," the first man mumbled.

"I do," said his companion. "We always get suspicious looks and second glances. Nobody wants to talk to us, let alone help in any way. We asked at lots of farms, but nobody wanted to take a chance on us. Strange, innit, after serving King and country, and now we're treated worse than scum. Which is why we thought we'd see if you would help us, sir, seeing as you understand how hard life is now after the war."

His heart stirred with compassion. Which was surely what Captain Balfour had hoped, that Adam might prove a soft touch. "I need to speak to my father. He will not be best pleased to learn about the missing sheep."

"Aye. We be sorry about that. You can take it off our wages."

Adam smothered a smile at the cheeky comment. These men thought he was really going to hire them. "As I said, there are others who must be consulted. But I'm hopeful we might be able to help in some way."

"We'd be that grateful, sir."

He could hear the genuine hope in their voices. "I will see what I can do."

One of them coughed. "Would . . . would it be all right if we stayed in the hut a little longer? We have nowhere else to go."

"No families?"

"None that wants us."

It didn't bear thinking about why that might be. "Very well. For another week. And if you wish to help, then you might consider doing what you can to clean the place. Including burying the sheep remains, so that others do not see."

"You be a good man, Lieutenant."

"Not a good man. None of us are. But I'm one who is trying to live a different life after war."

A twig broke as someone stepped forwards or away.

Frank barked, and Adam suddenly knew himself to be vulnerable, to be at their mercy. *God, protect me.* He nodded, willing his voice to remain affable. "And if you happen to return here before dusk, I'll ensure there's food for you both. As to the matter of employment, please come to the farmhouse this time next week, and I can give you my answer."

"We'll do that. Thank ye, sir."

He nodded and remained standing, while Frank growled, until receding footsteps suggested they'd gone away.

He exhaled, dusting off his hands. Seemed he had yet another thing to arrange.

But at least he had tomorrow morning to fix the most important thing.

Dear God, give me wisdom.

For tomorrow morning he would—one way or another—finally speak to Mary.

Today was Sunday and attending services would be her first public outing since her return from Upton Pike and all the associated scandal. She hoped—she was tempted to pray—that Adam Edgerton would stay away from church today.

Such hopes withered the moment she walked in. He sat with his parents, head turned as if he could see her. Dread slicked her fingers within her gloves, and she hurriedly turned away.

But not before a quick glance around the whispering congregants confirmed Adam's presence had garnered notice, and the way attention swung from him to her—well, she didn't need to be a prophet to predict what was being said.

"Ignore them," Joanna whispered, patting her arm.

Mary nodded, and resumed the pretense of listening to the sermon, then mouthing along to the final prayers and hymn. She needed to escape. She needed to flee the flinty stares and murmurs of this scandal-minded crowd. She was innocent, but insistence of the fact would only feed doubts in those so inclined. Oh, if only she had enough nerve to assume Joanna's insouciance, but the weight of recent grief and pain made such a thing impossible. As soon as she was able, she hurried to the side aisle, sliding past those waiting to shake the reverend's hand.

She could not shake Mr. Ponsonby's hand today. He was so unlikely to understand or offer a modicum of sympathy.

Outside gave space to breathe, and she hurried to Susan's grave, unpinning the lavender from her brooch and placing it gently on the turned earth. She bit her quavering lip, whispered another prayer for Susan's father. She would visit again, but she was so tired.

"Here you are." Joanna pulled on her shoulder. "Mother was wondering where you were. Are you ready?"

No. But she meekly followed as Joanna led her past a clutch of congregants whose voices dropped as they drew near.

Her sister gripped her arm. "Don't worry about what people are saying, hear me?"

"About Susan? Well, when people dare to speak ill of the dead—"

"About you," Joanna hissed. "Look, just ignore Mrs. Endicott and Mrs. Payne and their nasty tongues."

Touched by her sister's unsought consideration, Mary nodded and excused herself. "I see Mrs. Croker there, and would like to learn how Betsy is these days."

"Of course. I will speak with Mrs. Hardy and find out news of Emily."

Emily. Mary's heart twisted as she made her way to where Sally Croker stood. With all the whispers accompanying Mary's slow procession, it seemed a long walk. Would they cast aspersions on Mary as they had Susan? Emotions tipped, turned. Somehow she'd need to find the courage and opportunity to speak with Emily about exactly why Mary had encouraged her to move away.

Adam stepped into her path. "Miss Bloomfield."

She stopped, Sally Croker still ten yards away. Keeping herself very still and upright, face devoid of anything that might be mistaken by the gossips, she said, "Mr. Edgerton, hello."

"Mary, I must speak with you."

She winced, knowing the words he'd been asked to say. "I have nothing to say to you, sir, except things that might give pain. Please excuse me."

"I cannot, not yet. Just give me a chance to talk."

Conscious of all the eyes watching and that the determination she sensed within him was unlikely to make him desist, she finally sighed.

"Very well, but not here, not now. Come to the house tomorrow afternoon."

"Thank you."

She nodded, as if he could see her, and finally reached Sally Croker's side. "Hello, Sally."

"Hello, Mary. What did Adam Edgerton want with you?"

Mary drew her away a little, to the yew-shaded corner away from prying ears and eyes. "I'm surprised you have not heard. He is supposed to make me an offer."

Sally's eyes grew round. "Truly? Does this concern your night together on Upton Pike?"

Mary cringed. "You make it sound so sordid, when really it was only a sudden storm that forced us to take shelter. And even then, I was unconscious for much of that."

"Is that why Mrs. Hardy is looking at you with such daggers?"

"Oh, Sally, don't. I just cannot bear it today."

Sally laid a hand on Mary's shoulder. "Today has been hard. I will be praying for you."

Moisture burned at the back of Mary's eyes, and she blinked it away. "Thank you," she whispered. Then, drawing herself up, she said, "I wanted to enquire about Betsy. Is she fully recovered yet?"

"Oh, she is much better now, thank you. Enjoying time with her sister, whom she treats as her little doll. She loves to dress her and play peekaboo."

A knot of tension left her. "I'm glad. I'd like to visit again, if I may."

They fixed on a day later in the week, and after brief farewells, Mary made her way to where her parents and sister waited, ever-conscious of the eyes that tracked her progress and of the certainty of tomorrow afternoon's unpleasant task.

⁂

The next day, Mary twisted her skirt between nervous fingers, dread filling her stomach as Adam stood in the drawing room, hat in hands, his sightless eyes turned towards her.

"Miss Bloomfield, Mary, I wish to ask for your hand in marriage."

Now he had finally spoken, his words pierced like arrows to her soul. If only she held his heart. If only he cared for her beyond the proprieties.

Or maybe—a fresh burst of pain—her refusal would be a relief to him. Then he could be said to have done his duty and his honor would be intact when it was known eccentric Mary Bloomfield had turned him down. She drew in a deep breath. "Sir, you do me a great honor, but as I said before, I fear I cannot give you a favorable answer."

His lips pressed together. "May I be so bold as to ask why? I do not need a nursemaid, if that is what concerns you."

"And I do not need a husband, if protecting my reputation is what concerns you."

He shifted his weight. "But everyone will gossip."

"Everyone already is."

"All the more reason to be wed."

"Excuse me, sir, but I hardly think gossip is sufficient reason to marry." She forced cheer into her voice. "Come, sir, you really can't expect me to be concerned about such things at my advanced age."

"How old are you?"

"Nine-and-twenty."

He shook his head, a slight smile on his face. "Advanced, indeed."

A savage pain caught her breast, refusing speech. She glanced down, tears blurring the muted carpet. He might smile, as if jesting, but such words only made her feel plain and old and unwanted. Where was his denial? His reassurance that she wasn't too old? This was not how she wished her first—her only!—proposal to be.

"Miss Bloomfield, Mary, I know I am not much of a catch, but as a gentleman you have my assurance that I would do my best for you."

She swallowed, willed the tears in her eyes to not infect her voice. "Thank you for your kind offer, but I'm afraid I must refuse."

He frowned. "You have said that my blindness does not make me unmarriageable."

"That is not the reason I turn you down." She could not marry a man who professed nothing of his regard or affection.

"Is it the farm you have no wish for?"

"Not at all. It is one of the loveliest places I've seen."

"But the work involved is not to your liking."

"I'm not afraid of hard work. And . . . and it is exciting to see what the future holds for you."

"Exciting?" His lips twisted in an expression devoid of humor.

In that moment she realized just what she was saying no to. Rejection today would likely mean she should but rarely visit the Edgertons, and all the hopeful possibilities for the future would not be ones in which she'd partake. Someone else would likely soon have that right. Would enjoy his company. Would know his embrace. Would know his kiss. Her soul shuddered.

"But you have no wish to marry me."

God forgive her the untruth, for her breaking their pact of honesty, as she had many wishes that weren't coming true, but "No."

"I did not think you like—" He appeared to bite off what he was about to say. "Forgive me. I should not argue." Something like sadness— or was it resignation?—washed over his features. "I shall not waste any more of your valuable time. Good day, Miss Bloomfield."

She watched him go, as sudden knowledge of how her words might be construed filtered into her brain. But how to clarify? "Mr. Edgerton!" The words rushed out before she could stop them. "Wait."

He paused, turned partway, as if half-poised to leave. "Yes?"

"Please understand, I'm truly touched by your kind offer."

"Though you deny it, you have no wish to marry a blind man. I do not blame you."

"No." She laid a hand on his arm, felt the ripple of corded muscle. "It is not that. The truth is I barely notice your inability, and I would not have you think that I—that is, I do not . . ." Oh dear. Her mouth had run ahead of wisdom and propriety again. "Sir, I do thank you for your very kind offer, but I do not wish to be married." Not from an act of pitying chivalry.

"But I thought—" He bit his lip.

"I assure you that I am content with my lot and have no wish to be married." Not to an unwilling bridegroom whom social expectation had dragged to the altar.

"Truly?"

"It's as I say." And as she qualified in her own mind.

He exhaled. "Forgive me. I am sure this has proved most discomfiting. I will not be so reckless as to mention this again."

"No," she whispered, as her heart slowly tore to pieces.

"Good day." His farewell was stiff, his mien unsmiling.

She watched him depart, knowing her one chance at happiness was walking away.

But she could not marry unless for real affection, she told herself fiercely. Knowing it would forever be a one-sided attraction, she could not.

Chapter 26

The room was still, save for Frankie's snores, Adam's arguments still hanging in the air. "Father, I believe it only behooves us to give these men a chance."

"I cannot like it."

"Nor I," said John Davis.

"They served with Captain Balfour, and their injuries meant they were released to home, but home would not have them. Surely you can understand their need for purpose. I certainly can." And in recent days he'd understood it all the more. He hadn't realized until Mary's rejection how much purpose he'd found in dreaming of a life with her, a life that seemed so much hollower now, thus demanding all-consuming distraction through plans for the farm.

"We know nowt about them."

Adam fought for patience. "Please reread Balfour's note. He said—"

"I know, I know," his father said. "But what I don't know is why this Captain Balfour friend of yours cannot manage to find work for these men on his estates."

"Balfour has no estates," said Adam. "He's worked his way up through the ranks, as I did, and certainly never had the privileges of some." Like other captains he had come across, such as Captain Stamford, who might be privileged and the son of the Earl of Hawkesbury, yet still proved to have more mettle and battle wisdom than most and a genuine concern for his men. "Balfour is an ordinary man."

"Hmm. How do we know this Conway and Gilroy aren't taking advantage of you?"

"We need the workers, Father. And they need the work." As did he. Anything that could take his mind off, take his heart off, the humiliation of three days ago.

Why had Mary rejected him? He had a feeling it was more than what she'd said. Was she more like Emily than he'd imagined? No. He couldn't come at that. It must be something else. But what?

"Adam? Do you have more to add?"

"Forgive me, Father. I was thinking."

"Well, we're waiting."

He drew in a breath and turned slightly to where he judged his father might be. "I know what it is to be rejected over circumstances over which I have no control. I know what it is like to have others think I cannot do things because they judge me without daring to imagine possibilities." He hoped his father did not take offense. "But I also know what it is like to have someone believe in you and encourage you to imagine a world beyond the confines of the past or your physical limitations." His voice grew shaky. *Oh Mary, why?* "And I cannot help but want to extend the same level of support to those who might not experience it otherwise." He exhaled, and turned away, before they saw the emotion on his face. Why had she rejected him? Why had she not allowed him to offer the protection of his name?

"You speak most eloquently, son," his father said.

He shrugged. Was his father willing to relent?

"I didn't realize just how much this meant to you personally."

Adam nodded, unable to speak.

"Very well. We'll give them a month's trial. But they will need to stay in the shepherd's hut and must always have a sighted man nearby to supervise."

"Thank you, Father."

His father dismissed Davis and drew nearer. "Adam? You seem distressed. Is there more to this? These men, they have not threatened you, have they?"

"What? No. It is not that."

"But it is something."

Adam turned away. "I should go—"

"Not before you tell me what is wrong." His father gripped Adam's arm. "What troubles you, son?"

His father's care broke his reserve. "Mary Bloomfield rejected me."

"What?"

"I spoke with her, offered my hand, and she said no. That is all. Now I must go."

"But—"

"Oh, here you both are." His mother's voice awakened Frankie, who barked. "Adam? Why do you look woebegone?"

"I'm tired, that is all."

"Well, you best put away that gloomy face, for you have a visitor."

"Miss Bloomfield?" His heart thumped with hope. *Please, Lord.*

"No. It's Mrs. Hardy."

"And how are you feeling, little Betsy?"

"Oh, much better, thank you, Miss Bloomfield."

"And you're enjoying your little sister?"

"It's good to have a sister, isn't it, miss?"

Mary nodded. Joanna's support these past few days had been so very welcome, a crutch against the challenges of the impertinent remarks. Such as Mrs. Payne, who had stopped Mary on her walk to the Crokers', and, amidst generalized observations about one's duty to propriety and her reflection that she was thankful no scandal had ever plagued *her* household, had asked if Mary entertained any thought of marriage soon.

"Why, no," Mary responded, offering as bland a smile as she could, before begging to be excused.

"Before you go, I wondered if you had heard who had arrived back in town."

She was clearly waiting to be asked, so Mary fulfilled the obligation.

"Emily Hardy has returned."

Her heart missed a beat. "Is that so?"

"Perhaps she'll pick things up with Adam Edgerton again, now he's so much better than before."

"Perhaps she will." She congratulated herself inwardly on her mild tone. "If so, I hope they will be very happy."

"They are so very well-suited, don't you agree?" she cooed.

"I always thought so." She hated that her departure might lead Mrs. Payne to think she was not immune to the pain her words had caused. "I shall look forward to offering them both my congratulations. Now, please excuse me. I'm due to be at the Crokers'."

"Oh, of course. I would not detain you."

Mary had affixed a brittle smile and hastened to Sally Croker's, where the warmth and busy nothings of domesticity soon soothed the tumbling in her breast.

As the children's play and laughter continued, absolving Mary of the need to chat, her thoughts returned to what Emily's return must mean.

Mary would have to speak with her, to ascertain if Emily still held Adam in regard.

Mary would have to speak to her, to explain her reasons for encouraging Emily to depart.

Mary would have to speak with her, and apologize, for wishing to steal Adam's heart.

Dear God, please give me strength.

"Mary?" Sally stood, babe at breast. Her color was not good. "I feel a little strange."

"Here." Mary hurried to retrieve the child, propping Marigold against her shoulder. "Sit down."

Sally sat in the proffered chair, her breaths coming quick and light. "I feel rather dizzy."

"You have been very busy. And no doubt are quite tired. Just rest and close your eyes."

"Mama?" Betsy turned to Mary. "What is wrong with Mama?"

"She's a little weary, that is all. Here, would you place Marigold in her bed?"

Betsy obeyed, and Mary—conscious of a sticky trickle of something down her neck—could finally devote her full attention to Sally. "Just breathe, and here, put your feet up." She grasped Sally's hand, feeling for the pulse as her father had taught her. "Heavenly Father," she murmured, "please heal and comfort Sally, help her now."

Heat began to flow.

Sally drew in a deep breath and opened her eyes. "Mary, why is it that whenever you pray, I feel better?"

"God is good."

"Yes. But how can that happen every time?"

"It doesn't." Her smile faded. "I wish it did, but sometimes God has other plans."

Like with Susan. Like with Adam.

Her spirits dipped and she turned away. "Shall I make some tea?"

"Oh, yes, please. Betsy can help if you need."

Mary busied herself for the next few minutes, glad for the distraction of small children who wanted to know if she'd brought any more currant buns or her apple cake. Which brought to mind another person who'd expressed a fondness for her apple cake, a thought that pricked new tears.

"Mary? What is it?"

"Nothing. I'm sorry, you will have to excuse me. I have something of the headache."

"Something of the heartache, too, I warrant."

Mary glanced at her, shook her head.

"No, don't you go shaking your head at me, young lady. Now, make yourself a cup of tea and tell me what happened. Did you receive a certain offer?"

Mary's lip trembled. She bit down hard, concentrating on steadying her emotions, steadying her heart, as she fixed both cups of tea and returned to the table. "I did."

"Why has it taken until now before you told me? I am so very happy—"

"I refused him."

Sally's eyes widened. "What? Why?"

Mary sipped her tea. She could not share her reasons, and instead focused on the excuse offered by Mrs. Payne's news from earlier today. "Emily Hardy has returned. I will not stand in the way of them when I know she was his choice, not merely his obligation."

Sally's eyes grew shrewd. "You think he does not care for you."

"I know he does not."

"Then you are not nearly the sharp-witted woman I took you for."

"Perhaps." She offered a hollow smile. "A more intelligent person would have ensured I had a chaperone on that walk to Upton Pike."

"Stuff and nonsense," Sally exclaimed, then, noting her children's enquiring faces, said in a lower voice, "Such miserly minds some people have."

"Indeed." Mary had to go; she could not put up with this pretense any longer. She swallowed the rest of her tea and pushed away her cup, pushed out a tired smile. "If you are sure you are feeling better, I might leave."

"I feel as though I might suffer a relapse!" Sally fanned herself, opening her eyes wide. "Please stay and tell me more."

"There is nothing more to tell. Now I really must go. Thank you for the tea."

The joviality drained from Sally's eyes, replaced by kindness. "Thank you for coming. You will continue to be in my prayers."

Mary nodded, hugged the children, and departed.

There was nothing more to tell—until she had conversation with Emily Hardy.

⸙

Upon her return to the cottage infirmary, she busied herself in the still room, getting lost in the preparations and medicines, glad for the distraction they offered. She would *not* cry. She would not pity her situation. God would be her comfort. Wasn't there a verse in the Old Testament about God being as a husband? He must be that to her. She pressed her lips together.

From without she grew aware of the sound of a door knock, a door answered, voices. She was no coward but she didn't want to see who that might be. She had yet to figure out how to frame her words of regret and apology.

There came a sound of feet drawing near.

She quickly turned, humming, and pretended ignorance there was a visitor.

The door creaked open. "Here she is. Look, Mary, who has come to pay us a visit. It is Emily."

Bracing herself, Mary affixed a smile, and turned. "Emily! How wonderful to see you."

Emily smiled, the epitome of loveliness in her primrose gown and smooth coiffure. She glanced interestedly around, then her focus settled on Mary. "It is good to see you, too, Mary."

Would she still think so after Mary's awkward explanation? How long was she staying? Surely the answer to that would determine everything about Adam Edgerton. She finally dared ask the question burning in her heart. "Have you returned for good or are you returning to your aunt's soon?"

"Oh, I'm not sure." She gave Mary a swift glance, then turned to Joanna. "Do you mind if we talk elsewhere?"

"Of course. I believe the drawing room is free." Joanna gestured to Mary to join them, whispering as Emily moved ahead, "Mary, you have something white and rather ghastly-looking down your back." She drew nearer, sniffed, and made a face. "You smell rather peculiar, too."

Mary exhaled, mortification stealing over her. "I think that is the posset of Marigold."

Joanna wrinkled her nose in an expression of disgust. "It's also in your hair!"

Perhaps this was her escape. "I best go and change. Please make my excuses—"

"Oh, no. You're not getting out of things this way."

"Out of things? Whatever do you mean?"

"Emily specifically asked to talk to you. So go, get yourself cleaned up a little, but don't you dare run away."

Mary grimaced and hurried upstairs. *Lord, help me. What do I say to her?*

Upon her return to their guest, she was somewhat calmer. She would simply do her best to explain and beg forgiveness. Perhaps Emily would be understanding.

"Emily." She smiled as she sat near Joanna on the settee. "I'm sorry for keeping you. I was unaware of the evidence of my earlier visit to the Crokers and had not known you were planning to visit, so did not realize my need to change."

"Oh, never mind. Joanna has been telling me about what's happened in recent days."

A twinge a fear shot through her body, as Emily's face held a stiff quality she did not recognize. A quick glance at her sister's shrug revealed Joanna was none the wiser. "How has York been?"

"York has proved most interesting." Emily quickly thawed, offering her opinions of the wonders of the architecture and society and the opportunities to be found in such a place. "But I wanted to speak more about the happenings of Amberley." She glanced down at the lace trimming her gown. "My mother told me about you and Adam."

Her chest constricted. "That I have been assisting him, at my father's request."

"That you have been spending a great deal of time with him, that is true." Emily's face, usually so expressive, still revealed no clue.

Mary waited, sure Emily would finally speak whatever she had come to say.

"I . . ." Emily glanced away at the fire, then returned her gaze to look Mary in the eyes. "Did you encourage me to leave because you wanted to spend time with him yourself?"

Mary swallowed. Glanced at Joanna. Back at Emily. "I have asked myself the same question."

Emily's lips pursed. "Mama said you had always liked him, that she remembered you used to trail behind him when you were a girl."

"When I was a girl, yes." When Emily was but an infant. But that likely wasn't helpful to point this out.

"Adam is very engaging," offered Joanna.

"Exactly." Emily eyed Mary once more. "He has a way about him that can make people think more than what they ought."

Mary drew back as if she'd been slapped. She willed her countenance to impassivity. "I assure you I have no thought of him having any thought of me."

"But do you want him to? Is that why you were keen to send me away?"

"I assure you, I never meant to hurt you. I was thinking of what might be for your best and my intent—"

"Don't you remember how distraught you were at the thought of being bound to a blind man?" Joanna interposed, frowning at Emily.

"Yes, but—"

"Do you still wish to marry him?" Joanna persisted. "You have decided to marry a blind man, a farmer?"

Mary's breath suspended. Such was the heart of the matter.

"Well . . ." Emily raised her chin. "Well, no."

Moisture pricked Mary's eyes, and her chest loosened as breath silently released.

"Then what is it you've really come to say?" Joanna asked. "Do you want Mary's assurance that she will never marry him? Did your mother tell you that they were trapped on Upton Pike, and that people thought he was duty bound to offer for her? Because he did propose—"

Emily gasped.

"—and she refused him."

Emily's disbelieving eyes swung back to Mary. "You refused him?"

"He doesn't love me." Mary offered a twisted smile. "How could he, after loving you?"

Emily fell back against the cushion, her eyes on Mary still. "You must think me very selfish."

"Perhaps you are a little unaware of what options you have. Mr. Edgerton has so few these days." And Mary had virtually none. A long and lonely road of spinsterhood lay before her.

"I heard he is getting more involved with the farm." Emily studied Mary. "That he owes this to you."

"I've done very little."

"She's actually done quite a lot," insisted Joanna. "And I hope you will forgive me, Emily, but if you mean to sit there and tell Mary she is to not have anything more to do with Adam, then I will not hesitate to say you're acting like a spoilt child who cannot share any of the sweets you have been handed."

"Joanna," Mary cautioned, as Emily paled.

"No, it's only fair that she knows how hard you've worked to help poor Adam. Helping him to learn to walk, and reading to him, assisting him with training that dog. And I don't mind telling you, Emily, that I think it is very boldfaced to come here and tell Mary whom she may or may not love."

Emily's expression shifted from affronted to abashed. "I . . . I am not saying that."

"No? Then Mary has your blessing, should Adam ask again?"

Mary startled. "He will not do so—"

"No," Emily said. "You . . . you have my blessing."

It wasn't many more minutes before Joanna closed the door on their guest and turned to Mary with upraised brows. "Have you ever met with such effrontery?"

"I appreciate your efforts, and the love that motivates them, but I'm afraid it will have no effect."

"What do you mean?" Joanna demanded. "You can now tell Adam that you'll have him, that it was simply a moment of maidenly shyness or whatever, and you have changed your mind."

"No." Mary forced a wobbly smile. "I might have long admired Adam, and I didn't need Emily's blessing. That is not the issue."

"Then what in heaven's name *is* it?"

"He does not love me."

Joanna stared at her. "Is that all?"

"All?" Mary uttered a bitter chuckle. "It is everything."

Chapter 27

The weeks held a kind of blurring nothingness as he tried to overcome the savage pain of her rejection through renewed focus on the farm, on learning fields, on learning sheep. Gilroy and Conway were proving malleable, following instruction, so Father and John Davis said. He was glad and hoped and prayed they might find some way to settle in, for they spoke often of the landscape, the vast beauty of which seemed to possess the power to heal.

He knew what they meant, had found some comfort in the out-of-doors, but truly it was more his focus on God and the way the wind had of filling his ears until he couldn't hear the sound of her refusal anymore.

Until he returned home in the afternoons. Despite his mother's affection and his father's tolerance for his ideas and the warm comfort of young Frankie, he knew himself to be lonesome. He'd sit and try not to sink into low spirits, but the darkness these days felt very black.

Mary Bloomfield did not love him, could not care for him save as a patient. His stomach churned, his heart felt weighted, all light and hope seemed to have faded from the world.

He barely noticed his mother's entrance, or her offer of tea, or her disappearance, then return to the room. Why could Mary not hold him in some regard?

He felt around for the cup of the ubiquitous tea his mother made, conscious she was speaking, hardly caring what she might say.

"Adam? Are you listening to the letter?"

He shifted to where his mother's voice had spoken. "Yes. Please, go on."

Papers rustled. "Very well. I was reading about what Captain Balfour had to say about another acquaintance, a certain Langley. From Northumberland, apparently."

"Captain Langley." A foolhardy man of means with a reckless way of drinking.

"Apparently he's now a major, so there you go. Captain Balfour writes that he too has become a Christian."

"Truly? Well, that is something." If God could redeem James Langley, He could do miracles indeed.

"Yes."

She said nothing more for a long moment. "I saw Mrs. Hardy at the grocer's today."

"Did you?"

"She mentioned what she said to you that day."

He said nothing.

"I can't believe the nerve of that woman. Demanding you not marry Mary Bloomfield. What right did she have?"

"It doesn't matter, Mama." Except it actually mattered so much that it hurt.

"Why do you sit here looking so glum if it does not—" She broke off at the sound of the maid. "Oh, what *is* it, Meggie?"

"Miss Bloomfield is here to see the young master."

She'd relented? Come back to see him? Oh, how he'd ached to see her. "Send her in," he commanded.

"Oh, Adam, do you want me to stay?" his mother asked, voice lined with hope.

"I need to see her. Alone."

"Very well. I shall be in the garden if you need me."

And he heard her walk away.

"Miss Bloomfield, sir," Meggie said.

He rose, affixed a smile. "Mary? You've come at last. I thought you never would. You'll never know how much I missed you—"

"It's not Mary, sir. It's Joanna."

"Oh." His heart dropped like a stone. "Forgive me." He gestured to a seat and forced himself to act the genial host and to listen, until her words brought new hope and a clear path for him to follow.

⁂

"Oh, Mary, did you hear? Charles Payne has disappeared."

"What?" Mary dropped the lavender bag she was stitching at the kitchen table and stared at her sister, whose wide eyes and pallor spoke of distress.

"Mr. Payne was just in the drawing room talking with Father, and I distinctly heard him say that Charles has left the village."

"He's probably just gone to visit family or friends."

"It didn't sound like that by the way they were talking in such hushed tones."

Mary's brows rose. "And just how exactly did you manage to hear these things?"

"Oh, never mind that." Joanna gave an impatient wave of her hand. "It is a mystery! For why would his father not know where he's gone?"

"That seems quite strange, but not something we should concern ourselves with." Mary managed a wry smile. "It's not exactly pleasant to be at the receiving end of village speculation."

Joanna bit her lip and looked contrite. "Hopefully Father will tell us soon."

"Tell you what?"

Mary glanced up.

Her father's features had never looked so weary. He seemed quite pulled, and even somewhat sad.

She pulled out a chair at the kitchen table, begged him to sit, and hurried to pour him some tea.

"Oh, Father, is it true that Charles Payne has left the village?" Joanna asked excitedly. "Is it true he's disappeared?"

Their father settled in his chair. "It's true he's gone, but not that he's disappeared. He was"—he eyed Mary carefully—"obliged to depart for other places."

What would the son of the magistrate be forced to leave for? Oh. No. Her heart lurched. The wicked scoundrel! "I see." She thought so, anyway. Her hand shook as she handed Father his tea.

Joanna looked disappointed. "Well, there's little mystery in that."

"Hmm." Father glanced at her. "You know, my dear Joanna, it really doesn't behoove a young lady to be listening at doors."

"I wasn't listening at doors, Father." She sat upright, nose tilted in the air. "The door was ajar, and I was simply standing in the hallway. I could not help it if you spoke of private matters with the door open."

His gaze narrowed, and Joanna seemed to judge it prudent to make an exit, while making sure the door was closed quite firmly, as if to make a point.

"I'm glad to speak with you. I did not want to say in front of Joanna, but it does concern Charles Payne."

"What's happened?"

He took a sip, placed the cup on the table. "It seems young Susan's death has finally pierced Payne's son's conscience. He wrote a note to his father confessing his wicked deed."

"He was the evil villain who raped her?"

"Payne was mortified to think his own flesh and blood could be responsible for such a thing, and felt it only fair, as he's the magistrate, to inform those of us who were involved."

"Has he spoke with Mr. Oakley yet?"

"He's going there now." He sighed. "He came to speak to me as he's wondering if he should offer Lord Carstairs his resignation."

"And so he should!"

"But his was not the evil action. That was his son's doing, the coward who judged it best to board a ship to America and change his name."

"Wicked, wicked man!" Heat streamed through her chest. "Responsible for two deaths, and yet he gets away with it."

"He knows he will find no mercy here."

"Did you advise against Mr. Payne's resignation?"

"I only told him that whatever decision he makes should be guided by Mr. Oakley." He exhaled heavily. "But at least we now know who the culprit was."

"And it probably wouldn't help anyone to spread such news around. Poor Mr. and Mrs. Payne."

"Gossip never helps anyone, especially the innocent." Her father sipped his tea, then settled the cup back into the saucer. "Which reminds me. Have you had enough time to reconsider?"

"Reconsider what, Father?"

He eyed her seriously. "This is important, Mary."

"I know it is. But I cannot marry him. I cannot marry because of obligation."

"If he esteemed you?"

"He does not."

"And you know this how?"

"How could he? Why would he choose me after Emily Hardy? She's so young and pretty and vivacious. Everything I am not."

"She's everything you are not, that's true."

Hurt filled her chest, moisture lined her eyes, and she glanced down.

"Mary, you are considerate, steadfast, willing to see the best in others, unselfish. Yes, you're not like her at all."

The earlier tears were dashed away. "You are biased, Father."

"Indeed, I am." His smile grew tender. "But I do wish you would reconsider Adam's proposal."

"There is no point."

"I wouldn't be so sure."

"Why? What have you heard?"

But he didn't answer, only smiled and exited.

She shook her head—how dare her foolish hopes try to breathe again?—and refocused on her stitching. The scent of lavender filled the air, testimony to the sachet she was making for her mother's birthday.

"Mary!" called Joanna. "Can you help me, please?"

She sighed and put aside her needlework. "Where are you?"

"In the drawing room," Joanna replied.

She moved through the room into the hall, touching the wall gently as she recalled making such movements with her eyes closed to put herself in Adam's world. It was best she not visit him anymore. It would not do to fuel village speculation, despite her noble intentions to ignore it. Perhaps she should move away. Perhaps Aunt Margaret might be persuadable for Mary to come and stay.

"What do you want help with?" She rounded the door, then stumbled to a halt.

Joanna sat, a big grin on her face, on the sofa in front of Adam Edgerton. "Look who is here to see you."

A fluttering sensation, like the wings of a dozen sparrows, took residence within. "I . . . I thought you needed my help—"

"Oh, but I do." Joanna rushed over and pulled Mary closer. "I fear Mr. Edgerton thinks I'm nothing but a silly goose, and I desperately need your help to entertain him."

"You *are* a silly goose," Mary murmured.

Joanna chuckled. "Not as much as someone who refuses to listen to a proposal."

Before Mary could reply, Joanna had whisked out the door and closed it very firmly.

Mary sighed. "I must apologize for my sister, sir."

"Why? I think she's quite enterprising. And definitely not a silly goose, as far as I'm concerned."

That was debatable. Mary perched herself on the edge of a stiff chair, bracing herself for a painful interview. She might as well be uncomfortable in body, too. "Mr. Edgerton, I'm sorry you have made this visit for no purpose, but—"

"What do you mean no purpose? Is it not enough to enjoy your company and listen to your voice? You know, I've always liked the sound of your voice. In fact, I remember being so comforted by it when I first arrived and was in the throes of fever."

"I fear, sir, that I know why you have come, and that you won't like hearing what I have to say."

"Forgive me, but that sounds a little presumptuous, Miss Bloomfield."

She almost fell from her chair. "I beg your pardon?"

"How can you possibly know what I have come here to say?"

"Joanna said that you . . . that you were here to propose again. Well, let me save you the trouble. As I mentioned the last time you were so obliging to make such an offer, I have no intention of accepting."

He drew back, eyebrows raised. "Exactly as I said. Presumptuous."

"I'm sorry. I thought . . . do you mean you were not coming here to propose?"

"No."

She blinked. "You mean you were?"

"I still am," he said, smiling a little.

Her mind, her heart whirled. Dare she believe? No. "Regardless," she said sternly, tamping down the desire to return his smile, "I still cannot accept your very kind offer."

"But I've made no offer. Not yet today."

"You, sir, are proving most obstreperous. Very well, make your offer, but I warn you that I shall then refuse."

"Dear Miss Bloomfield, will you marry me?"

Her heart knew a fierce pang. "Thank you for your very kind offer, sir, but no."

His countenance betrayed no disappointment. "Why do you seem determined to refuse me?"

"Because I know you ask only from a sense of obligation, and my father"—she winced—"had to convince you to propose in the first place."

"Let me understand this clearly. You believe that I ask you to marry me to observe the conventions, or because you think I wish to obey your father, who has been very good to me, after all."

"You think you should make me an offer because you fear social ostracism if you don't."

"But I don't."

Oh. "Then perhaps you're concerned that I might face social ostracism, and you feel it your duty to protect me in this way."

"But I don't."

"I assure you, Mr. Edgerton, that I do not care about my reputation."

"I know."

"You do?"

He nodded, his expression growing grave. "We agreed, did we not, to always speak truthfully. So it saddens me to doubt your claim that you do not wish to marry me because I'm blind."

"That is not it."

"As hard as it would be to imagine a future with one who cannot see, I did not think you a young lady who required constant admiration of your face, or hair, or whatever gown you might choose to wear."

"I'm not like that at all!"

"I know." He sighed. "Which means I can only assume then that you do not like me."

"But I do."

"Not enough to marry me, it seems."

"You, sir—"

"My name is Adam," he said humbly.

"—are proving most—"

"Obstreperous was the word I believe you used before."

"—disruptive to my train of thought!"

"I'm sorry." His expression looked anything but contrite.

"I don't think you really are."

"Then you would be right. Again. For I do not want to leave here without an acceptance."

"But why? You do not love me."

The words, so baldly put, seemed to echo in the air.

"Why do you say that?" he asked softly.

"Because you don't. You cannot. I know you long cared for Emily. You need not pretend otherwise."

"I did care for Emily," he said slowly, "and for a long time I believed myself in love with her. And then I learned what love truly is. That love is about patience and compassion and forbearance and long-suffering."

Her eyes filled with tears. "How romantic you make it sound," she choked out.

"Would you prefer me to say that I also learned love is about friendship and laughter and knowing someone really understands you?"

He felt that too? Oh . . .

"Mary, you are the person who makes the darkness go away."

Her heart constricted.

"And I have come to realize that I love you in a way I never cared for anyone else before, and I do not want to live my life without you."

The joy his words induced shrunk in the memory of her mother's words. "Because I'm so dependable?"

"Because, my dearest Mary, because I love you. I enjoy you. I love spending time with you, I love your perspective on life, your willingness to help, your delightful sense of humor."

"Because it matches yours?"

"See? A delightful sense of humor, and someone so very wise."

She groped back the former emotion. Affixed a smile he'd never see to her face. "You are full of nonsense, sir. Shall I fetch my father? He should know what remedy you need."

"The only remedy I need is right in front of me. You are my tonic, remember? Sweet, and good for one's soul, and quite necessary to have on a daily basis."

Her smile softened at the corners—that wasn't *quite* how she remembered his earlier description—but any more she could not say.

"Dearest Mary, what would it take to convince you?"

"Convince me of what?"

"That my affections are engaged. That they have long been engaged by you."

"No. I am little and plain and blunt-spoken. You cannot be serious."

"But I am. I want to marry my dearest friend."

His dearest friend? New moisture pricked her eyes.

"Forgive me, I know I am a poor bargain—"

"No, you're not." He was kind and courageous and true. His eyesight might be wanting, but his heart was perfect and good.

"It's not just my affections that are towards you, but my hopes, my thoughts, my dreams." He stood, stepped forwards, and held out his hands, a small smile on his lips. "I love you."

"You cannot," she said, nearly through tears.

"Come here. Please."

She rose and moved—feet like lead—and placed her hands in his.

He gently squeezed and then released them, reached up to capture her face in his large hands.

She closed her eyes as his fingers traced her cheekbones, her jaw, her lips. Her chest constricted as his breath warmed her skin. Then came the press of his lips to her brow, to one cheek, then the other, then her nose, and then her mouth.

He kissed her softly, then soundly, then most thoroughly indeed. Such intensity drew strength from her knees, requiring her to hold on to his shoulders, to slip her arms around him to feel the muscles on his back, as her lips held his and her mind and heart spun with the wondrous impossibility of it all.

She finally pulled away to breathe.

"Was that convincing enough?" he whispered.

"Well, it was a good attempt, but—"

"I'll try again." And he drew her closer, closed his mouth on hers again, and this time wrapped her firmly in his arms as he deepened the kiss, his lips exploring hers.

Delightful, delicious sensations welled warmth within. Oh, this was heavenly, was romantic, was better than any dream.

"What about now?" he eventually asked, a smile playing about his mouth.

It took a moment for the head whirling to still, for her thoughts, her reason, to cohere. "That was quite persuasive," she eventually managed. If only it were true. "But what of Emily?"

"Who?" His grin faded, his look turning serious. "I have no thought of her."

"But wouldn't she be hurt?"

"According to your sister, she has already given her blessing on our marriage. I plan to take her at her word."

It still did not seem real. She dared ask for assurance. "You really love me?"

"I really do," he said in tones of staunch conviction.

He really did? He really did.

Something warm and delightful filled her chest, cascading upwards, outwards, in the form of euphoric pleasure.

"Are you laughing at me?" He drew her near, pressed another kiss to her brow. "I'm starting to wonder if you even care."

"Oh, Adam, you know I do."

"You do what?" he pressed.

"I love you." She smiled. "Most deeply. I suspect I always have, even since I was a little girl."

"Truly?" He looked surprised. "And I barely noticed you."

"Until you could not see."

"Which was when I finally saw what was most important and realized how wonderful you really are. And how kind." He kissed the top of her head. "How sweet." He kissed her jaw. "And how beautiful you are to me." He murmured this last against her lips, with a repeated plea. "Have I convinced you enough, dearest sweetest Mary?"

"Convinced me to—"

"Marry me?"

Joy pushed out in a chuckle, as she wrapped her arms around his neck. She whispered against his lips, "Yes. Oh, Adam, yes. A thousand times yes."

Knowing she was loved, knowing God was with them, they could walk together into a future lit with promise, lit with hope, and leave the shores of darkness for the promised land of love.

Author's Note

John Metcalf was an extraordinary man who lived in Knaresborough, England. He went blind at age five from smallpox, but his indomitable spirit meant he let little stop him. He became accomplished at playing the fiddle, riding horses, swimming, diving, and hunting, and he became one of Yorkshire's leading road builders. He died in 1810 and is commemorated in Knaresborough today, one of England's truly inspirational men. His story, hard as it may be to believe, forms the basis of Adam's transformation from shocked misery to someone daring to believe God has a purpose for him yet.

I love finding snippets of history and weaving them into fiction. When I came across letters recounting the sickness of English soldiers who fought in Walcheren and the peninsula, and discovered the horrific loss of life and conditions these men endured, I wanted to show something of how life might really have been for soldiers returning from the Napoleonic campaigns. Walcheren fever saw an army of forty thousand men, who had been sent to this part of the Dutch coast, decimated through an unknown (and therefore largely untreatable) disease that seemed to combine the worst of malaria, typhoid, typhus, and dysentery. Unbelievably, some of these sufferers were then shipped to Portugal and Spain, where they continued to fight, even though greatly weakened. Through frequent recurring bouts of fever, and sight-stealing combat, I imagine life would have been most challenging for those veterans fortunate enough to return to England.

The Complete Herbal by Nicholas Culpeper, MD, is a fabulous resource outlining various herbs, traditional medical treatments, and recipes that I imagine would have held similar treatments to those used by Dr. Bloomfield and Mary.

Of course, medicine cannot solve every problem—even with an additional two hundred years of medical knowledge, some things remain inexplicable.

I grew up in a church that dared to believe that the miracle-working God of the Bible also wants to heal people today. Later, ministry experience showed God's healing power at work time and time again: a baby healed of water on the brain. Deaf people who could hear. My husband prayed and saw a person's clouded eyes recover so that they could see. We have friends in the Philippines who saw their cousin come back to life at his funeral. My friend, Aussie young-adult author Jenny Glazebrook, astounded her doctors recently when people prayed and her sight was restored. I believe God heals. I believe He is a miracle-working God.

But He doesn't always heal. We can pray, and sometimes God doesn't give us the answers we wish for. What then? Does that mean He's not real?

God isn't Santa. He isn't a magician. He's God, and is not obliged to fulfill our wish list. So does that mean when our prayers aren't answered, it's because He has a higher purpose? It's hard to give a definitive answer, especially when we're suffering, but I believe God, who loves us, who has good plans for His children, is ultimately able to work all things together for the good of those who love Him and are called together for His purpose. He is all powerful. He delights in showing Himself strong on behalf of His children. And yes, He's looking for people to trust Him.

But I don't believe it's our level of faith that determines whether our prayers are answered. Jesus commended those with strong faith, but even the Apostle Paul didn't see every prayer answered. I think the bigger question God is challenging us with is this: Are we willing to trust Him even when things go wrong? That is deep faith, gritty faith. My prayer is that each of us is prepared to dare to believe God, even in the midst of strife and anguish. To let Him truly be God, directing our paths, no matter the circumstances. To dare to believe that the Jesus who walked this earth two thousand years ago died on a barbaric cross so that we would be forgiven all our sin. To dare to believe that we need simply pray and we can see salvation, and a guaranteed place in heaven when we die. To know the peace that comes from being friends with God. That is my prayer for me, for my family, and for all of us.

For behind-the-book details and a discussion guide, and to sign up for my newsletter, please visit www.carolynmillerauthor.com.

And if you have enjoyed reading this or any of the books in the Regency Brides series, please consider leaving a review on Amazon, Goodreads, or your favorite bookish site.

Finally, thank you, lovely readers, for all your wonderful support! God bless you.

Acknowledgments

A book doesn't just become. It takes a team of amazing people behind the scenes who encourage and help nurture an author's initial idea into what you see now.

So, thank you, God, for your amazing blessings, for your constant love, care, and life-giving power that transforms darkness into light. Thank you for Jesus Christ, whose death on a cross means salvation is possible for anyone who dares to believe. Thank you for the hope and peace this brings.

Huge hugs to my husband, Joshua, for believing in and supporting my writing dream. Thank you, Caitlin, Jackson, Asher, and Tim, for understanding why your mum talks as if imaginary people and problems are real. Thank you to my extended family and friends, in particular my beta reader, Roslyn Weaver, and Diana Clarke for sharing about her occupational therapist experience.

Thanks, too, to my English-born friend Joan, who allowed me to use her experience atop a Lake District mountain of hearing angelic-like singing—when nobody else was around! I love how God cannot be boxed.

A very special thank-you to Rick Vinckx, who shared so openly about his challenges with being legally blind, and who proves through his participation in everything from music (he plays drums) to chainsawing (!) that blindness need not keep a good man down.

Huge thanks to my agent, Tamela Hancock Murray, and the wonderful team at Kregel Publications for allowing me to write books that can be considered unapologetically Christian. I continue to be so thankful that you took a chance on an unknown Aussie and published my first book, *The Elusive Miss Ellison*, back in 2017. Thanks to my editors, Janyre and Christina, for forcing me to dig deeper to find the gold, and the wonderful designers who make such beautiful covers that always get high praise.

Thanks also to the authors and bloggers and influencers who have endorsed, and encouraged, and opened doors along the way. You are truly appreciated.

And thank *you*, wonderful readers, for choosing to read this book (and hopefully others of mine also!). Thank you for buying my books and sharing the love with others through your kind reviews and your encouraging messages and emails.

I hope you enjoyed Mary and Adam's story. God bless you.

Don't miss the second book of the Regency Wallflowers series

COMING SPRING 2022

Midnight's Budding Morrow

Chapter 1

YORKSHIRE
1811

"Oh, Sarah, please. Please? What would it take for you to reconsider?"

"But I am needed here," Sarah Drayton said, smiling to ease her friend's disappointment. Well, not exactly here—a thousand balls could take place and she would neither be needed nor missed—but at her aunt and uncle's in nearby Hartsdale.

"But *I* need you more," Beatrice Langley complained. "And really, why would you not want to come visit me? Am I not your oldest friend?" Her bottom lip protruded in a childlike pout.

"You are certainly my oldest friend, and you must know such an invitation holds a measure of interest. To be sure, I would enjoy the chance to finally see the sea," she teased.

"I see, I'm merely a measure of interest, am I?" Beatrice asked, brows aloft, before pleading further. "You simply must come. Langley is a little shabby these days, but it *is* interesting. And I know you would enjoy seeing a place which has hosted many important people over the years."

Sarah laughed. "You are incorrigible, that's what you are."

"Runs in the family, so I'm told," Beatrice said, lips curving with wryness.

Another flicker of curiosity pulsed. No, she would *not* ask about her former school friend's older brother. But incorrigibility and James Langley went hand in hand, or so the rumors said.

"Please, Sarah. You have no idea just how lonesome it can be living at Langley."

"Yes, with all that family, and all those servants, and all those parties you write about in your letters. I imagine it must be terribly hard."

Beatrice's eyes shadowed. "There is only Father and James now, and there have been far fewer parties of late. I'm afraid the place is falling into decay, so it seems overwhelming at times," she admitted. "Which is why I was ever so glad to learn you would be here tonight, so I could speak in person about such things."

Sarah's heart twisted. Perhaps her aunt and uncle would be sympathetic to her leaving them to spend some time with a friend whose situation somewhat resembled her own.

"I will ask my aunt and uncle and see if they can spare me."

"Oh, Sarah, you are the truest of friends."

Sarah offered a smile, as anticipation surged through her veins. To exchange the drear of duty to live in a castle by the sea? Who else would hesitate? Had she not prayed only this morning for God to direct her paths? Was this something of His leading?

A slightly older gentleman moved into view, his attention fixed on Beatrice, as had been the case all evening. Not that Sarah minded. Fading into the background was her wont, after all.

"Ah, Miss Langley. We are honored with your presence tonight."

"Good evening, Sir John. May I introduce you to my dear friend, Miss Drayton? Sarah, this is Sir John Willoughby, one of our neighbors."

He spared Sarah barely a glance, the merest nod, a brief word. She looked enquiringly at Beatrice, who seemed to recognize her feeling of awkwardness and drew Sarah's arm through her own. "I don't think you understand, Sir John. Miss Drayton is one of my oldest friends—we have known each other from the schoolroom, have we not, Sarah?—and she has promised to come and pay me a lengthy visit in the not very distant future. Is that not quite marvelous?"

"Why, ahem, quite marvelous, I am sure." His lips turned up in the semblance of a smile. "Anyone who is a friend of my dear Miss Langley is sure to be a friend of mine."

Sarah bowed her head, hiding her amusement at the man's pomposity, as she struggled to discern the nature of their friendship. That the man was enamored of Beatrice was plain, but did her bright-eyed friend return his regard? She could not say. She would have to wait for a gap in this post-dinner conversation to make polite enquiry.

She remained by the pillar, knowing that with her unadorned cream gown and plain pale features, she would almost blend into the wall. Her attire was several years out of date, and she had been made acutely aware of this by the dismissive glances cast her way from Durham's fashionable and rich. Normally she did not mind, but tonight . . .

Something astringent seemed to have entered the room at the arrival of Sir John. Something that tipped her heart towards unease, towards a vague sense of fear. She shook her head at herself, lifted her chin higher. How foolish. She wasn't normally one taken in by such fancies.

She looked around the rest of the room, noting the titled, the wealthy and assured. There was Lord Danver, a peer in his late forties said to be abominably wealthy, his politeness to all evident in the way he patiently listened, even as his dark eyes appeared tinged with weary sorrow. There was Miss Georgiana Barnstaple, a fussily dressed blonde whom Beatrice had said was one of her blackguard brother's greatest admirers, "But he never has any time for her." There were other notables too, most of whom apparently observed Sarah with indifference, unless it involved a raised-nose sneer at her clothes. Ah, well. It was a good thing she would but rarely meet with such people.

Sarah accepted a glass of punch from a passing waiter, watching as the couples assembled for the first dance. The music began, and she wondered how best to approach her aunt about the proposed visit. It was not as if her mother's sister actually had any meaningful work for her to do, save act as an unpaid housekeeper of sorts. And at Sarah's advanced age, she was certainly not bound by any duty save that of the familial, something which Aunt Patricia had exploited to such an extent that Sarah felt none of the warmer feelings of family connections at all. Perhaps an appeal to her aunt's well-developed sense of economies might work: one less mouth to feed, one less person constantly in the way.

She grew aware of a voice speaking behind her, her ears pricking at the name Langley.

"Such a temper I've never seen!"

"Gets it from the old man, if you ask me."

"Aye, that's for sure and for certain. How that lass ever got her sweetness I'll never know."

"They say—" Here the voices dipped in volume to make the words indiscernible.

Sarah's ears strained, wishing to hear more, even as she despised herself for being so low as to want to know gossip about her friend and her relations. She wrinkled her nose at herself and inched away from temptation.

A disturbance came at the door. Two men pushed into view, one grey and stooped, one handsome and brimming with vitality and good looks. The younger man scanned the room, his features narrowing when he saw Beatrice and her swain. He muttered something to the older man, then hurried down the steps to speak to her.

"Bea." He clutched her arm, drawing her away from Sir John without apology. "I've come at last."

"Oh, thank goodness!" Beatrice's previously bored features now lit with an internal glow. She caught Sarah's gaze and motioned her forwards, her body angling in such a way that Sir John was excluded. "Peter, I want you to meet my dear friend, Sarah Drayton."

The man's green eyes sparkled. "Ah, the famous Miss Drayton. At last we meet."

"Indeed we do, Mister . . . ?"

"Oh, forgive me," Beatrice said. "This is Peter Grayson, a . . . a friend."

"A friend?" His quick glance at Bea held a degree of disappointment. "Is that all?" he added in an undertone.

"All for now," Beatrice murmured.

Sarah curtsied to his short bow, heart alive with interest. Now *this* was more the sort of man she could envisage her pretty friend having as a suitor.

She peeked over her shoulder, saw the rumpled brow of Sir John before he noticed her noticing him and hurried away to speak to the elderly man who had entered the room with Mr. Grayson. Urgent whispers and gesticulations made it apparent that neither man was enamored with Beatrice's choice of beau, but neither Bea nor Mr. Grayson noticed, caught in their bubble of mutual admiration.

Sarah sighed, moving her attention away, only to see the dance had concluded and couples were re-forming lines to prepare for the next. At the door, the elderly man and Sir John continued their discussion, ignoring the two new guests stumbling their way down the steps, even as the shorter one shot the older men a look. Who were these gentlemen? A few years older than Beatrice, of a similar vintage to Bea's beau, they appeared careless of their presentation, careless of their lurching movements that suggested they had imbibed rather too heavily before their attendance tonight. The taller one with blond hair seemed oblivious to the whispers behind raised hands, while the shorter, dark-haired man almost reveled in it, eyes taking in the room as if glorying in the attention.

He paused, his focus fixing on Beatrice and Mr. Grayson, and he moved through the twirling couples without care for how his movements impeded theirs. "Beatrice," he pronounced loudly.

Definitely drunk, Sarah thought, eyeing him with disapproval. Who dared speak to a young lady so?

"Whatever are you doing with this puppy?" he slurred, gesturing to Mr. Grayson.

Beatrice blanched. Mr. Grayson seemed dumbstruck.

As if sensing Sarah's disfavor, the newcomer turned to her. "Something to say, Miss Prim?"

"Prim?" Beatrice protested. "No, no, this is Miss Drayton, my friend."

His eyes narrowed. "Looking down her nose at me like she thinks I'm spoony drunk."

He lurched closer, his beery breath igniting a spark of fear.

"Forgive me, sir," Sarah murmured. "I did not mean to give offense."

"Leave her," Beatrice implored. "Go talk to Papa instead."

"Father?" The man uttered a curse word. "Barely looked at me when I walked in. Too busy talking to Sir Pompous Jack O'Dandy."

Breath suspended. Did this mean this man was—?

"Sarah, allow me to introduce my brother, Captain James Langley."

The captain gave a mock bow, the movement tipping him to his knees, where he gave a great shout of laughter, unmindful of the humiliation of his sister.

Around them the music paused, the dancing stilled, the atmosphere grew thick with shame and ignominy. "Cap'n Blackwood, get us another pot of Sir John Barleycorn," he cried. "And a shovel of port for Miss Sour-Sides here. She looks like she could do with a good drink."

Sarah blinked, took a step back, as his taller friend grinned and enquired loudly for two large strong drinks.

"Afraid of me, are you?" With surprising quickness Captain Langley rose and drew close, his eyes fixed on her, his mouth a twisted sneer. "I'll give you something to remember me by."

And in one swift motion he closed the space between them, his hands jerking her to himself as his alcohol-soaked mouth pressed down on hers.

She struggled for air, pushed away, slapping his cheek with a thwack that echoed off the walls, and then wiped a hand across her contaminated lips as she stumbled back. "How dare you?"

"Oh, Sarah, I'm so sorry." Beatrice hurried forwards and grasped her arm, then whisked her up the stairs and into an anteroom, away from the shocked whispers and stares. "Forgive me, forgive him. James is so lost, he doesn't know what he does anymore."

"Has . . . had he done that before?" Sarah asked, heart still wildly thumping, wishing she could scrub away the scent of his breath, the feel of his arms, the shocking violence of her first kiss.

"He's not well," Beatrice said, evading Sarah's gaze. "Please don't let this stop your visit."

Sarah shook her head. "I cannot visit if he is there. I *will* not visit if he is there."

"He shan't be, I assure you. James is returning to the army, which is probably why he's here for one last merriment before he ships abroad. How I wish I could make this up to you. You have no idea how sorry I am."

Shame and sorrow shone in her friend's eyes. Beatrice could not be blamed for her unfortunate brother.

"You are sure he will not come?"

"He won't. He and Papa do not get on."

"Really?" The sarcasm was thick.

"Please, I beg of you. Do not hold his behavior against me."

Sarah exhaled and slumped into a round-backed wooden chair. "You promise I need never see him again?"

"Cross my heart." Beatrice suited the action to the words. "If he does happen to visit, I'll see you are locked inside the tower room."

"How reassuring," she said dryly, even as her heart prickled. Beatrice's castle had a tower?

"Please, Sarah?"

She sighed. "Oh, very well."

She would not permit Captain James Langley to impede her one chance to grasp a new life. She would go as Beatrice's friend, and pray she'd never see the scoundrel again.

REGENCY BRIDES
DAUGHTERS *of* AYNSLEY

"*Miller's inclusion of faith issues with an authentic portrayal of
Regency society will continue to delight her growing fan base.*"
—Publishers Weekly